Famous Detective Stories in Large Print

Also available in Large Print:

Favorite Poems in Large Print
*Favorite Short Stories in Large
  Print*
*Best-Loved Poems in Large
  Print*

Famous Detective Stories in Large Print

Edited by Virginia S. Reiser
and Mary Allen

G.K.HALL &CO.
Boston, Massachusetts
1984

Library of Congress Cataloging in Publication Data

Main entry under title:
  Famous detective stories in large print.

  Includes index.
  1. Detective and mystery stories, American.
2. Detective and mystery stories, English.   3. Large
type books.   I. Reiser, Virginia S.   II. Allen, Mary
[PS648.D4F35 1984]   813'.0872'08   84–12779
ISBN 0–8161–3681–5

Acknowledgments

The editors gratefully acknowledge permission to reproduce copyright short stories in this book.

"The Case of the White Elephant," Margery Allingham, reprinted by courtesy of P. & M. Youngman Carter Limited.

"The Sweet Shot," E. C. Bentley, copyright 1938 by E. C. Bentley. Reprinted by kind permission of Curtis Brown Group Ltd. on behalf of the Estate of E. C. Bentley.

"The Incautious Burglar," John Dickson Carr, copyright 1940 by John Dickson Carr. Reprinted by permission of Harold Ober Associates, Inc.

"The Pencil," Raymond Chandler, copyright 1971 by Helga Greene, Executrix. Reprinted by permission of Houghton Mifflin Company. Reprinted in the British Commonwealth by permission of Hamish Hamilton Ltd.

"A Chess Problem," Agatha Christie, from *The Big Four* by Agatha Christie. Copyright 1927 by Dodd, Mead & Company, Inc. Copyright renewed 1955 by Agatha Christie Mallowan. Reprinted by permission of Harold Ober Associates, Inc.

"Introducing Susan Dare," Mignon Eberhart, from *The Cases of Susan Dare,* published by Doubleday, Doran & Company. Copyright 1934, 1962, by Mignon Eberhart. Reprinted by permission of Brandt & Brandt Literary Agents Inc.

Contents

Famous Detective Stories in Large Print

The Boscombe Valley Mystery

Arthur Conan Doyle

WE WERE SEATED at breakfast one morning, my wife and I, when the maid brought in a telegram. It was from Sherlock Holmes and ran in this way:

> Have you a couple of days to spare? Have just been wired for from the west of England in connection with Boscombe Valley tragedy. Shall be glad if you will come with me. Air and scenery perfect. Leave Paddington by the 11:15.

"What do you say, dear?" said my wife, looking across at me. "Will you go?"

"I really don't know what to say. I have a fairly long list at present."

"Oh, Anstruther would do your work for you. You have been looking a little pale lately. I think that the change would do you good, and you are always so interested in Mr. Sherlock Holmes's cases."

1

"I should be ungrateful if I were not, seeing what I gained through one of them," I answered. "But if I am to go, I must pack at once, for I have only half an hour."

My experience of camp life in Afghanistan had at least had the effect of making me a prompt and ready traveller. My wants were few and simple, so that in less than the time stated I was in a cab with my valise, rattling away to Paddington Station. Sherlock Holmes was pacing up and down the platform, his tall, gaunt figure made even gaunter and taller by his long gray travelling-cloak and close-fitting cloth cap.

"It is really very good of you to come, Watson," said he. "It makes a considerable difference to me, having someone with me on whom I can thoroughly rely. Local aid is always either worthless or else biassed. If you will keep the two corner seats I shall get the tickets."

We had the carriage to ourselves save for an immense litter of papers which Holmes had brought with him. Among these he rummaged and read, with intervals of note-taking and of meditation, until we were past Reading. Then he suddenly rolled them all into a gigantic ball and tossed them up onto the rack.

"Have you heard anything of the case?" he asked.

"Not a word. I have not seen a paper for some days."

"The London press has not had very full accounts. I have just been looking through all the recent papers in order to master the particulars. It seems, from what I gather, to be one of those simple cases which are so extremely difficult."

"That sounds a little paradoxical."

"But it is profoundly true. Singularity is almost invariably a clue. The more feature-less and commonplace a crime is, the more difficult it is to bring it home. In this case, however, they have established a very serious case against the son of the murdered man."

"It is a murder, then?"

"Well, it is conjectured to be so. I shall take nothing for granted until I have the opportunity of looking personally into it. I will explain the state of things to you, as far as I have been able to understand it, in a very few words.

"Boscombe Valley is a country district not very far from Ross, in Herefordshire. The largest landed proprietor in that part is a Mr. John Turner, who made his money in Australia and returned some years ago to the old country. One of the farms which he held, that of Hatherley, was let to Mr. Charles McCarthy, who was also an ex-Australian. The men had known each other in the colonies, so that it was not unnatural that when they came to settle down they should do so as near each other as possible. Turner was

3

apparently the richer man, so McCarthy became his tenant but still remained, it seems, upon terms of perfect equality, as they were frequently together. McCarthy had one son, a lad of eighteen, and Turner had an only daughter of the same age, but neither of them had wives living. They appear to have avoided the society of the neighbouring English families and to have led retired lives, though both the McCarthys were fond of sport and were frequently seen at the race-meetings of the neighbourhood. McCarthy kept two servants — a man and a girl. Turner had a considerable household, some half-dozen at the least. That is as much as I have been able to gather about the families. Now for the facts.

"On June 3d, that is, on Monday last, McCarthy left his house at Hatherley about three in the afternoon and walked down to the Boscombe Pool, which is a small lake formed by the spreading out of the stream which runs down the Boscombe Valley. He had been out with his serving-man in the morning at Ross, and he had told the man that he must hurry, as he had an appointment of importance to keep at three. From that appointment he never came back alive.

''From Hatherley Farmhouse to the Boscombe Pool is a quarter of a mile, and two people saw him as he passed over this ground. One was an old woman, whose name is not mentioned, and the other was William

Crowder, a game-keeper in the employ of Mr. Turner. Both these witnesses depose that Mr. McCarthy was walking alone. The game-keeper adds that within a few minutes of his seeing Mr. McCarthy pass he had seen his son, Mr. James McCarthy, going the same way with a gun under his arm. To the best of his belief, the father was actually in sight at the time, and the son was following him. He thought no more of the matter until he heard in the evening of the tragedy that had occurred.

"The two McCarthys were seen after the time when William Crowder, the game-keeper, lost sight of them. The Boscombe Pool is thickly wooded round, with just a fringe of grass and of reeds round the edge. A girl of fourteen, Patience Moran, who is the daughter of the lodge-keeper of the Boscombe Valley estate, was in one of the woods picking flowers. She states that while she was there she saw, at the border of the wood and close by the lake, Mr. McCarthy and his son, and that they appeared to be having a violent quarrel. She heard Mr. McCarthy the elder using very strong language to his son, and she saw the latter raise up his hand as if to strike his father. She was so frightened by their violence that she ran away and told her mother when she reached home that she had left the two McCarthys quarrelling near Boscombe Pool, and that she was afraid that they were going to fight. She had hardly said the words when young Mr. McCarthy came running up to the lodge to say that he had found his father dead in the wood, and to ask for the help of the lodge-keeper. He was much excited, without either his gun or his hat, and his right hand and sleeve were observed to be stained with fresh blood. On following him they found the dead body stretched out upon the grass beside the pool. The head had been beaten in by repeated blows of some heavy and blunt weapon. The injuries were such as might very well have been inflicted by the butt-end of his son's gun, which was found lying on the grass within a few paces of the body. Under these circumstances the young man was instantly arrested, and a verdict of 'wilful murder' having been returned at the inquest on Tuesday, he was on Wednesday brought before the magistrates at Ross, who have referred the case to the next Assizes. Those are the main facts of the case as they came out before the coroner and the police-court."

"I could hardly imagine a more damning case," I remarked. "If ever circumstantial evidence pointed to a criminal it does so here."

"Circumstantial evidence is a very tricky thing," answered Holmes thoughtfully. "It may seen to point very straight to one thing, but if you shift your own point of view a little,

6

you may find it pointing in an equally uncompromising manner to something entirely different. It must be confessed, however, that the case looks exceedingly grave against the young man, and it is very possible that he is indeed the culprit. There are several people in the neighbourhood, however, and among them Miss Turner, the daughter of the neighbouring land-owner, who believe in his innocence, and who have retained Lestrade, whom you may recollect in connection with 'A Study in Scarlet', to work out the case in his interest. Lestrade, being rather puzzled, has referred the case to me, and hence it is that two middle-aged gentlemen are flying westward at fifty miles an hour instead of quietly digesting their breakfasts at home.''

"I am afraid,'' said I, ''that the facts are so obvious that you will find little credit to be gained out of this case.''

"There is nothing more deceptive than an obvious fact,'' he answered, laughing. "Besides, we may chance to hit upon some other obvious facts which may have been by no means obvious to Mr. Lestrade. You know me too well to think that I am boasting when I say that I shall either confirm or destroy his theory by means which he is quite incapable of employing, or even of understanding. To take the first example to hand, I very clearly perceive that in your bedroom the window is upon the right-hand side, and yet I question

7

whether Mr. Lestrade would have noted even so self-evident a thing as that."

"How on earth ——"

"My dear fellow, I know you well. I know the military neatness which characterizes you. You shave every morning, and in this season you shave by the sunlight; but since your shaving is less and less complete as we get farther back on the left side, until it becomes positively slovenly as we get round the angle of the jaw, it is surely very clear that that side is less illuminated than the other. I could not imagine a man of your habits looking at himself in an equal light and being satisfied with such a result. I only quote this as a trivial example of observation and inference. Therein lies my *métier,* and it is just possible that it may be of some service in the investigation which lies before us. There are one or two minor points which were brought out in the inquest, and which are worth considering."

"What are they?"

"It appears that his arrest did not take place at once, but after the return to Hatherley Farm. On the inspector of constabulary informing him that he was a prisoner, he remarked that he was not surprised to hear it, and that it was no more than his deserts. This observation of his had the natural effect of removing any traces of doubt which might have remained in the minds of the

8

coroner's jury."

"It was a confession," I ejaculated.

"No, for it was followed by a protestation of innocence."

"Coming on the top of such a damning series of events, it was at least a most suspicious remark."

"On the contrary," said Holmes, "it is the brightest rift which I can at present see in the clouds. However innocent he might be, he could not be such an absolute imbecile as not to see that the circumstances were very black against him. Had he appeared surprised at his own arrest, or feigned indignation at it, I should have looked upon it as highly suspicious, because such surprise or anger would not be natural under the circumstances, and yet might appear to be the best policy to a scheming man. His frank acceptance of the situation marks him as either an innocent man, or else as a man of considerable self-restraint and firmness. As to his remark about his deserts, it was also not unnatural if you consider that he stood beside the dead body of his father, and that there is no doubt that he had that very day so far forgotten his filial duty as to bandy words with him, and even, according to the little girl whose evidence is so important, to raise his hand as if to strike him. The self-reproach and contrition which are displayed in his remark appear to me to be the signs of a healthy mind rather than of a guilty one."

I shook my head. "Many men have been hanged on far slighter evidence," I remarked.

"So they have. And many men have been wrongfully hanged."

"What is the young man's own account of the matter?"

"It is, I am afraid, not very encouraging to his supporters, though there are one or two points in it which are suggestive. You will find it here, and may read it for yourself."

He picked out from his bundle a copy of the local Herefordshire paper, and having turned down the sheet he pointed out the paragraph in which the unfortunate young man had given his own statement of what had occurred. I settled myself down in the corner of the carriage and read it very carefully. It ran in this way:

Mr. James McCarthy, the only son of the deceased, was then called and gave evidence as follows: "I had been away from home for three days at Bristol, and had only just returned upon the morning of last Monday, the 3d. My father was absent from home at the time of my arrival, and I was informed by the maid that he had driven over to Ross with John Cobb, the groom. Shortly after my return I heard the wheels of his trap in the yard, and, looking out of my window, I saw him get out and walk rapidly out of the yard, though I was not aware in which direction he was going. I then took my gun and strolled out in the direction of the Boscombe Pool, with the intention of visiting the rabbit-warren which is upon the other side. On my way I saw William Crowder, the game-keeper, as he had stated in his evidence; but he is mistaken in thinking that I was following my father. I had no idea that he was in front of me. When about a hundred yards from the pool I heard a cry of 'Cooee!' which was a usual signal between my father and myself. I then hurried forward, and found him standing by the pool. He appeared to be much surprised at seeing me and asked me rather roughly what I was doing there. A conversation ensued which led to high words and almost to blows, for my father was a man of a very violent temper. Seeing that his passion was becoming ungovernable, I left him and returned toward Hatherley Farm. I had not gone more than 150 yards, however, when I heard a hideous outcry behind me, which caused me to run back again. I found my father expiring upon the ground, with his head terribly injured. I dropped my gun and held him in my arms, but he almost instantly expired. I knelt beside him for some minutes, and then made my way to Mr. Turner's lodge-keeper, his house being the nearest, to ask for assistance. I saw no one near my father when I returned, and I have no idea how he came by his injuries. He was not a popular man, being somewhat cold and forbidding in his manners; but he had, as far as I know, no active enemies. I know nothing further of the matter."

The Coroner: Did your father make any statement to you before he died?

Witness: He mumbled a few words, but I could only catch some allusion to a rat.

The Coroner: What did you understand by that?

Witness: It conveyed no meaning to me. I thought that he was delirous.

The Coroner: What was the point upon which you and your father had this final quarrel?

Witness: I should prefer not to answer.

The Coroner: I am afraid that I must press it.

Witness: It is really impossible for me to tell you. I can assure you that it has nothing to do with the sad tragedy which followed.

The Coroner: That is for the court to decide. I need not point out to you that your refusal to answer will prejudice your case considerably in any future proceedings which may arise.

Witness: I must still refuse.

The Coroner: I understand that the cry of "Cooee" was a common signal between you and your father?

Witness: It was.

The Coroner: How was it, then, that he uttered it before he saw you, and before he even knew that you had returned from Bristol?

Witness (with considerable confusion): I do not know.

A Juryman: Did you see nothing which aroused your suspicions when you returned on hearing the cry and found your father fatally injured?

Witness: Nothing definite.

The Coroner: What do you mean?

Witness: I was so disturbed and excited as I rushed out into the open, that I could think of nothing except of my father. Yet I have a vague impression that as I ran forward something lay upon the ground to the left of me. It seemed to me to be something gray in colour, a coat of some sort, or a plaid perhaps. When I rose from my father I looked round for it, but it was gone.

"Do you mean that it disappeared before you went for help?"

"Yes, it was gone."

"You cannot say what it was?"

"No, I had a feeling something was there."

"How far from the body?"

"A dozen yards or so."

"And how far from the edge of the wood?"

"About the same."

"Then if it was removed it was while you were within a dozen yards of it?"

"Yes, but with my back towards it."

This concluded the examination of the witness.

"I see," said I as I glanced down the column, "that the coroner in his concluding remarks was rather severe upon young McCarthy. He calls attention, and with reason, to the discrepancy about his father having signalled to him before seeing him, also to his refusal to give details of his conversation with his father, and his singular account of his father's dying words. They are all, as he remarks, very much against the son."

Holmes laughed softly to himself and stretched himself out upon the cushioned seat. "Both you and the coroner have been at some pains," said he, "to single out the very strongest points in the young man's favour. Don't you see that you alternately give him credit for having too much imagination and too little? Too little, if he could not invent a cause of quarrel which would give him the sympathy of the jury; too much, if he evolved from his own inner consciousness anything so *outré* as a dying reference to a rat, and the incident of the vanishing cloth.

14

No, sir, I shall approach this case from the point of view that what this young man says is true, and we shall see whither that hypothesis will lead us. And now here is my pocket Petrarch, and not another word shall I say of this case until we are on the scene of action. We lunch at Swindon, and I see that we shall be there in twenty minutes."

It was nearly four o'clock when we at last, after passing through the beautiful Stroud Valley, and over the broad gleaming Severn, found ourselves at the pretty little country-town of Ross. A lean, ferret-like man, furtive and sly-looking, was waiting for us upon the platform. In spite of the light brown dustcoat and leather-leggings which he wore in deference to his rustic surroundings, I had no difficulty in recognizing Lestrade, of Scotland Yard. With him we drove to the Hereford Arms where a room had already been engaged for us.

"I have ordered a carriage," said Lestrade as we sat over a cup of tea. "I knew your energetic nature, and that you would not be happy until you had been on the scene of the crime."

"It was very nice and complimentary of you," Holmes answered. "It is entirely a question of barometric pressure."

Lestrade looked startled. "I do not quite follow," he said.

"How is the glass? Twenty-nine, I see. No

wind, and not a cloud in the sky. I have a caseful of cigarettes here which need smoking, and the sofa is very much superior to the usual country hotel abomination. I do not think that it is probable that I shall use the carriage to-night."

Lestrade laughed indulgently. "You have, no doubt, already formed your conclusions from the newspapers," he said. "The case is as plain as a pikestaff, and the more one goes into it the plainer it becomes. Still, of course, one can't refuse a lady, and such a very postive one, too. She had heard of you, and would have your opinion, though I repeatedly told her that there was nothing which you could do which I had not already done. Why, bless my soul! here is her carriage at the door."

He had hardly spoken before there rushed into the room one of the most lovely young women that I have ever seen in my life. Her violet eyes shining, her lips parted, a pink flush upon her cheeks, all thought of her natural reserve lost in her overpowering excitement and concern.

"Oh, Mr. Sherlock Holmes!" she cried, glancing from one to the other of us, and finally, with a woman's quick intuition, fastening upon my companion, "I am so glad that you have come. I have driven down to tell you so. I know that James didn't do it. I know it, and I want you to start upon your work knowing it, too. Never let yourself doubt upon that point. We have known each other since we were little children, and I know his faults as no one else does; but he is too tenderhearted to hurt a fly. Such a charge is absurd to anyone who really knows him."

"I hope we may clear him, Miss Turner," said Sherlock Holmes. "You may rely upon my doing all that I can."

"But you have read the evidence. You have formed some conclusion? Do you not see some loophole, some flaw? Do you not yourself think that he is innocent?"

"I think that it is very probable."

"There, now!" she cried, throwing back her head and looking defiantly at Lestrade. "You hear! He gives me hopes."

Lestrade shrugged his shoulders. "I am afraid that my colleague has been a little quick in forming his conclusions," he said.

"But he is right. Oh! I know that he is right. James never did it. And about his quarrel with his father, I am sure that the reason why he would not speak about it to the coroner was because I was concerned in it."

"In what way?" asked Holmes.

"It is no time for me to hide anything. James and his father had many disagreements about me. Mr. McCarthy was very anxious that there should be a marriage between us. James and I have always loved each other as brother and sister; but of course he is young and has seen very little of life yet, and — and — well, he naturally did not wish to do anything like that yet. So there were quarrels, and this, I am sure, was one of them."

"And your father?" asked Holmes. "Was he in favour of such a union?"

"No, he was averse to it also. No one but Mr. McCarthy was in favour of it." A quick blush passed over her fresh young face as Holmes shot one of his keen, questioning glances at her.

"Thank you for this information," said he. "May I see your father if I call tomorrow?"

"I am afraid the doctor won't allow it."

"The doctor?"

"Yes, have you not heard? Poor father has never been strong for years back, but this has broken him down completely. He has taken to his bed, and Dr. Willows says that he is a wreck and that his nervous system is shattered. Mr. McCarthy was the only man alive who had known dad in the old days in Victoria."

"Ha! In Victoria! That is important."

"Yes, at the mines."

"Quite so; at the gold-mines, where, as I understand, Mr. Turner made his money."

"Yes, certainly."

"Thank you, Miss Turner. You have been of material assistance to me."

"You will tell me if you have any news tomorrow. No doubt you will go to the prison to see James. Oh, if you do, Mr. Holmes, do tell him that I know him to be innocent."

"I will, Miss Turner."

"I must go home now, for dad is very ill, and he misses me so if I leave him. Good-bye, and God help you in your undertaking." She hurried from the room as impulsively as she had entered, and we heard the wheels of her carriage rattle off down the street.

"I am ashamed of you, Holmes," said Lestrade with dignity after a few minutes' silence. "Why should you raise up hopes which you are bound to disappoint? I am not over-tender of heart, but I call it cruel."

"I think that I see my way to clearing James McCarthy," said Holmes. "Have you an order to see him in prison?"

"Yes, but only for you and me."

"Then I shall reconsider my resolution about going out. We have still time to take a train to Hereford and see him to-night?"

"Ample."

"Then let us do so. Watson, I fear that you will find it very slow, but I shall only be away a couple of hours."

I walked down to the station with them, and then wandered through the streets of the little town, finally returning to the hotel, where I lay upon the sofa and tried to interest myself in a yellow-backed novel. The puny plot of the story was so thin, however, when compared to the deep mystery through which we were groping, and I found my attention wander so continually from the fiction to the fact, that I at last flung it across the room and gave myself up entirely to a consideration of the events of the day. Supposing that this unhappy young man's story were absolutely true, then what hellish thing, what absolutely unforeseen and extraordinary calamity could have occurred between the time when he parted from his father, and the moment when, drawn back by his screams, he rushed into the glade? It was something terrible and deadly. What could it be? Might not the nature of the injuries reveal something to my medical instincts? I rang the bell and called for the weekly county paper, which contained a verbatim account of the inquest. In the surgeon's deposition it was stated that the posterior third of the left parietal bone and the left half of the occipital bone had been shattered by a heavy blow from a blunt weapon. I marked the spot upon my own head. Clearly such a blow must have been struck from behind. That was to some extent in favour of the accused, as when seen quarrelling he was face to face with his father. Still, it did not go for very much, for the older man might have turned his back before the blow fell. Still, it might be worth while to call Holmes's attention to it. Then there was the peculiar reference to a rat. What could that mean? It could not be delirium. A man dying

20

from a sudden blow does not commonly become delirious. No, it was more likely to be an attempt to explain how he met his fate. But what could it indicate? I cudgelled my brains to find some possible explanation. And then the incident of the gray cloth seen by young McCarthy. If that were true the murderer must have dropped some part of his dress, presumably his overcoat, in his flight, and must have had the hardihood to return and to carry it away at the instant when the son was kneeling with his back turned not a dozen paces off. What a tissue of mysteries and improbabilities the whole thing was! I did not wonder at Lestrade's opinion, and yet I had so much faith in Sherlock Holmes's insight that I could not lose hope as long as every fresh fact seemed to strengthen his conviction of young McCarthy's innocence.

It was late before Sherlock Holmes returned. He came back alone, for Lestrade was staying at lodgings in the town.

"The glass still keeps very high," he remarked as he sat down. "It is of importance that it should not rain before we are able to go over the ground. On the other hand, a man should be at his very best and keenest for such nice work as that, and I did not wish to do it when fagged by a long journey. I have seen young McCarthy."

"And what did you learn from him?"

"Nothing."

"Could he throw no light?"

"None at all. I was inclined to think at one time that he knew who had done it and was screening him or her, but I am convinced now that he is as puzzled as everyone else. He is not a very quick-witted youth, though comely to look at and, I should think, sound at heart."

"I cannot admire his taste," I remarked, "if it is indeed a fact that he was averse to a marriage with so charming a young lady as this Miss Turner."

"Ah, thereby hangs a rather painful tale. This fellow is madly, insanely. in love with her, but some two years ago, when he was only a lad, and before he really knew her, for she had been away five years at a boarding-school, what does the idiot do but get into the clutches of a barmaid in Bristol and marry her at a registry office? No one knows a word of the matter, but you can imagine how maddening it must be to him to be upbraided for not doing what he would give his very eyes to do, but what he knows to be abso-lutely impossible. It was sheer frenzy of this sort which made him throw his hands up into the air when his father, at their last interview, was goading him on to propose to Miss Turner. On the other hand, he had no means of supporting himself, and his father, who was by all accounts a very hard man, would have thrown him over utterly had he known the truth. It was with his barmaid wife that he had spent the last three days in Bristol, and his father did not know where he was. Mark that point. It is of importance. Good has come out of evil, however, for the barmaid, finding from the papers that he is in serious trouble and likely to be hanged, has thrown him over utterly and has written to him to say that she has a husband already in the Bermuda Dockyard, so that there is really no tie between them. I think that that bit of news has consoled young McCarthy for all that he has suffered."

"But if he is innocent, who has done it?"

"Ah! who? I would call your attention very particularly to two points. One is that the murdered man had an appointment with someone at the pool, and that the someone could not have been his son, for his son was away, and he did not know when he would return. The second is that the murdered man was heard to cry "Cooee!" before he knew that his son had returned. Those are the crucial points upon which the case depends. And now let us talk about George Meredith, if you please, and we shall leave all minor matters until to-morrow."

There was no rain, as Holmes had foretold, and the morning broke bright and cloudless. At nine o'clock Lestrade called for us with the carriage, and we set off for Hatherley Farm and the Boscombe Pool.

"There is serious news this morning," Lestrade observed. "It is said that Mr. Turner, of the Hall, is so ill that his life is despaired of."

"An elderly man, I presume?" said Holmes.

"About sixty; but his constitution has been shattered by his life abroad, and he has been in failing health for some time. This business has had a very bad effect upon him. He was an old friend of McCarthy's, and, I may add, a great benefactor to him, for I have learned that he gave him Hatherley Farm rent free."

"Indeed! That is interesting," said Holmes.

"Oh, yes! In a hundred other ways he has helped him. Everybody about here speaks of his kindness to him."

"Really! Does it not strike you as a little singular that this McCarthy, who appears to have had little of his own, and to have been under such obligations to Turner, should still talk of marrying his son to Turner's daughter, who is, presumably, heiress to the estate, and that in such a very cocksure manner, as if it were merely a case of a proposal and all else would follow? It is the more strange, since we know that Turner himself was averse to the idea. The daughter told us as much. Do you not deduce something from that?"

"We have got to the deductions and the inferences," said Lestrade, winking at me. "I find it hard enough to tackle facts, Holmes, without flying away after theories and fancies.''

''You are right,'' said Holmes demurely; ''you do find it very hard to tackle the facts.''

''Anyhow, I have grasped one fact which you seem to find it difficult to get hold of,'' replied Lestrade with some warmth.

''And that is ——''

''That McCarthy senior met his death from McCarthy junior and that all theories to the contrary are the merest moonshine.''

''Well, moonshine is a brighter thing than fog,'' said Holmes, laughing. ''But I am very much mistaken if this is not Hatherley Farm upon the left.''

''Yes, that is it.'' It was a widepsread, comfortable-looking building, two-storied, slate-roofed, with great yellow blotches of lichen upon the gray walls. The drawn blinds and the smokeless chimneys, however, gave it a stricken look, as though the weight of this horror still lay heavy upon it. We called at the door, when the maid, at Holmes's request, showed us the boots which her master wore at the time of his death, and also a pair of the son's, though not the pair which he had then had. Having measured these very carefully from seven or eight different points, Holmes desired to be led to the court-yard, from which we all followed the winding track which led to Boscombe Pool.

Sherlock Holmes was transformed when he

25

was hot upon such a scent as this. Men who had only known the quiet thinker and logician of Baker Street would have failed to recognize him. His face flushed and darkened. His brows were drawn into two hard black lines, while his eyes shone out from beneath them with a steely glitter. His face was bent downward, his shoulders bowed, his lips compressed, and the veins stood out like whipcord in his long, sinewy neck. His nostrils seemed to dilate with a purely animal lust for the chase, and his mind was so absolutely concentrated upon the matter before him that a question or remark fell unheeded upon his ears, or, at the most, only provoked a quick, impatient snarl in reply. Swiftly and silently he made his way along the track which ran through the meadows, and so by way of the woods to the Boscombe Pool. It was damp, marshy ground, as is all that district, and there were marks of many feet, both upon the path and amid the short grass which bounded it on either side. Sometimes Holmes would hurry on, sometimes stop dead, and once he made quite a little detour into the meadow. Lestrade and I walked behind him, the detective indifferent and contemptuous, while I watched my friend with the interest which sprang from the conviction that every one of his actions was directed towards a definite end.

The Boscombe Pool, which is a little reed-girt sheet of water some fifty yards across, is situated at the boundary between the Hatherley Farm and the private park of the wealthy Mr. Turner. Above the woods which lined it upon the farther side we could see the red, jutting pinnacles which marked the site of the rich landowner's dwelling. On the Hatherley side of the pool the woods grew very thick, and there was a narrow belt of sodden grass twenty paces across between the edge of trees and the reeds which lined the lake. Lestrade showed us the exact spot at which the body had been found, and, indeed, so moist was the ground, that I could plainly see the traces which had been left by the fall of the stricken man. To Holmes, as I could see by his eager face and peering eyes, very many other things were to be read upon the trampled grass. He ran round, like a dog who is picking up a scent, and then turned upon my companion.

"What did you go into the pool for?" he asked.

"I fished about with a rake. I thought there might be some weapon or other trace. But how on earth ——"

"Oh, tut, tut! I have no time! That left foot of yours with its inward twist is all over the place. A mole could trace it, and there it vanishes among the reeds. Oh, how simple it would all have been had I been here before they came like a herd of buffalo and wallowed all over it. Here is where the party with the lodge-keeper came, and they have covered all tracks for six or eight feet round the body. But here are three separate tracks of the same feet." He drew out a lens and lay down upon his waterproof to have a better view, talking all the time rather to himself than to us. "These are young McCarthy's feet. Twice he was walking, and once he ran swiftly, so that the soles are deeply marked and the heels hardly visible. That bears out his story. He ran when he saw his father on the ground. Then here are the father's feet as he paced up and down. What is this, then? It is the butt-end of the gun as the son stood listening. And this? Ha, ha! What have we here? Tiptoes! tiptoes! Square, too, quite unusual boots! They come, they go, they come again — of course that was for the cloak. Now where did they come from?" He ran up and down, sometimes losing, sometimes finding the track until we were well within the edge of the wood and under the shadow of a great beech, the largest tree in the neighbourhood. Holmes traced his way to the farther side of this and lay down once more upon his face with a little cry of satisfaction. For a long time he remained there, turning over the leaves and dried sticks, gathering up what seemed to me to be dust into an envelope and examining with his lens not only the ground but even the bark of the tree as far as he could reach.

A jagged stone was lying among the moss, and this also he carefully examined and retained. Then he followed a pathway through the wood until he came to the high-road, where all traces were lost.

"It has been a case of considerable interest," he remarked, returning to his natural manner. "I fancy that this gray house on the right must be the lodge. I think that I will go in and have a word with Moran, and perhaps write a little note. Having done that, we may drive back to our luncheon. You may walk to the cab, and I shall be with you presently."

It was about ten minutes before we regained our cab and drove back into Ross, Holmes still carrying with him the stone which he had picked up in the wood.

"This may interest you, Lestrade," he remarked, holding it out. "The murder was done with it."

"I see no marks."

"There are none."

"How do you know, then?"

"The grass was growing under it. It had only lain there a few days. There was no sign of a place whence it had been taken. It corresponds with the injuries. There is no sign of any other weapon."

"And the murderer?"

"Is a tall man, left-handed, limps with the right leg, wears thick-soled shooting-boots and a gray cloak, smokes Indian cigars, uses a cigar-holder, and carries a blunt pen-knife in his pocket. There are several other indications, but these may be enough to aid us in our search."

Lestrade laughed. "I am afraid that I am still a sceptic," he said. "Theories are all very well, but we have to deal with a hard-headed British jury."

"Nous verrons," answered Holmes calmly. "You work your own method, and I shall work mine. I shall be busy this afternoon, and shall probably return to London by the evening train."

"And leave your case unfinished?"

"No, finished."

"But the mystery?"

"It is solved."

"Who was the criminal, then?"

"The gentleman I describe."

"But who is he?"

"Surely it would not be difficult to find out. This is not such a populous neighbourhood."

Lestrade shrugged his shoulders. "I am a practical man," he said, "and I really cannot undertake to go about the country looking for a left-handed gentleman with a game-leg. I should become the laughing-stock of Scotland Yard."

"All right," said Holmes quietly. "I have given you the chance. Here are your lodgings. Good-bye. I shall drop you a line before

I leave."

Having left Lestrade at his rooms, we drove to our hotel, where we found lunch upon the table. Holmes was silent and buried in thought with a pained expression upon his face, as one who finds himself in a perplexing position.

"Look here, Watson," he said when the cloth was cleared; "just sit down in this chair and let me preach to you for a little. I don't know quite what to do, and I should value your advice. Light a cigar and let me expound."

"Pray do so."

"Well, now, in considering this case there are two points about young McCarthy's narrative which struck us both instantly, although they impressed me in his favour and you against him. One was the fact that his father should, according to his account, cry 'Cooee!' before seeing him. The other was his singular dying reference to a rat. He mumbled several words, you understand, but that was all that caught the son's ear. Now from this double point our research must commence, and we will begin it by presuming that what the lad says is absolutely true."

"What of this 'Cooee!' then?"

"Well, obviously it could not have been meant for the son. The son, as far as he knew, was in Bristol. It was mere chance that he was within earshot. The 'Cooee!' was meant to attract the attention of whoever it was that he had the appointment with. But 'Cooee' is a distinctly Australian cry, and one which is used between Australians. There is a strong presumption that the person whom McCarthy expected to meet him at Boscombe Pool was someone who had been in Australia."

"What of the rat, then?"

Sherlock Holmes took a folded paper from his pocket and flattened it out on the table. "This is a map of the Colony of Victoria," he said. "I wired to Bristol for it last night." He put his hand over part of the map. "What do you read?"

"ARAT," I read.

"And now?" He raised his hand.

"BALLARAT."

"Quite so. That was the word the man uttered, and of which his son only caught the last two syllables. He was trying to utter the name of his murderer. So and so, of Ballarat."

"It is wonderful!" I exclaimed.

"It is obvious. And now, you see, I had narrowed the field down considerably. The possession of a gray garment was a third point which, granting the son's statement to be correct, was a certainty. We have come now out of mere vagueness to the definite conception of an Australian from Ballaret with a gray cloak."

"Certainly."

"And one who was at home in the district, for the pool can only be approached by the farm or by the estate, where strangers could hardly wander."

"Quite so."

"Then comes our expedition of to-day. By an examination of the ground I gained the trifling details which I gave to that imbecile Lestrade, as to the personality of the criminal."

"But how did you gain them?"

"You know my method. It is founded upon the observation of trifles."

"His height I know that you might roughly judge from the length of his stride. His boots, too, might be told from their traces."

"Yes, they were peculiar boots."

"But his lameness?"

"The impression of his right foot was always less distinct than his left. He put less weight upon it. Why? Because he limped — he was lame."

"But his left-handedness."

"You were yourself struck by the nature of the injury as recorded by the surgeon at the inquest. The blow was struck from immediately behind, and yet was upon the left side. Now, how can that be unless it were by a left-handed man? He had stood behind that tree during the interview between the father and son. He had even smoked there. I found the ash of a cigar, which my special knowledge of tobacco ashes enables me to pronounce as an Indian cigar. I have, as you know, devoted some attention to this, and written a little monograph on the ashes of 140 different varieties of pipe, cigar, and cigarette tobacco. Having found the ash, I then looked round and discovered the stump among the moss where he had tossed it. It was an Indian cigar, of the variety which are rolled in Rotterdam."

"And the cigar-holder?"

"I could see that the end had not been in his mouth. Therefore he used a holder. The tip had been cut off, not bitten off, but the cut was not a clean one, so I deduced a blunt pen-knife."

"Holmes," I said, "you have drawn a net round this man from which he cannot escape, and you have saved an innocent human life as truly as if you had cut the cord which was hanging him. I see the direction in which all this points. The culprit is ——"

"Mr. John Turner," cried the hotel waiter, opening the door of our sitting-room, and ushering in a visitor.

The man who entered was a strange and impressive figure. His slow, limping step and bowed shoulders gave the appearance of decrepitude, and yet his hard, deep-lined, craggy features, and his enormous limbs showed that he was possessed of unusual strength of body and of character. His tangled beard, grizzled hair, and outstanding, droop-ping eyebrows combined to give an air of dignity and power to his appearance, but his face was of an ashen white, while his lips and the corners of his nostrils were tinged with a shade of blue. It was clear to me at a glance that he was in the grip of some deadly and chronic disease.

"Pray sit down on the sofa," said Holmes gently. "You had my note?"

"Yes, the lodge-keeper brought it up. You said that you wished to see me here to avoid scandal."

"I thought people would talk if I went to the Hall."

"And why did you wish to see me?" He looked across at my companion with despair in his weary eyes, as though his question was already answered.

"Yes," said Holmes, answering the look rather than the words. "It is so. I know all about McCarthy."

The old man sank is face in his hands. "God help me!" he cried. "But I would not have let the young man come to harm. I give you my word that I would have spoken out if it went against him at the Assizes."

"I am glad to hear you say so," said Holmes gravely.

"I would have spoken now had it not been for my dear girl. It would break her heart — it will break her heart when she hears that I am arrested."

"It may not come to that," said Holmes.

"What?"

"I am no official agent. I understand that it was your daughter who required my presence here, and I am acting in her interests. Young McCarthy must be got off, however."

"I am a dying man," said old Turner. "I have had diabetes for years. My doctor says it is a question whether I shall live a month. Yet I would rather die under my own roof than in a jail."

Holmes rose and sat down at the table with his pen in his hand and a bundle of paper before him. "Just tell us the truth," he said. "I shall jot down the facts. You will sign it, and Watson here can witness it. Then I could produce your confession at the last extremity to save young McCarthy. I promise you that I shall not use it unless it is absolutely needed."

"It's as well," said the old man; "it's a question whether I shall live to the Assizes, so it matters little to me, but I should wish to spare Alice the shock. And now I will make the thing clear to you; it has been a long time in the acting, but will not take me long to tell.

"You didn't know this dead man, McCarthy. He was a devil incarnate. I tell you that. God keep you out of the clutches of such a man as he. His grip has been upon me these twenty years, and he had blasted

36

my life. I'll tell you first how I came to be in his power.

"It was in the early '60's at the diggings. I was a young chap then, hot-blooded and reckless, ready to turn my hand at anything; I got among bad companions, took to drink, had no luck with my claim, took to the bush, and in a word became what you would call over here a highway robber. There were six of us, and we had a wild free life of it, sticking up a station from time to time, or stopping the wagons on the road to the diggings. Black Jack of Ballarat was the name I went under, and our party is still remembered in the colony as the Ballarat Gang.

"One day a gold convoy came down from Ballarat to Melbourne, and we lay in wait for it and attacked it. There were six troopers and six of us, so it was a close thing, but we emptied four of their saddles at the first volley. Three of our boys were killed, however, before we got the swag. I put my pistol to the head of the wagon-driver, who was this very man McCarthy. I wish to the Lord that I had shot him then, but I spared him, though I saw his wicked little eyes fixed on my face, as though to remember every feature. We got away with the gold, became wealthy men, and made our way over to England without being suspected. There I parted from my old pals and determined to settle down to a quiet and respectable life. I bought this estate, which chanced to be in the market, and I set myself to do a little good with my money, to make up for the way in which I had earned it. I married, too, and though my wife died young she left me my dear little Alice. Even when she was a baby her wee hand seemed to lead me down the right path as nothing else had ever done. In a word, I turned over a new leaf and did my best to make up for the past. All was going well when McCarthy laid his grip upon me.

"I had gone up to town about an investment, and I met him in Regent Street with hardly a coat to his back or a boot to his foot.

" 'Here we are, Jack' says he, touching me on the arm; 'we'll be as good as a family to you. There's two of us, me and my son, and you can have the keeping of us. If you don't — it's a fine, law-abiding country is England, and there's always a policeman within hail.'

"Well, down they came to the west country, there was no shaking them off, and there they have lived rent free on my best land ever since. There was no rest for me, no peace, no forgetfulness; turn where I would, there was his cunning, grinning face at my elbow. It grew worse as Alice grew up, for he soon saw I was more afraid of her knowing my past than of the police. Whatever he wanted he must have, and whatever it was I gave him without question, land, money, houses, until at last he asked a thing which I could not give.

He asked for Alice.

"His son, you see, had grown up, and so had my girl, and as I was known to be in weak health, it seemed a fine stroke to him that his lad should step into the whole property. But there I was firm. I would not have his cursed stock mixed with mine; not that I had any dislike to the lad, but his blood was in him, and that was enough. I stood firm. McCarthy threatened. I braved him to do his worst. We were to meet at the pool midway between our houses to talk it over.

"When I went down there I found him talking with his son, so I smoked a cigar and waited behind a tree until he should be alone. But as I listened to his talk all that was black and bitter in me seemed to come uppermost. He was urging his son to marry my daughter with as little regard for what she might think as if she were a slut from off the streets. It drove me mad to think that I and all that I held most dear should be in the power of such a man as this. Could I not snap the bond? I was already a dying and a desperate man. Though clear of mind and fairly strong of limb, I knew that my own fate was sealed. But my memory and my girl! Both could be saved if I could but silence that foul tongue. I did it, Mr. Holmes. I would do it again. Deeply as I have sinned, I have led a life of martyrdom to atone for it. But that my girl should be entangled in the same meshes which held me was more than I could suffer. I struck him down with no more compunction than if he had been some foul and venomous beast. His cry brought back his son; but I had gained the cover of the wood, though I was forced to go back to fetch the cloak which I had dropped in my flight. That is the true story, gentlemen, of all that occurred."

"Well, it is not for me to judge you," said Holmes as the old man signed the statement which has been drawn out. "I pray that we may never be exposed to such a temptation."

"I pray not, sir. And what do you intend to do?"

"In view of your health, nothing. You are yourself aware that you will soon have to answer for your deed at a higher court than the Assizes. I will keep your confession, and if McCarthy is condemned I shall be forced to use it. If not, it shall never be seen by mortal eye; and your secret, whether you be alive or dead, shall be safe with us."

"Farewell, then," said the old man solemnly. "Your own deathbeds, when they come, will be the easier for the thought of the peace which you have given to mine." Tottering and shaking in all his giant frame, he stumbled slowly from the room.

"God help us!" said Holmes after a long silence. "Why does fate play such tricks with poor, helpless worms? I never hear of such a case as this that I do not think of Baxter's words, and say, 'There, but for the grace of God, goes Sherlock Holmes.' "

James McCarthy was acquitted at the Assizes on the strength of a number of objections which had been drawn out by Holmes and submitted to the defending counsel. Old Turner lived for seven months after our interview, but he is now dead; and there is every propsect that the son and daughter may come to live happily together in ignorance of the black cloud which rests upon their past.

The Sweet Shot

E. C. Bentley

No; I HAPPENED to be abroad at the time,"
Philip Trent said. "I wasn't in the way of
seeing the English papers, so until I came here
this week I never heard anything about your
mystery."

Captain Royden, a small, spare, brown-
faced man, was engaged in the delicate — and
forbidden — task of taking his automatic
telephone instrument to pieces. He now
suspended his labours and reached for the
tobacco jar. The large window of his office
in the Kempshill clubhouse looked down
upon the eighteenth green of that delectable
golf course, and his eye roved over the whin-
clad slopes beyond as he called on his recollection.

"Well, if you call it a mystery," he said as
he filled a pipe. "Some people do, because
they like mysteries, I suppose. For instance,
Colin Hunt, the man you're staying with, calls
it that. Others won't have it, and say there was

a perfectly natural explanation. I could tell you as much as anybody could about it, I dare say."

"As being secretary here, you mean?"

"Not only that. I was one of the two people who were in at the death, so to speak — or next door to it," Captain Royden said. He limped to the mantelshelf and took down a silver box embossed on the lid with the crest and mottoes of the Corps of Royal Engineers. "Try one of these cigarettes, Mr. Trent. If you'd like to hear the yarn, I'll give it you. You have heard something about Arthur Freer, I suppose?"

"Hardly anything," Trent said. "I just gathered that he wasn't a very popular character."

"No," Captain Royden said with reserve. "Did they tell you he was my brother-in-law? No? Well, now, it happened about four months ago, on a Monday — let me see — yes, the second Monday in May. Freer had a habit of playing nine holes before breakfast. Barring Sundays — he was strict about Sunday — he did it most days, even in the beastliest weather, going round all alone usually, carrying his own clubs, studying every shot as if his life depended on it. That helped to make him the very good player he was. His handicap here was two, and at Undershaw he used to be scratch, I believe.

"At a quarter to eight he'd be on the first

tee, and by nine he'd be back at his house — it's only a few minutes from here. That Monday morning he started off as usual ——"

"And at the usual time?"

"Just about. He had spent a few minutes in the clubhouse blowing up the steward about some trifle. And that was the last time he was seen alive by anybody — near enough to speak to, that is. No one else went off the first tee until a little after nine, when I started round with Browson — he's our local padre; I had been having breakfast with him at the Vicarage. He's got a game leg, like me, so we often play together when he can fit it in.

"We had holed out on the first green, and were walking on to the next tee, when Browson said, 'Great Scott! Look there. Something's happened.' He pointed down the fairway of the second hole; and there we could see a man lying sprawled on the turf, face down and motionless. Now there is this point about the second hole — the first half of it is in a dip in the land, just deep enough to be out of sight from any other point on the course, unless you're standing right above it — you'll see when you go round yourself. Well, on the tee, you *are* right above it; and we saw this man lying. We ran to the spot.

"It was Freer, as I had known it must be at that hour. He was dead, lying in a

44

disjointed sort of way no live man could have lain in. His clothing was torn to ribbons, and it was singed too. So was his hair — he used to play bareheaded — and his face and hands. His bag of clubs was lying a few yards away, and the brassie, which he had just been using, was close by the body.

"There wasn't any wound showing, and I had seen far worse things often enough, but the padre was looking sickish, so I asked him to go back to the clubhouse and send for a doctor and the police while I mounted guard. They weren't long coming, and after they had done their job the body was taken away in an ambulance. Well, that's about all I can tell you at first hand, Mr. Trent. If you are staying with Hunt, you'll have heard about the inquest and all that, probably."

Trent shook his head. "No," he said. "Colin was just beginning to tell me, after breakfast this morning, about Freer having been killed on the course in some incomprehensible way, when a man came to see him about something. So, as I was going to apply for a fortnight's run of the course, I thought I would ask you about the affair."

"All right," Captain Royden said. "I can tell you about the inquest anyhow — had to be there to speak my own little piece, about finding the body. As for what had happened to Freer, the medical evidence was rather confusing. It was agreed that he had been

45

killed by some tremendous shock, which had jolted his whole system to pieces and dislocated several joints, but had been not quite violent enough to cause any visible wound. Apart from that, there was a disagreement. Freer's own doctor, who saw the body first, declared he must have been struck by lightning. He said it was true there hadn't been a thunderstorm, but that there had been thunder about all that week-end, and that sometimes lightning did act in that way. But the police surgeon, Collins, said there would be no such displacement of the organs from a lightning stroke, even if it did ever happen that way in our climate, which he doubted. And he said that if it had been lightning, it would have struck the steel-headed clubs; but the clubs lay there in their bag quite undamaged. Collins thought there must have been some kind of explosion, though he couldn't suggest what kind."

Trent shook his head. "I don't suppose that impressed the court," he said. "All the same, it may have been all the honest opinion he could give." He smoked in silence a few moments, while Captain Royden attended to the troubles of his telephone instrument with a camel-hair brush. "But surely," Trent said at length, "if there had been such an explosion as that, somebody would have heard the sound of it."

"Lots of people would have heard it,"

Captain Royden answered. "But there you are, you see — nobody notices the sound of explosions just about here. There's the quarry on the other side of the road there, and any time after seven a.m. there's liable to be a noise of blasting."

"A dull, sickening thud?"

"Jolly sickening," Captain Royden said, "for all of us living near by. And so that point wasn't raised. Well, Collins is a very sound man; but as you say, his evidence didn't really explain the thing, and the other fellow's did, whether it was right or wrong. Besides, the coroner and the jury had heard about a bolt from a clear sky, and the notion appealed to them. Anyhow, they brought it in death from misadventure."

"Which nobody could deny, as the song says," Trent remarked. "And was there no other evidence?"

"Yes; some. But Hunt can tell you about it as well as I can; he was there. I shall have to ask you to excuse me now," Captain Royden said. "I have an appointment in the town. The steward will sign you on for a fortnight, and probably get you a game too, if you want one to-day."

Colin Hunt and his wife, when Trent returned to their house for luncheon, were very willing to complete the tale. The verdict, they declared, was tripe. Dr. Collins knew his job, whereas Dr. Hoyle was an old footler, and Freer's death had never been reasonably explained.

As for the other evidence, it had, they agreed, been interesting, though it didn't help at all. Freer had been seen after he had played his tee shot at the second hole, when he was walking down to the bottom of the dip towards the spot where he met his death.

"But according to Royden," Trent said, "that was a place where he couldn't be seen, unless one was right above him."

"Well, this witness *was* right above him," Hunt rejoined. "About one thousand feet above him, so he said. He was an R.A.F. man, piloting a bomber from Bexford Camp, not far from here. He was up doing some sort of exercise, and passed over the course just at that time. He didn't know Freer, but he spotted a man walking down from the second tee, because he was the only living soul visible on the course. Gossett, the other man in the plane, is a temporary member here, and he did know Freer quite well — or as well as anybody cared to know him — but he never saw him. However, the pilot was quite clear that he saw a man just at the time in question, and they took his evidence so as to prove that Freer was absolutely alone just before his death. The only other person who saw Freer was another man who knew him well; used to be a caddy here, and then got a job at the

48

quarry. He was at work on the hillside, and he watched Freer play the first hole and go on to the second — nobody with him, of course."

"Well, that was pretty well established then," Trent remarked. "He was about as alone as he could be, it seems. Yet something happened somehow."

Mrs. Hunt sniffed sceptically, and lighted a cigarette. "Yes, it did," she said. "However, I didn't worry much about it, for one. Edith — Mrs. Freer, that is: Royden's sister — must have had a terrible life of it with a man like that. Not that she ever said anything — she wouldn't. She is not that sort."

"She is a jolly good sort, anyhow," Hunt declared.

"Yes, she is; too good for most men. I can tell you," Mrs. Hunt added for the benefit of Trent, "if Colin ever took to cursing me and knocking me about, my well-known loyalty wouldn't stand the strain for very long."

"That's why I don't do it. It's the fear of exposure that makes me the perfect husband, Phil. She would tie a can to me before I knew what was happening. As for Edith, it's true she never said anything, but the change in her since it happened tells the story well enough. Since she's been living with her brother she has been looking far better and happier than she ever succeeded in doing while

49

Freer was alive."

"She won't be living with him for very long, I dare say," Mrs. Hunt intimated darkly.

"No. I'd marry her myself if I had the chance," Hunt agreed cordially.

"Pooh! You wouldn't be in the first six," his wife said. "It will be Rennie, or Gossett, or possibly Sandy Butler — you'll see. But perhaps you've had enough of the local tittle-tattle, Phil. Did you fix up a game for this afternoon?"

"Yes; with the Jarman Professor of Chemistry in the University of Cambridge," Trent said. "He looked at me as if he thought a bath of vitriol would do me good, but he agreed to play me."

"You've got a tough job," Hunt observed. "I believe he is almost as old as he looks, but he is a devil at the short game, and he knows the course blindfold, which you don't. And he isn't so cantankerous as he pretends to be. By the way, he was the man who saw the finish of the last shot Freer ever played — a sweet shot if ever there was one. Get him to tell you."

"I shall try to," Trent said. "The steward told me about that, and that was why I asked the professor for a game."

Colin Hunt's prediction was fulfilled that afternoon. Professor Hyde, receiving five strokes, was one up at the seventeenth, and at the last hole sent down a four-foot putt to win the match. As they left the green he remarked, as if in answer to something Trent had that moment said, "Yes: I can tell you a curious circumstance about Freer's death."

Trent's eye brightened; for the professor had not said a dozen words during their game, and Trent's tentative allusion to the subject after the second hole had been met merely by an intimidating grunt.

"I saw the finish of the last shot he played," the old gentleman went on, "without seeing the man himself at all. A lovely brassie it was, too — though lucky. Rolled to within two feet of the pin."

Trent considered. "I see," he said, "what you mean. You were near the second green, and the ball came over the ridge and ran down to the hole."

"Just so," Professor Hyde said. "That's how you play it — if you can. You might have done it yourself to-day, if your second shot had been thirty yards longer. I've never done it; but Freer often did. After a really good drive, you play a long second, blind, over the ridge; and with a perfect shot, you may get the green. Well, my house is quite near that green. I was pottering about in the garden before breakfast, and just as I happened to be looking towards the green a ball came hopping down the slope and trickled right across to the hole. Of course, I knew whose

51

it must be — Freer always came along about that time. If it had been anyone else, I'd have waited to see him get his three, and congratulate him. As it was, I went indoors, and didn't hear of his death until long afterwards."

"And you never saw him play the shot," Trent said thoughtfully.

The professor turned a choleric blue eye on him. "How the deuce could I?" he said huffily. "I can't see through a mass of solid earth."

"I know, I know," Trent said. "I was only trying to follow your mental process. Without seeing him play the shot, you knew it was his second — you say he would have been putting for a three. And you said, too — didn't you? — that it was a brassie shot."

"Simply because, my young friend" — the Professor was severe — "I happened to know the man's game. I had played that nine holes with him before breakfast often, until one day he lost his temper more than usual, and made himself impossible. I knew he practically always carried the ridge with his second — I won't say he always got the green — and his brassie was the only club that would do it. It is conceivable, I admit," Professor Hyde added a little stiffly, "that some mishap took place, and that the shot in question was not actually Freer's second; but it did not occur to me to allow for that highly speculative contingency."

On the next day, after those playing a morning round were started on their perambulation, Trent indulged himself with an hour's practice, mainly on the unsurveyed stretch of the second hole. Afterwards he had a word with the caddy master; then visited the professional's shop, and won the regard of that expert by furnishing himself with a new mid-iron. Soon he brought up the subject of the last shot played by Arthur Freer. A dozen times that morning, he said, he had tried, after a satisfying drive, to reach the green with his second; but in vain. Fergus MacAdam shook his head. Not many, he said, could strike the ball with yon force. He could get there himself, whiles, but never for a certainty. Mr. Freer had the strength, and he kenned how to use it forbye.

What sort of clubs, Trent asked, had Freer preferred? "Lang and heavy, like himsel'. Noo ye mention it," MacAdam said, "I hae them here. They were brocht here after the ahccident." He reached up to the top of a rack. "Ay, here they are. They shouldna be, of course; but naebody came to claim them, and it juist slippit ma mind."

Trent, extracting the brassie, looked thoughtfully at the heavy head with the strip of hard white material inlaid in the face. "It's a powerful weapon, sure enough," he remarked.

"Ay, for a man that could control it," MacAdam said. "I dinna care for yon ivorine face mysel'. Some fowk think it gies mair reseelience, ye ken; but there's naething in it."

"He didn't get it from you, then," Trent suggested, still closely examining the head.

"Ay, but he did. I had a lot down from Nelsons while the fashion for them was on. Ye'll find my name," MacAdam added, "stampit on the wood in the usual place, if yer een are seein' richt."

"Well, I don't — that's just it. The stamp is quite illegible."

"Tod! Let's see," the professional said, taking the club in hand. "Guid reason for its being illegible," he went on after a brief scrutiny. "It's been obleeterated — that's easy seen. Who ever saw sic a daft-like thing! The wood has juist been crushed some gait — in a vice, I wouldna wonder. Noo, why would onybody want to dae a thing like yon?"

"Unaccountable, isn't it?" Trent said. "Still, it doesn't matter, I suppose. And anyhow, we shall never know."

It was twelve days later that Trent, looking in at the open door of the secretary's office, saw Captain Royden happily engaged with the separated parts of some mechanism in which coils of wire appeared to be the

54

leading motive.

"I see you're busy," Trent said.

"Come in! Come in!" Royden said heart-ily. "I can do this any time — another hour's work will finish it." He laid down a pair of sharp-nosed pliers. "The electricity people have just changed us over to A.C., and I've got to re-wind the motor of our vacuum cleaner. Beastly nuisance," he added, looking down affectionately at the bewildering jumble of disarticulated apparatus on his table.

"You bear your sorrow like a man," Trent remarked; and Royden laughed as he wiped his hands on a towel.

"Yes," he said, "I do love tinkering about with mechanical jobs, and if I do say it myself, I'd rather do a thing like this with my own hands than risk having it faultily done by a careless workman. Too many of them about. Why, about a year ago the company sent a man here to fit a new main fuse box, and he made a short circuit with his screwdriver that knocked him right across the kitchen and might very well have killed him." He reached down his cigarette box and offered it to Trent, who helped himself; then looked down thoughtfully at the device on the lid.

"Thanks very much. When I saw this box before, I put you down for an R.E. man. *Ubique,* and *Quo fas et gloria ducunt.* Hm! I wonder why Engineers were given that motto in particular."

"Lord knows," the captain said. "In my experience, Sappers don't exactly go where right and glory lead. The dirtiest of all the jobs and precious little of the glory — that's what they get."

"Still, they have the consolation," Trent pointed out, "of feeling that they are at home in a scientific age, and that all the rest of the Army are amateurs compared with them. That's what one of them once told me, anyhow. Well now, Captain, I have to be off this evening. I've looked in just to say how much I've enjoyed myself here."

"Very glad you did," Captain Royden said. "You'll come again, I hope, now you know that the golf here is not so bad."

"I like it immensely. Also the members. And the secretary." Trent paused to light his cigarette. "I found the mystery rather interesting, too."

Captain Royden's eyebrows lifted slightly. "You mean about Freer's death? So you made up your mind it *was* a mystery."

"Why, yes," Trent said. "Because I made up my mind he had been killed by somebody, and probably killed intentionally. Then, when I had looked into the thing a little, I washed out the 'probably.' "

Captain Royden took up a penknife from his desk and began mechanically to sharpen a pencil. "So you don't agree with the coroner's jury?"

"No: as the verdict seems to have been meant to rule out murder or any sort of human agency, I don't. The lightning idea, which apparently satisfied them, or some of them, was not a very bright one, I thought. I was told what Dr. Collins had said against it at the inquest; and it seemed to me he had disposed of it completely when he said that Freer's clubs, most of them steel ones, were quite undamaged. A man carrying his clubs puts them down, when he plays a shot, a few feet away at most; yet Freer was supposed to have been electrocuted without any notice having been taken of them, so to speak."

"Hm! No, it doesn't seem likely. I don't know that that quite decides the point, though," the captain said. "Lightning plays funny tricks, you know. I've seen a small tree struck when it was surrounded by trees twice the size. All the same, I quite agree there didn't seem to be any sense in the lightning notion. It was thundery weather, but there wasn't any storm that morning in this neighbourhood."

"Just so. But when I considered what had been said about Freer's clubs, it suddenly occurred to me that nobody had said anything about *the* club, so far as my information about the inquest went. It seemed clear, from what you and the parson saw, that he had just played a shot with his brassie when he was struck down; it way lying near him, not in the

57

bag. Besides, old Hyde actually saw the ball he had hit roll down the slope on to the green. Now, it's a good rule to study every little detail when you are on a problem of this kind. There weren't many left to study, of course, since the thing had happened four months before; but I knew Freer's clubs must be somewhere, and I thought of one or two places where they were likely to have been taken, in the circumstances, so I tried them. First, I reconnoitred the caddy-master's shed, asking if I could leave my bag there for a day or two; but I was told that the regular place to leave them was the pro's shop. So I went and had a chat with MacAdam, and sure enough it soon came out that Freer's bag was still in his rack. I had a look at the clubs, too.''

''And did you notice anything peculiar about them?'' Captain Royden asked.

''Just one little thing. But it was enough to set me thinking, and next day I drove up to London, where I paid a visit to Nelsons, the sporting outfitters. You know the firm, of course.''

Captain Royden, carefully fining down the point of his pencil, nodded. ''Everybody knows Nelsons.''

''Yes; and MacAdam, I knew, had an account there for his stocks. I wanted to look over some clubs of a particular make — a brassie, with a slip of ivorine let into the face,

58

such as they had supplied to MacAdam. Freer had had one of them from him."

Again Royden nodded.

"I saw the man who shows clubs at Nelsons. We had a talk, and then — you know how little things come out in the course of conversation ——"

"Especially," put in the captain with a cheerful grin, "when the conversation is being steered by an expert."

"You flatter me," Trent said. "Anyhow, it did transpire that a club of that particular make had been bought some months before by a customer whom the man was able to remember. Why he remembered him was because, in the first place, he insisted on a club of rather unusual length and weight — much too long and heavy for himself to use, as he was neither a tall man nor of powerful build. The salesman had suggested as much in a delicate way; but the customer said no, he knew exactly what suited him, and he bought the club and took it away with him."

"Rather an ass, I should say," Royden observed thoughtfully.

"I don't think he was an ass, really. He was capable of making a mistake, though, like the rest of us. There were some other things, by the way, that the salesman recalled about him. He had a slight limp, and he was, or had been, an Army officer. The salesman was an ex-Serviceman, and he couldn't be mistaken, he said, about that."

Captain Royden had drawn a sheet of paper towards him, and was slowly drawing little geometrical figures as he listened. "Go on, Mr. Trent," he said quietly.

"Well, to come back to the subject of Freer's death. I think he was killed by someone who knew Freer never played on Sunday, so that his clubs would be — or ought to be, shall we say? — in his locker all that day. All the following night, too, of course — in case the job took a long time. And I think this man was in a position to have access to the lockers in this clubhouse at any time he chose, and to possess a master key to those lockers. I think he was a skilful amateur craftsman. I think he had a good practical knowledge of high explosives. There is a branch of the Army" — Trent paused a moment and looked at the cigarette box on the table — "in which that sort of knowledge is specially necessary, I believe."

Hastily, as if just reminded of the duty of hospitality, Royden lifted the lid of the box and pushed it towards Trent. "Do have another," he urged.

Trent did so with thanks. "They have to have it in the Royal Engineers," he went on, "because — so I'm told — demolition work is an important part of their job."

"Quite right," Captain Royden observed, delicately shading one side of a cube.

"*Ubique!*" Trent mused, staring at the box lid. "If you are 'everywhere,' I take it you can be in two places at the same time. You could kill a man in one place, and at the same time be having breakfast with a friend a mile away. Well, to return to our subject yet once more; you can see the kind of idea I was led to form about what happened to Freer. I believe that his brassie was taken from his locker on the Sunday before his death. I believe the ivorine face of it was taken off and a cavity hollowed out behind it; and in that cavity a charge of explosive was placed. Where it came from I don't know, for it isn't the sort of thing that is easy to come by, I imagine."

"Oh, there would be no diffculty about that," the captain remarked. "If this man you're speaking of knew all about H.E., as you say, he could have compounded the stuff himself from materials anybody can buy. For instance, he could easily make tetranitroaniline — that would be just the thing for him, I should say."

"I see. Then perhaps there would be a tiny detonator attached to the inner side of the ivorine face, so that a good smack with the brassie would set it off. Then the face would be fixed on again. It would be a delicate job, because the weight of the club-head would have to be exactly right. The feel and balance of the club would have to be just the same as

61

before the operation."

"A delicate job, yes," the captain agreed. "But not an impossible one. There would be rather more to it than you say, as a matter of fact; the face would have to be shaved down thin, for instance. Still, it could be done."

"Well, I imagined it done. Now, this man I have in mind knew there was no work for a brassie at the short first hole, and that the first time it would come out of the bag was at the second hole, down at the bottom of the dip, where no one could see what happened. What certainly did happen was that Freer played a sweet shot, slap on to the green. What else happened at the same moment we don't know for certain, but we can make a reasonable guess. And then, of course, there's the question what happened to the club — or what was left of it; the handle, say. But it isn't a difficult question, I think, if we remember how the body was found."

"How do you mean?" Royden asked.

"I mean, by whom it was found. One of the two players who found it was too much upset to notice very much. He hurried back to the clubhouse; and the other was left alone with the body for, as I estimate it, at least fifteen minutes. When the police came on the scene, they found lying near the body a perfectly good brassie, an unusually long and heavy club, exactly like Freer's brassie in every respect — except one. The name stamped on the wood of the club head had been obliterated by crushing. That name, I think, was not F. MacAdam, but W. J. Nelson; and the club had been taken out of a bag that was not Freer's — a bag which had the remains, if any, of Freer's brassie at the bottom of it. And I believe that's all." Trent got to his feet and stretched his arms. "You can see what I meant when I said I found the mystery interesting."

For some moments Captain Royden gazed thoughtfully out of the window; then he met Trent's inquiring eye. "If there was such a fellow as you imagine," he said coolly, "he seems to have been careful enough — lucky enough too, if you like — to leave nothing at all of what you could call proof against him. And probably he had personal and private reasons for what he did. Suppose that somebody whom he was much attached to was in the power of a foul-tempered, bullying brute; and suppose he found that the bullying had gone to the length of physical violence; and suppose that the situation was hell by day and by night to this man of yours; and suppose there was no way on earth of putting an end to it except the way he took. Yes, Mr. Trent; suppose all that!"

"I will — I do!" Trent said. "That man — if he exists at all — must have been driven pretty hard, and what he did is no business of mine anyway. And now — still in the conditional mood — suppose I take myself off."

The Avenging Chance

Anthony Berkeley

ROGER SHERINGHAM WAS inclined to think afterwards that the Poisoned Chocolates Case, as the papers called it, was perhaps the most perfectly planned murder he had ever encountered. The motive was so obvious, when you knew where to look for it — but you didn't know; the method was so significant when you had grasped its real essentials — but you didn't grasp them; the traces were so thinly covered, when you had realised what was covering them — but you didn't realise. But for a piece of the merest bad luck, which the murderer could not possibly have foreseen, the crime must have been added to the classical list of great mysteries.

This is the gist of the case, as Chief Inspector Moresby told it one evening to Roger in the latter's rooms in the Albany a week or so after it happened: —

On the past Friday morning, the fifteenth of

November, at half past ten o'clock, in accordance with his invariable custom, Sir William Anstruther walked into his club in Piccadilly, the very exclusive Rainbow Club, and asked for his letters. The porter handed him three and a small parcel. Sir William walked over to the fireplace in the big lounge hall to open them.

A few minutes later another member entered the club, a Mr. Graham Beresford. There were a letter and a couple of circulars for him, and he also strolled over to the fireplace, nodding to Sir William, but not speaking to him. The two men only know each other very slightly, and had probably never exchanged more than a dozen words in all.

Having glanced through his letters, Sir William opened the parcel and, after a moment, snorted with disgust. Beresford looked at him, and with a grunt Sir William thrust out a letter which had been enclosed in the parcel. Concealing a smile (Sir William's ways were a matter of some amusement to his fellow members), Beresford read the letter. It was from a big firm of chocolate manufacturers, Mason & Sons, and set forth that they were putting on the market a new brand of liqueur chocolates designed especially to appeal to men; would Sir William do them the honour of accepting the enclosed two-pound box and letting the firm have his candid opinion on them?

"Do they think I'm a blank chorus girl?" fumed Sir William. "Write 'em testimonials about their blank chocolates, indeed! Blank 'em! I'll complain to the blank committee. That sort of blank thing can't blank well be allowed here."

"Well, it's an ill wind so far as I'm concerned," Beresford soothed him. "It's reminded me of something. My wife and I had a box at the Imperial last night. I bet her a box of chocolates to a hundred cigarettes that she wouldn't spot the villain by the end of the second act. She won. I must remember to get them. Have you seen it — *The Creaking Skull?* Not a bad show."

Sir William had not seen it, and said so with force.

"Want a box of chocolates, did you say?" he added, more mildly. "Well, take this blank one. I don't want it."

For a moment Beresford demurred politely and then, most unfortunately for himself, accepted. The money so saved meant nothing to him for he was a wealthy man; but trouble was always worth saving.

By an extraordinarily lucky chance neither the outer wrapper of the box nor its covering letter were thrown into the fire, and this was the more fortunate in that both men had tossed the envelopes of their letters into the flames. Sir William did, indeed, make a bundle of the wrapper, letter and string, but he handed it over to Beresford, and the latter simply dropped it inside the fender. This bundle the porter subsequently extracted and, being a man of orderly habits, put it tidily away in the waste paper basket, whence it was retrieved later by the police.

Of the three unconscious protagonists in the impending tragedy, Sir William was without doubt the most remarkable. Still a year or two under fifty, he looked, with his flaming red face and thickset figure, a typical country squire of the old school, and both his manners and his language were in accordance with tradition. His habits, especially as regards women, were also in accordance with tradition — the tradition of the bold, bad baronet which he undoubtedly was.

In comparison with him, Beresford was rather an ordinary man, a tall, dark, not handsome fellow of two-and-thirty, quiet and reserved. His father had left him a rich man, but idleness did not appeal to him, and he had a finger in a good many business pies.

Money attracts money. Graham Beresford had inherited it, he made it, and, inevitably, he had married it, too. The daughter of a late shipowner in Liverpool, with not far off half a million in her own right. But the money was incidental, for he needed her and would have married her just as inevitably (said his friends) if she had not had a farthing. A tall, rather serious-minded, highly cultured girl, not so young that her character had not had time to form (she was twenty-five when Beresford married her, three years ago), she was the ideal wife for him. A bit of a Puritan perhaps in some ways, but Beresford, whose wild oats, though duly sown, had been a sparse crop, was ready enough to be a Puritan himself by that time if she was. To make no bones about it, the Beresfords succeeded in achieving that eighth wonder of the modern world, a happy marriage.

And into the middle of it there dropped with irretrievable tragedy, the box of chocolates.

Beresford gave them to her after lunch as they sat over their coffee, with some jesting remark about paying his honourable debts, and she opened the box at once. The top layer, she noticed, seemed to consist only of kirsch and maraschino. Beresford, who did not believe in spoiling good coffee, refused when she offered him the box, and his wife ate the first one alone. As she did so she exclaimed in surprise that the filling seemed exceedingly strong and positively burnt her mouth.

Beresford explained that they were samples of a new brand and then, made curious by what his wife had said, took one too. A burning taste, not intolerable but much too strong to be pleasant, followed the release of the liquid, and the almond flavouring seemed quite excessive.

"By Jove," he said, "they are strong. They must be filled with neat alcohol."

"Oh, they wouldn't do that, surely," said his wife, taking another. "But they are very strong. I think I rather like them, though."

Beresford ate another, and disliked it still more "I don't," he said with decision. "They make my tongue feel quite numb. I shouldn't eat any more of them if I were you. I think there's something wrong with them."

"Well, they're only an experiment, I suppose," she said. "But they do burn. I'm not sure whether I like them or not."

A few minutes later Beresford went out to keep a business appointment in the City. He left her still trying to make up her mind whether she liked them, and still eating them to decide. Beresford remembered that scrap of conversation afterwards very vividly, because it was the last time he saw his wife alive.

That was roughly half past two. At a quarter to four Beresford arrived at his club from the City in a taxi, in a state of collapse. He was helped into the building by the driver and the porter, and both described him subsequently as pale to the point of ghastliness, with staring eyes and livid lips, and his skin damp and clammy. His mind seemed unaffected, however, and when they had got him up the steps he was able to walk, with the porter's help, into the lounge.

The porter, thoroughly alarmed, wanted to send for a doctor at once, but Beresford, who was the last man in the world to make a fuss, refused to let him, saying that it must be indigestion and he would be all right in a few minutes. To Sir William Anstruther, however, who was in the lounge at the time, he added after the porter had gone:

"Yes, and I believe it was those infernal chocolates you gave me, now I come to think of it. I thought there was something funny about them at the time. I'd better go and find out if my wife ——" He broke off abruptly. His body, which had been leaning back limply in his chair, suddenly heaved rigidly upright; his jaws locked together, the livid lips drawn back in a horrible grin, and his hands clenched on the arms of his chair. At the same time Sir William became aware of an unmistakable smell of bitter almonds.

Thoroughly alarmed, believing indeed that the man was dying under his eyes, Sir William raised a shout for the porter and a doctor. The other occupants of the lounge hurried up, and between them they got the convulsed body of the unconscious man into a more comfortable position. Before the doctor could arrive a telephone message was received at the club from an agitated butler asking if Mr. Beresford was there, and if so would he come home at once as Mrs. Beresford had been taken seriously ill. As a matter of fact she was already dead.

Beresford did not die. He had taken less of the poison than his wife, who after his departure must have eaten at least three more of the chocolates, so that its action was less rapid and the doctor had time to save him. As a matter of fact it turned out afterwards that he had not had a fatal dose. By about eight o'clock that night he was conscious; the next day he was practically convalescent.

As for the unfortunate Mrs. Beresford, the doctor had arrived too late to save her, and she passed away very rapidly in a deep coma.

The police had taken the matter in hand as soon as Mrs. Beresford's death was reported to them and the fact of poison established, and it was only a very short time before things had become narrowed down to the chocolates as the active agent.

Sir William was interrogated, the letter and wrapper were recovered from the waste paper basket, and, even before the sick man was out of danger, a detective inspector was asking for an interview with the managing director of Mason & Sons. Scotland Yard moves quickly.

It was the police theory at this stage, based on what Sir William and the two doctors had been able to tell them, that by an act of criminal carelessness on the part of one of Mason's employees, an excessive amount of oil of bitter almonds had been included in the filling mixture of the chocolates, for that was what the doctor had decided must be the poisoning ingredient. However, the managing director quashed this idea at once: oil of bitter almonds, he asserted, was never used by Mason's.

He had more interesting news still. Having read with undisguised astonishment the covering letter, he at once declared that it was a forgery. No such letter, no such samples had been sent out by the firm at all; a new variety of liqueur chocolates had never even been mooted. The fatal chocolates were their ordinary brand.

Unwrapping and examining one more closely, he called the Inspector's attention to a mark on the underside, which he suggested was the remains of a small hole drilled in the case, through which the liquid could have been extracted and the fatal filling inserted, the hole afterwards being stopped up with softened chocolate, a perfectly simple operation.

He examined it under a magnifying glass and the Inspector agreed. It was now clear to him that somebody had been trying deliberately to murder Sir William Anstruther.

Scotland Yard doubled its activities. The chocolates were sent for analysis, Sir William was interviewed again, and so was the now conscious Beresford. From the latter the doctor insisted that the news of his wife's death must be kept till the next day, as in his weakened condition the shock might be fatal, so that nothing very helpful was obtained from him.

Nor could Sir William throw any light on the mystery or produce a single person who might have any grounds for trying to kill him. He was living apart from his wife, who was the principal beneficiary in his will, but she was in the South of France, as the French police subsequently confirmed. His estate in Worcestershire, heavily mortgaged, was entailed and went to a nephew; but as the rent he got for it barely covered the interest on the mortgage, and the nephew was considerably better off than Sir William himself, there was no motive there. The police were at a dead end.

The analysis brought one or two interesting facts to light. Not oil of bitter almonds but nitrobenzine, a kindred substance, chiefly used in the manufacture of aniline dyes, was the somewhat surprising poison employed. Each chocolate in the upper layer contained exactly six minims of it, in a mixture of kirsch and maraschino. The chocolates in the other layers were harmless.

As to the other clues, they seemed equally useless. The sheet of Mason's note paper was identified by Merton's, the printers, as of their work, but there was nothing to show

how it had got into the murderer's possession. All that could be said was that, the edges
being distinctly yellowed, it must be an old
piece. The machine on which the letter had
been typed, of course, could not be traced.
From the wrapper, a piece of ordinary brown
paper with Sir William's address hand-printed
on it in large capitals, there was nothing to
be learnt at all beyond that the parcel had
been posted at the office in Southhampton
Street between the hours of 8:30 and 9:30 on
the previous evening.

Only one thing was quite clear. Whoever
had coveted Sir William's life had no intention of paying for it with his or her own.

"And now you know as much as we do, Mr.
Sheringham," concluded Chief Inspector
Moresby; "and if you can say who sent those
chocolates to Sir William, you'll know a good
deal more."

Roger nodded thoughtfully.

"It's a brute of a case. I met a man only
yesterday who was at school with Beresford.
He didn't know him very well because Beresford was on the modern side and my friend
was a classical bird, but they were in the same
house. He says Beresford's absolutely
knocked over by his wife's death. I wish you
could find out who sent those chocolates,
Moresby."

"So do I, Mr. Sheringham," said Moresby

75

gloomily.

"It might have been anyone in the whole world," Roger mused. "What about feminine jealousy, for instance? Sir William's private life doesn't seem to be immaculate. I dare say there's a good deal of off with the old light-o'-love and on with the new."

"Why, that's just what I've been looking into, Mr. Sheringham, sir," retorted Chief Inspector Moresby reproachfully. "That was the first thing that came to me. Because if anything does stand out about this business it is that it's a woman's crime. Nobody but a woman would send poisoned chocolates to a man. Another man would send a poisoned sample of whisky, or something like that."

"That's a very sound point, Moresby," Roger meditated. "Very sound indeed. And Sir William couldn't help you?"

"Couldn't," said Moresby, not without a trace of resentment, "or wouldn't. I was inclined to believe at first that he might have his suspicions and was shielding some woman. But I don't think so now."

"Humph!" Roger did not seem quite so sure. "It's reminiscent, this case, isn't it? Didn't some lunatic once send poisoned choc-olates to the Commissioner of Police himself? A good crime always gets imitated, as you know."

Moresby brightened.

"It's funny you should say that, Mr. Sher-

76

ingham, because that's the very conclusion I've come to. I've tested every other theory, and so far as I know there's not a soul with an interest in Sir William's death, whether from motives of gain, revenge, or what you like, whom I haven't had to rule quite out of it. In fact, I've pretty well made up my mind that the person who sent those chocolates was some irresponsible lunatic of a woman, a social or religious fanatic who's probably never even seen him. And if that's the case," Moresby sighed, "a fat chance I have of ever laying hands on her."

"Unless Chance steps in, as it so often does," said Roger brightly, "and helps you. A tremendous lot of cases get solved by a stroke of sheer luck, don't they? *Chance the Avenger*. It would make an excellent film title. But there's a lot of truth in it. If I were superstitious, which I'm not, I should say it wasn't chance at all, but Providence avenging the victim."

"Well, Mr. Sheringham," said Moresby, who was not superstitious either, "to tell the truth, I don't mind what it is, so long as it lets me get my hands on the right person."

If Moresby had paid his visit to Roger Sheringham with any hope of tapping that gentleman's brains, he went away disappointed.

To tell the truth, Roger was inclined to agree with the Chief Inspector's conclusion, that the attempt on the life of Sir William Anstruther and the actual murder of the unfortunate Mrs. Beresford must be the work of some unknown criminal lunatic. For this reason, although he thought about it a good deal during the next few days, he made no attempt to take the case in hand. It was the sort of affair, necessitating endless inquiries that a private person would have neither the time nor the authority to carry out, which can be handled only by the official police. Roger's interest in it was purely academic.

It was hazard, a chance encounter nearly a week later, which translated this interest from the academic into the personal.

Roger was in Bond Street, about to go through the distressing ordeal of buying a new hat. Along the pavement he suddenly saw bearing down on him Mrs. Verreker-le-Flemming. Mrs. Verreker-le-Flemming was small, exquisite, rich, and a widow, and she sat at Roger's feet whenever he gave her the opportunity. But she talked. She talked, in fact, and talked, and talked. And Roger, who rather liked talking himself, could not bear it. He tried to dart across the road, but there was no opening in the traffic stream. He was cornered.

Mrs. Verreker-le-Flemming fastened on him gladly.

"Oh, Mr. Sheringham! *Just* the person I wanted to see. Mr. Sheringham, *do* tell me.

In confidence. *Are* you taking up this dreadful business of poor Joan Beresford's death?"

Roger, the frozen and imbecile grin of civilised intercourse on his face, tried to get a word in; without result.

"I was horrified when I heard of it — simply horrified. You see, Joan and I were such *very* close friends. Quite intimate. And the awful thing, the truly *terrible* thing is that Joan brought the whole business on herself. Isn't that *appalling?*"

Roger no longer wanted to escape.

"What did you say?" he managed to insert incredulously.

"I suppose it's what they call tragic irony," Mrs. Verreker-le-Flemming chattered on. "Certainly it was tragic enough, and I've never heard anything so terribly ironical. You know about that bet she made with her husband, of course, so that he had to get her a box of chocolates, and if he hadn't Sir William would never have given him the poisoned ones and he'd have eaten them and died himself and good riddance? Well, Mr. Sheringham —" Mrs. Verreker-le-Flemming lowered her voice to a conspirator's whisper and glanced about her in the approved manner. "I've never told anybody else this, but I'm telling you because I know you'll appreciate it. *Joan wasn't playing fair!*"

"How do you mean?" Roger asked, bewildered.

Mrs. Verreker-le-Flemming was artlessly pleased with her sensation.

"Why, she'd seen the play before. We went together, the very first week it was on. She *knew* who the villain was all the time."

"By Jove!" Roger was as impressed as Mrs. Verreker-le-Flemming could have wished. "Chance the Avenger! We're none of us immune from it."

"Poetic justice, you mean?" twittered Mrs. Verreker-le-Flemming, to whom these remarks had been somewhat obscure. "Yes, but Joan Beresford of all people! That's the extraordinary thing. I should never have thought Joan *would* do a thing like that. She was such a *nice* girl. A little close with money, of course, considering how well-off they are, but that isn't anything. Of course it was only fun, and pulling her husband's leg, but I always used to think Joan was such a *serious girl,* Mr. Sheringham. I mean, ordinary people don't talk about honour, and truth, and playing the game, and all those things one takes for granted. But Joan did. She was always saying that this wasn't honourable, or that wouldn't be playing the game. Well, she paid herself for not playing the game, poor girl, didn't she? Still, it all goes to show the truth of the old saying, doesn't it?"

"What old saying?" said Roger, hypnotised by this flow.

"Why, that still waters run deep. Joan must

been deep, I'm afraid." Mrs. Verreker-le-Flemming sighed. It was evidently a social error to be deep. "I mean, she certainly took me in. She can't have been quite so honourable and truthful as she was always pretending, can she? And I can't help wondering whether a girl who'd deceive her husband in a little thing like that might not — oh, well, I don't want to say anything against poor Joan now she's dead, poor darling, but she can't have been *quite* such a plaster saint after all, can she? I mean," said Mrs. Verreker-le-Flemming, in hasty extenuation of these suggestions, "I do think psychology is so very interesting, don't you, Mr. Sheringham?"

"Sometimes, very," Roger agreed gravely. "But you mentioned Sir William Anstruther just now. Do you know him, too?"

"I used to," Mrs. Verreker-le-Flemming replied, without particular interest. "Horrible man! Always running after some woman or other. And when he's tired of her, just drops her — biff! — like that. At least," added Mrs. Verreker-le-Flemming somewhat hastily, "so I've heard."

"And what happens if she refuses to be dropped?"

"Oh dear, I'm sure I don't know. I suppose you've heard the latest."

Mrs. Verreker-le-Flemming hurried on, perhaps a trifle more pink than the delicate aids to nature on her cheeks would have warranted.

"He's taken up with that Bryce woman now. You know, the wife of the oil man, or petrol, or whatever he made his money in. It began about three weeks ago. You'd have thought that dreadful business of being responsible, in a way, for poor Joan Beresford's death would have sobered him up a little, wouldn't you? But not a bit of it; he ——"

Roger was following another line of thought.

"What a pity you weren't at the Imperial with the Beresfords that evening. She'd never have made that bet if you had been." Roger looked extremely innocent. "You weren't, I suppose."

"I?" queried Mrs. Verreker-le-Flemming in surprise. "Good gracious, no. I was at the new revue at the Pavilion. Lady Gavelstoke had a box and asked me to join her party."

"Oh, yes. Good show, isn't it? I thought that sketch *The Sempiternal Triangle* very clever. Didn't you?"

"*The Sempiternal Triangle?*" wavered Mrs. Verreker-le-Flemming.

"Yes, in the first half."

"Oh! Then I didn't see it. I got there disgracefully late, I'm afraid. But then," said Mrs. Verreker-le-Flemming with pathos, "I always do seem to be late for simply everything."

Roger kept the rest of the conversation resolutely upon theatres. But before he left her he had ascertained that she had photographs of both Mrs. Beresford and Sir William Anstruther, and had obtained permission to borrow them some time. As soon as she was out of view he hailed a taxi and gave Mrs. Verreker-le-Flemming's address. He thought it better to take advantage of her permission at a time when he would not have to pay for it a second time over.

The parlourmaid seemed to think there was nothing odd in his mission, and took him up to the drawing-room at once. A corner of the room was devoted to the silver-framed photographs of Mrs. Verreker-le-Flemming's friends, and there were many of them. Roger examined them with interest, and finally took away with him not two photographs but six, those of Sir William, Mrs. Beresford, Beresford, two strange males who appeared to belong to the Sir William period, and, lastly, a likeness of Mrs. Verreker-le-Flemming herself. Roger liked confusing his trail.

For the rest of the day he was very busy.

His activities would have no doubt seemed to Mrs. Verreker-le-Flemming not merely baffling but pointless. He paid a visit to a public library, for instance, and consulted a work of reference, after which he took a taxi and drove to the offices of the Anglo-Eastern Perfumery Company, where he inquired for a certain Mr. Joseph Lea Hardwick and seemed much put out on hearing that no such gentleman was known to the firm and was certainly not employed in any of their branches. Many questions had to be put about the firm and its branches before he consented to abandon the quest.

After that he drove to Messrs. Weall and Wilson, the well-known institution which protects the trade interests of individuals and advises its subscribers regarding investments. Here he entered his name as a subscriber, and explaining that he had a large sum of money to invest, filled in one of the special inquiry forms which are headed Strictly Confidential.

Then he went to the Rainbow Club, in Piccadilly.

Introducing himself to the porter without a blush as connected with Scotland Yard, he asked the man a number of questions, more or less trivial, concerning the tragedy.

"Sir William, I understand," he said finally, as if by the way, "did not dine here the evening before."

There it appeared that Roger was wrong. Sir William had dined in the club, as he did about three times a week.

"But I quite understood he wasn't here that evening," Roger said plaintively.

The porter was emphatic. He remembered quite well. So did a waiter, whom the porter summoned to corroborate him. Sir William had dined, rather late, and had not left the dining-room till about nine o'clock. He spent the evening there, too, the waiter knew, or at least some of it, for he himself had taken him a whisky and soda in the lounge not less than half an hour later.

Roger retired.

He retired to Merton's, in a taxi.

It seemed that he wanted some new note paper printed, of a very special kind, and to the young woman behind the counter he specified at great length and in wearisome detail exactly what he did want. The young woman handed him the books of specimen pieces and asked him to see if there was any style there which would suit him. Roger glanced through them, remarking garrulously to the young woman that he had been recommended to Merton's by a very dear friend, whose photograph he happened to have on him at that moment. Wasn't that a curious coincidence? The young woman agreed that it was.

"About a fortnight ago, I think, my friend was in here last," said Roger, producing the photograph. "Recognise this?"

The young woman took the photograph, without apparent interest.

"Oh, yes. I remember. About some note

paper, too, wasn't it? So that's your friend. Well, it's a small world. Now this is a line we're selling a good deal of just now."

Roger went back to his rooms to dine. Afterwards, feeling restless, he wandered out of the Albany and turned up Piccadilly. He wandered round the Circus, thinking hard, and paused for a moment out of habit to inspect the photographs of the new revue hung outside the Pavilion. The next thing he realised was that he had got as far as Jermyn Street and was standing outside the Imperial Theatre. Glancing at the advertisements of *The Creaking Skull,* he saw that it began at half past eight. Glancing at his watch, he saw that the time was twenty-nine minutes past the hour. He had an evening to get through somehow. He went inside.

The next morning, very early for Roger, he called on Moresby at Scotland Yard.

"Moresby," he said without preamble, "I want you to do something for me. Can you find me a taximan who took a fare from Piccadilly Circus or its neighbourhood at about ten past nine on the evening before the Beresford crime to the Strand somewhere near the bottom of Southampton Street, and another who took a fare back between those points? I'm not sure about the first. Or one taxi might have been used for the double journey, but I doubt that. Anyhow, try to find out for me, will you?"

"What are you up to now, Mr. Sheringham?" Moresby asked suspiciously.

"Breaking down an interesting alibi," replied Roger serenely. "By the way, I know who sent those chocolates to Sir William. I'm just building up a nice structure of evidence for you. Ring up my rooms when you've got those taximen."

He strolled out, leaving Moresby positively gaping after him.

The rest of the day he spent apparently trying to buy a secondhand typewriter. He was very particular that it should be a Hamilton No. 4. When the shop people tried to induce him to consider other makes he refused to look at them, saying that he had had the Hamilton No.4 so strongly recommended to him by a friend who had bought one about three weeks ago. Perhaps it was at this very shop? No? They hadn't sold a Hamilton No. 4 for the last three months? How odd.

But at one shop they had sold a Hamilton No. 4 within the last month, and that was odder still.

At half past four Roger got back to his rooms to await the telephone message from Moresby. At half past five it came.

"There are fourteen taxidrivers here, littering up my office," said Moresby offensively. "What do you want me to with 'em?"

"Keep them till I come, Chief Inspector,"

returned Roger with dignity.

The interview with the fourteen was brief enough, however. To each man in turn Roger showed a photograph, holding it so that Moresby could not see it, and asked if he could recognise his fare. The ninth man did so, without hesitation.

At a nod from Roger, Moresby dismissed them, then sat at his table and tried to look official. Roger seated himself on the table, looking most unofficial, and swung his legs. As he did so, a photograph fell unnoticed out of his pocket and fluttered, face downwards, under the table. Moresby eyed it but did not pick it up.

"And now, Mr. Sheringham, sir," he said, "perhaps you'll tell me what you've been doing?"

"Certainly, Moresby," said Roger blandly. "Your work for you. I really have solved the thing, you know. Here's your evidence." He took from his notecase an old letter and handed it to the Chief Inspector. "Was that typed on the same machine as the forged letter from Mason's, or was it not?"

Moresby studied it for a moment, then drew the forged letter from a drawer of his table and compared the two minutely.

"Mr. Sheringham," he said soberly, "where did you get hold of this?"

"In a secondhand typewriter shop in St. Martin's Lane. The machine was sold to an unknown customer about a month ago. They identified the customer from that same photograph. As it happened, this machine had been used for a time in the office after it was repaired, to see that it was O.K., and I easily got hold of that specimen of its work."

"And where is the machine now?"

"Oh, at the bottom of the Thames, I expect," Roger smiled. "I tell you, this criminal takes no unnecessary chances. But that doesn't matter. There's your evidence."

"Humph! It's all right so far as it goes," conceded Moresby. "But what about Mason's paper?"

"That," said Roger calmly, "was extracted from Merton's book of sample note papers, as I'd guessed from the very yellowed edges might be the case. I can prove contact of the criminal with the book, and there is a gap which will certainly turn out to have been filled by that piece of paper."

"That's fine," Moresby said more heartily.

"As for the taximan, the criminal had an alibi. You've heard it broken down. Between ten past nine and twenty-five past, in fact during the time when the parcel must have been posted, the murderer took a hurried journey to that neighbourhood, going probably by bus or Underground, but returning, as I expected, by taxi, because time would be getting short."

"And the murderer, Mr. Sheringham?"

"The person whose photograph is in my pocket," Roger said unkindly. "By the way, do you remember what I was saying the other day about Chance the Avenger, my excellent film title? Well, it's worked again. By a chance meeting in Bond Street with a silly woman I was put, by the merest accident, in possession of a piece of information which showed me then and there who had sent those chocolates addressed to Sir William. There were other possibilities, of course, and I tested them, but then and there on the pavement I saw the whole thing, from first to last."

"Who was the murderer, then, Mr. Sheringham?" repeated Moresby.

"It was so beautifully planned," Roger went on dreamily. "We never grasped for one moment that we were making the fundamental mistake that the murderer all along intended us to make."

"And what was that?" asked Moresby.

"Why, that the plan had miscarried. That the wrong person had been killed. That was just the beauty of it. The plan had *not* miscarried. It had been brilliantly successful. The wrong person was *not* killed. Very much the right person was."

Moresby gasped.

"Why, how on earth do you make that out, sir?"

"Mrs. Beresford was the objective all the

time. That's why the plot was so ingenious. Everything was anticipated. It was perfectly natural that Sir William should hand the chocolates over to Beresford. It was foreseen that we should look for the criminal among Sir William's associates and not the dead woman's. It was probably even foreseen that the crime would be considered the work of a woman!"

Moresby, unable to wait any longer, snatched up the photograph.

"Good heavens! But Mr. Sheringham, you don't mean to tell me that . . . Sir William himself!"

"He wanted to get rid of Mrs. Beresford," Roger continued. "He had liked her well enough at the beginning, no doubt, though it was her money he was after all the time.

"But the real trouble was that she was too close with her money. He wanted it, or some of it, pretty badly; and she wouldn't part. There's no doubt about the motive. I made a list of the firms he's interested in and got a report on them. They're all rocky, every one. He'd got through all his own money, and had to get more.

"As for the nitrobenzine which puzzled us so much, that was simple enough. I looked it up and found that beside the uses you told me, it's used largely in perfumery. And he's got a perfumery business. The Anglo-Eastern Perfumery Company. That's how he'd know

91

about it being poisonous, of course. But I shouldn't think he got his supply from there. He'd be cleverer than that. He probably made the stuff himself. Any schoolboy knows how to treat benzol with nitric acid to get nitro-benzine."

"But," stammered Moresby, "but Sir William . . . He was at Eton."

"Sir William?" said Roger sharply. "Who's talking about Sir William? I told you the photograph of the murderer was in my pocket." He whipped out the photograph in question and confronted the astounded Chief Inspector with it. "Beresford, man! Beresford's the murderer of his own wife.

"Beresford, who still had handerings after a gay life," he went on more mildly, "didn't want his wife but did want her money. He contrived this plot, providing as he thought against every contingency that could possibly arise. He established a mild alibi, if suspicion ever should arise, by taking his wife to the Imperial, and slipped out of the theatre at the first interval. (I sat through the first act of the dreadful thing myself last night to see when the interval came.) Then he hurried down to the Strand, posted his parcel, and took a taxi back. He had ten minutes, but nobody would notice if he got back to the box a minute late.

"And the rest simply followed. He knew Sir William came to the club every morning at ten thirty, as regularly as clockwork; he knew that for a psychological certainty he could get the chocolates handed over to him if he hinted for them; he knew that the police would go chasing after all sorts of false trails starting from Sir William. And as for the wrapper and the forged letter, he carefully didn't destroy them because they were calculated not only to divert suspicion but actually to point away from him to some anonymous lunatic."

"Well, it's very smart of you, Mr. Sheringham," Moresby said, with a little sigh, but quite ungrudgingly. "Very smart indeed. What was it the lady told you that showed you the whole thing in a flash?"

"Why, it wasn't so much what she actually told me as what I heard between her words, so to speak. What she told me was that Mrs. Beresford knew the answer to that bet; what I deduced was that, being the sort of person she was, it was quite incredible that she should have made a bet to which she knew the answer. *Ergo*, she didn't. *Ergo*, there never was such a bet. *Ergo*, Beresford was lying. *Ergo,* Beresford wanted to get hold of those chocolates for some reason other than he stated. After all, we only had Beresford's word for the bet, hadn't we?

"Of course he wouldn't have left her that afternoon till he'd seen her take, or somehow made her take, at least six of the chocolates, more than a lethal dose. That's why the stuff was in those meticulous six-minim doses. And so that he could take a couple himself, of course. A clever stroke, that."

Moresby rose to his feet.

"Well, Mr. Sheringham, I'm much obliged to you, sir. And now I shall have to get busy myself." He scratched his head. "Chance the Avenger, eh? Well, I can tell you one pretty big thing Beresford left to Chance the Avenger, Mr. Sheringham. Suppose Sir William hadn't handed over the chocolates after all? Supposing he'd kept 'em, to give to one of his own ladies?"

Roger positively snorted. He felt a personal pride in Beresford by this time.

"Really, Moresby! It wouldn't have had any serious results if Sir William had. Do give my man credit for being what he is. You don't imagine he sent the poisoned ones to Sir William, do you? Of course not! He'd send harmless ones, and exchange them for the others on his way home. Dash it all, he wouldn't go right out of his way to present opportunities to Chance.

"If," added Roger, "Chance really is the right word."

The Vindictive Story of the Footsteps That Ran

Dorothy L. Sayers

MR. BUNTER WITHDREW his head from beneath the focusing cloth.

"I fancy that will be quite adequate, sir," he said deferentially, "unless there are any further patients, if I may call them so, which you would wish put on record."

"Not today," replied the doctor. He took the last stricken rat gently from the table, and replaced it in its cage with an air of satisfaction. "Perhaps on Wednesday, if Lord Peter can kindly spare your services once again ——"

"What's that?" murmured his lordship, withdrawing his long nose from the investigation of a number of unattractive-looking glass jars. "Nice old dog," he added vaguely. "Wags his tail when you mention his name, what? Are these monkey-glands, Hartman, or a southwest elevation of Cleopatra's duodenum?"

95

"You don't know anything, do you?" said the young physician, laughing. "No use playing your bally-fool-with-an-eyeglass tricks on me, Wimsey. I'm up to them. I was saying to Bunter that I'd be no end grateful if you'd let him turn up again three days hence to register the progress of the specimens — always supposing they do progress, that is."

"Why ask, dear old thing?" said his lordship. "Always a pleasure to assist a fellow-sleuth, don't you know. Trackin' down murderers — all in the same way of business and all that. All finished? Good egg! By the way, if you don't have that cage mended you'll lose one of your patients — Number 5. The last wire but one is workin' loose — assisted by the intelligent occupant. Jolly little beasts, ain't they? No need of dentists — wish I was a rat — wire much better for the nerves than that fizzlin' drill."

Dr. Hartman uttered a little exclamation.

"How in the world did you notice that, Wimsey? I didn't think you'd even looked at the cage."

"Built noticin' — improved by practice," said Lord Peter quietly. "Anythin' wrong leaves a kind of impression on the eye; brain trots along afterwards with the warnin'. I saw that when we came in. Only just grasped it. Can't say my mind was glued on the matter. Shows the victim's improvin', anyhow. All serene, Bunter?"

"Everything perfectly satisfactory, I trust, my lord," replied the manservant. He had packed up his camera and plates, and was quietly restoring order in the little laboratory, whose fittings — compact as those of an ocean liner — had been disarranged for the experiment.

"Well," said the doctor, "I am enormously obliged to you, Lord Peter, and to Bunter too. I am hoping for a great result from these experiments, and you cannot imagine how valuable an assistance it will be to me to have a really good series of photographs. I can't afford this sort of thing — yet," he added, his rather haggard young face wistful as he looked at the great camera, "and I can't do the work at the hospital. There's no time; I've got to be here. A struggling G.P. can't afford to let his practice go, even in Bloomsbury. There are times when even a half-crown visit makes all the difference between making both ends meet and having an ugly hiatus."

"As Mr. Micawber said," replied Wimsey, " 'Income twenty pounds, expenditure nineteen, nineteen, six — result: happiness; expenditure twenty pounds, ought, six — result: misery.' Don't prostrate yourself in gratitude, old bean; nothin' Bunter loves like messin' round with pyro and hyposulphite. Keeps his hand in. All kinds of practice welcome. Fingerprints and process plates spell seventh what-you-may-call-it of bliss, but focal-plane work on scurvy-ridden rodents (good phrase!) acceptable if no crime forthcoming. Crimes have been rather short lately. Been eatin' our heads off, haven't we, Bunter? Don't know what's come over London. I've taken to prying into my neighbor's affairs to keep from goin' stale. Frightened the postman into a fit the other day by askin' him how his young lady at Croydon was. He's a married man, livin' in Great Ormond Street."

"How did you know?"

"Well, I didn't really. But he lives just opposite to a friend of mine — Inspector Parker; and his wife — not Parker's; he's unmarried; the postman's, I mean — asked Parker the other day whether the flyin' shows at Croydon went on all night. Parker, bein' flummoxed, said 'No,' without thinkin'. Bit of a give-away, what? Thought I'd give the poor devil a word in season, don't you know. Uncommonly thoughtless of Parker."

The doctor laughed. "You'll stay to lunch, won't you?" he said. "Only cold meat and salad, I'm afraid. My woman won't come Sundays. Have to answer my own door. Deuced unprofessional, I'm afraid, but it can't be helped."

"Pleasure," said Wimsey, as they emerged from the laboratory and entered the dark little flat by the back door. "Did you build this place on?"

"No," said Hartman; "the last tenant did that. He was an artist. That's why I took the place. It comes in very useful, ramshackle as it is, though this glass roof is a bit sweltering on a hot day like this. Still, I had to have something on the ground floor, cheap, and it'll do till times get better."

"Till your vitamin experiments make you famous, eh?" said Peter cheerfully. "You're goin' to be the comin' man, you know. Feel it in my bones. Uncommonly neat little kitchen you've got, anyhow."

"It does," said the doctor. "The lab makes it a bit gloomy, but the woman's only here in the daytime."

He led the way into a narrow little dining-room, where the table was laid for a cold lunch. The one window at the end farthest from the kitchen looked out into Great James Street. The room was little more than a passage, and full of doors — the kitchen door, a door in the adjacent wall leading into the entrance-hall, and a third on the opposite side, through which his visitor caught a glimpse of a moderate-sized consulting-room.

Lord Peter Wimsey and his host sat down to table, and the doctor expressed a hope that Mr. Bunter would sit down with them. That correct person, however, deprecated any such suggestion.

"If I might venture to indicate my own preference, Sir," he said, "it would be to wait upon you and his lordship in the usual manner."

"It's no use," said Wimsey. "Bunter likes me to know my place. Terrorizin' sort of man, Bunter. Can't call my soul my own. Carry on, Bunter; we wouldn't presume for the world."

Mr. Bunter handed the salad, and poured out the water with a grave decency appropriate to a crusted old tawny port.

It was a Sunday afternoon in that halcyon summer of 1921. The sordid little street was almost empty. The ice-cream man alone seemed thriving and active. He leaned luxuriously on the green post at the corner, in the intervals of driving a busy trade. Bloomsbury's swarm of able-bodied and able-voiced infants were still; presumably within-doors, eating steamy Sunday dinners inappropriate to the tropical weather. The only disturbing sounds came from the flat above, where heavy footsteps passed rapidly to and fro.

"Who's the merry-and-bright bloke above?" enquired Lord Peter presently. "Not an early riser, I take it. Not that anybody is on a Sunday mornin'. Why an inscrutable Providence ever inflicted such a ghastly day on people livin' in town I can't imagine. I ought to be in the country, but I've got to meet a friend at Victoria this afternoon. Such a day to choose. . . . Who's the lady? Wife or accomplished friend? Gather she takes a properly submissive view of woman's duties in the home, either way. That's the bedroom overhead, I take it."

Hartman looked at Lord Peter in some surprise.

"'Scuse my beastly inquisitiveness, old thing," said Wimsey. "Bad habit. Not my business."

"How did you ——?"

"Guesswork," said Lord Peter, with disarming frankness. "I heard the squawk of an iron bedstead on the ceiling and a heavy fellow get out with a bump, but it may quite well be a couch or something. Anyway, he's been potterin' about in his stocking feet over these few feet of floor for the last half-hour, while the woman has been clatterin' to and fro, in and out of the kitchen and away into the sittin'-room, with her high heels on, ever since we've been here. Hence deduction as to domestic habits of the first-floor tenants."

"I thought," said the doctor, with an aggrieved expression, "you'd been listening to my valuable exposition of the beneficial effects of Vitamin B, and Lind's treatment of scurvy with lemons in 1755."

"I was listenin'," agreed Lord Peter hastily, "but I heard the footsteps as well. Fellow's toddled into the kitchen — only wanted the matches, though; he's gone off into the sittin'-room and left her to carry on the good work. What was I sayin'? Oh, yes! You see, as I was

101

sayin' before, one hears a thing or sees it without knowin' or thinkin' about it. Then afterwards one starts meditatin', and it all comes back, and one sorts out one's impressions. Like those plates of Bunter's. Picture's all there, l — la — what's the word I want, Bunter?"

"Latent, my lord."

"That's it. My right-hand man, Bunter; couldn't do a thing without him. The picture's latent till you put the developer on. Same with the brain. No mystery. Little grey matter's all you want to remember things with. As a matter of curiosity, was I right about those people above?"

"Perfectly. The man's a gas-company's inspector. A bit surly, but devoted (after his own fashion) to his wife. I mean, he doesn't mind hulking in bed on a Sunday morning and letting her do the chores, but he spends all the money he can spare on giving her pretty hats and fur coats and what not. They've only been married about six months. I was called in to her when she had a touch of 'flu in the spring, and he was almost off his head with anxiety. She's a lovely little woman, I must say — Italian. He picked her up in some eating-place in Soho, I believe. Glorious dark hair and eyes: Venus sort of figure; proper contours in all the right places; good skin — all that sort of thing. She was a bit of a draw to that restaurant while she was there, I fancy. Lively. She had an old admirer round here one day — awkward little Italian fellow with a knife — active as a monkey. Might have been unpleasant, but I happened to be on the spot, and her husband came along. People are always laying one another out in these streets. Good for business, of course, but one gets tired of tying up broken heads and slits in the jugular. Still, I suppose the girl can't help being attractive, though I don't say she's what you might call stand-offish in her manner. She's sincerely fond of Brotherton, I think, though — that's his name."

Wimsey nodded inattentively. "I suppose life is a bit monotonous here," he said.

"Professionally, yes. Births and drunks and wife-beatings are pretty common. And all the usual ailments, of course. God!" cried the doctor explosively, "if only I could get away, and do my experiments!"

"Ah!" said Peter, "where's that eccentric old millionaire with a mysterious disease, who always figures in the novels? A lightning diagnosis — a miraculous cure — 'God bless you, doctor; here are five thousand pounds' — Harley Street——"

"That sort doesn't live in Bloomsbury," said the doctor.

"It must be fascinatin', diagnosin' things," said Peter thoughtfully. "How d'you do it? I mean, is there a regular set of symptoms for each disease, like callin' a club to show you want your partner to go no trumps? You don't just say: 'This fellow's got a pimple on his nose, therefore he has fatty degeneration of the heart——' "

"I hope not," said the doctor drily.

"Or is it more like gettin' a clue to a crime?" went on Peter. "You see somethin' — a room, or a body, say, all knocked about anyhow, and there's a damn sight of symptoms of somethin' wrong, and you've got just to pick out the ones which tell the story?"

"That's more like it," said Dr. Hartman. "Some symptoms are significant in themselves — like the condition of the gums in scurvy, let us say — others in conjunction with——"

He broke off, and both sprang to their feet as a shrill scream sounded suddenly from the flat above, followed by a heavy thud. A man's voice cried out lamentably; feet ran violently to and fro; then, as the doctor and his guests stood frozen in consternation, came the man himself — falling down the stairs in his haste, hammering at Hartman's door.

"Help! Help! Let me in! My wife! He's murdered her!"

They ran hastily to the door and let him in. He was a big, fair man, in his shirt-sleeves and stockings. His hair stood up, and his face was set in bewildered misery.

"She is dead — dead. He was her lover," he groaned. "Doctor! I have lost my wife! My Maddalena——" He paused, looked wildly for a moment, and then said hoarsely, "Someone's been in — somehow — stabbed her — murdered her. I'll have the law on him, doctor. Come quickly — she was cooking the chicken for my dinner — Ah-h-h!"

He gave a long, hysterical shriek, which ended in a hiccupping laugh. The doctor took him roughly by the arm and shook him. "Pull yourself together, Mr. Brotherton," he said sharply. "Perhaps she is only hurt. Stand out of the way!"

"Only hurt?" said the man, sitting heavily down on the nearest chair. "No — no — she is dead — little Maddalena — Oh, my God!"

Dr. Hartman had snatched a roll of bandages and a few surgical appliances from the consulting-room, and he ran upstairs, followed closely by Lord Peter. Bunter remained for a few moments to combat hysterics with cold water. Then he stepped across to the dining-room window and shouted.

"Well, wot is it?" cried a voice from the street.

"Would you be so kind as to step in here a minute, officer?" said Mr. Bunter. "There's been murder done."

When Brotherton and Bunter arrived upstairs

with the constable, they found Dr. Hartman and Lord Peter in the little kitchen. The doctor was kneeling beside the woman's body. At their entrance he looked up, and shook his head.

"Death instantaneous," he said. "Clean through the heart. Poor child. She cannot have suffered at all. Oh, constable, it is very fortunate you are here. Murder appears to have been done — though I'm afraid the man has escaped. Probably Mr. Brotherton can give us some help. He was in the flat at the time."

The man had sunk down on a chair, and was gazing at the body with a face from which all meaning seemed to have been struck out. The policeman produced a notebook.

"Now, sir," he said, "don't let's waste any time. Sooner we can get to work the more likely we are to catch our man. Now, you was 'ere at the time, was you?"

Brotherton stared a moment, then, making a violent effort, he answered steadily:

"I was in the sitting-room, smoking and reading the paper. My — *she* — was getting the dinner ready in here. I heard her give a scream, and I rushed in and found her lying on the floor. She didn't have time to say anything. When I found she was dead, I rushed to the window, and saw the fellow scrambling away over the glass roof there. I yelled at him, but he disappeared. Then I ran down ——"

"'Arf a mo'," said the policeman. "Now, see 'ere, sir, didn't you think to go after 'im at once?"

"My first thought was for her," said the man. "I thought maybe she wasn't dead. I tried to bring her round——" His speech ended in a groan.

"You say he came in through the window," said the policeman.

"I beg your pardon, officer," interrupted Lord Peter, who had been apparently making a mental inventory of the contents of the kitchen. "Mr. Brotherton suggested that the man went *out* through the window. It's better to be accurate."

"It's the same thing," said the doctor. "It's the only way he could have come in. These flats are all alike. The staircase door leads into the sitting-room, and Mr. Brotherton was there, so the man couldn't have come that way."

"And," said Peter, "he didn't get in through the bedroom window, or we should have seen him. We were in the room below. Unless, indeed, he let himself down from the roof. Was the door between the bedroom and the sitting-room open?" he asked suddenly, turning to Brotherton.

The man hesitated a moment. "Yes," he said finally. "Yes, I'm sure it was."

"Could you have seen the man if he had

come through the bedroom window?"

"I couldn't have helped seeing him."

"Come, come, sir," said the policeman, with some irritation, "better let *me* ask the questions. Stands to reason the fellow wouldn't get in through the bedroom window in full view of the street."

"How clever of you to think of that," said Wimsey. "Of course not. Never occurred to me. Then it must have been this window, as you say."

"And, what's more, here's his marks on the window-sill," said the constable triumphantly, pointing to some blurred traces among the London soot. "That's right. Down he goes by that drainpipe, over the glass roof down there — what's that the roof of?"

"My laboratory," said the doctor. "Heavens! to think that while we were at dinner this murdering villain——"

"Quite so, sir," agreed the constable. "Well, he'd get away over the wall into the court be'ind. 'E'll 'ave been seen there, no fear; you needn't anticipate much trouble in layin' 'ands on 'im, sir. I'll go round there in 'arf a tick. Now then, sir" — turning to Brotherton — "'ave you any idea wot this party might have looked like?"

Brotherton lifted a wild face, and the doctor interposed.

"I think you ought to know, constable," he said, "that there was — well, not a murderous attack, but what might have been one, made on this woman before — about eight weeks ago — by a man named Marinetti — an Italian waiter — with a knife.''

"Ah!" The policeman licked his pencil eagerly. "Do you know this party as 'as been mentioned?" he enquired of Brotherton.

"That's the man," said Brotherton, with concentrated fury. "Coming here after my wife — God curse him! I wish to God I had him dead here beside her!"

"Quite so," said the policeman. "Now, sir" — to the doctor — "'ave you got the weapon wot the crime was committed with?"

"No," said Hartman, "there was no weapon in the body when I arrived."

"Did *you* take it out?" pursued the constable, to Brotherton.

"No," said Brotherton, "he took it with him."

"Took it with 'im," the constable entered the fact in his notes. "Phew! Wonderful 'ot it is in 'ere, ain't it, sir?" he added, mopping his brow.

"It's the gas-oven, I think," said Peter mildly. "Uncommon hot thing, a gas-oven, in the middle of July. D'you mind if I turn it out? There's the chicken inside, but I don't suppose you want——"

Brotherton groaned, and the constable said: "Quite right sir. A man wouldn't 'ardly fancy 'is dinner after a thing like this. Thank

109

you, sir. Well now, doctor, wot kind of weapon do you take this to 'ave been?''

"It was a long, narrow weapon — something like an Italian stiletto, I imagine,'' said the doctor, "about six inches long. It was thrust in with great force under the fifth rib, and I should say it had pierced the heart centrally. As you see, there has been practically no bleeding. Such a wound would cause instant death. Was she lying just as she is now when you first saw her, Mr. Brotherton?''

"On her back, just as she is,'' replied the husband.

"Well, that seems clear enough,'' said the policeman. "This 'ere Marinetti, or wotever 'is name is, 'as a grudge against the poor young lady——''

"I believe he was an admirer,'' put in the doctor.

"Quite so,'' agreed the constable. "Of course, these foreigners are like that — even the decentest of 'em. Stabbin' and such-like seems to come natural to them, as you might say. Well, this 'ere Marinetti climbs in 'ere, sees the poor young lady standin' 'ere by the table all alone, gettin' the dinner ready; 'e comes in be'ind, catches 'er round the waist, stabs 'er — easy job, you see; no corsets nor nothink — she shrieks out, 'e pulls 'is stiletty out of 'er an' makes tracks. Well, now we've got to find 'im, and by your leave, sir, I'll be gettin' along. We'll 'ave 'im by the 'eels

110

before long, sir, don't you worry. I'll 'ave to put a man in charge 'ere, sir, to keep folks out, but that needn't worry you. Good mornin', gentlemen."

"May we move the poor girl now?" asked the doctor.

"Certainly. Like me to 'elp you, sir?"

"No. Don't lose any time. We can manage." Dr. Hartman turned to Peter as the constable clattered downstairs. "Will you help me, Lord Peter?"

"Bunter's better at that sort of thing," said Wimsey, with a hard mouth.

The doctor looked at him in some surprise, but said nothing, and he and Bunter carried the still form away. Brotherton did not follow them. He sat in a grief-stricken heap, with his head buried in his hands. Lord Peter walked about the little kitchen, turning over the various knives and utensils, peering into the sink bucket, and apparently taking an inventory of the bread, butter, condiments, vegetables, and so forth which lay about in preparation for the Sunday meal. There were potatoes in the sink, half peeled, a pathetic witness to the quiet domestic life which had been so horribly interrupted. The colander was filled with green peas. Lord Peter turned these things over with an inquisitive finger, gazed into the smooth surface of a bowl of drippings as though it were a divining-crystal, ran his hands several times right through a

111

bowl of flour — then drew his pipe from his pocket and filled it slowly.

The doctor returned, and put his hand on Brotherton's shoulder.

"Come," he said gently, "we have laid her in the other bedroom. She looks very peaceful. You must remember that, except for that moment of terror when she saw the knife, she suffered nothing. It is terrible for you, but you must try not to give way. The police——"

"The police can't bring her back to life," said the man savagely. "She's dead. Leave me alone, curse you! Leave me alone I say!"

He stood up, with a violent gesture.

"You must not sit here," said Hartman firmly. "I will give you something to take, and you must try to keep calm. Then we will leave you, but if you don't control yourself——"

After some further persuasion, Brotherton allowed himself to be led away.

"Bunter," said Lord Peter, as the kitchen door closed behind them, "do you know why I am doubtful about the success of those rat experiments?"

"Meaning Dr. Hartman's, my lord?"

"Yes. Dr. Hartman has a theory. In any investigation, my Bunter, it is most damnably dangerous to have a theory."

"I have heard you say so, my lord."

"Confound you — you know it as well as I

112

do! What is wrong with the doctor's theories, Bunter?"

"You wish me to reply, my lord, that he only sees the facts which fit in with the theory."

"Thought-reader!" exclaimed Lord Peter bitterly.

"And that he supplies them to the police, my lord."

"Hush!" said Peter, as the doctor returned.

"I have got him to lie down," said Dr. Hartman, "and I think the best thing we can do is to leave him to himself."

"D'you know," said Wimsey, "I don't cotton to that idea, somehow."

"Why? Do you think he's likely to destroy himself?"

"That's as good a reason to give as any other, I suppose," said Wimsey, "when you haven't got any reason which can be put into words. But my advice is, don't leave him for a moment."

"But why? Frequently, with a deep grief like this, the presence of other people is merely an irritant. He begged me to leave him."

"Then for God's sake go back to him," said Peter.

"Really, Lord Peter," said the doctor, "I think I ought to know what is best for my patient."

"Doctor," said Wimsey, "this is not a

question of your patient. A crime has been committed."

"But there is no mystery."

"There are twenty mysteries. For one thing, when was the window-cleaner here last?"

"The window-cleaner?"

"Who shall fathom the ebony-black enigma of the window-cleaner?" pursued Peter lightly, putting a match to his pipe. "You are quietly in your bath, in a state of more or less innocent nature, when an intrusive head appears at the window, like the ghost of Hamilton Tighe, and a gruff voice, suspended between earth and heaven, says, 'Good morning sir.' Where do window-cleaners go between visits?" Do they hibernate, like busy bees? Do they ——"

"Really, Lord Peter," said the doctor, "don't you think you're going a bit beyond the limit?"

"Sorry you feel like that," said Peter, "but I really want to know about the window-cleaner. Look how clear these panes are."

"He came yesterday, if you want to know," said Dr. Hartman, rather stiffly.

"You are sure?"

"He did mine at the same time."

"I thought as much," said Lord Peter. "In that case, it is absolutely imperative that Brotherton should not be left alone for a moment. Bunter! Confound it all, where's that fellow got to?"

114

The door into the bedroom opened.

"My lord?" Mr. Bunter unobtrusively appeared, as he had unobtrusively stolen out to keep an unobtrusive eye on the patient.

"Good," said Wimsey. "Stay where you are." His lackadaisical manner had gone, and he looked at the doctor as four years previously he might have looked at a refractory subaltern.

"Dr. Hartman," he said, "something is wrong. Cast your mind back. We were talking about symptoms. Then came the scream. Then came the sound of feet running. *Which direction did they run in?*"

"I'm sure I don't know."

"Don't you? Symptomatic though, doctor. They have been troubling me all the time, subconsciously. Now I know why. They ran *from the kitchen.*"

"Well?"

"Well! And now the window-cleaner ——"

"What about him?"

"Could you swear that it wasn't the window-cleaner who made those marks on the sill?"

"And the man Brotherton saw ——"

"Have we examined your laboratory for his footsteps?"

"But the weapon? Wimsey, this is madness! Someone took the weapon."

"I know. But did you think the edge of the wound was clean enough to have been made by a smooth stiletto? It looked ragged to me."

"Wimsey, what are you driving at?"

"There's a clue here in the flat — and I'm damned if I can remember it. I've seen it — I know I've seen it. It'll come to me presently. Meanwhile, don't let Brotherton ——"

"What?"

"Do whatever it is he's going to do."

"But what is it?"

"If I could tell you that I could show you the clue. Why couldn't he make up his mind whether the bedroom door was open or shut? Very good story, but not quite thought out. Anyhow — I say, doctor, make some excuse, and strip him, and bring me his clothes. And send Bunter to me."

The doctor stared at him, puzzled. Then he made a gesture of acquiescence and passed into the bedroom. Lord Peter followed him, casting a ruminating glance at Brotherton as he went. Once in the sitting-room, Lord Peter sat down on a red velvet armchair, fixed his eyes on a gilt-framed oleograph, and became wrapped in contemplation.

Presently Bunter came in, with his arms full of clothing. Wimsey took it, and began to search it, methodically enough, but listlessly. Suddenly he dropped the garments, and turned to the manservant.

"No," he said, "this is a precaution, Bunter mine, but I'm on the wrong track. It wasn't

116

here I saw — whatever I did see. It was in the kitchen. Now, what was it?"

"I could not say, my lord, but I entertain a conviction that I was also in a manner of speaking, conscious — not consciously conscious, my lord, if you understand me, but still conscious of an incongruity."

"Hurray!" said Wimsey suddenly. "Cheer-oh! for the subconscious what's-his-name! Now let's remember the kitchen. I cleared out of it because I was gettin' obfuscated. Now then. Begin at the door. Fryin'-pans and sauce-pans on the wall. Gas-stove — oven goin' — chicken inside. Rack of wooden spoons on the wall, gas-lighter, pan-lifter. Stop me when I'm gettin' hot. Mantelpiece. Spice-boxes and stuff. Anything wrong with them? No. Dresser. Plates. Knives and forks — all clean; flour dredger — milk-jug — sieve on the wall — nutmeg-grater. Three-tier steamer. Looked inside — no grisly secrets in the steamer."

"Did you look in all the dresser drawers, my lord?"

"No. That could be done. But the point is, I *did* notice somethin'. What did I notice? That's the point. Never mind. On with the dance — let joy be unconfined! Knife-board. Knife-powder. Kitchen table. Did you speak?"

"No," said Bunter, who had moved from his attitude of wooden deference.

"Table stirs a chord. Very good. On table. Choppin'-board. Remains of ham and herb stuffin'. Packet of suet. Another sieve. Several plates. Butter in a glass dish. Bowl of drippin' — "

"Ah!"

"Drippin'——! Yes, there was ——"

"Something unsatisfactory, my lord ——"

"About the drippin'! Oh, my head! What's that they say in *Dear Brutus,* Bunter? 'Hold on to the workbox.' That's right. Hold on to the drippin'. Beastly slimy stuff to hold on to —— Wait!"

There was a pause.

"When I was a kid," said Wimsey, "I used to love to go down into the kitchen and talk to old cookie. Good old soul she was, too. I can see her now, gettin' chicken ready, with me danglin' my legs on the table. *She* used to pluck an' draw 'em herself. I revelled in it. Little beasts boys are, ain't they, Bunter? Pluck it, draw it, wash it, stuff it, tuck its little tail through its little what-you-may-call-it, truss it, grease the dish —— Bunter?"

"My lord!"

"Hold on to the dripping!"

"The bowl, my lord ——"

"The bowl — visualize it — what was wrong?"

"It was full, my lord!"

"Got it — got it — *got* it! The bowl was full — smooth surface. Golly! I knew there

118

was something queer about it. Now why shouldn't it be full? Hold on to the ——"

"The bird was in the oven."

"Without dripping!"

"Very careless cookery, my lord."

"The bird — in the oven — no dripping. Bunter! Suppose it was never put in till after she was dead? Thrust in hurriedly by someone who had something to hide — horrible!"

"But with what object, my lord?"

"Yes, why? That's the point. One more mental association with the bird. It's just coming. Wait a moment. Pluck, draw, wash, stuff, tuck up, truss —— By God!"

"My lord?"

"Come on, Bunter. Thank Heaven we turned off the gas!"

He dashed through the bedroom, disregarding the doctor and the patient, who sat up with a smothered shriek. He flung open the oven door and snatched out the baking-tin. The skin of the bird had just begun to discolour. With a little gasp of triumph, Wimsey caught the iron ring that protruded from the wing, and jerked out — *the six-inch spiral skewer.*

The doctor was struggling with the excited Brotherton in the doorway. Wimsey caught the man as he broke away, and shook him into the corner with a jiu-jitsu twist.

"Here is the weapon," he said.

"Prove it, blast you!" said Brotherton

savagely.

"I will," said Wimsey. "Bunter, call in the policeman at the door. Doctor, we shall need your microscope."

In the laboratory the doctor bent over the microscope. A thin layer of blood from the skewer had been spread upon the slide.

"Well?" said Wimsey impatiently.

"It's all right," said Hartman. "The roasting didn't get anywhere near the middle. My God, Wimsey, yes, you're right — round corpuscles, diameter $\frac{1}{3621}$ — mammalian blood — probably human ——"

"Her blood," said Wimsey.

"It was very clever, Bunter," said Lord Peter, as the taxi trundled along on the way to his flat in Piccadilly. "If that fowl had gone on roasting a bit longer the blood-corpuscles might easily have been destroyed beyond all hope of recognition. It all goes to show that the unpremeditated crime is usually the safest."

"And what does your lordship take the man's motive to have been?"

"In my youth," said Wimsey meditatively, "they used to make me read the Bible. Trouble was, the only books I ever took to naturally were the ones they weren't over and above keen on. But I got to know the Song of Songs pretty well by heart. Look it up, Bunter; at your age it won't hurt you; it talks sense about jealousy."

"I have perused the work in question, your lordship," replied Mr. Bunter, with a sallow blush. "It says, if I remember rightly: *'Jealousy is cruel as the grave.'*"

A Chess Problem

Agatha Christie

POIROT AND I often dined at a small restaurant in Soho. We were there one evening, when we observed a friend at an adjacent table. It was Inspector Japp, and as there was room at our table, he came and joined us. It was some time since either of us had seen him.

"Never do you drop in to see us nowadays," declared Poirot reproachfully. "Not since the affair of the Yellow Jasmine have we met, and that is nearly a month ago."

"I've been up north — that's why. Take any interest in chess, Moosior Poirot?" Japp asked.

"I have played it, yes."

"Did you see that curious business yesterday? Match between two players of world-wide reputation, and one died during the game?"

"I saw a mention of it. Dr. Savaronoff, the Russian champion, was one of the players, and the other, who succumbed to heart failure, was the brilliant young American, Gilmour Wilson.''

"Quite right. Savaronoff beat Rubinstein and became Russian champion some years ago. Wilson is said to be a second Capablanca.''

"A very curious occurrence,'' mused Poirot. "If I mistake not, you have a particular interest in the matter.''

Japp gave a rather embarrassed laugh.

"You've hit it, Moosior Poirot. I'm puzzled. Wilson was sound as a bell — no trace of heart trouble. His death is quite inexplicable.''

"You suspect Dr. Savaronoff of putting him out of the way?'' I cried.

"Hardly that,'' said Japp dryly. "I don't think even a Russian would murder another man in order not to be beaten at chess — and anyway, from all I can make out, the boot was likely to be on the other leg. The doctor is supposed to be very hot stuff — second to Lasker they say he is.''

Poirot nodded thoughtfully.

"Then what exactly is your little idea?'' he asked. "Why should Wilson be poisoned? For, I assume, of course, that it is poison you suspect.''

"Naturally. Heart failure means your heart stops beating — that's all there is to that. That's what a doctor says officially at the moment, but privately he tips us the wink that he's not satisfied."

"When is the autopsy to take place?"

"To-night. Wilson's death was extraordinarily sudden. He seemed quite as usual and was actually moving one of the pieces when he suddenly fell forward — dead!"

"There are very few poisons would act in such a fashion," objected Poirot.

"I know. The autopsy will help us, I expect. But why should any one want Gilmour Wilson out of the way — that's what I'd like to know. Harmless unassuming young fellow. Just come over here from the States, and apparently hadn't an enemy in the world."

"It seems incredible," I mused.

"Not at all," said Poirot, smiling. "Japp has his theory, I can see."

"I have, Moosior Poirot. I don't believe the poison was meant for Wilson — it was meant for the other man."

"Savaronoff?"

"Yes. Savaronoff fell foul of the Bolsheviks at the outbreak of the Revolution. He was even reported killed. In reality he escaped, and for three years endured incredible hardships in the wilds of Siberia. His sufferings were so great that he is now a changed man. His friends and acquaintances declare they would hardly have recognized him. His hair is white, and his whole aspect that of a man terribly aged. He is a semi-invalid, and seldom goes out, living alone with a niece, Sonia Daviloff, and a Russian manservant in a flat down Westminster way. It is possible that he still considers himself a marked man. Certainly he was very unwilling to agree to this chess contest. He refused several times point blank, and it was only when the newspapers took it up and began making a fuss about the 'unsportsmanlike refusal' that he gave in. Gilmour Wilson had gone on challenging him with real Yankee pertinacity, and in the end he got his way. Now I ask you, Moosior Poirot, why wasn't he willing? Because he didn't want attention drawn to him. Didn't want somebody or other to get on his track. That's my solution — Gilmour Wilson got pipped by mistake."

"There is no one who has any private reason to gain by Savaronoff's death?"

"Well, his niece, I suppose. He's recently come into an immense fortune. Left him by Madame Gospoja whose husband was a sugar profiteer under the old regime. They had an affair together once, I believe, and she refused steadfastly to credit the reports of his death."

"Where did the match take place?"

"In Savaronoff's own flat. He's an invalid, as I told you."

"Many people there to watch it?"

"At least a dozen — probably more."

Poirot made an expressive grimace.

"My poor Japp, your task is not an easy one."

"Once I know definitely that Wilson was poisoned, I can get on."

"Has it occurred to you that, in the meantime, supposing your assumption that Savaronoff was the intended victim to be correct, the murderer may try again?"

"Of course it has. Two men are watching Savaronoff's flat."

"That will be very useful if any one should call with a bomb under his arm," said Poirot dryly.

"You're getting interested, Moosior Poirot," said Japp, with a twinkle. "Care to come round to the mortuary and see Wilson's body before the doctors start on it? Who knows, his tie pin may be askew, and that may give you a valuable clue that will solve the mystery."

"My dear Japp, all through dinner my fingers have been itching to rearrange your own tie pin. You permit, yes? Ah! that is much more pleasing to the eye. Yes, by all means, let us go to the mortuary."

I could see that Poirot's attention was completely captivated by this new problem. It was so long since he had shown any interest over any outside case that I was quite rejoiced to see him back in his old form.

For my own part, I felt a deep pity as I looked down upon the motionless form and convulsed face of the hapless young American who had come by his death in such a strange way. Poirot examined the body attentively. There was no mark on it anywhere, except a small scar on the left hand.

"And the doctor says that's a burn, not a cut," explained Japp.

Poirot's attention shifted to the contents of the dead man's pockets which a constable spread out for our inspection. There was nothing much — a handkerchief, keys, notecase filled with notes, and some unimportant letters. But one object standing by itself filled Poirot with interest.

"A chessman!" he exclaimed. "A white bishop. Was that in his pocket?"

"No, clasped in his hand. We had quite a difficulty to get it out of his fingers. It must be returned to Dr. Savaronoff sometime. It's part of a very beautiful set of carved ivory chessmen."

"Permit me to return it to him. It will make an excuse for my going there."

"Aha!" cried Japp. "So you want to come in on this case."

"I admit it. So skilfully have you aroused my interest."

"That's fine. Got you away from your brooding. Captain Hastings is pleased, too, I can see."

"Quite right," I said, laughing.

Poirot turned back towards the body.

"No other little detail you can tell me about — him?" he asked.

"I don't think so."

"Not even — that he was left-handed?"

"You're a wizard, Moosior Poirot. How did you know that? He *was* left-handed. Not that it's anything to do with the case."

"Nothing whatever," agreed Poirot hastily, seeing that Japp was slightly ruffled. "My little joke — that was all. I like to play you the trick, you see."

We went out upon an amicable understanding.

The following morning saw us wending our way to Dr. Savaronoff's flat in Westminster.

"Sonia Daviloff," I mused. "It's a pretty name."

Poirot stopped, and threw me a look of despair.

"Always looking for romance! You are incorrigible."

The door of the flat was opened to us by a manservant with a peculiarly wooden face. It seemed impossible to believe that that impassive countenance could ever display emotion.

Poirot presented a card on which Japp had scribbled a few words of introduction, and we were shown into a low, long room furnished with rich hangings and curios. One or two wonderful ikons hung upon the walls, and exquisite Persian rugs lay upon the floor. A samovar stood upon a table.

I was examining one of the ikons which I judged to be of considerable value, and turned to see Poirot prone upon the floor. Beautiful as the rug was, it hardly seemed to me to necessitate such close attention.

"Is it such a very wonderful specimen?" I asked.

"Eh? Oh! the rug? But no, it was not the rug I was remarking. But it *is* a beautiful specimen, far too beautiful to have a large nail wantonly driven through the middle of it. No, Hastings," as I came forward, "the nail is not there now. But the hole remains."

A sudden sound behind us made me spin round, and Poirot spring nimbly to his feet. A girl was standing in the doorway. Her eyes, full upon us, were dark with suspicion. She was of medium height, with a beautiful, rather sullen face, dark-blue eyes, and very black hair which was cut short. Her voice, when she spoke, was rich and sonorous, and completely un-English.

"I fear my uncle will be unable to see you. He is a great invalid."

"That is a pity, but perhaps you will kindly help me instead. You are Mademoiselle Daviloff, are you not?"

"Yes, I am Sonia Daviloff. What is it you want to know?"

"I am making some inquiries about that sad affair the night before last — the death of M. Gilmour Wilson. What can you tell me about it?"

The girl's eyes opened wide.

"He died of heart failure — as he was playing chess."

"The police are not so sure that it was — heart failure, mademoiselle."

The girl gave a terrified gesture.

"It was true then," she cried. "Ivan was right."

"Who is Ivan, and why do you say he was right?"

"It was Ivan who opened the door to you — and he has already said to me that in his opinion Gilmour Wilson did not die a natural death — that he was poisoned by mistake."

"By mistake."

"Yes, the poison was meant for my uncle."

She had quite forgotten her first distrust now, and was speaking eagerly.

"Why do you say that, mademoiselle? Who should wish to poison Dr. Savaronoff?"

She shook her head.

"I do not know. I am all in the dark. And my uncle, he will not trust me. It is natural, perhaps. You see, he hardly knows me. He saw me as a child, and not since till I came to live with him here in London. But this much I do know, he is in fear of something. We have many secret societies in Russia, and one day I overheard something which made me think it was of just such a society he went in fear."

"Mademoiselle, your uncle is still in danger. I must save him. Now recount to me exactly the events of that fatal evening. Show me the chessboard, the table, how the two men sat — everything."

She went to the side of the room and brought out a small table. The top of it was exquisite, inlaid with squares of silver and black to represent a chessboard.

"This was sent to my uncle a few weeks ago as a present, with the request that he would use it in the next match he played. It was in the middle of the room — so."

Poirot examined the table with what seemed to me quite unnecessary attention. He was not conducting the inquiry at all as I would have done. Many of his questions seemed to me pointless, and upon really vital matters he seemed to have no questions to ask.

After a minute examination of the table and the exact position it had occupied, he asked to see the chessmen. Sonia Daviloff brought them to him in a box. He examined one or two of them in a perfunctory manner.

"An exquisite set," he murmured absent-mindedly.

Still not a question as to what refreshments there had been, or what people had been present.

I cleared my throat significantly.

"Don't you think, Poirot, that —"

He interrupted me peremptorily.

"Do not think, my friend. Leave all to me. Mademoiselle, is it quite impossible that I should see your uncle?"

A faint smile showed itself on her face.

"He will see you, yes. You understand, it is my part to interview all strangers first."

She disappeared. I heard a murmur of voices in the next room, and a minute later she came back and motioned us to pass into the adjoining room.

The man who lay there on a couch was an imposing figure. Tall, gaunt, with huge bushy eyebrows and white beard, and a face haggard as the result of starvation and hardships, Dr. Savaronoff was a distinct personality. I noted the peculiar formation of his head, its unusual height. A great chess player must have a great brain, I knew. I could easily understand Dr. Savaronoff being the second greatest player in the world.

Poirot bowed.

"*M. le Docteur*, may I speak to you alone?"

Savaronoff turned to his niece.

"Leave us, Sonia."

She disappeared obediently.

"Now, sir, what is it?"

"Dr. Savaronoff, you have recently come into an enormous fortune. If you should — die unexpectedly, who inherits it?"

"I have made a will leaving everything to

my niece, Sonia Daviloff. You do not suggest —"

"I suggest nothing, but you have not seen
your niece since she was a child. It would
have been easy for any one to impersonate
her."

Savaronoff seemed thunderstruck by the
suggestion. Poirot went on easily.

"Enough as to that. I give you the word of
warning, that is all. What I want you to do
now is to describe to me the game of chess
the other evening."

"How do you mean — describe it?"

"Well, I do not play the chess myself, but
I understand that there are various regular
ways of beginning — the gambit, do they not
call it?"

Dr. Savaronoff smiled a little.

"Ah! I comprehend you now. Wilson
opened Ruy Lopez — one of the soundest
openings there is, and one frequently adopted
in tournaments and matches."

"And how long had you been playing when
the tragedy happened?"

"It must have been about the third or fourth
move when Wilson suddenly fell forward over
the table, stone dead."

Poirot rose to depart. He flung out his last
question as though it was of absolutely no
importance, but I knew better.

"Had he had anything to eat or drink?"

"A whisky and soda, I think."

"Thank you, Dr. Savaronoff. I will disturb you no longer."

Ivan was in the hall to show us out. Poirot lingered on the threshold.

"The flat below this, do you know who lives there?"

"Sir Charles Kingwell, a member of Parliament, sir. It has been let furnished lately, though."

"Thank you."

We went out into the bright winter sunlight.

"Well, really, Poirot," I burst out. "I don't think you've distinguished yourself this time. Surely your questions were very inadequate."

"You think so, Hastings?" Poirot looked at me appealingly. "I was *bouleversé,* yes. What would you have asked?"

I considered the question carefully, and then outlined my scheme to Poirot. He listened with what seemed to be close interest. My monologue lasted until we had nearly reached home.

"Very excellent, very searching, Hastings," said Poirot, as he inserted his key in the door and preceded me up the stairs. "But quite unnecessary."

"Unnecessary!" I cried, amazed. "If the man was poisoned —"

"Aha," cried Poirot, pouncing upon a note which lay on the table. "From Japp. Just as I thought." He flung it over to me. It was brief and to the point. No traces of poison had been found, and there was nothing to show how the man came by his death.

"You see," said Poirot, "our questions would have been quite unnecessary."

"You guessed this beforehand?"

" 'Forecast the probable result of the deal,' " quoted Poirot from a recent bridge problem on which I had spent much time. *"Mon ami,* when you do that successfully, you do not call it guessing."

"Don't let's split hairs," I said impatiently. "You foresaw this?"

"I did."

"Why?"

Poirot put his hand into his pocket and pulled out — a white bishop.

"Why," I cried, "you forgot to give it back to Dr. Savaronoff."

"You are in error, my friend. That bishop still reposes in my left-hand pocket. I took its fellow from the box of chessmen Mademoiselle Daviloff kindly permitted me to examine. The plural of one bishop is two bishops."

He sounded the final *s* with a great hiss. I was completely mystified.

"But why did you take it?"

"Parbleu, I wanted to see if they were exactly alike."

He stood them on the table side by side.

"Well, they are, of course," I said, "exactly

alike."

Poirot looked at them with his head on one side.

"They seem so, I admit. But one should take no fact for granted until it is proved. Bring me, I pray you, my little scales."

With infinite care he weighed the two chessmen, then turned to me with a face alight with triumph.

"I was right. See you, I was right. Impossible to deceive Hercule Poirot!"

He rushed to the telphone — waited impatiently.

"Is that Japp? Ah! Japp, it is you. Hercule Poirot speaks. Watch the manservant, Ivan. On no account let him slip through your fingers. Yes, yes, it is as I say."

He dashed down the receiver and turned to me.

"You see it not, Hastings? I will explain. Wilson was not poisoned, he was electrocuted. A thin metal rod passes up the middle of one of those chessmen. The table was prepared beforehand and set upon a certain spot on the floor. When the bishop was placed upon one of the silver squares, the current passed through Wilson's body, killing him instantly. The only mark was the electric burn upon his hand — his left hand, because he was left-handed. The 'special table' was an extremely cunning piece of mechanism. The table I examined was a duplicate, perfectly innocent. It was substituted for the other immediately after the murder. The thing was worked from the flat below, which, if you remember, was let furnished. But one accomplice at least was in Savaronoff's flat. The girl is an agent of a Russian secret society, working to inherit Savaronoff's money."

"And Ivan?"

"I strongly suspect that Ivan is the girl's confederate."

"It's amazing," I said at last. "Everything fits in. Savaronoff had an inkling of the plot, and that's why he was so averse to playing the match."

Poirot looked at me without speaking. Then he turned abruptly away, and began pacing up and down.

"Have you a book on chess by any chance, *mon ami?*" he asked suddenly.

"I believe I have somewhere."

It took me some time to ferret it out, but I found it at last, and brought it to Poirot, who sank down in a chair and started reading it with the greatest attention.

In about a quarter of an hour the telephone rang. I answered it. It was Japp. Ivan had left the flat, carrying a large bundle. He had sprung into a waiting taxi, and the chase had begun. He was evidently trying to lose his pursuers. In the end he seemed to fancy that he had done so, and had then driven to a big empty house at Hampstead. The house was surrounded.

I recounted all this to Poirot. He merely stared at me as though he scarcely took in what I was saying. He held out the chess book.

"Listen to this, my friend. This is the Ruy Lopez opening. 1 P-K4, P-K4; 2 Kt-KB3, Kt-QB3; 3B-Kt5. Then there comes a question as to Black's best third move. He has the choice of various defences. It was White's third move that killed Gilmour Wilson, 3B-Kt5. Only the third move — does that say nothing to you?"

I hadn't the least idea what he meant, and told him so.

"I suppose, Hastings, that while you were sitting in this chair, you heard the front door being opened and shut, what would you think?"

"I should think some one had gone out, I suppose."

"Yes — but there are always two ways of looking at things. Some one gone out — some one come *in* — two totally different things, Hastings. But if you assumed the wrong one, presently some little discrepancy would creep in and show you that you were on the wrong track."

"What does all this mean, Poirot?"

Poirot sprang to his feet with sudden energy.

"It means that I have been a triple imbecile. Quick, quick, to the flat in Westminster. We may yet be in time."

We tore off in a taxi. Poirot returned no answer to my excited questions. We raced up the stairs. Repeated rings and knocks brought no reply, but listening closely I could distinguish a hollow groan coming from within.

The hall porter proved to have a master key, and after a few difficulties he consented to use it.

Poirot went straight to the inner room. A whiff of chloroform met us. On the floor was Sonia Daviloff, gagged and bound, with a great wad of saturated cotton wool over her nose and mouth. Poirot tore it off and began to take measures to restore her. Presently a doctor arrived, and Poirot handed her over to his charge and drew aside with me. There was no sign of Dr. Savaronoff.

"What does it all mean?" I asked, bewildered.

"It means that before two equal deductions I chose the wrong one. You heard me say that it would be easy for any one to impersonate Sonia Daviloff because her uncle had not seen her for so many years?"

"Yes?"

"Well, precisely the opposite held good also. It was equally easy for any one to *impersonate the uncle!*"

"What?"

"Savaronoff *did* die at the outbreak of the Revolution. The man who pretended to have escaped with such terrible hardships, the man so changed 'that his own friends could hardly recognise him,' the man who successfully laid claim to an enormous fortune — is an impostor. He guessed I should get on the right track in the end, so he sent off the honest Ivan on a tortuous wild-goose chase, chloroformed the girl, and got out, having by now doubtless realised most of the securities left by Madame Gospoja."

"But — but who tried to kill him?"

"Nobody tried to kill *him*. Wilson was the intended victim all along."

"But why?"

"My friend, the real Savaronoff was the second greatest chess player in the world. In all probability his impersonator did not even know the rudiments of the game. Certainly he could not sustain the fiction of a match. He tried all he knew to avoid the contest. When that failed, Wilson's doom was sealed. At all costs he must be prevented from discovering that the great Savaronoff did not even know how to play chess. Wilson was fond of the Ruy Lopez opening, and was certain to use it. The false Savaronoff arranged for death to come with the third move, before any complications of defence set in."

"But, my dear Poirot," I persisted, "are we

dealing with a lunatic? I quite follow your reasoning, and admit that you must be right, but to kill a man just to sustain his rôle! Surely there were simpler ways out of the difficulty than that! He could have said that his doctor forbade the strain of a match."

Poirot wrinkled his forehead.

"*Certainement,* Hastings," he said, "there were other ways, but none so convincing. Besides, you are assuming that to kill a man is a thing to avoid, are you not? Our impostor's mind, it does not act that way. I put myself in his place, a thing impossible for you. I picture his thoughts. He enjoys himself as the professor at that match. I doubt not he has visited the chess tourneys to study his part. He sits and frowns in thought; he gives the impression that he is thinking great plans, and all the time he laughs in himself. He is aware that two moves are all that he knows — and all that he *need know.* Again, it would appeal to his mind to foresee the events and to make Wilson his own executioner. . . . Oh, yes, Hastings, I begin to understand our friend and his psychology."

I shrugged.

"Well, I suppose you're right, but I can't understand any one running a risk he could so easily avoid."

"Risk!" Poirot snorted. "Where then lay the risk? Would Japp have solved the problem? No; if the false Savaronoff had not made one small mistake he would have run no risk."

"And his mistake?" I asked, although I suspected the answer.

"*Mon ami,* he overlooked the little gray cells of Hercule Poirot."

Poirot has his virtues, but modesty is not one of them.

The Case of the White Elephant

Margery Allingham

MR CAMPION, PILOTING his companion through the crowded courtyard at Burlington House, became aware of the old lady in the Daimler partly because her chauffeur almost ran over him and partly because she gave him a stare of such vigorous and personal disapproval that he felt she must either know him very well indeed or have mistaken him for someone else entirely.

Juliet Fysher-Sprigge, who was leaning on his arm with all the weariness of a two-hour trek round the academy's Summer Exhibition, enlightened him.

"We were *not* amused, were we?" she said. "Old-fashioned people have minds that are just too prurient, my dear. After all, I have known you for years, haven't I, and I'm not even married to Philip. Besides, the academy is so respectable. It isn't as though she'd seen me sneaking out of the National Gallery."

Mr Campion handed her into a taxicab.

"Who was she?" he enquired, hoisting his lank form in after her.

Juliet laughed. Her laughter was one of her most charming attributes, for it wiped the sophistication from her débutante's face and left her the schoolgirl he had known three years before.

"My dear, didn't you recognize her? That would have been the last straw for the poor darling! That's Florence, Dowager Countess of Marle. Philip's Auntie Flo."

Mr Campion's pale blue eyes grew momentarily more intelligent behind his horn-rimmed spectacles.

"Ah, hence the disgust," he said. "You'll have to explain me away. The police are always doing it."

Juliet turned to him with the wide-eyed ingenuousness of one who perceives a long-awaited opening.

"You still dabble in police and detection and things, then?" she said breathlessly and not very tactfully, since his reputation as a criminologist was considerable. "Do tell me, what is the low-down on these terribly exciting burglaries? Are the police really beaten or are they being bribed? No one talks of anything else these days. I just had to see you and find out."

Her companion leant back in the leathery depths of the cab and sighed regretfully.

"When you phoned me and demanded to

be taken to this execrable exhibition I was vain enough to think it was my companionship you were after," he said. "Now it turns out to be merely a vulgar pursuit of the material for gossip. Well, my girl, you're going to be disappointed. The clever gentleman doesn't know a thing and, what's more, he doesn't care. Have you lost anything yourself?"

"Me?" Juliet's gratification at the implied compliment all but outweighed her disappointment. "Of course I haven't. It's only the really worth-while collections that have gone. That's why it's so interesting. The De Breuil diamonds went first. Then the Denver woman lost her emeralds and the glorious Napoleon necklace. Josephine Pharoah had her house burgled and just lost her tiara, which was the one really good thing she had, and now poor old Mrs Dacre has had her diamonds and rubies pinched, including the famous dog collar. Forty-two diamonds, my dear! — each one quite as big as a pea. They say it's a cat burglar and the police know him quite well but they can't find him — at least, that's one story. The other one is that it's all being done for the insurance and the police are in it. What do you think?"

Mr Campion glanced at her affectionately and noted that the gold hair under her small black hat curled as naturally as ever.

"Both stories are equally good," he

announced placidly. "Come and have some tea, or has Philip's Auntie Flo got spies everywhere?"

Miss Fysher-Sprigge blushed. "I don't care if she has," she said. "I've quarelled with Philip, anyway."

It took Mr Campion several minutes, until they were seated at a table on the edge of the Hotel Monde's smaller dance floor, in fact, before he fully digested this piece of information. Juliet was leaning back in her chair, her eyes roving over the gathering in a frank search for old acquaintances, when he spoke again.

"Seriously?" he enquired.

Juliet met his eyes and again he saw her sophistication vanish.

"I hope not," she said soberly. "I've been rather an ass. Can I tell you about it?"

Mr Campion smiled ruefully. It was a sign of the end of the thirties, he supposed, when one submitted cheerfully to the indignity of taking a young woman out only to hear about her hopes and fears concerning a younger man. Juliet went on blissfully, lowering her voice so that the heart searchings of the balalaika orchestra across the floor concealed it from adjoining tables.

"Philip is a dear, but he has to be so filthily careful about the stupidest things," she said, accepting a rhumbaba. "The F.O. casts a sort of white light over people, have you noticed?

146

His relations are like it, too, only worse. You can't talk of anything without getting warned off. The aunt we saw today bit my head off the other evening for merely mentioning these cat burglaries, which, after all, are terribly exciting. 'My child,' she said, 'we can't afford to know about such things,' and went on talking about her old White Elephant until I nearly wept."

"White Elephant?" Mr Campion looked blank. "The charity?"

Juliet nodded. " 'Send your white elephant to Florence, Countess of Marle, and she will find it a home where it will be the pet of the family,' " she quoted. "It's quite an important affair, patronised by royalty and blessed by every archbishop in the world. I pointed out it was only a glorified jumble sale and she nearly had a fit. She works herself to death for it. I go and help pack up parcels sometimes — or I did before this row with Philip. I've been rather silly. I've done something infuriating. Philip's livid with me now and I don't know what's going to happen when he finds out everything. I must tell somebody. Can I tell you?"

A faint smile passed over Mr Campion's thin face.

"You're quite a nice girl," he said, "but you won't stay twenty-one for ever. Stop treating me as though I was a maiden uncle."

"You must be thirty-six at least," said Miss

Fysher-Sprigge brutally, "and I'm rather glad, because presumably you're sensible. Look here, if a man has a criminal record it doesn't mean he's always going to be stealing things, does it? Not if he promises to go straight?"

Her companion frowned. "I don't quite follow," he said. "Age is stopping the brain from functioning. I thought we were talking about Philip Graysby, Auntie Flo's nephew?"

"So we are," said Juliet. "He hasn't got the record, of course, but Henry Swan has. Henry Swan is — or, rather, was — Philip's man. He'd been with Philip for eighteen months and been perfectly good, and then this came out about him. Philip said he was awfully sorry but he'd have to go. Philip couldn't help it, I suppose — I do see that now – but at the time I was furious. It seemed so unfair, and we had a quarrel. I said some beastly things and so did he, but he wouldn't give in and Swan went."

She paused and eyed her companion dubiously. Mr Campion shrugged his shoulders.

"It doesn't seem very serious," he said.

Juliet accepted the cigarette he offered her and seemed engrossed in the tip of it.

"No," she agreed. "That part isn't. But you see, I'm a very impulsive person and I was stupidly cross at the time and so when I had a wonderful idea for getting my own back I acted on it. I got Swan a job with the most respectable person I knew and, in order to do it, I gave him a reference. To make it a good reference I didn't say anything about the record. How's that?"

"Not so good," he admitted. "Who's the most respectable person harbouring this human bomb?"

Juliet avoided his eyes. "Philip's Auntie Flo," she said. "She's the stiffest, thorniest, most conventional of them all. Philip doesn't go there often so he hasn't seen Swan yet, but when he does and makes enquiries and hears about me — well, it's going to be awkward. D'you think he'll ever forgive me? He stands to get a fortune from Auntie Flo if he doesn't annoy her. It was a silly thing of me to do, wasn't it?"

"Not bright," agreed Mr Campion. "Are you in love with Philip?"

"Horribly," said Juliet Fysher-Sprigge and looked away across the dance floor.

Mr Campion had spent some time expounding a wise course of action, in which a clean breast to all concerned figured largely, when he became aware that he was not being heard. Juliet was still staring across the room, her eyes puzzled.

"I say," she said unexpectedly, "this place is wildly expensive, isn't it?"

"I hope not," said Mr Campion mildly.

Juliet did not smile. Her cheeks were faintly flushed and her eyes questioning.

"Don't be a fool. You know what I mean. This is probably the most expensive place in London, isn't it? How queer! It looks as though Auntie Flo really has got her spies everywhere. That's her manicurist over there, having tea alone."

He glanced casually across the room.

"The woman sitting directly under the orchestra?" he enquired. "The one who looks like a little bull in a navy hat? She's an interesting type, isn't she? Not very nice."

Juliet's eyes were still thoughtful.

"That's her. Miss Matisse. A visiting manicurist," she said. "She goes to dozens of people I know. I believe she's very good. How funny for her to come to tea alone, here of all places . . ."

Mr Campion's casual interest in the small square figure who managed somehow to look flamboyant in spite of her sober clothes showed signs of waning.

"She may be waiting for someone," he suggested.

"But she's ordered her tea and started it."

"Oh well, perhaps she just felt like eating."

"Rubbish!" said Juliet. "You pay ten and sixpence just to sit in this room because you can dance if you want to."

Her host laughed. "Auntie Flo has a pretty turn of speed if she tracked us down here and then whipped round and set her manicuring bloodhound on us, all in half an hour," he said.

Juliet ignored him. Her attention had wandered once again.

"I say," she murmured, "can you see through that mirror over there? See that man eating alone? I thought at first he was watching Miss Matisse, but I believe it's you he's most interested in."

Her companion turned his head and his eyes widened.

"Apologies," he said. "I underestimated you. That's Detective Sergeant Blower, one of the best men in the public-school and night-club tradition. I wonder who he's tailing. Don't watch him — it's unkind."

Juliet laughed. "You're a most exciting person to have tea with," she said. "I do believe . . ."

The remainder of her remark was lost as, in common with all but one visitor in the room, she was silenced by what was, for the Hotel Monde, a rather extraordinary incident.

The balalaika orchestra had ceased to play for a moment or so and the dance floor was practically deserted when, as though taking advantage of the lull, the woman in the navy hat rose from her chair and shouted down the whole length of the long room, in an effort, apparently, to attract the attention of a second woman who had just entered.

"Mrs. Gregory!" Her voice was powerful

and well articulated. "Mrs. Gregory! Mrs. Gregory!"

The newcomer halted as all eyes were turned upon her, and her escort expostulated angrily to the excited maître d'hotel who hurried forward.

Miss Matisse sat down, and in the silence Mr Campion heard her explaining in a curiously flat voice to the waiter who came up to her.

"I am sorry. I thought I recognised a friend. I was mistaken. Bring me my bill, please."

Juliet stared across the table, her young face shocked.

"What a very extraordinary thing to do," she said.

Mr Campion did not reply. From his place of vantage he could see in the mirror that Detective Sergeant Blower had also called for his bill and was preparing to leave.

Some little time later, when Mr Campion deposited Juliet on her Mount Street doorstep, she was in a more cheerful mood.

"Then you think if I go to Philip and tell him the worst and say that I'm sorry he'll forgive me?" she said as they parted.

"If he's human he'll forgive you anything," Mr Campion assured her gallantly.

Juliet sighed. "Age does improve the manners," she said unnecessarily. "I'll forgive you for disappointing me about the burglaries. I really had hoped to get all the dirt. Good-bye."

"Damn the burglaries!" said Mr Campion and took a taxi home.

Three days later he said the same thing again but for a different reason. This reason arrived by post. It came in a fragrant green box designed to contain a large flask of familiar perfume and it lay upon his breakfast table winking at him with evil amusement. It was Mrs Dacre's ruby-and-diamond dog collar and it was not alone. In a nest of cotton wool beneath it were five diamond rings of considerable value, a pair of exquisite ruby ear clips, and a small hooped bracelet set with large alternate stones.

Mr Campion, who was familiar with the "stolen" list which the police send round to their local stations and circularise to the jewellers and pawnbrokers of the kingdom, had no difficulty in recognising the collection as the haul of the last cat burglary.

The sender of so dubious a gift might have been harder to identify had it not been for the familiarity of the perfume and the presence of a small card on which was printed in shaky, ill-disguised characters a simple request and a specious promise:

Get these back where they belong and I'll love you for ever, darling.

Mr Campion had a considerable respect for

the law but he spent some time that morning in acquiring a box of similar design but different and more powerful perfume, and it was not until the jewelry was freshly housed and the card burned that he carried his responsibility to Scotland Yard and laid it with a sigh of relief on the desk of Chief Detective Inspector Stanislaus Oates, his friend and partner in many adventures.

The original wrapping he decided to retain. Its ill-written address might have been scrawled by anyone and the fact that it was grossly overfranked showed that it had been dropped into a public box and not passed over a post-office counter.

He let the chief, who was a tall, disconsolate personage with a grey face and dyspepsia, recover from his first transports of mingled relief and suspicion before regretting his inability to help him further. Oates regarded him.

"It's my duty to warn you that you're under suspicion," he said with the portentous solemnity which passed with him for wit.

Campion laughed. "My cat-burglary days are over," he said. "Or am I the fence?"

"That's more like it." The chief passed his cigarette case. "I can't tell you how glad I am to see this lot. But it doesn't help us very much unless we know where it came from. These cat jobs are done by The Sparrow. We knew that as soon as we saw the first one.

You remember him, Campion? — a sleek, handsome chap with an insufferable manner. These jobs have his trademarks all over them. Pane cut out with a diamond and the glass removed with a sucker — no fingerprints, no noise, no mistakes." He paused and caressed his ear sadly. "It's getting on my nerves," he said. "The commissioner is sarcastic and the papers are just libellous. It's hard on us. We know who and where the fellow is but we can't get him. We've held him as long as we dared, three separate times this summer, but we haven't got a thing we can fix on him. I've been trusting the stuff would turn up somewhere so that we could work back on him from that angle, but frankly this is the first scrap of it I've seen. Where's all the early swag? This was only pinched five days ago."

Mr Campion remained unhelpful. "I got it this morning," he said. "It just came out of the air. Ask the postman."

"Oh, I know . . ." The chief waved the suggestion aside. "You'll help us just as much as you can, which means as much as you care to. Some society bit is mixed up in this somewhere, I'm sure of it. Look here, I'll tell you what I'll do. I'll put my cards on the table. This isn't official; this is the truth. Edward Borringer, alias The Sparrow, is living with his wife in digs in Kilburn. They're very respectable at the moment, just a quiet hardworking couple. He takes classes in the local

155

gym and she does visiting manicure work."

"Under the name of Matisse?"

"Exactly!" The inspector was jubilant. "Now you've given yourself away, my lad. What do you know about Margot Matisse?"

"Not much," his visitor confessed affably. "She was pointed out to me as a manicurist at a thé dansant at the Hotel Monde on Tuesday. Looking round, I saw Blower on her trail, so naturally when you mentioned manicurists I put two and two together."

"Who pointed her out to you?"

"A lady who had seen her at work in a relation's house."

"All right." The policeman became depressed again. "Well, there you are. It's quite obvious how they're working it. She goes round to the big houses and spots the stuff and the lie of the land, and then he calls one night and does the job. It's the old game worked very neatly. Too neatly, if you ask me. What we can't fathom is how they're disposing of the stuff. They certainly haven't got it about them, and their acquaintance just now is so respectable, not to say aristocratic, that we can barely approach it. Besides, to make this big stuff worth the risk they must be using an expert. Most of these stones are so well known that they must go to a first-class fellow to be recut."

Mr Campion hesitated. "I seem to remember that Edward Borringer was once associated with our old friend Bertrand Meyer and his ménage," he ventured. "Are they still functioning?"

"Not in England." The chief was emphatic. "And if these two are getting their stuff out of the country I'll eat my hat. The customs are co-operating with us. We thought a maid in one of the houses which the Matisse woman visits might be in it and so if you've heard a squawk from your society pals about severity at the ports, that's our work. I don't mind telling you it's all very difficult. You can see for yourself. These are the Matisse clients."

Mr Campion scanned the typewritten page and his sympathy for his friend deepened.

"Oh yes, Caesar's wives," he agreed. "Every one of 'em. Servants been in the families for years, I suppose?"

"Unto the third and fourth generations," said the chief bitterly.

His visitor considered the situation.

"I suppose they've got alibis fixed up for the nights of the crimes?" he enquired.

"Fixed up?" The chief's tone was eloquent. "The alibis are so good that we ought to be able to arrest 'em on suspicion alone. An alibi these days doesn't mean anything except that the fellow knows his job. Borringer does, too, and so does his wife. We've had them both on the carpet for hours without getting a glimmer from them. No, it's no use, Campion; we've got to spot the middleman

157

and then the fence, and pin it on to them that way. Personally, I think the woman actually passes the stuff, but we've had Blower on her for weeks and he swears she doesn't speak to a soul except these superior clients of hers. Also, of course, neither of them post anything. We thought we'd got something once and got the postal authorities to help us, but all we got for our trouble was a p.c. to a viscountess about an appointment for chiropody."

Mr Campion was silent for some time.

"It was funny, her shouting out like that in the Hotel Monde," he said at last.

The chief grunted. "Mrs Gregory," he said. "Yes, I heard about that. A little show for Blower's benefit, if you ask me. Thought she'd give him something to think about. The Borringers are like that, cocky as hell."

Once again there was thoughtful silence in the light airy office and this time it was Stanislaus Oates who spoke first.

"Look here, Campion," he said, "you and I know one another. Let this be a word of friendly warning. If you suspect anyone you know of getting mixed up in this – for a bit of fun, perhaps – see that she's careful. If The Sparrow and his wife are still tied up with the Meyer lot, and they very well may be, the Meyer crowd aren't a pretty bunch. In fact, you know as well as I do, they're dirty and they're dangerous."

His visitor picked up the list again. Philip Graysby's aunt's name headed the second column. He made up his mind.

"I don't know anything," he said. "I'm speaking entirely from guesswork and I rely on you to go into this in stockinged feet and with your discretion wrapping you like a blanket. But if I were you I should have a little chat with one Henry Swan, employed by Florence, Dowager Countess of Marle."

"Ah," said the chief with relief, "that's where the wind blows, does it? I thought you'd come across."

"I don't promise anything," Campion protested.

"Who does?" said Stanislaus Oates and pulled a pad towards him. . . .

Mr Campion kept late hours. He was sitting up by the open window of his flat in Bottle Street, the cul-de-sac off Piccadilly, when the chief detective inspector called upon him just after midnight on the evening of his visit to Scotland Yard. The policeman was unusually fidgety. He accepted a drink and sat down before mentioning the purpose of his visit, which was, in fact, to gossip.

Campion, who knew him, let him take his time.

"We pulled the chap Swan in this afternoon," he volunteered at last. "He's a poor weedy little beggar who did a stretch for larceny in twenty-three and seems to have gone straight since. We had quite a time with him. He wouldn't open his mouth at first. Fainted when he thought we were going to jug him. Finally, of course, out it came, and a very funny story it was. Know anything about the White Elephant Society, Campion?"

His host blinked. "Nothing against it," he admitted. "Ordinary charity stunt. Very decently run, I believe. The dowager does it herself."

"I know." There was a note of mystification in the chief's voice. "See this?"

From his wallet he took a small green stick-on label. It was an ornate product embellished with a design of angels in the worst artistic taste. Across the top was a printed heading:

This is a gift from the White Elephant Society (Secy, Florence, Countess of Marle) and contains — A blank space had been filled up with the legend *Two Pairs of Fancy Woollen Gloves* in ink. The address, which was also in ink, was that of a well-known orphanage and the addressee was the matron.

"That's how they send the white elephants out," Oates explained. "There's a word or two inside in the countess's own handwriting. This is a specimen label. See what it means? It's as good as a diplomatic pass with that old woman's name on it."

"Who to?" demanded Mr Campion

160

dubiously.

"Anyone," declared the chief trium-phantly. "Especially the poor chap in the customs office who's tired of opening parcels. Even if he does open 'em he's not going to examine 'em. Now here's Swan's story. He admits he found the jewlery, which he passed on to a friend whose name he will not divulge. That friend must have sent it to you. It sounds like a woman to me but I'm not interested in her at the moment."

"Thank God for that," murmured his host devoutly. "Go on. Where did he find the stuff?"

"In a woollen duck inside one of these White Elephant parcels," said the chief unex-pectedly. "We've got the duck; homemade toy with little chamois pockets under its wings. The odd thing is that Swan swears the old lady gave the parcel to him herself, told him to post it, and made such a fuss about it that he became suspicious and opened it up."

"Do you believe that?" Mr Campion was grinning and Oates frowned.

"I do," he said slowly. "Curiously enough I do, in the main. In the first place, this chap honestly wants to go straight. One dose of clink has put him in terror of it for life. Secondly, if he was in on the theft why give the whole game away? Why produce the duck? What I do think is that he recognised the address. He says he can't remember

anything about it except that it was somewhere abroad, but that's just what he would
say if he recognised it and thought it was
dangerous and was keeping quiet for fear of
reprisals. Anyway, I believed him sufficiently
to go down and interview the old lady."

"Did you, by Jove!" murmured Mr
Campion with respect.

Stanislaus Oates smiled wryly and ran his
finger round the inside of his collar.

"Not a homely woman," he observed.
"Ever met someone who made you feel you
wanted a haircut, Campion? I was very
careful, of course. Kid gloves all the way. Had
to. I tell you one funny thing, though: she
was rattled."

Mr Campion sat up. He knew his friend to
be one of the soberest judges of humanity in
the police force, where humanity is deeply
studied.

"Sure?" he demanded incredulously.

"Take my dying oath on it," said the chief.
"Scared blue, if you ask me."

The young man in the horn-rimmed spectacles made polite but depreciating noises.
The chief shook his head.

"It's the truth. I gave her the facts — well,
most of them. I didn't explain how we came
to open the parcel, since that part of the business wasn't strictly orthodox. But I gave her
the rest of the story just as I've given it to
you, and instead of being helpful she tried to

send me about my business with a flea in my ear. She insisted that she had directed each outgoing parcel during the last four weeks herself and swore that the Matisse woman could never have had access to any of them. Also, which is significant, she would not give me a definite reply about the duck. She was not sure if she'd ever seen it before. I ask you! a — a badly made yellow duck in a blue pullover. Anyone'd know it again."

Mr Campion grinned. "What was the upshot of this embarrassing interview?" he enquired.

The chief coughed. "When she started talking about her son in the Upper House I came away," he said briefly. "I thought I'd let her rest for a day or two. Meanwhile, we shall keep a wary eye on Swan and the Borringers, although if those three are working together I'll resign."

He was silent for a moment.

"She certainly was rattled," he repeated at last. "I'd swear it. Under that magnificent manner of hers she was scared. She had that set look about the eyes. You can't mistake it. What d'you make of that, my lad?"

"I don't," said Campion discreetly. "It's absurd."

Oates sighed. "Of course it is," he agreed. "And so what?"

"Sleep on it," his host suggested and the chief took the hint. . . .

It was unfortunate for everyone concerned that Mr Campion should have gone into the country early the following morning on a purely personal matter concerning a horse which he was thinking of buying and should not have returned to his flat until the evening. When he did get back he found Juliet and the dark, good-looking Philip Graysby, with whom she had presumably made up her differences, waiting for him. To Mr Campion they both seemed very young and very distressed. Juliet appeared to have been crying and it was she who broke the news.

"It's Auntie Flo," she said in a small tragic voice. "She's bunked, Albert."

It took Mr Campion some seconds to assimilate this interesting development, and by that time young Graysby had launched into hurried explanations.

"That's putting it very crudely," he said. "My aunt caught the Paris plane this morning. Certainly she travelled alone, which was unusual, but that may not mean anything. Unfortunately, she did not leave an address, and although we've got into touch with the Crillon she doesn't seem to have arrived there."

He hesitated and his dark face became suddenly ingenuous.

"It's so ridiculously awkward, her going off like this without telling anyone just after Detective Inspector Oates called on her last night. I don't know what the interview was about, of course — nobody does — but there's an absurd feeling in the household that it wasn't very pleasant. Anyway, the inspector was very interested to hear that she had gone away when he called round this afternoon. It was embarrassing not being able to give him any real information about her return, and precious little about her departure. You see, we shouldn't have known she'd taken the plane if the chauffeur hadn't driven her to Croydon. She simply walked out of the house this morning and ordered the car. She didn't even take a suitcase, which looks as though she meant to come back tonight, and, of course, there's every possibility that she will."

Mr Campion perched himself on the table and his eyes were grave.

"Tell me," he said quietly, "had Lady Florence an appointment with her manicurist today?"

"Miss Matisse?" Juliet looked up. "Why, yes, she had, as a matter of fact. I went round there quite early this morning. Swan phoned me and told me Aunt had left rather hurriedly so I — er — I went to see him."

She shot an appealing glance at Philip, who grimaced at her, and she hurried on.

"While I was there Miss Matisse arrived and Bennett, Aunt's maid, told her all the gossip before I could stop her. Oh my dear, you don't think . . .?"

Instead of replying Mr Campion reached for the telephone and dialled a famous Whitehall number. Chief Detective Inspector Oates was glad to hear his voice. He said so. He was also interested to know if Mr Campion had heard of the recent developments in The Sparrow case.

"No," he said in reply to Mr Campion's sharp question. "The two Borringers are behaving just as usual. Blower's had the girl under his eye all day. . . . No, she hasn't communicated with anyone. . . . What? . . . Wait a minute. I've got notes on Blower's telephoned report here. Here we are. 'On leaving the Dowager Countess of Marle's house Miss Matisse went to the Venetian Cinema in Regent Street for the luncheon programme.' Nothing happened there except that she pulled Blower's leg again."

"Did she shout to someone?" Mr Campion's tone was urgent.

"Yes. Called to a woman named Mattie, who she said she thought was in the circle. Same silly stunt as last time. What's the matter?"

Campion checked his exasperation. He was desperately in earnest and his face as he bent over the instrument was frighteningly grave.

"Oates," he said quietly, "I'm going to ring you again in ten minutes and then you've got to get busy. Remember our little talk about the Meyers? This may be life or death."

"Good . . ." began the chief and was cut off.

Mr Campion hustled his visitors out of the flat.

"We're going down to see Swan," he said, "and the quicker we get there the better."

Henry Swan proved to be a small frightened man who was inclined to be more than diffident until he had had matters explained to him very thoroughly. Then he was almost pathetically anxious to help.

"The address on the duck parcel, sir?" he said, echoing Mr Campion's question nervously. "I daren't tell the police that. It might have been more than my life was worth. But if you think her ladyship ——"

"Let's have it," cut in Graysby irritably.

"Please," murmured Juliet.

Mr Swan came across. "Nineteen A, Rue Robespierre, Lyons, France," he blurted out. "I've burned the label but I remember the address. In fact, to tell you the truth, it was because of the address I opened the box in the first place. I never had such a fright in all me life, sir, really."

"I see. Who was the parcel sent to?" Mr Campion's manner was comfortingly reassuring.

Henry Swan hesitated. "Maurice Bonnet," he said at last, "and I once met a man who called himself that."

Mr Campion's eyes flickered. "On those occasions when he wasn't calling himself Meyer, I suppose?" he remarked.

The small man turned a shade or so paler and dropped his eyes.

"I shouldn't like to say, sir," he murmured.

"Very wise," Campion agreed. "But you've got nothing to worry about now. We've got the address and that's all that matters. You run along. Graysby, you and I have got to hurry. I'll just have a word with Oates on the phone and then we'll nip down to Croydon and charter a plane."

Juliet caught his arm. "You don't mean Philip's aunt might be in *danger?*" she said.

Mr Campion smiled down at her. "Some people do resent interference so, my dear," he said, "especially when they have quite a considerable amount to lose. . . ."

The Rue Robespierre is not in the most affluent quarter of Lyons and just before midnight on a warm spring evening it is not seen at its best. There silent figures loll in the dark doorways of houses which have come down in the world, and the night life has nothing to do with gaiety.

From Scotland Yard the wires had been busy and Campion and Graysby were not alone as they hurried down the centre of the wide street. A military little capitaine and four gendarmes accompanied them, but even so they were not overstaffed.

As their small company came to a stop before the crumbling façade of number nineteen A an upper window was thrown open and a shot spat down upon them. The capitaine drew his own gun and fired back, while the others put their shoulders to the door.

As they pitched into the dark musty hall a rain of fire met them from the staircase. A bullet took Mr Campion's hat from his head, and one of the gendarmes stepped back swearing, his left hand clasping a shattered right elbow.

The raiding party defended itself. For three minutes the darkness was streaked with fire, while the air became heavy with the smell of cordite.

The end came suddenly. There was a scream from the landing and a figure pitched over the balustrade onto the flags below, dragging another with it in its flight, while pattering footsteps flying up to the top story testified to the presence of a fugitive.

Mr Campion plunged forward, the others at his heels. They found Florence, Dowager Countess of Marle, at last in a locked bedroom on the third floor. She had defended herself and had suffered for it. Her black silk was torn and dusty and her coiffure dishevelled. But her spirit was unbroken and the French police listened to her tirade with a respect all the more remarkable since they could not understand one word of it.

Graysby took his aunt back to her hotel in a police car and Mr Campion remained to assist in the cleaning up.

Bertrand Meyer himself actually succeeded in getting out onto the roof, but he was brought back finally and the little capitaine had the satisfaction of putting the handcuffs on him.

One of the gang had been killed outright when his head had met the flagstones of the hall, and the remaining member was hurried off to a prison hospital with a broken thigh.

Mr Campion looked at Meyer with interest. He was an oldish man, square and powerful, with strong sensitive hands and the hot angry eyes of a fanatic. His workroom revealed many treasures. A jeweller's bench, exquisitely fitted with all the latest appliances, contained also a drawer which revealed the dismembered fragments of the proceeds of the first three London burglaries, together with some French stones in particular request by the Sûreté.

Campion looked round him. "Ah," he said with satisfaction, "and there's the wireless set. I wondered when some of you fellows were going to make use of the outside broadcasting programmes. How did you work it? Had someone listening to the first part of the first programme to be broadcast from a London public place each day, I suppose? It really is amazing how clearly those asides come, her voice quite fearless and yet so natural that it wasn't until some time afterwards that I realised she had been standing just below the orchestra's live microphone."

Meyer did not answer. His face was sullen and his eyes were fixed on the stones which the Frenchmen were turning out of little chamois leather bags onto the baize surface of the bench. . . .

It was some days later, back in the flat in Bottle Street, when Chief Detective Inspector Oates sipped a whisky and soda and beamed upon his friend.

"I take off my hat to the old girl," he said disrespectfully. "She's got courage and a great sense of justice. She says she'll go into the witness box if we need her and she apologised handsomely to me for taking the law into her own hands."

"Good," said Mr Campion. "You've got the Borringers, of course?"

The chief grinned. "We've got 'em as safe as a couple of ferrets in a box," he declared. "The man's an expert, but the woman's a genius. The story she told the old lady, for instance. That was more than brains. After she'd got her ladyship interested in her she broke down one day and told a pretty little yarn about her cruel husband in France who had framed a divorce and got the custody of the kid. She told a harrowing story about the

171

little presents she had made for it herself and had had sent back to her pronto. It didn't take her long to get the old woman to offer to send them as though they'd come from the White Elephant Society. Every woman has a streak of sentimentality in her somewhere. So all the Borringer — alias Matisse — girl had to do was to bring along the toys in her manicure case from time to time and have 'em despatched free, gratis, with a label which almost guaranteed 'em a free pass. Very nice, eh?"

"Very," Campion agreed. "Almost simple."

The chief nodded. "She did it well," he said; "so well that even after I'd given the old lady the facts she didn't trust me. She believed so strongly in this fictitious kid that she went roaring over to Lyons to find out the truth for herself before she gave the girl away. Unfortunately, the Borringers had that means of wireless communication with Meyer and so when she arrived the gang was ready for her. It's a good thing you got there, Campion. They're a hot lot. I wonder what they'd have done with her."

"Neat," muttered Mr Campion. "That wireless stunt, I mean."

"It was." Oates was still impressed. "The use of the names made it sound so natural. What was the code exactly? Do you know?"

His host pulled a dictionary from a shelf at

his side and turned over the leaves until he came to a small section at the end.

"It's childish," he said. "Funny how these people never do any inventing if they can help it. Look it all up."

The chief took the book and read the heading aloud.

"*The More Common British Christian Names and Their Meanings.*"

He ran his eyes down the columns.

"*Gregory,*" he read. "A *watcher.* Good Lord, that was to tell 'em Blower was on their track, I suppose. And Mattie . . . what's Mattie?"

He paused. "*Diminutive of Matilda,*" he said at last. "*Mighty Battle Maid.* I don't get that."

"Dangerous, indignant and female," translated Mr Campion. "It rather sums up Philip Graysby's Auntie Flo, don't you think?"

It was after the chief had gone and he was alone that Juliet phoned. She was jubilant and her clear voice bubbled over the wire.

"I can't thank you," she said. "I don't know what to say. Aunt Florence is perfectly marvellous about everything. And I say, Albert . . ."

"Yes?"

"Philip says we can keep Swan if we have him at the country house. We're going to be married quite soon, you know. Our reconciliation rather hurried things along. . . . Oh, what did you say?"

Mr Campion smiled. "I said I'll have to send you a wedding present then," he lied.

There was a fraction of silence at the other end of the wire.

"Well, darling . . . it would be just too terribly sweet if you really *wanted* to," said Miss Fysher-Sprigge.

The Mad Tea Party

Ellery Queen

THE TALL YOUNG man in the dun raincoat thought that he had never seen such a downpour. It gushed out of the black sky in a roaring flood, gray-gleaming in the feeble yellow of the station lamps. The red tails of the local from Jamaica had just been drowned out in the west. It was very dark beyond the ragged blur of light surrounding the little railroad station, and unquestionably very wet. The tall young man shivered under the eaves of the platform roof and wondered what insanity had moved him to venture into the Long Island hinterland in such wretched weather. And where, damn it all, was Owen?

He had just miserably made up his mind to seek out a booth, telephone his regrets, and take the next train back to the City, when a lowslung coupé came splashing and snuffling out of the darkness, squealed to a stop, and a man in chauffeur's livery leaped out and dashed across the gravel for the protection of

175

the eaves.

"Mr. Ellery Queen?" he panted, shaking out his cap. He was a blond young man with a ruddy face and sun-squinted eyes.

"Yes," said Ellery with a sigh. Too late now.

"I'm Millan, Mr. Owen's chauffeur, sir," said the man. "Mr. Owen's sorry he couldn't come down to meet you himself. Some guests — This way, Mr. Queen."

He picked up Ellery's bag and the two of them ran for the coupé. Ellery collapsed against the mohair in an indigo mood. Damn Owen and his invitations! Should have known better. Mere acquaintance, when it came to that. One of J. J.'s questionable friends. People were always pushing so. Put him up on exhibition, like a trained seal. Come, come, Rollo; here's a juicy little fish for you! . . . Got vicarious thrills out of listening to crime yarns. Made a man feel like a curiosity. Well, he'd be drawn and quartered if they got him to mention crime once! But then Owen had said Emmy Willowes would be there, and he'd always wanted to meet Emmy. Curious woman, Emmy, from all the reports. Daughter of some blueblood diplomat who had gone to the dogs — in this case, the stage. Stuffed shirts, her tribe, probably. Atavi! There were some people who still lived in mediaeval . . . Hmm. Owen wanted him to see "the house." Just taken a month

176

ago. Ducky, he'd said. "Ducky!" The big brute . . .

The coupé splashed along in the darkness, its headlights revealing only remorseless sheets of speckled water and occasionally a tree, a house, a hedge.

Millan cleared his throat. "Rotten weather, isn't it, sir. Worst this spring."

Ah, the conversational chauffeur! thought Ellery with an inward groan. "Pity the poor sailor on a night like this," he said piously.

"Ha, ha," said Millan. "Isn't it the truth, though. You're a little late, aren't you, sir? That was the eleven-fifty. Mr. Owen told me this morning you were expected tonight on the nine-thirty."

"Detained," murmured Ellery, wishing he were dead.

"A case, Mr. Queen?" asked Millan eagerly, rolling his squinty eyes.

Even he, O Lord. . . . "No, no. My father had his annual attack of elephantiasis. Poor Dad! We thought for a bad hour there that it was the end."

The chauffeur gaped. Then, looking puzzled, he returned his attention to the soggy pelted road. Ellery closed his eyes with a sigh of relief.

But Millan's was a persevering soul, for after a moment of silence he grinned — true, a trifle dubiously — and said: "Lots of excitement at Mr. Owen's tonight, sir. You see,

Master Jonathan —"

"Ah," said Ellery, starting a little. Master Jonathan, eh? Ellery recalled him as a stringy, hot-eyed brat in the indeterminate years between seven and ten who possessed a perfectly fiendish ingenuity for making a nuisance of himself. Master Jonathan. . . . He shivered again, this time from apprehension. He had quite forgotten Master Jonathan.

"Yes, sir, Jonathan's having a birthday party tomorrow, sir — ninth, I think — and Mr. and Mrs. Owen've rigged up something special." Millan grinned again, mysteriously. "Something very special, sir. It's a secret, y'see. The kid — Master Jonathan doesn't know about it yet. Will he be surprised!"

"I doubt it, Millan," groaned Ellery, and lapsed into a dismal silence which not even the chauffeur's companionable blandishments were able to shatter.

Richard Owen's "ducky" house was a large rambling affair of gables and ells and colored stones and bright shutters, set at the terminal of a winding driveway flanked by soldierly trees. It blazed with light and the front door stood ajar.

"Here we are, Mr. Queen!" cried Millan cheerfully, jumping out and holding the door open. "It's only a hop to the porch; you won't get wet, sir."

Ellery descended and obediently hopped to the porch. Millan fished his bag out of the car and bounded up the steps. "Door open 'n' everything," he grinned. "Guess the help are all watchin' the show."

"Show?" gasped Ellery with a sick feeling at the pit of his stomach.

Millan pushed the door wide open. "Step in, step in, Mr. Queen. I'll go get Mr. Owen. . . . They're rehearsing, y'see. Couldn't do it while Jonathan was up, so they had to wait till he'd gone to bed. It's for tomorrow, y'see. And he was very suspicious; they had an awful time with him —"

"I can well believe that," mumbled Ellery. Damn Jonathan and all his tribe! He stood in a small foyer looking upon a wide brisk living room, warm and attractive. "So they're putting on a play. Hmm. . . . Don't bother, Millan; I'll just wander in and wait until they've finished. Who am I to clog the wheels of Drama?"

"Yes, sir," said Millan with a vague disappointment; and he set down the bag and touched his cap and vanished in the darkness outside. The door closed with a click curiously final, shutting out both rain and night.

Ellery reluctantly divested himself of his drenched hat and raincoat, hung them dutifully in the foyer closet, kicked his bag into a corner, and sauntered into the living room to warm his chilled hands at the good fire.

179

He stood before the flames soaking in heat, only half-conscious of the voices which floated through one of the two open doorways beyond the fireplace.

A woman's voice was saying in odd childish tones: "No, please go on! I won't interrupt you again. I dare say there may be *one.*"

"Emmy," thought Ellery, becoming conscious very abrupty. "What's going on here?" He went to the first doorway and leaned against the jamb.

An astonishing sight. They were all — as far as he could determine — there. It was a large bookish room done in the modern manner. The farther side had been cleared and a home-made curtain, manufactured out of starchy sheets and a pulley, stretched across the room. The curtain was open, and in the cleared space there was a long table covered with a white cloth and with cups and saucers and things on it. In an armchair at the head of the table sat Emmy Willowes, whimsically girlish in a pinafore, her gold-brown hair streaming down her back, her slim legs sheathed in white stockings, and black pumps with low heels on her feet. Beside her sat an apparition, no less; a rabbity creature the size of a man, his huge ears stiffly up, an enormous bow tie at his furry neck, his mouth clacking open and shut as human sounds came from his throat. Beside the hare there was another apparition: a creature with an amiably rodent little face and slow sleepy movements. And beyond the little one, who looked unaccountably like a dormouse, sat the most remarkable of the quartet — a curious creature with shaggy eyebrows and features reminiscent of George Arliss's, at his throat a dotted bow tie, dressed Victorian-wise in a quaint waistcoat, on his head an extraordinary tall cloth hat in the band of which was stuck a placard reading: "For This Style ¹⁰%."

The audience was composed of two women: an old lady with pure white hair and the stubbornly sweet facial expression which more often than not conceals a chronic acerbity; and a very beautiful young woman with full breasts, red hair, and green eyes. Then Ellery noticed that two domestic heads were stuck in another doorway, gaping and giggling decorously.

"The mad tea party," thought Ellery, grinning. "I might have known, with Emmy in the house. Too good for that merciless brat!"

"They were learning to draw," said the little dormouse in a high-pitched voice, yawning and rubbing its eyes, "and they drew all manner of things — everything that begins with an M —"

"Why with an M?" demanded the woman-child.

"Why not?" snapped the hare, flapping his ears indignantly.

The dormouse began to doze and was instantly beset by the tophatted gentleman, who pinched him so roundly that he awoke with a shriek and said: " — that begins with an M, such as mousetraps, and the moon, and memory, and muchness — you know you say things are 'much of a muchness' — did you ever see such a thing as a drawing of a muchness?"

"Really, now you ask me," said the girl, quite confused, "I don't think —"

"Then you shouldn't talk," said the Hatter tartly.

The girl rose in open disgust and began to walk away, her white legs twinkling. The dormouse fell asleep and the hare and the Hatter stood up and grasped the dormouse's little head and tried very earnestly to push it into the mouth of a monstrous teapot on the table.

And the little girl cried, stamping her right foot: "At any rate I'll never go *there* again. It's the stupidest tea party I was ever at in all my life!"

And she vanished behind the curtain; an instant later it swayed and came together as she operated the rope of the pulley.

"Superb," drawled Ellery, clapping his hands. "*Brava,* Alice. And a couple of *bravi* for the zoölogical characters, Messrs. Dormouse and March Hare, not to speak of my good friend the Mad Hatter."

The Mad Hater goggled at him, tore off his hat, and came running across the room. His vulturine features under the make-up were both good-humored and crafty; he was a stoutish man in his prime, a faintly cynical and ruthless prime. "Queen! When on earth did you come? What held you up?"

"Family matter. Millan did the honors. Owen, that's your natural costume, I'll swear. I don't know what ever possessed you to go into Wall Street. You were born to be the Hatter."

"Think so?" chuckled Owen, pleased. "I guess I always did have a yen for the stage; that's why I backed Emmy Willowes's *Alice* show. Here, I want you to meet the gang. Mother," he said to the white-haired old lady, "may I present Mr. Ellery Queen. Laura's mother, Queen — Mrs. Mansfield." The old lady smiled a sweet, sweet smile; but Ellery noticed that her eyes were very sharp. "Mrs. Gardner," continued Owen, indicating the buxom young woman with the red hair and green eyes. "Believe it or not, she's the wife of that hairy Hare over there. Ho, ho, ho!"

There was something a little brutal in Owen's laughter. Ellery bowed to the beautiful woman and said quickly: "Gardner? You're not the wife of Paul Gardner, the architect?"

"Guilty," said the March Hare in a cavernous voice; and he removed his head and disclosed a lean face with twinkling eyes. "How are you, Queen? I haven't seen you since I testified for your father in that Schultz murder case in the Village."

They shook hands. "Surprise," said Ellery. "This *is* nice. Mrs. Gardner, you have a clever husband. He set the defense by their respective ears with his expert testimony in that case."

"Oh, I've always said Paul is a genius," smiled the red-haired woman. She had a queer husky voice. "But he won't believe me. He thinks I'm the only one in the world who doesn't appreciate him."

"Now, Carolyn," protested Gardner with a laugh; but the twinkle had gone out of his eyes and for some odd reason he glanced at Richard Owen.

"Of course you remember Laura," boomed Owen, taking Ellery forcibly by the arm. "That's the Dormouse. Charming little rat, isn't she?"

Mrs. Mansfield lost her sweet expression for a fleeting instant; very fleeting indeed. What the Dormouse thought about being publicly characterized as a rodent, however charming, by her husband was concealed by the furry little head; when she took it off she was smiling. She was a wan little woman with tired eyes and cheeks that had already begun to sag.

"And this," continued Owen with the pride

of a stock raiser exhibiting a prize milch cow, "is the one and only Emmy. Emmy, meet Mr. Queen, that murder-smelling chap I've been telling you about. Miss Willowes."

"You see us, Mr. Queen," murmured the actress, "in character. I hope you aren't here on a professional visit? Because if you are, we'll get into mufti at once and let you go to work. I know *I've* a vicariously guilty conscience. If I were to be convicted of every mental murder I've committed, I'd need the nine lives of the Cheshire Cat. Those damn' critics —"

"The costume," said Ellery, not looking at her legs, "is most fetching. And I think I like you better as Alice." She made a charming Alice; she was curved in her slimness, half boy, half girl. "Whose idea was this, anyway?"

"I suppose you think we're fools or nuts," chuckled Owen. "Here, sit down, Queen. Maud!" he roared. "A cocktail for Mr. Queen. Bring some more fixin's." A frightened domestic head vanished. "We're having a dress rehearsal for Johnny's birthday party tomorrow; we've invited all the kids of the neighborhood. Emmy's brilliant idea; she brought the costumes down from the theatre. You know we closed Saturday night."

"I hadn't heard. I thought *Alice* was playing to S.R.O."

"So it was. But our lease at the Odeon ran

out and we've our engagements on the road to keep. We open in Boston next Wednesday."

Slim-legged Maud set a pinkish liquid concoction before Ellery. He sipped slowly, succeeding in not making a face.

"Sorry to have to break this up," said Paul Gardner, beginning to take off his costume. "But Carolyn and I have a bad trip before us. And then tomorrow . . . The road must be an absolute washout."

"Pretty bad," said Ellery politely, setting down his three-quarters-full glass.

"I won't hear of it," said Laura Owen. Her pudgy little Dormouse's stomach gave her a peculiar appearance, tiny and fat and sexless. "Driving home in this storm! Carolyn, you and Paul must stay over."

"It's only four miles, Laura," murmured Mrs. Gardner.

"Nonsense, Carolyn! More like forty on a night like this," boomed Owen. His cheeks were curiously pale and damp under the makeup. "That's settled! We've got more room than we know what to do with. Paul saw to that when he designed this development."

"That's the insidious part of knowing architects socially," said Emmy Willowes with a grimace. She flung herself in a chair and tucked her long legs under her. "You can't fool 'em about the number of available

186

guest rooms."

"Don't mind Emmy," grinned Owen. "She's the Peck's Bad Girl of show business: no manners at all. Well, well! This is great. How's about a drink, Paul?"

"No, thanks."

"You'll have one, won't you, Carolyn? Only good sport in the crowd." Ellery realized with embarrassment that his host was, under the jovial glaze of the exterior, drunk.

Mrs. Gardner raised her heavily-lidded green eyes to Owen's. "I'd love it, Dick." They stared with frank hunger at each other. Mrs. Owen suddenly smiled and turned her back, struggling with her cumbersome costume.

And, just as suddenly, Mrs. Mansfield rose and smiled her unconvincing sweet smile and said in her sugary voice to no one in particular: "*Will* you all excuse me? It's been a trying day, and I'm an old woman. . . . Laura, my darling." She went to her daughter and kissed the lined, averted forehead.

Everybody murmured something; including Ellery, who had a headache, a slow pinkish fire in his vitals, and a consuming wishfulness to be far, far away.

Mr. Ellery Queen came to with a start and a groan. He turned over in bed, feeling very poorly. He had dozed in fits since one o'clock, annoyed rather than soothed by the splash of the rain against the bedroom windows. And now he was miserably awake, attacked by an inexplicable insomnia. He sat up and reached for his wrist watch, which was ticking thunderously away on the night table beside his bed. By the radium hands he saw that it was five past two.

He lay back, tucking his palms behind his head, and stared into the half-darkness. The mattress was deep and downy, as one had a right to expect of the mattress of a plutocrat, but it did not rest his restless bones. The house was cosy, but it did not comfort him. His hostess was thoughtful, but uncomfortably woebegone. His host was a disturbing force, like the storm. His fellow guests; Master Jonathan snuffling away in his junior bed — Ellery was positive that Master Jonathan snuffled. . . .

At two-fifteen he gave up the battle and, rising, turned on the light and got into his dressing gown and slippers. That there was no book or magazine on or in the night table he had ascertained before retiring. Shocking hospitality! Sighing, he went to the door and opened it and peered out. A small night light glimmered at the landing down the hall. Everything was quiet.

And suddenly he was attacked by the strangest diffidence. He definitely did not want to leave the bedroom.

Analyzing the fugitive fear, and arriving

nowhere, Ellery sternly reproached himself for an imaginative fool and stepped out into the hall. He was not habitually a creature of nerves, nor was he psychic; he laid the blame to lowered physical resistance due to fatigue, lack of sleep. This was a nice house with nice people in it. It was like a man, he thought, saying: "Nice doggie, nice doggie," to a particularly fearsome beast with slavering jaws. That woman with the sea-green eyes. Put to sea in a sea-green boat. Or was it pea-green. . . . "No room! No room!" . . . "There's *plenty* of room," said Alice indignantly. . . . And Mrs. Mansfield's smile did make you shiver.

Berating himself bitterly for the ferment his imagination was in, he went down the carpeted stairs to the living room.

It was pitch-dark and he did not know where the light switch was. He stumbled over a hassock and stubbed his toe and cursed silently. The library should be across from the stairs, next to the fireplace. He strained his eyes toward the fireplace, but the last embers had died. Stepping warily, he finally reached the fireplace wall. He groped about in the rain-splattered silence, searching for the library door. His hand met a cold knob, and he turned the knob rather noisily and swung the door open. His eyes were oriented to the darkness now and he had already begun to make out in the mistiest black haze the unrecognizable outlines of still objects.

The darkness from beyond the door however struck him like a blow. It was darker darkness. . . . He was about to step across the sill when he stopped. It was the wrong room. Not the library at all. How he knew he could not say, but he was sure he had pushed open the door of the wrong room. Must have wandered orbitally to the right. Lost men in the dark forest. . . . He stared intently straight before him into the absolute, unrelieved blackness, sighed, and retreated. The door shut noisily again.

He groped along the wall to the left. A few feet. . . . There it was! The very next door. He paused to test his psychic faculties. No, all's well. Grinning, he pushed open the door, entered boldly, fumbled on the nearest wall for the switch, found it, pressed. The light flooded on to reveal, triumphantly, the library.

The curtain was closed, the room in disorder as he had last seen it before being conducted upstairs by his host.

He went to the built-in bookcases, scanned several shelves, hesitated between two volumes, finally selected *Huckleberry Finn* as blithe reading on a dour night, put out the light, and felt his way back across the living room to the stairway. Book tucked under his arm, he began to climb the stairs. There was a footfall from the landing above. He looked up. A man's dark form was silhouetted below the tiny landing light.

"Owen?" whispered a dubious male voice.

Ellery laughed. "It's Queen, Gardner. Can't you sleep, either?"

He heard the man sigh with relief. "Lord, no! I was just coming downstairs for something to read. Carolyn — my wife's asleep, I guess, in the room adjoining mine. How she can sleep —! There's something in the air tonight."

"Or else you drank too much," said Ellery cheerfully, mounting the stairs.

Gardner was in pajamas and dressing gown, his hair mussed. "Didn't drink at all to speak of. Must be this confounded rain. My nerves are all shot."

"Something in that. Hardy believed, anyway, in the Green unities. . . . If you can't sleep, you might join me for a smoke in my room, Gardner."

"You're sure I won't be —"

"Keeping me up? Nonsense. The only reason I fished about downstairs for a book was to occupy my mind with something. Talk's infinitely better than Huck Finn, though he does help at times. Come on."

They went to Ellery's room and Ellery produced cigarettes and they relaxed in chairs and chatted over tobacco about Inspector Queen, old books, and the price of green cheese until the early dawn began struggling to emerge from behind the fine gray wet bars of the rain outside. Then Gardner went yawning back to his room and Ellery fell into a heavy, uneasy slumber.

He was on the rack in a tall room of the Inquisition and his left arm was being torn out of his shoulder socket. The pain was almost pleasant. Then he awoke to find Millan's ruddy face in broad daylight above him, his blond hair tragically dishevelled. He was jerking at Ellery's arm for all he was worth.

"Mr. Queen!" he was crying. "Mr. Queen! For God's sake, wake up!"

Ellery sat up quickly, startled. "What's the matter, Millan?"

"Mr. Owen, sir. He's — he's gone!"

Ellery sprang out of bed. "What d'ye mean, man?"

"Disappeared, Mr. Queen. We — can't find him. Just gone. Mrs. Owen is all —"

"You go downstairs, Millan," said Ellery calmly, stripping off his pajama coat, "and pour yourself a drink. Please tell Mrs. Owen not to do anything until I come down. And nobody's to leave or telephone. You understand?"

"Yes, sir," said Millan in a low voice, and blundered off.

Ellery dressed like a fireman, splashed his face, spat water, adjusted his necktie, and ran downstairs. He found Laura Owen in a crumpled négligé on the sofa, sobbing. Mrs. Mansfield was patting her daughter's shoulder. Master Jonathan Owen was scowling at his grandmother, Emmy Willowes silently smoked a cigarette, and the Gardners were pale and quiet by the gray-washed windows.

"Mr. Queen," said the actress quickly. "It's a drama, hot off the script. At least Laura Owen thinks so. Won't you assure her that it's all probably nothing?"

"I can't do that," smiled Ellery, "until I learn the facts. Owen's gone? How? When?"

"Oh, Mr. Queen," choked Mrs. Owen, raising a tear-stained face. "I know something — something dreadful's happened. I had a feeling — You remember last night, after Richard showed you to your room?"

"Yes."

"Then he came back downstairs and said he had some work to do in his den for Monday, and told me to go to bed. Everybody else had gone upstairs. The servants, too. I warned him not to stay up too late and I went up to bed. I — I was exhausted, and I fell right asleep —"

"You occupy one bedroom, Mrs. Owen?"

"Yes. Twin beds. I fell asleep and didn't wake up until a half-hour ago. Then I saw —" She shuddered and began to sob again. Her mother looked helpless and angry.

"His bed hadn't been slept in. His clothes — the ones he'd taken off when he got into the costume — were still where he had left them on the chair by his bed. I was shocked, and ran downstairs; but he was gone. . . ."

"Ah," said Ellery queerly. "Then, as far as you know, he's still in that Mad Hatter's rig? Have you looked over his wardrobe? Are any of his regular clothes missing?"

"No, no; they're all there. Oh, he's dead. I know he's dead."

"Laura, dear, please," said Mrs. Mansfield in a tight quavery voice.

"Oh, Mother, it's too horrible —"

"Here, here," said Ellery. "No hysterics. Was he worried about anything? Business, for instance?"

"No, I'm sure he wasn't. In fact, he said only yesterday things were picking up beautifully. And he isn't — isn't the type to worry, anyway."

"Then it probably isn't amnesia. He hasn't had a shock of some sort recently?"

"No, no."

"No possibility, despite the costume, that he went to his office?"

"No. He never goes down Saturdays."

Master Jonathan jammed his fists into the pockets of his Eton jacket and said bitterly: "I bet he's drunk again. Makin' Mamma cry. I hope he *never* comes back."

"Jonathan!" screamed Mrs. Mansfield.

194

"You go up to your room this very minute, do you hear, you nasty boy? This minute!"

No one said anything; Mrs. Owen continued to sob; so Master Jonathan thrust out his lower lip, scowled at his grandmother with unashamed dislike, and stamped upstairs.

"Where," said Ellery with a frown, "was your husband when you last saw him, Mrs. Owen? In this room?"

"In his den," she said with difficulty. "He went in just as I went upstairs. I saw him go in. That door, there." She pointed to the door at the right of the library door. Ellery started; it was the door to the room he had almost blundered into during the night in his hunt for the library.

"Do you think —" began Carolyn Gardner in her husky voice, and stopped. Her lips were dry, and in the gray morning light her hair did not seem so red and her eyes did not seem so green. There was, in fact, a washed-out look about her, as if all the fierce vitality within her had been quenched by what had happened.

"Keep out of this, Carolyn," said Paul Gardner harshly. His eyes were red-rimmed from lack of sleep.

"Come, come," murmured Ellery, "we may be, as Miss Willowes has said, making a fuss over nothing at all. If you'll excuse me . . . I'll have a peep at the den."

195

He went into the den, closing the door behind him, and stood with his back squarely against the door. It was a small room, so narrow that it looked long by contrast; it was sparsely furnished and seemed a business-like place. There was a simple neatness about its desk, a modern severity about its furnishings that were reflections of the direct, brutal character of Richard Owen. The room was as trim as a pin; it was almost ludicrous to conceive of its having served as the scene of a crime.

Ellery gazed long and thoughtfully. Nothing out of place, so far as he could see; and nothing, at least perceptible to a stranger, added. Then his eyes wavered and fixed themselves upon what stood straight before him. That *was* odd. . . . Facing him as he leaned against the door there was a bold naked mirror set flush into the opposite wall and reaching from floor to ceiling — a startling feature of the room's decorations. Ellery's lean figure, and the door behind him, were perfectly reflected in the sparkling glass. And there, above . . . In the mirror he saw, above the reflection of the door against which he was leaning, the reflection of the face of a modern electric clock. In the dingy grayness of the light there was a curious lambent quality about its dial. . . . He pushed away from the door and turned and stared up. It was a chromium-and-onyx clock, about a foot in diameter.

He opened the door and beckoned Millan, who had joined the silent group in the living room. "Have you a stepladder?"

Millan brought one. Ellery shut the door firmly, mounted the ladder, and examined the clock. Its electric outlet was behind, concealed from view. The plug was in the socket, as he saw at once. The clock was going; the time — he consulted his wrist watch — was reasonably accurate. But then he cupped his hands as best he could to shut out what light there was and stared hard and saw that the numerals and the hands, as he had suspected, were radium-painted. They glowed faintly.

He decended, opened the door, gave the ladder into Millan's keeping, and sauntered into the living room. They looked up at him trustfully.

"Well," said Emmy Willowes with a light shrug, "has the Master Mind discovered the all-important clue? Don't tell us that Dickie Owen is out playing golf at the Meadowbrook links in that Mad Hatter's get-up!"

"Well, Mr. Queen?" asked Mrs. Owen anxiously.

Ellery sank into an armchair and lighted a cigarette. "There's something curious in there. Mrs. Owen, did you get this house furnished?"

She was puzzled. "Furnished? Oh, no. We

bought it, you know; brought all our own things.''

''Then the electric clock above the door in the den is yours?''

''The clock?'' They all stared at him. ''Why, of course. What has that —''

''Hmm,'' said Ellery. ''That clock has a disappearing quality, like the Cheshire Cat — since we may as well continue being Carrollish, Miss Willowes.''

''But what can the clock possibly have to do with Richard's being gone?'' asked Mrs. Mansfield with asperity.

Ellery shrugged. *''Je n'sais.* The point is that a little after two this morning, being unable to sleep, I ambled downstairs to look for a book. In the dark I blundered to the door of the den, mistaking it for the library door. I opened it and looked in. But I saw nothing, you see.''

''But how could you, Mr. Queen?'' said Mrs. Gardner in a small voice; her breasts heaved. ''If it was dark —''

''That's the curious part of it,'' drawled Ellery. ''I *should* have seen something *because* it was so dark, Mrs. Gardner.''

''But —''

''The clock over the door.''

''Did you go in?'' murmured Emmy Willowes, frowning. ''I can't say I understand. The clock's above the door, isn't it?''

''There is a mirror facing the door,''

198

explained Ellery absently, "and the fact that it was so dark makes my seeing nothing quite remarkable. Because that clock has luminous hands and numerals. Consequently I should have seen their reflected glow very clearly indeed in that pitch darkness. But I didn't, you see. I saw literally nothing at all."

They were silent, bewildered. Then Gardner muttered: "I still don't see — You mean something, somebody was standing in front of the mirror, obscuring the reflection of the clock?"

"Oh, no. The clock's above the door — a good seven feet or more from the floor. The mirror reaches to the ceiling. There isn't a piece of furniture in that room seven feet high, and certainly we may dismiss the possibility of an intruder seven feet or more tall. No, no, Gardner. It does seem as if the clock wasn't above the door at all when I looked in."

"Are you sure, young man," snapped Mrs. Mansfield, "that you know what you're talking about? I thought we were concerned with my son-in-law's absence. And how on earth could the clock not have been there?"

Ellery closed his eyes. "Fundamental. *It was moved from its position.* Wasn't above the door when I looked in. After I left, it was returned."

"But why on earth," murmured the actress, "should anyone want to move a mere clock from a wall, Mr. Queen? That's almost as nonsensical as some of the things in *Alice*."

"That," said Ellery, "is the question I'm propounding to myself. Frankly I don't know." Then he opened his eyes. "By the way, has anyone seen the Mad Hatter's hat?"

Mrs. Owen shivered. "No, that — that's gone, too."

"You've looked for it?"

"Yes. Would you like to look yours —"

"No, no, I'll take your word for it, Mrs. Owen. Oh, yes. Your husband has no enemies?" He smiled. "That's the routine question, Miss Willowes. I'm afraid I can't offer you anything startling in the way of technique."

"Enemies? Oh, I'm sure not," quavered Mrs. Owen. "Richard was — is strong and — and sometimes rather curt and contemptuous, but I'm sure no one would hate him enough to — to kill him." She shivered again and drew the silk of her négligé closer about her plump shoulders.

"Don't say that, Laura," said Mrs. Mansfield sharply. "I do declare, you people are like children! It probably has the simplest explanation."

"Quite possible," said Ellery in a cheerful voice. "It's the depressing weather, I suppose. . . . There! I believe the rain's stopped." They dully looked out the windows. The rain had perversely ceased, and

200

the sky was growing brighter. "Of course," continued Ellery, "there are certain possibilities. It's conceivable — I say conceivable, Mrs. Owen — that your husband has been . . . well, kidnaped. Now, now, don't look so frightened. It's a theory only. The fact that he has disappeared in the costume does seem to point to a very abrupt — and therefore possibly enforced — departure. You haven't found a note of some kind? Nothing in your letter box? The morning mail —"

"Kidnaped," whispered Mrs. Owen feebly.

"Kidnaped?" breathed Mrs. Gardner, and bit her lip. But there was a brightness in her eye, like the brightness of the sky outdoors.

"No note, no mail," snapped Mrs. Mansfield. "Personally, I think this is ridiculous. Laura, this is your house, but I think I have a duty. . . . You should do one of two things. Either take this seriously and telephone the *regular* police, or forget all about it. *I'm* inclined to believe Richard got befuddled — he *had* a lot to drink last night, dear — and wandered off drunk somewhere. He's probably sleeping it off in a field somewhere and won't come back with anything worse than pneumonia."

"Excellent suggestion," drawled Ellery. "All except for the summoning of the *regular* police, Mrs. Mansfield. I assure you I possess — er — *ex officio* qualifications. Let's not call the police and say we did. If there's any explaining to do — afterward — I'll do it. Meanwhile, I suggest we try to forget all this unpleasantness and wait. If Mr. Owen hasn't returned by nightfall, we can go into conference and decide what measures to take. Agreed?"

"Sounds reasonable," said Gardner disconsolately. "May I —" he smiled and shrugged — "this *is* exciting! — telephone my office, Queen?"

"Lord, yes."

Mrs. Owen shrieked suddenly, rising and tottering toward the stairs. "Jonathan's birthday party! I forgot all about it! And all those children invited — What *will* I say?"

"I suggest," said Ellery in a sad voice, "that Master Jonathan is indisposed, Mrs. Owen. Harsh, but necessary. You might phone all the potential spectators of the mad tea party and voice your regrets." And Ellery rose and wandered into the library.

It was a depressing day for all the lightening skies and the crisp sun. The morning wore on and nothing whatever happened. Mrs. Mansfield firmly tucked her daughter into bed, made her swallow a small dose of Luminal from a big bottle in the medicine chest, and remained with her until she dropped off to exhausted sleep. Then the old lady telephoned to all and sundry the collective Owen regrets over the unfortunate turn of events.

202

Jonathan *would* have to run a fever when . . . Master Jonathan, apprised later by his grandmother of the *débâcle,* sent up a healthy howl of anguish that caused Ellery, poking about downstairs in the library, to feel prickles slither up and down his spine. It took the combined labors of Mrs. Mansfield, Millan, the maid, and the cook to pacify the Owen hope. A five-dollar bill ultimately restored a rather strained *entente.* . . . Emmy Willowes spent the day serenely reading. The Gardners listlessly played gin-rummy.

Luncheon was a dismal affair. No one spoke in more than monosyllables.

During the afternoon they wandered about, restless. Even the actress began to show signs of tension: she consumed innumerable cigarettes and cocktails and lapsed into almost sullen silence. No word came; the telephone rang only once, and then it was merely the local confectioner protesting the cancellation of the ice cream order. Ellery spent most of the afternoon in mysterious activity in the library and den. What he was looking for remained his secret. At five o'clock he emerged from the den, rather gray of face. There was a deep crease between his brows. He went out onto the porch and leaned against a pillar, sunk in thought. The gravel was dry; the sun had quickly sopped up the rain. When he went back into the house it was already dusk and growing darker each moment with the swiftness of the country nightfall.

There was no one about; the house was quiet, its miserable occupants having retired to their rooms. Ellery sought a chair. He buried his face in his hands and thought for long minutes, completely still.

And then at last something happened to him and he went to the foot of the stairs and listened. No sound. He tiptoed back, reached for the telephone, and spent the next fifteen minutes in low-voiced, earnest conversation with someone in New York. When he had finished, he went upstairs to his room.

An hour later, while the others were downstairs gathering for dinner, he slipped down the rear stairway and out of the house unobserved even by the cook in the kitchen. He spent some time in the thick darkness of the grounds.

How it happened Ellery never knew. He felt its effects soon after dinner; and on retrospection he recalled that the others, too, had seemed drowsy at approximately the same time. It was a late dinner and a cold one, Owen's disappearance apparently having disrupted the culinary organization as well; so that it was not until a little after eight that the coffee — Ellery was certain later it had been the coffee — was served by the trim-legged maid. The drowsiness came on less than half an hour later. They were seated in the living room, chatting dully about nothing at all. Mrs. Owen, pale and silent, had gulped her coffee thirstily; had called for a second cup, in fact. Only Mrs. Mansfield had been belligerent. She had been definitely of a mind, it appeared, to telephone the police. She had great faith in the local constabulary of Long Island, particularly in one Chief Naughton, the local prefect; and she left no doubt in Ellery's mind of *his* incompetency. Gardner had been restless and a little rebellious; he had tinkered with the piano in the alcove. Emmy Willowes had drawn herself into a slant-eyed shell, no longer amused and very, very quiet. Mrs. Gardner had been nervous. Jonathan, packed off screaming to bed. . . .

It came over their senses like a blanket of snow. Just a pleasant sleepiness. The room was warm, too, and Ellery rather hazily felt perspiration on his forehead. He was half-gone before his dulled brain sounded a warning note. And then, trying in panic to rise, to use his muscles, he felt himself slipping, slipping into unconsciousness, his body as leaden and remote as Vega. His last conscious thought, as the room whirled dizzily before his eyes and he saw blearily the expressions of his companions, was that they had all been drugged. . . .

The dizziness seemed merely to have taken up where it had left off. Specks danced before his closed eyes and somebody was hammering petulantly at his temples. Then he opened his eyes and saw glittering sun fixed upon the floor at his feet. Good God, all night. . . .

He sat up groaning and feeling his head. The others were sprawled in various attitudes of labored-breathing coma about him — without exception. Someone — his aching brain took it in dully; it was Emmy Willowes — stirred and sighed. He got to his feet and stumbled toward a portable bar and poured himself a stiff, nasty drink of Scotch. Then, with his throat burning, he felt unaccountably better; and he went to the actress and pummeled her gently until she opened her eyes.

"What — when —"

"Drugged," croaked Ellery. "The crew of us. Try to revive these people, Miss Willowes, while I scout about a bit. And see if anyone's shamming."

He wove his way a little uncertainly, but with purpose, toward the rear of the house. Groping, he found the kitchen. And there were the trim-legged maid and Millan and the cook unconscious in chairs about the kitchen table over cold cups of coffee. He made his way back to the living room, nodded at Miss Willowes working over Gardner at the piano, and staggered upstairs. He discovered Master Jonathan's bedroom after a short search; the boy was still sleeping — a deep natural sleep punctuated by nasal snuffles. Lord, he *did* snuffle! Groaning, Ellery visited the lavatory adjoining the master bedroom. After a little while he went downstairs and into the den. He came out almost at once, haggard and wild-eyed. He took his hat from the foyer closet and hurried outdoors into the warm sunshine. He spent fifteen minutes poking about the grounds; the Owen house was shallowly surrounded by timber and seemed isolated as a Western ranch. . . . When he returned to the house, looking grim and disappointed, the others were all conscious, making mewing little sounds and holding their heads like scared children.

"Queen, for God's sake," began Gardner hoarsely.

"Whoever it was used that Luminal in the lavatory upstairs," said Ellery, flinging his hat away and wincing at a sudden pain in his head. "The stuff Mrs. Mansfield gave Mrs. Owen yesterday to make her sleep. Except that almost the whole of that large bottle was used. Swell sleeping draught! Make yourselves comfortable while I conduct a little investigation in the kitchen. I think it was the Java." But when he returned he was grimacing. "No luck. *Madame la Cuisinière,* it seems, had to visit the bathroom at one period; Millan was out in the garage looking at the cars; and the maid was off somewhere, doubtless primping. Result: our friend the Luminalist had an opportunity to pour most of the powder from the bottle into the coffeepot. Damn!"

"I *am* going to call the police!" cried Mrs. Mansfield hysterically, striving to rise. "We'll be murdered in our beds, next thing we know! Laura, I positively insist —"

"Please, please, Mrs. Mansfield," said Ellery wearily. "No heroics. And you would be of greater service if you went into the kitchen and checked the insurrection that's brewing there. The two females are on the verge of packing, I'll swear.'

Mrs. Mansfield bit her lip and flounced off. They heard her no longer sweet voice raised in remonstrance a moment later.

"But, Queen," protested Gardner, "we can't go unprotected —"

"What I want to know in my infantile way," drawled Emmy Willowes from pale lips, "is who did it, and why. That bottle upstairs . . . It looks uncomfortably like one of us, doesn't it?"

Mrs. Gardner gave a little shriek. Mrs. Owen sank back into her chair.

"One of us?" whispered the red-haired woman.

Ellery smiled without humor. Then his smile faded and he cocked his head toward the foyer. "What was that?" he snapped.

They turned, terror-stricken, and looked. But there was nothing to see. Ellery strode toward the front door.

"What is it now, for heaven's sake?" faltered Mrs. Owen.

"I thought I heard a sound —" He flung the door open. The early morning sun streamed in. Then they saw him stoop and pick up something from the porch and rise and look swiftly about outside. But he shook his head and stepped back, closing the door.

"Package," he said with a frown. "I *thought* someone . . ."

They looked blankly at the brown-paper bundle in his hands. "Package?" asked Mrs. Owen. Her face lit up. "Oh, it may be from Richard!" And then the light went out, to be replaced by fearful pallor. "Oh, do you think —?"

"It's addressed," said Ellery slowly, "to you, Mrs. Owen. No stamp, no postmark, written in pencil in disguised block letters. I think I'll take the liberty of opening this, Mrs. Owen." He broke the feeble twine and tore away the wrapping of the crude parcel. And then he frowned even more deeply. For the package contained only a pair of large men's shoes, worn at the heels and soles — sport Oxfords in tan and white.

Mrs. Owen rolled her eyes, her nostrils quivering with nausea. "Richard's!" she gasped. And she sank back, half-fainting.

"Indeed?" murmured Ellery. "How interesting. Not, of course, the shoes he wore Friday night. You're positive they're his,

209

Mrs. Owen?"

"Oh, he *has* been kidnaped!" quavered Mrs. Mansfield from the rear doorway. "Isn't there a note, b-blood . . ."

"Nothing but the shoes. I doubt the kidnap theory now, Mrs. Mansfield. These weren't the shoes Owen wore Friday night. When did you see these last, Mrs. Owen?"

She moaned: "In his wardrobe closet upstairs only yesterday afternoon."

"There. You see?" said Ellery cheerfully. "Probably stolen from the closet while we were all unconscious last night. And now returned rather spectacularly. So far, you know, there's been no harm done. I'm afraid," he said with severity, "we're nursing a viper at our bosoms."

But they did not laugh. Miss Willowes said strangely: "Very odd. In fact, insane, Mr. Queen. I can't see the slightest purpose in it."

"Nor I, at the moment. Somebody's either playing a monstrous prank, or there's a devilishly clever and warped mentality behind all this." He retrieved his hat and made for the door.

"Wherever are you going?" gasped Mrs. Gardner.

"Oh, out for a thinking spell under God's blue canopy. But remember," he added quietly, "that's a privilege reserved to detectives. No one is to set foot outside this house."

He returned an hour later without explanation.

At noon they found the second package. It was a squarish parcel wrapped in the same brown paper. Inside there was a cardboard carton, and in the carton, packed in crumpled tissue paper, there were two magnificent toy sailing boats such as children race on summer lakes. The package was addressed to Miss Willowes.

"This is getting dreadful," murmured Mrs. Gardner, her full lips trembling. "I'm all goose pimples."

"I'd feel better," muttered Miss Willowes, "if it was a bloody dagger, or something. Toy boats!" She stepped back and her eyes narrowed. "Now, look here, good people, I'm as much a sport as anybody, but a joke's a joke and I'm just a bit fed up on this particular one. Who's manoeuvring these monkeyshines?"

"Joke," snarled Gardner. He was white as death. "It's the work of a madman, I tell you!"

"Now, now," murmured Ellery, staring at the green-and-cream boats. "We shan't get anywhere this way. Mrs. Owen, have you ever seen these before?"

Mrs. Owen, on the verge of collapse, mumbled: "Oh, my good dear God. Mr.

211

Queen, I don't — Why, they're — they're Jonathan's!"

Ellery blinked. Then he went to the foot of the stairway and yelled: "Johnny! Come down here a minute."

Master Jonathan descended sluggishly, sulkily. "What you want?" he asked in a cold voice.

"Come here, son." Master Jonathan came with dragging feet. "When did you see these boats of yours last?"

"Boats!" shrieked Master Jonathan, springing into life. He pounced on them and snatched them away, glaring at Ellery. "My boats! Never seen such a place. My boats! You stole 'em!"

"Come, come," said Ellery, flushing, "be a good little man. When did you see them last?"

"Yest'day! In my toy chest! My boats! Scan'lous," hissed Master Jonathan, and fled upstairs, hugging his boats to his scrawny breast.

"Stolen at the same time," said Ellery helplessly. "By thunder, Miss Willowes, I'm almost inclined to agree with you. By the way, who bought those boats for your son, Mrs. Owen?"

"H-his father."

"Damn," said Ellery for the second time that impious Sunday, and he sent them all on a search of the house to ascertain if anything else were missing. But no one could find that anything had been taken.

It was when they came down from upstairs that they found Ellery regarding a small white envelope with puzzlement.

"Now what?" demanded Gardner wildly.

"Stuck in the door," he said thoughtfully. "Hadn't noticed it before. This *is* a queer one."

It was a rich piece of stationery, sealed with blue wax on the back and bearing the same penciled scrawl, this time addressed to Mrs. Mansfield.

The old lady collapsed in the nearest chair, holding her hand to her heart. She was speechless with fear.

"Well," said Mrs. Gardner huskily, "open it."

Ellery tore open the envelope. His frown deepened. "Why," he muttered, "there's nothing at all inside!"

Gardner gnawed his fingers and turned away, mumbling. Mrs. Gardner shook her head like a dazed pugilist and stumbled toward the bar for the fifth time that day. Emmy Willowes's brow was dark as thunder.

"You know," said Mrs. Owen almost quietly, "that's Mother's stationery."

Ellery muttered: "Queerer and queerer. I *must* get this organized. . . . The shoes are a puzzler. The toy boats might be construed as a gift; yesterday was Jonathan's birthday; the boats are his — a distorted practical joke. . . ." He shook his head. "Doesn't wash. And this third — an envelope without a letter in it. That would seem to point to the envelope as the important thing. But the envelope's the property of Mrs. Mansfield. The only other thing — ah, the wax!" He scanned the blue blob on the back narrowly, but it bore no seal-insignia of any kind.

"That," said Mrs. Owen again in the quiet unnatural voice, "looks like our wax, too, Mr. Queen, from the library."

Ellery dashed away, followed by a troubled company. Mrs. Owen went to the library desk and opened the top drawer.

"Was it here?" asked Ellery quickly.

"Yes," she said, and then her voice quivered. "I used it only Friday when I wrote a letter. Oh, good . . ."

There was no stick of wax in the drawer.

And while they stared at the drawer, the front doorbell rang.

It was a market basket this time, lying innocently on the porch. In it, nestling crisp and green, were two large cabbages.

Ellery shouted for Gardner and Millan, and himself led the charge down the steps. They scattered, searching wildly through the brush and woods surrounding the house. But they found nothing. No sign of the bell ringer, no sign of the ghost who had cheerfully left a basket of cabbages at the door as his fourth odd gift. It was as if he were made of smoke and materialized only for the instant he needed to press his impalpable finger to the bell.

They found the women huddled in a corner of the living room, shivering and white-lipped. Mrs. Mansfield, shaking like an aspen, was at the telephone ringing for the local police. Ellery started to protest, shrugged, set his lips, and stooped over the basket.

There was a slip of paper tied by string to the handle of the basket. The same crude pencil scrawl. . . . "Mr. Paul Gardner."

"Looks," muttered Ellery, "as if you're elected, old fellow, this time."

Gardner stared as if he could not believe his eyes. "Cabbages!"

"Excuse me," said Ellery curtly. He went away. When he returned he was shrugging. "From the vegetable bin in the outside pantry, says Cook. She hadn't thought to look for missing *vegetables,* she told me with scorn."

Mrs. Mansfield was babbling excitedly over the telephone to a sorely puzzled officer of the law. When she hung up she was red as a newborn baby. "That will be *quite* enough of this crazy nonsense, Mr. Queen!" she snarled. And then she collapsed in a chair and laughed hysterically and shrieked: "Oh, I knew you were making the mistake of your life when you married that beast, Laura!'' and laughed again like a madwoman.

The law arrived in fifteen minutes, accompanied by a howling siren and personified by a stocky, brick-faced man in chief's stripes and a gangling young policeman.

"I'm Naughton," he said shortly. "What the devil's goin' on here?"

Ellery said: "Ah, Chief Naughton. I'm Queen's son — Inspector Richard Queen of Centre Street. How d'ye do?"

"Oh!" said Naughton. He turned on Mrs. Mansfield sternly. "Why didn't you say Mr. Queen was here, Mrs. Mansfield? You ought to know —"

"Oh, I'm sick of the lot of you!" screamed the old lady. "Nonsense, nonsense, nonsense from the instant this week-end began! First that awful actress-woman there, in her short shirt and legs and things, and then this — this —"

Naughton rubbed his chin. "Come over here, Mr. Queen, where we can talk like human beings. What the deuce happened?"

Ellery with a sigh told him. As he spoke, the Chief's face grew redder and redder. "You mean you're serious about this business?" he rumbled at last. "It sounds plain crazy to me. Mr. Owen's gone off his nut and he's playing jokes on you people. Good God, you can't take this thing serious!"

"I'm afraid," murmured Ellery, "we must. . . . What's that? By heaven, if that's another manifestation of our playful ghost —!" And he dashed toward the door while Naughton gaped and pulled it open, to be struck by a wave of dusk. On the porch lay the fifth parcel, a tiny one this time.

The two officers darted out of the house, flashlights blinking and probing. Ellery picked up the packet with eager fingers. It was addressed in the now familiar scrawl to Mrs. Paul Gardner. Inside were two identically shaped objects: chessmen, kings. One was white and the other was black.

"Who plays chess here?" he drawled.

"Richard," shrieked Mrs. Owen. "Oh, my God, I'm going mad!"

Investigation proved that the two kings from Richard Owen's chess-set were gone.

The local officers came back, rather pale, and panting. They had found no one outside. Ellery was silently studying the two chessmen.

"Well?" said Naughton, drooping his shoulders.

"Well," said Ellery quietly. "I have the most brilliant notion, Naughton. Come here a moment." He drew Naughton aside and began to speak rapidly in a low voice. The others stood limply about, twitching with nervousness. There was no longer any pretense of self-control. If this was a joke, it

217

was a ghastly one indeed. And Richard Owen looming in the background . . .

The Chief blinked and nodded. "You people," he said shortly, turning to them, "get into that library there." They gaped. "I mean it! The lot of you. This tomfoolery is going to stop right now."

"But, Naughton," gasped Mrs. Mansfield, "it couldn't be any of us who sent those things. Mr. Queen will tell you we weren't out of his sight today —"

"Do as I say, Mrs. Mansfield," snapped the officer.

They trooped, puzzled, into the library. The policeman rounded up Millan, the cook, the maid, and went with them. Nobody said anything; nobody looked at anyone else. Minutes passed; a half-hour; an hour. There was the silence of the grave from beyond the door to the living room. They strained their ears. . . .

At seven-thirty the door was jerked open and Ellery and the Chief glowered in on them. "Everybody out," said Naughton shortly. "Come on, step on it."

"Out?" whispered Mrs. Owen. "Where? Where is Richard? What —"

The policeman herded them out. Ellery stepped to the door of the den and pushed it open and switched on the light and stood aside.

"Will you please come in here and take

seats," he said dryly; there was a tense look on his face and he seemed exhausted.

Silently, slowly, they obeyed. The policeman dragged in extra chairs from the living room. They sat down. Naughton drew the shades. The policeman closed the door and set his back against it.

Ellery said tonelessly: "In a way this has been one of the most remarkable cases in my experience. It's been unorthodox from every angle. Utterly nonconforming. I think, Miss Willowes, the wish you expressed Friday night has come true. You're about to witness a slightly cock-eyed exercise in criminal ingenuity."

"Crim —" Mrs. Gardner's full lips quivered. "You mean — there's been a crime?"

"Quiet," said Naughton harshly.

"Yes," said Ellery in gentle tones, "there has been a crime. I might say — I'm sorry to say, Mrs. Owen — a major crime."

"Richard's d —"

"I'm sorry." There was a litle silence. Mrs. Owen did not weep; she seemed dried out of tears. "Fantastic," said Ellery at last. "Look here." He sighed. "The crux of the problem was the clock. The Clock That Wasn't Where It Should Have Been, the clock with the invisible face. You remember I pointed out that, since I hadn't seen the reflection of the luminous hands in that mirror there, the clock must have been moved. That was a tenable theory. But it wasn't the *only* theory."

"Richard's dead," said Mrs. Owen, in a wondering voice.

"Mr. Gardner," continued Ellery quickly, "pointed out one possibility: that the clock may still have been over this door, but that something or someone may have been standing in front of the mirror. I told you why that was impossible. But," and he went suddenly to the tall mirror, "there was still another theory which accounted for the fact that I hadn't seen the luminous hands' reflection. And that was: that when I opened the door in the dark and peered in and saw nothing, the clock was still there but the *mirror* wasn't!"

Miss Willowes said with a curious dryness: "But how could that be, Mr. Queen? That — that's silly."

"Nothing is silly, dear lady, until it is proved so. I said to myself: How could it be that the mirror wasn't there at that instant? It's apparently a solid part of the wall, a built-in section in this modern room." Something glimmered in Miss Willowes's eyes. Mrs. Mansfield was staring straight before her, hands clasped tightly in her lap. Mrs. Owen was looking at Ellery with glazed eyes, blind and deaf. "Then," said Ellery with another sigh, "there was the very odd nature of the packages which have been descending upon us all day like manna from heaven. I said this

220

was a fantastic affair. Of course it must have ocurred to you that someone was trying desperately to call our attention to the secret of the crime."

"Call our at —" began Gardner, frowning.

"Precisely. Now, Mrs. Owen," murmured Ellery softly, "the first package was addressed to you. What did it contain?" She stared at him without expression. There was a dreadful silence. Mrs. Mansfield suddenly shook her, as if she had been a child. She started, smiled vaguely; Ellery repeated the question.

And she said, almost brightly: "A pair of Richard's sport Oxfords."

He winced. "In a word, *shoes*. Miss Willowes," and despite her nonchalance she stiffened a little, "you were the recipient of the second package. And what did that contain?"

"Jonathan's toy boats," she murmured.

"In a word, again — *ships*. Mrs. Mansfield, the third package was sent to you. It contained what, precisely?"

"Nothing." She tossed her head. "I still think this is the purest drivel. Can't you see you're driving my daughter — all of us — insane? Naughton, are you going to permit this farce to continue? If you know what's happened to Richard, for goodness' sake tell us!"

"Answer the question," said Naughton with a scowl.

"Well," she said defiantly, "a silly envelope, empty, and sealed with our own wax."

"And again in a word," drawled Ellery, *"sealing-wax.* Now, Gardner, to you fell the really whimsical fourth bequest. It was —?"

"Cabbage," said Gardner with an uncertain grin.

"Cabbage*s*, my dear chap; there were two of them. And finally, Mrs. Gardner, you received what?"

"Two chessmen," she whispered.

"No, no. Not just two chessmen, Mrs. Gardner. Two *kings.*" Ellery's gray eyes glittered. "In other words, in the order named we were bombarded with gifts . . ." he paused and looked at them, and continued softly, " *'of shoes and ships and sealing-wax, of cabbages and kings.' "*

There was the most extraordinary silence. Then Emmy Willowes gasped: " 'The Walrus and the Carpenter.' *Alice's Adventures in Wonderland!"*

"I'm ashamed of you, Miss Willowes. Where precisely does Tweedledee's Walrus speech come in Carroll's duology?"

A great light broke over her eager features. *"Through the Looking Glass!"*

"Through the Looking Glass," murmured Ellery in the crackling silence that followed. "And do you know what the subtitle of *Through the Looking Glass* is?"

She said in an awed voice: *"And What Alice Found There."*

"A perfect recitation, Miss Willowes. We were instructed, then, to go through the looking glass and, by inference, find something on the other side connected with the disappearance of Richard Owen. Quaint idea, eh?" He leaned forward and said brusquely: "Let me revert to my original chain of reasoning. I said that a likely theory was that the mirror didn't reflect the luminous hands because the mirror wasn't there. But since the wall at any rate is solid, the mirror itself must be movable to have been shifted out of place. How was this possible? Yesterday I sought for two hours to find the secret of that mirror — or should I say . . . looking glass?" Their eyes went with horror to the tall mirror set in the wall, winking back at them in the glitter of the bulbs. "And when I discovered the secret, I looked *through the looking glass* and what do you suppose I — a clumsy Alice, indeed! — found there?"

No one replied.

Ellery went swiftly to the mirror, stood on tiptoe, touched something, and something happened to the whole glass. It moved forward as if on hinges. He hooked his fingers in the crack and pulled. The mirror, like a door, swung out and away, revealing a shallow closet-like cavity.

The women with one breath screamed and

covered their eyes.

The stiff figure of the Mad Hatter, with Richard Owen's unmistakable features, glared out at them — a dead, horrible, baleful glare.

Paul Gardner stumbled to his feet, choking and jerking at his collar. His eyes bugged out of his head. "O-O-Owen," he gasped. "Owen. He *can't* be here. I b-b-buried him myself under the big rock behind the house in the woods. Oh, my God." And he smiled a dreadful smile and his eyes turned over and he collapsed in a faint on the floor.

Ellery sighed. "It's all right now, De Vere," and the Mad Hatter moved and his features ceased to resemble Richard Owen's magically. "You may come out now. Admirable bit of statuary histrionics. And it turned the trick, as I thought it would. There's your man, Mr. Naughton. And if you'll question Mrs. Gardner, I believe you'll find that she's been Owen's mistress for some time. Gardner obviously found it out and killed him. Look out — there *she* goes, too!"

"What I can't understand," murmured Emmy Willowes after a long silence late that night, as she and Mr. Ellery Queen sat side by side in the local bound for Jamaica and the express for Pennsylvania Station, "is —" She stopped helplessly. "I can't understand so many things, Mr. Queen."

224

"It was simple enough," said Ellery wearily, staring out the window at the rushing dark countryside.

"But who is that man — that De Vere?"

"Oh, he! A Thespian acquaintance of mine temporarily 'at liberty.' He's an actor — does character bits. You wouldn't know him, I suppose. You see, when my deductions had led me to the looking glass and I examined it and finally discovered its secret and opened it, I found Owen's body lying there in the Hatter costume —"

She shuddered. "Much too realistic drama to my taste. Why didn't you announce your discovery at once?"

"And gain what? There wasn't a shred of evidence against the murderer. I wanted time to think out a plan to make the murderer give himself away. I left the body there —"

"You mean to sit there and say you knew Gardner did it all the time?" she demanded, frankly skeptical.

He shrugged. "Of course. The Owens had lived in that house barely a month. The spring on that compartment is remarkably well concealed; it probably would never be discovered unless you knew it existed and were looking for it. But I recalled that Owen himself had remarked Friday night that Gardner had designed 'this development.' I had it then, naturally. Who more likely than the architect to know the secret of such a hidden closet? Why he designed and had built a secret panel I don't know; I suppose it fitted into some architectural whim of his. So it had to be Gardner, you see." He gazed thoughtfully at the dusty ceiling of the car. "I reconstructed the crime easily enough. After we retired Friday night Gardner came down to have it out with Owen about Mrs. Gardner — a lusty wench, if I ever saw one. They had words; Gardner killed him. It must have been an unpremeditated crime. His first impulse was to hide the body. He couldn't take it out Friday night in that awful rain without leaving traces on his night clothes. Then he remembered the panel behind the mirror. The body would be safe enough there, he felt, until he could remove it, when the rain stopped and the ground dried, to a permanent hiding place; dig a grave, or whatnot. . . . He was stowing the body away in the closet when I opened the door of the den; that was why I didn't see the reflection of the clock. Then, while I was in the library, he closed the mirror door and dodged upstairs. I came out quickly, though, and he decided to brazen it out; even pretended he thought I might be 'Owen' coming up.

"At any rate, Saturday night he drugged us all, took the body out, buried it, and came back and dosed himself with the drug to make his part as natural as possible. He didn't know I had found the body behind the mirror

Saturday afternoon. When, Sunday morning, I found the body gone, I knew of course the reason for the drugging. Gardner by burying the body in a place unknown to anyone — without leaving, as far as he knew, even a clue to the fact that murder had been committed at all — was naturally doing away with the primary piece of evidence in any murder case . . . the *corpus delicti.* . . . Well, I found the opportunity to telephone De Vere and instruct him in what he had to do. He dug up the Hatter's costume somewhere, managed to get a photo of Owen from a theatrical office, came down here. . . . We put him in the closet while Naughton's man was detaining you people in the library. You see, I had to build up suspense, make Gardner give himself away, break down his moral resistance. He had to be forced to disclose where he had buried the body; and he was the only one who could tell us. It worked."

The actress regarded him sidewise out of her clever eyes. Ellery sighed moodily, glancing away from her slim legs outstretched to the opposite seat. "But the most puzzling thing of all," she said with a pretty frown. "Those perfectly fiendish and fantastic packages. Who sent them, for heaven's sake?"

Ellery did not reply for a long time. Then he said drowsily, barely audible above the clatter of the train: "You did, really."

227

"I?" She was so startled that her mouth flew open.

"Only in a manner of speaking," murmured Ellery, closing his eyes. "Your idea about running a mad tea party out of *Alice* for Master Jonathan's delectation — the whole pervading spirit of the Reverend Dodgson — started a chain of fantasy in my own brain, you see. Just opening the closet and saying that Owen's body had been there, or even getting De Vere to act as Owen, wasn't enough. I had to prepare Gardner's mind psychologically, fill him with puzzlement first, get him to realize after a while where the gifts with their implications were leading . . . . Had to torture him, I suppose. It's a weakness of mine. At any rate, it was an easy matter to telephone my father, the Inspector; and he sent Sergeant Velie down and I managed to smuggle all those things I'd filched from the house out into the woods behind and hand good Velie what I had. . . . He did the rest, packaging and all."

She sat up and measured him with a severe glance. *"Mr.* Queen! Is that cricket in the best detective circles?"

He grinned sleepily. "Drama, Miss Willowes. You ought to be able to understand that. Surround a murderer with things he doesn't understand, bewilder him, get him mentally punch-drunk, and then spring the knock-out blow, the crusher. . . . Oh, it was devilish clever of me, I admit."

She regarded him for so long and in such silence and with such supple twisting of her boyish figure that he stirred uncomfortably. "And what, if I may ask," he said lightly, "brings that positively lewd expression to your Peter Pannish face? You must be feeling —"

"As Alice would say," she said softly, leaning a little toward him, "curiouser and curiouser."

The Incautious Burglar

John Dickson Carr

TWO GUESTS, WHO were not staying the night at Cranleigh Court, left at shortly past eleven o'clock. Marcus Hunt saw them to the front door. Then he returned to the dining-room, where the poker-chips were now stacked into neat piles of white, red, and blue.

"Another game?" suggested Rolfe.

"No good," said Derek Henderson. His tone, as usual, was weary. "Not with just the three of us."

Their host stood by the sideboard and watched them. The long, low house, overlooking the Weald of Kent, was so quiet that their voices rose with startling loudness. The dining-room, large and panelled, was softly lighted by electric wall-candles which brought out the sombre colours of the paintings. It is not often that anybody sees, in one room of an otherwise commonplace country house, two Rembrandts and a Van Dyck. There was a kind of defiance about those paintings.

To Arthur Rolfe — the art dealer — they represented enough money to make him shiver. To Derek Henderson — the art critic — they represented a problem. What they represented to Marcus Hunt was not apparent.

Hunt stood by the sideboard, his fists on his hips, smiling. He was a middle-sized, stocky man, with a full face and a high complexion. Equip him with a tuft of chin-whisker, and he would have looked like a Dutch burgher for a Dutch brush. His shirt-front bulged out untidily. He watched with ironical amusement while Henderson picked up a pack of cards in long fingers, cut them into two piles, and shuffled with a sharp flick of each thumb which made the cards melt together like a conjuring trick.

Henderson yawned.

"My boy," said Hunt, "you surprise me."

"That's what I try to do," answered Henderson, still wearily. He looked up. "But why do you say so, particuarly?"

Henderson was young, he was long, he was lean, he was immaculate; and he wore a beard. It was a reddish beard, which moved some people to hilarity. But he wore it with an air of complete naturalness.

"I'm surprised," said Hunt, "that you enjoy anything so bourgeois — so plebeian — as poker."

"I enjoy reading people's characters," said

231

Henderson. "Poker's the best way to do it, you know."

Hunt's eyes narrowed. "Oh? Can you read my character, for instance?"

"With pleasure," said Henderson. Absently he dealt himself a poker-hand, face up. It contained a pair of fives, and the last card was the ace of spades. Henderson remained staring at it for a few seconds before he glanced up again.

"And I can tell you," he went on, "that *you* surprise *me*. Do you mind if I'm frank? I had always thought of you as the Colossus of Business; the smasher; the plunger; the fellow who took the long chances. Now, you're not like that at all."

Marcus Hunt laughed. But Henderson was undisturbed.

"You're tricky, but you're cautious. I doubt if you ever took a long chance in your life. Another surprise" — he dealt himself a new hand — "is Mr. Rolfe here. He's the man who, given the proper circumstancs, would take the long chances."

Arthur Rolfe considered this. He looked startled, but rather flattered. Though in height and build not unlike Hunt, there was nothing untidy about him. He had a square, dark face, with thin shells of eyeglasses, and a worried forehead.

"I doubt that," he declared, very serious about this. Then he smiled. "A person who took long chances in my business would find himself in the soup." He glanced round the room. "Anyhow, I'd be too cautious to have three pictures, with an aggregate value of thirty thousand pounds, hanging in an unprotected downstairs room with French windows giving on a terrace." An almost frenzied note came into his voice. "Great Scot! Suppose a burglar —— "

"Damn!" said Henderson unexpectedly.

Even Hunt jumped.

Ever since the poker-party, an uneasy atmosphere had been growing. Hunt had picked up an apple from a silver fruit-bowl on the sideboard. He was beginning to pare it with a fruit-knife, a sharp wafer-thin blade which glittered in the light of the wall-lamps.

"You nearly made me slice my thumb off," he said, putting down the knife. "What's the matter with you?"

"It's the ace of spades," said Henderson, still languidly. "That's the second time it's turned up in five minutes."

Arthur Rolfe chose to be dense. "Well? What about it?"

"I think our young friend is being psychic," said Hunt, good-humoured again. "Are you reading characters, or only telling fortunes?"

Henderson hesitated. His eyes moved to Hunt, and then to the wall over the sideboard where Rembrandt's "Old Woman with Cap" stared back with the immobility and skin-colouring of a red Indian. Then Henderson looked towards the French windows opening on the terrace.

"None of my affair," shrugged Henderson. "It's your house and your collection and your responsibility. But this fellow Butler: what do you know about him?"

Marcus Hunt looked boisterously amused.

"Butler? He's a friend of my niece's. Harriet picked him up in London, and asked me to invite him down here. Nonsense! Butler's all right. What are you thinking, exactly?"

"Listen!" said Rolfe, holding up his hand.

The noise they heard, from the direction of the terrace, was not repeated. It was not repeated because the person who had made it, a very bewildered and uneasy young lady, had run lightly and swiftly to the far end, where she leaned against the balustrade.

Lewis Butler hesitated before going after her. The moonlight was so clear that one could see the mortar between the tiles which paved the terrace, and trace the design of the stone urns along the balustrade. Harriet Davis wore a white gown with long and filmy skirts, which she lifted clear of the ground as she ran.

Then she beckoned to him.

She was half sitting, half leaning against the rail. Her white arms were spread out, fingers gripping the stone. Dark hair and dark eyes became even more vivid by moonlight. He could see the rapid rise and fall of her breast; he could even trace the shadow of her eyelashes.

"That was a lie, anyhow," she said.

"What was?"

"What my Uncle Marcus said. You heard him." Harriet Davis's fingers tightened still more on the balustrade. But she nodded her head vehemently, with fierce accusation. "About my knowing you. And inviting you here. I never saw you before this week-end. Either Uncle Marcus is going out of his mind, or. . . . will you answer me just one question?"

"If I can."

"Very well. Are you by any chance a crook?"

She spoke with as much simplicity and directness as though she had asked him whether he might be a doctor or a lawyer. Lewis Butler was not unwise enough to laugh. She was in that mood where, to any woman, laughter is salt to a raw wound; she would probably have slapped his face.

"To be quite frank about it," he said, "I'm not. Will you tell me why you asked?"

"This house," said Harriet, looking at the moon, "used to be guarded with burglar alarms. If you as much as touched a window, the whole place started clanging like a fire-station. He had all the burglar alarms removed last week. Last week." She took her hands off the balustrade, and pressed them together hard. "The pictures used to be upstairs, in a locked room next to his bedroom. He had them moved downstairs — last week. It's almost as though my uncle *wanted* the house to be burgled."

Butler knew that he must use great care here.

"Perhaps he does." (Here she looked at Butler quickly, but did not comment.) "For instance," he went on idly, "suppose one of his famous Rembrandts turned out to be a fake? It might be a relief not to have to show it to his expert friends."

The girl shook her head.

"No." She said. "They're all genuine. You see, I thought of that too."

Now was the time to hit, and hit hard. To Lewis Butler, in his innocence, there seemed to be no particular problem. He took out his cigarette-case, and turned it over without opening it.

"Look here, Miss Davis, you're not going to like this. But I can tell you of cases in which people were rather anxious to have their property 'stolen.' If a picture is insured for more than its value, and then it is mysteriously 'stolen' one night ——?"

"That might be all very well too," answered Harriet, still calmly. "Except that not one of those pictures has been insured."

The cigarette-case, which was of polished metal, slipped through Butler's fingers and fell with a clatter on the tiles. It spilled cigarettes, just as it spilled and confused his theories. As he bent over to pick it up, he could hear a church clock across the Weald strike the half-hour after eleven.

"You're sure of that?"

"I'm perfectly sure. He hasn't insured any of his pictures for as much as a penny. He says it's a waste of money."

"But ——"

"Oh, I know! And I don't know why I'm talking to you like this. You're a stranger, aren't you?" She folded her arms, drawing her shoulders up as though she were cold. Uncertainty, fear, and plain nerves flicked at her eyelids. "But then Uncle Marcus is a stranger too. Do you know what I think? I think he's going mad."

"Hardly as bad as that, is it?"

"Yes, go on," the girl suddenly stormed at him. "*Say* it: go on and say it. That's easy enough. But you don't see him when his eyes seem to get smaller, and all that genial-country-squire look goes out of his face. He's not a fake: he hates fakes, and goes out of his way to expose them. But, if he hasn't gone clear out of his mind, what's he up to? What can he be up to?"

In something over three hours, they

found out.

The burglar did not attack until half-past two in the morning. First he smoked several ciga-rettes in the shrubbery below the rear terrace. When he heard the church clock strike, he waited a few minutes more, and then slipped up the steps to the French windows of the dining-room.

A chilly wind stirred at the turn of the night, in the hour of suicides and bad dreams. It smoothed grass and trees with a faint rustling. When the man glanced over his shoulder, the last of the moonlight distorted his face: it showed less a face than the blob of a black cloth mask, under a greasy cap pulled down over his ears.

He went to work on the middle window, with the contents of a folding tool-kit not so large as a motorist's. He fastened two short strips of adhesive tape to the glass just beside the catch. Then his glass-cutter sliced out a small semi-circle inside the tape.

It was done not without noise: it crunched like a dentist's drill in a tooth, and the man stopped to listen.

There was no answering noise. No dog barked.

With the adhesive tape holding the glass so that it did not fall and smash, he slid his gloved hand through the opening and twisted the catch. The weight of his body deadened the creaking of the window when he pushed inside.

He knew exactly what he wanted. He put the tool-kit into his pocket, and drew out an electric torch. Its beam moved across to the sideboard; it touched gleaming silver, a bowl of fruit, and a wicked little knife thrust into an apple as though into someone's body; finally, it moved up the hag-face of the "Old Woman with Cap."

This was not a large picture, and the burglar lifted it down easily. He pried out glass and frame. Though he tried to roll up the canvas with great care, the brittle paint cracked across in small stars which wounded the hag's face. The burglar was so intent on this that he never noticed the presence of another person in the room.

He was an incautious burglar: he had no sixth sense which smelt murder.

Up on the second floor of the house, Lewis Butler was awakened by a muffled crash like that of metal objects falling.

He had not fallen into more than a half doze all night. He knew with certainty what must be happening, though he had no idea of why, or how, or to whom.

Butler was out of bed, and into his slippers, as soon as he heard the first faint clatter from downstairs. His dressing-gown would, as usual, twist itself up like a rolled umbrella and defy all attempts to find the arm-holes whenever he wanted to hurry. But the little flashlight was ready in the pocket.

That noise seemed to have roused nobody else. With certain possibilities in his mind, he had never in his life moved so fast once he managed to get out of his bedroom. Not using his light, he was down two flights of deep-carpeted stairs without noise. In the lower hall he could feel a draught, which meant that a window or door had been opened some-where. He made straight for the dining-room.

But he was too late.

Once the pencil-beam of Butler's flashlight had swept round, he switched on a whole blaze of lights. The burglar was still here, right enough. But the burglar was lying very still in front of the sideboard; and, to judge by the amount of blood on his sweater and trousers, he would neer move again.

"That's done it," Butler said aloud.

A silver service, including a tea-urn, had been toppled off the sideboard. Where the fruit-bowl had fallen, the dead man lay on his back among a litter of oranges, apples, and a squashed bunch of grapes. The mask still covered the burglar's face; his greasy cap was flattened still further on his ears; his gloved hands were thrown wide.

Fragments of smashed picture-glass lay round him, together with the empty frame, and the "Old Woman with Cap" had been half crumpled up under his body. From the position of the most conspicuous bloodstains, one judged that he had been stabbed through the chest with the stained fruit-knife beside him.

"What is it?" said a voice almost at Butler's ear.

He could not have been more startled if the fruit-knife had pricked his ribs. He had seen nobody turning on lights in the hall, nor had he heard Harriet Davis approach. She was standing just behind him, wrapped in a Japanese kimono, with her dark hair round her shoulders. But, when he explained what had happened, she would not look into the dining-room; she backed away, shaking her head violently, like an urchin ready for flight.

"You had better wake up your uncle," Butler said briskly, with a confidence he did not feel. "And the servants. I must use your telephone." Then he looked her in the eyes. "Yes, you're quite right. I think you've guessed it already. I'm a police-officer."

She nodded.

"Yes. I guessed. Who are you? And is your name really Butler?"

"I'm a sergeant of the Criminal Investigation Department. And my name really is Butler. Your uncle brought me here."

"Why?"

"I don't know. He hasn't got round to telling me."

This girl's intelligence, even when overshadowed by fear, was direct and disconcerting. "But, if he wouldn't say why he wanted a police-officer, how did they come to send you? He'd have to tell them, wouldn't he?"

Butler ignored it. "I must see your uncle. Will you go upstairs and wake him, please?"

"I can't," said Harriet. "Uncle Marcus isn't in his room."

"Isn't ——?"

"No. I knocked at the door on my way down. He's gone."

Butler took the stairs two treads at a time. Harriet had turned on all the lights on her way down, but nothing stirred in the bleak, over-decorated passages.

Marcus Hunt's bedroom was empty. His dinner-jacket had been hung up neatly on the back of a chair, shirt laid across the seat with collar and tie on top of it. Hunt's watch ticked loudly on the dressing-table. His money and keys were there too. But he had not gone to bed, for the bedspread was undisturbed.

The suspicion which came to Lewis Butler, listening to the thin insistent ticking of that watch in the drugged hour before dawn, was so fantastic that he could not credit it.

He started downstairs again, and on the way he met Arthur Rolfe blundering out of another bedroom down the hall. The art dealer's stocky body was wrapped in a flannel dressing-gown. He was not wearing his eyeglasses, which gave his face a bleary and rather caved-in expression. He planted himself in front of Butler, and refused to budge.

"Yes," said Butler. "You don't have to ask. It's a burglar."

"I knew it," said Rolfe calmly. "Did he get anything?"

"No. He was murdered."

For a moment Rolfe said nothing, but his hand crept into the breast of his dressing-gown as though he felt pain there.

"Murdered? You don't mean the *burglar* was murdered?"

"Yes."

"But why? By an accomplice, you mean? Who is the burglar?"

"That," snarled Lewis Butler, "is what I intend to find out."

In the lower hall he found Harriet Davis, who was now standing in the doorway of the dining-room and looking steadily at the body by the sideboard. Though her face hardly moved a muscle, her eyes brimmed over.

"You're going to take off the mask, aren't you?" she asked, without turning round.

Stepping with care to avoid squashed fruit and broken glass, Butler leaned over the dead man. He pushed back the peak of the greasy cap; he lifted the black cloth mask, which was clumsily held by an elastic band; and he found what he expected to find.

The burglar was Marcus Hunt–stabbed through the heart while attempting to rob his own house.

"You see, sir," Butler explained to Dr. Gideon Fell on the following afternoon, "that's the trouble. However you look at it, the case makes no sense."

Again he went over the facts.

"Why should the man burgle his own house and steal his own property? Every one of those paintings is valuable, and not a single one is insured! Consequently, why? Was the man a simple lunatic? What did he think he was doing?"

The village of Sutton Valence, straggling like a grey-white Italian town along the very peak of the Weald, was full of hot sunshine. In the apple orchard behind the white inn of the *Tabard,* Dr. Gideon Fell sat at a garden table among wasps, with a pint tankard at his elbow. Dr. Fell's vast bulk was clad in a white linen suit. His pink face smoked in the heat, and his wary lookout for wasps gave him a regrettably wall-eyed appearance as he pondered.

He said:

"Superintendent Hadley suggested that I might — harrumph — look in here. The local police are in charge, aren't they?"

"Yes. I'm merely standing by."

"Hadley's exact words to me were, 'It's so

244

crazy that nobody but you will understand it.' The man's flattery becomes more nauseating every day." Dr. Fell scowled. "I say. Does anything else strike you as queer about this business?"

"Well, why should a man burgle his own house?"

"No, no, no!" growled Dr. Fell. "Don't be obsessed with that point. Don't become hypnotized by it. For instance" — a wasp hovered near his tankard, and he distended his cheeks and blew it away with one vast puff like Father Neptune – "for instance, the young lady seems to have raised an interesting question. If Marcus Hunt wouldn't say why he wanted a detective in the house, why did the C.I.D. consent to send you?"

Butler shrugged his shoulders.

"Because," he said, "Chief Inspector Ames thought Hunt was up to funny business, and meant to stop it."

"What sort of funny business?"

"A faked burglary to steal his own pictures for the insurance. It looked like the old, old game of appealing to the police to divert suspicion. In other words, sir, exactly what this appeared to be: until I learned (and to-day proved) that not one of those damned pictures has ever been insured for a penny."

Butler hesitated.

"It can't have been a practical joke," he went on. "Look at the elaborateness of it!

Hunt put on old clothes from which all tailors' tabs and laundry marks were removed. He put on gloves and a mask. He got hold of a torch and an up-to-date kit of burglar's tools. He went out of the house by the back door; we found it open later. He smoked a few cigarettes in the shrubbery below the terrace; we found his footprints in the soft earth. He cut a pane of glass . . . but I've told you all that."

"And then," mused Dr. Fell, "somebody killed him."

"Yes. The last and worst 'why.' Why should anybody have killed him?"

"H'm. Clues?"

"Negative." Butler took out his notebook. "According to the police surgeon, he died of a direct heart-wound from a blade (presumably that fruit-knife) so thin that the wound was difficult to find. There were a number of his finger-prints, but nobody else's. We did find one odd thing, though. A number of pieces in the silver service off the sideboard were scratched in a queer way. It looked almost as though, instead of being swept off the sideboard in a struggle, they had been piled up on top of each other like a tower; and then pushed ——"

Butler paused, for Dr. Fell was shaking his big head back and forth with an expression of Gargantuan distress.

"Well, well, well," he was saying; "well, well, well. And you call that negative evidence?"

"Isn't it? It doesn't explain why a man burgles his own house."

"Look here," said the doctor mildly. "I should like to ask you just one question. What is the most important point in this affair? One moment! I did not say the most interesting; I said the most important. Surely it is the fact that a man has been murdered?"

"Yes, sir. Naturally."

"I mention the fact" — the doctor was apologetic — "because it seems in danger of being overlooked. It hardly interests you. You are concerned only with Hunt's senseless masquerade. You don't mind a throat being cut; but you can't stand a leg being pulled. Why not try working at it from the other side, and asking who killed Hunt?"

Butler was silent for a long time.

"The servants are out of it," he said at length. "They sleep in another wing on the top floor; and for some reason," he hesitated, "somebody locked them in last night." His doubts, even his dreads, were beginning to take form. "There was a fine blow-up over that when the house was roused. Of course, the murderer could have been an outsider."

"You know it wasn't," said Dr. Fell. "Would you mind taking me to Cranleigh Court?"

They came out on the terrace in the hottest

part of the afternoon.

Dr. Fell sat down on a wicker settee, with a dispirited Harriet beside him. Derek Henderson, in flannels, perched his long figure on the balustrade. Arthur Rolfe alone wore a dark suit and seemed out of place. For the pale green and brown of the Kentish lands, which rarely acquired harsh colour, now blazed. No air stirred, no leaf moved, in that brilliant thickness of heat; and down in the garden, towards their left, the water of the swimming-pool sparkled with hot, hard light. Butler felt it like a weight on his eyelids.

Derek Henderson's beard was at once languid and yet aggressive.

"It's no good," he said. "Don't keep on asking me why Hunt should have burgled his own house. But I'll give you a tip."

"Which is?" inquired Dr. Fell.

"Whatever the reason was," returned Henderson, sticking out his neck, "it was a good reason. Hunt was much too canny and cautious ever to do anything without a good reason. I told him so last night."

Dr. Fell spoke sharply. "Cautious? Why do you say that?"

"Well, for instance. I take three cards on the draw. Hunt takes one. I bet; he sees me and raises. I cover that, and raise again. Hunt drops out. In other words, it's fairly certain he's filled his hand, but not so certain I'm holding much more than a pair. Yet Hunt

248

drops out. So with my three sevens I bluff him out of his straight. He played a dozen hands last night just like that."

Henderson began to chuckle. Seeing the expression on Harriet's face, he checked himself and became preternaturally solemn.

"But then, of course," Henderson added, "he had a lot on his mind last night."

Nobody could fail to notice the change of tone.

"So? And what did he have on his mind?"

"Exposing somebody he had always trusted," replied Henderson coolly. "That's why I didn't like it when the ace of spades turned up so often."

"You'd better explain that," said Harriet, after a pause. "I don't know what you're hinting at, but you'd better explain that. He told you he intended to expose somebody he had always trusted?"

"No. Like myself, he hinted at it."

It was the stolid Rolfe who stormed into the conversation then. Rolfe had the air of a man determined to hold hard to reason, but finding it difficult.

"Listen to me," snapped Rolfe. "I have heard a great deal, at one time or another, about Mr. Hunt's liking for exposing people. Very well!" He slid one hand into the breast of his coat, in a characteristic gesture. "But where in the name of sanity does that leave us? He wants to expose someone. And, to do that, he puts on outlandish clothes and masquerades as a burglar. Is that sensible? I tell you, the man was mad! There's no other explanation."

"There are five other explanations," said Dr. Fell.

Derek Henderson slowly got up from his seat on the balustrade, but he sat down again at a savage gesture from Rolfe.

Nobody spoke.

"I will not, however," pursued Dr. Fell, "waste your time with four of them. We are concerned with only one explanation: the real one."

"And you know the real one?" asked Henderson sharply.

"I rather think so."

"Since when?"

"Since I had the opportunity of looking at all of you," answered Dr. Fell.

He settled back massively in the wicker settee, so that its frame creaked and cracked like a ship's bulkhead in a heavy sea. His vast chin was out-thrust and he nodded absently as though to emphasize some point that was quite clear in his own mind.

"I've already had a word with the local inspector," he went on suddenly. "He will be here in a few minutes. And, at my suggestion, he will have a request for all of you. I sincerely hope nobody will refuse."

"Request?" said Henderson. "What

request?"

"It's a very hot day," said Dr. Fell, blinking towards the swimming-pool. "He's going to suggest that you all go in for a swim."

Harriet uttered a kind of despairing mutter, and turned as though appealing to Lewis Butler.

"That," continued Dr. Fell, "will be the politest way of drawing attention to the murderer. In the meantime, let me call your attention to one point in the evidence which seems to have been generally overlooked. Mr. Henderson, do you know anything about direct heart-wounds, made by a steel blade as thin as a wafer?"

"Like Hunt's wound? No. What about them?"

"There is practically no exterior bleeding," answered Dr. Fell.

"But ——!" Harriet was beginning, when Butler stopped her.

"The police surgeon, in fact, called attention to that wound which was so 'difficult to find.' The victim dies almost at once; and the edges of the wound compress. But in that case," argued Dr. Fell, "how did the late Mr. Hunt come to have so much blood on his sweater, and even splashed on his trousers?"

"Well?"

"He didn't," answered Dr. Fell simply. "Mr. Hunt's blood never got on his clothes at all."

"I can't stand this," said Harriet, jumping to her feet. "I — I'm sorry, but have you gone mad yourself? Are you telling us we didn't see him lying by that sideboard, with blood on him?"

"Oh, yes. You saw that."

"Let him go on," said Henderson, who was rather white round the nostrils. "Let him rave."

"It is, I admit, a fine point," said Dr. Fell. "But it answers your question, repeated to the point of nausea, as to why the eminently sensible Mr. Hunt chose to dress up in burglar's clothes and play burglar. The answer is short and simple. He didn't."

"It must be plain to everybody," Dr. Fell went on, opening his eyes wide, "that Mr. Hunt was deliberately setting a trap for someone — the real burglar.

"He believed that a certain person might try to steal one or several of his pictures. He probably knew that this person had tried similar games before, in other country houses: that is, an inside job which was carefully planned to look like an outside job. So he made things easy for this thief, in order to trap him, with a police-officer in the house.

"The burglar, a sad fool, fell for it. This thief, a guest in the house, waited until well past two o'clock in the morning. He then put on his old clothes, mask, gloves, and the rest of it. He let himself out by the back door. He went through all the motions we have erroneously been attributing to Marcus Hunt. Then the trap snapped. Just as he was rolling up the Rembrandt, he heard a noise. He swung his light round. And he saw Marcus Hunt, in pyjamas and dressing-gown, looking at him.

"Yes, there was a fight. Hunt flew at him. The thief snatched up a fruit-knife and fought back. In that struggle, Marcus Hunt forced his opponent's hand back. The fruit-knife gashed the thief's chest, inflicting a superficial but badly bleeding gash. It sent the thief over the edge of insanity. He wrenched Marcus Hunt's wrist half off, caught up the knife, and stabbed Hunt to the heart.

"Then, in a quiet house, with a little beam of light streaming out from the torch on the sideboard, the murderer sees something that will hang him. He sees the blood from his own superficial wound seeping down his clothes.

"How is he to get rid of those clothes? He cannot destroy them, or get them away from the house. Inevitably the house will be searched, and they will be found. Without the blood-stains, they would seem ordinary clothes in his wardrobe. But with the blood-stains ——

"There is only one thing he can do."

Harriet Davis was standing behind the

wicker settee, shading her eyes against the glare of the sun. Her hand did not tremble when she said:

"He changed clothes with my uncle."

"That's it," growled Dr. Fell. "That's the whole sad story. The murderer dressed the body in his own clothes, making a puncture with the knife in sweater, shirt, and under-vest. He then slipped on Mr. Hunt's pyjamas and dressing-gown, which at a pinch he could always claim as his own. Hunt's wound had bled hardly at all. His dressing-gown, I think, had come open in the fight; so that all the thief had to trouble him was a tiny puncture in the jacket of the pyjamas.

"But, once he had done this, he had to hypnotize you all into the belief that there would have been no time for a change of clothes. He had to make it seem that the fight occurred just *then*. He had to rouse the house. So he brought down echoing thunders by pushing over a pile of silver, and slipped upstairs."

Dr. Fell paused.

"The burglar could never have been Marcus Hunt, you know," he added. "We learned that Hunt's fingerprints were all over the place. Yet the murdered man was wearing gloves."

There was a swishing of feet in the grass below the terrace, and a tread of heavy boots coming up the terrace steps. The local Inspector of police, buttoned up and steaming

254

in his uniform, was followed by two constables.

Dr. Fell turned round a face of satisfaction.

"Ah!" he said, breathing deeply. "They've come to see about that swimming-party, I imagine. It is easy to patch up a flesh-wound with lint and cotton, or even a handkerchief. But such a wound will become infernally conspicuous in anyone who is forced to climb into bathing-trunks."

"But it couldn't have been ——" cried Harriet. Her eyes moved round. Her fingers tightened on Lewis Butler's arm, an instinctive gesture which he was to remember long afterwards, when he knew her even better.

"Exactly," agreed the doctor, wheezing with pleasure. "It could not have been a long, thin, gangling fellow like Mr. Henderson. It assuredly could not have been a small and slender girl like yourself.

"There is only one person who, as we know, is just about Marcus Hunt's height and build; who could have put his own clothes on Hunt without any suspicion. That is the same person who, though he managed to staunch the wound in his chest, has been constantly running his hand inside the breast of his coat to make certain the bandage is secure. Just as Mr. Rolfe is doing now."

Arthur Rolfe sat very quiet, with his right hand still in the breast of his jacket. His face had grown smeary in the hot sunlight, but the eyes behind those thin shells of glasses remained inscrutable. He spoke only once, through dry lips, after they had cautioned him.

"I should have taken the young pup's warning," he said. "After all, he told me I would take long chances."

The Case of the Irate Witness

Erle Stanley Gardner

THE EARLY-MORNING SHADOWS cast by the mountains still lay heavily on the town's main street as the big siren on the roof of the Jebson Commercial Company began to scream shrilly.

The danger of fire was always present, and at the sound, men at breakfast rose and pushed their chairs back from the table. Men who were shaving barely paused to wipe lather from their faces; men who had been sleeping grabbed the first available garments. All of them ran to places where they could look for the first telltale wisps of smoke.

There was no smoke.

The big siren was still screaming urgently as the men formed into streaming lines, like ants whose hill has been attached. The lines all moved toward the Jebson Commercial Company.

There the men were told that the doors of the big vault had been found wide open. A jagged hole had been cut into one door with an acetylene torch.

The men looked at one another silently. This was the fifteenth of the month. The big, twice-a-month payroll, which had been brought up from the Ivanhoe National Bank the day before, had been the prize.

Frank Bernal, manager of the company's mine, the man who ruled Jebson City with an iron hand, arrived and took charge. The responsibility was his, and what he found was alarming.

Tom Munson, the night watchman, was lying on the floor in a back room, snoring in drunken slumber. The burglar alarm, which had been installed within the last six months, had been bypassed by means of an electrical device. This device was so ingenious that it was apparent that, if the work were that of a gang, at least one of the burglars was an expert electrician.

Ralph Nesbitt, the company accountant, was significantly silent. When Frank Bernal had been appointed manager a year earlier, Nesbitt had pointed out that the big vault was obsolete.

Bernal, determined to prove himself in his new job, had avoided the expense of tearing out the old vault and installing a new one by investing in an up-to-date burglar alarm and putting a special night watchman on duty.

Now the safe had been looted of $100,000

and Frank Bernal had to make a report to the main office in Chicago, with the disquieting knowledge that Ralph Nesbitt's memo stating that the antiquated vault was a pushover was at this moment reposing in the company files.

Some distance out of Jebson City, Perry Mason, the famous trial lawyer, was driving fast along a mountain road. He had planned a weekend fishing trip for a long time, but a jury which had waited until midnight before reaching its verdict had delayed Mason's departure and it was now 8:30 in the morning.

His fishing clothes, rod, wading boots, and creel were all in the trunk. He was wearing the suit in which he had stepped from the courtroom, and having driven all night he was eager for the cool, piny mountains.

A blazing red light, shining directly at him as he rounded a turn in the canyon road, dazzled his road-weary eyes. A sign, *STOP — POLICE,* had been placed in the middle of the road. Two men, a grim-faced man with a .30 — 30 rifle in his hands and a silver badge on his shirt and a uniformed motorcycle officer, stood beside the sign.

Mason stopped his car.

The man with the badge, deputy sheriff, said, "We'd better take a look at your driving license. There's been a big robbery at Jebson City."

"That so?" Mason said. "I went through

259

Jebson City an hour ago and everything seemed quiet."

"Where you been since then?"

"I stopped at a little service station and restaurant for breakfast."

"Let's take a look at your driving license."

Mason handed it to him.

The man started to return it, then looked at it again. "Say," he said, "you're Perry Mason, the big criminal lawyer!"

"Not a criminal lawyer," Mason said patiently, "a trial lawyer. I sometimes defend men who are accused of crime."

"What are you doing up in this country?"

"Going fishing."

The deputy looked at him suspiciously. "Why aren't you wearing your fishing clothes?"

"Because," Mason said, and smiled, "I'm not fishing."

"You said you were going fishing."

"I also intend," Mason said, "to go to bed tonight. According to you, I should be wearing my pajamas."

The deputy frowned. The traffic officer laughed and waved Mason on.

The deputy nodded at the departing car. "Looks like a live clue to me," he said, "but I can't find it in that conversation."

"There isn't any," the traffic officer said.

The deputy remained dubious, and later on, when a news-hungry reporter from the local paper asked the deputy if he knew of anything that would make a good story, the deputy said that he did.

And that was why Della Street, Perry Mason's confidential secretary, was surprised to read stories in the metropolitan papers stating that Perry Mason, the noted trial lawyer, was rumored to have been retained to represent the person or persons who had looted the vault of the Jebson Commercial Company. All this had been arranged, it would seem, before Mason's "client" had even been apprehended.

When Perry Mason called his office by long-distance the next afternoon, Della said, "I thought you were going to the mountains for a vacation."

"That's right. Why?"

"The papers claim you're representing whoever robbed the Jebson Commercial Company."

"First I've heard of it," Mason said. "I went through Jebson City before they discovered the robbery, stopped for breakfast a little farther on, and then got caught in a road-block. In the eyes of some officious deputy, that seems to have made me an accessory after the fact."

"Well," Della Street said, "they've caught a man by the name of Harvey L. Corbin, and apparently have quite a case against him.

261

They're hinting at mysterious evidence which won't be disclosed until the time of trial."

"Was he the one who committed the crime?" Mason asked.

"The police think so. He has a criminal record. When his employers at Jebson City found out about it, they told him to leave town. That was the evening before the robbery."

"Just like that, eh?" Mason asked.

"Well, you see, Jebson City is a one-industry town, and the company owns all the houses. They're leased to the employees. I understand Corbin's wife and daughter were told they could stay on until Corbin got located in a new place, but Corbin was told to leave town at once. You aren't interested, are you?"

"Not in the least," Mason said, "except that when I drive back I'll be going through Jebson City, and I'll probably stop to pick up the local gossip."

"Don't do it," she warned. "This man Corbin has all the earmarks of being an underdog, and you know how you feel about underdogs."

A quality in her voice made Perry suspicious. "You haven't been approached, have you, Della?"

"Well," she said, "in a way. Mrs. Corbin read in the papers that you were going to represent her husband, and she was overjoyed. It seems that she thinks her husband's implication in this is a raw deal. She hadn't known anything about his criminal record, but she loves him and is going to stand by him."

"You've talked with her?" Mason asked.

"Several times. I tried to break it to her gently. I told her it was probably nothing but a newspaper story. You see, Chief, they have Corbin dead to rights. They took some money from his wife as evidence. It was part of the loot."

"And she has nothing?"

"Nothing. Corbin left her forty dollars, and they took it all as evidence."

"I'll drive all night," he said. "Tell her I'll be back tomorrow."

"I was afraid of that," Della Street said. "Why did you have to call up? Why couldn't you have stayed up there fishing? Why did you have to get your name in the papers?"

Mason laughed and hung up.

Paul Drake, of the Drake Detective Agency, came in and sat in the big chair in Mason's office and said, "You have a bear by the tail, Perry."

"What's the matter, Paul? Didn't your detective work in Jebson City pan out?"

"It panned out all right, but the stuff in the pan isn't what you want, Perry," Drake explained.

"How come?"

"Your client's guilty."

"Go on," Mason said.

"The money he gave his wife was some of what was stolen from the vault."

"How do they know it was the stolen money?" Mason asked.

Drake pulled a notebook from his pocket. "Here's the whole picture. The plant manager runs Jebson City. There isn't any private property. The Jebson company controls everything."

"Not a single small business?"

Drake shook his head. "Not unless you want to consider garbage collecting as small business. An old coot by the name of George Addey lives five miles down the canyon; he has a hog ranch and collects the garbage. He's supposed to have the first nickel he ever earned. Buries his money in cans. There's no bank nearer than Ivanhoe City."

"What about the burglary? The men who did it must have moved in acetylene tanks and —"

"They took them right out of the company store," Drake said. And then he went on: "Munson, the watchman, likes to take a pull out of a flask of whiskey along about midnight. He says it keeps him awake. Of course, he's not supposed to do it, and no one was supposed to know about the whiskey, but someone did know about it. They doped the whiskey with a barbiturate. The watchman took his usual swig, went to sleep, and stayed asleep."

"What's the evidence against Corbin?" Mason asked.

"Corbin had a previous burglary record. It's a policy of the company not to hire anyone with a criminal record. Corbin lied about his past and got a job. Frank Bernal, the manager, found out about it, sent for Corbin about 8 o'clock the night the burglary took place, and ordered him out of town. Bernal agreed to let Corbin's wife and child stay on in the house until Corbin could get located in another city. Corbin pulled out in the morning, and gave his wife this money. It was part of the money from the burglary."

"How do they know?" Mason asked.

"Now there's something I don't know," Drake said. "This fellow Bernal is pretty smart, and the story is that he can prove Corbin's money was from the vault."

Drake paused, then continued: "The nearest bank is at Ivanhoe City, and the mine pays off in cash twice a month. Ralph Nesbitt, the cashier, wanted to install a new vault. Bernal refused to okay the expense. So the company has ordered both Bernal and Nesbitt back to its main office at Chicago to report. The rumor is that they may fire Bernal as manager and give Nesbitt the job. A couple of the directors don't like Bernal, and this thing has given them their chance. They dug out a report Nesbitt had made showing the vault was a pushover. Bernal didn't act on that report." He sighed and then asked, "When's the trial, Perry?"

"The preliminary hearing is set for Friday morning. I'll see then what they've got against Corbin."

"They're laying for you up there," Paul Drake warned. "Better watch out, Perry. That district attorney has something up his sleeve, some sort of surprise that's going to knock you for a loop."

In spite of his long experience as a prosecutor, Vernon Flasher, the district attorney of Ivanhoe County, showed a certain nervousness at being called upon to oppose Perry Mason. There was, however, a secretive assurance underneath that nervousness.

Judge Haswell, realizing that the eyes of the community were upon him, adhered to legal technicalities to the point of being pompous both in rulings and mannerisms.

But what irritated Perry Mason was in the attitude of the spectators. He sensed that they did not regard him as an attorney trying to safeguard the interests of a client, but as a legal magician with a cloven hoof. The looting of the vault had shocked the community, and there was a tight-lipped determination that no legal tricks were going to do Mason any good *this* time.

266

Vernon Flasher didn't try to save his surprise evidence for a whirlwind finish. He used it right at the start of the case.

Frank Bernal, called as a witness, described the location of the vault, identified photographs, and then leaned back as the district attorney said abruptly, "You had reason to believe this vault was obsolete?"

"Yes, sir."

"It had been pointed out to you by one of your fellow employees, Mr. Ralph Nesbitt?"

"Yes, sir."

"And what did you do about it?"

"Are you," Mason asked in some surprise, "trying to cross-examine your own witness?"

"Just let him answer the question, and you'll see," Flasher replied grimly.

"Go right ahead and answer," Mason said to the witness.

Bernal assumed a more comfortable position. "I did three things," he said, "to safeguard the payrolls and to avoid the expense of tearing out the old vault and installing a new vault in its place."

"What were those three things?"

"I employed a special night watchman; I installed the best burglar alarm money could buy; and I made arrangements with the Ivanhoe National Bank, where we have our payrolls made up, to list the number of each twenty-dollar bill which was a part of each payroll."

Mason suddenly sat up straight.

Flasher gave him a glance of gloating triumph. "Do you wish the court to understand, Mr. Bernal," he said smugly, "that you have the numbers of the bills in the payroll which was made up for delivery on the fifteenth?"

"Yes, sir. Not *all* the bills, you understand. That would have taken too much time, but I have the numbers of all the twenty-dollar bills."

"And who recorded those numbers?" the prosecutor asked.

"The bank."

"And do you have that list of numbers with you?"

"I do. Yes, sir." Bernal produced a list. "I felt," he said, glancing coldly at Nesbitt, "that these precautions would be cheaper than a new vault."

"I move the list be introduced in evidence," Flasher said.

"Just a moment," Mason objected. "I have a couple of questions. You say this list is not in your handwriting, Mr. Bernal?"

"Yes, sir."

"Whose handwriting is it, do you know?" Mason asked.

"The assistant cashier of the Ivanhoe National Bank."

"Oh, all right," Flasher said. "We'll do it the hard way, if we have to. Stand down, Mr.

268

Bernal, and I'll call the assistant cashier."

Harry Reedy, assistant cashier of the Ivanhoe Bank, had the mechanical assurance of an adding machine. He identified the list of numbers as being in his handwriting. He stated that he had listed the numbers of the twenty-dollar bills and put that list in an envelope which had been sealed and sent up with the money for the payroll.

"Cross-examine," Flasher said.

Mason studied the list. "These numbers are all in your handwriting?" he asked Reedy.

"Yes, sir."

"Did you yourself compare the numbers you wrote down with the numbers on the twenty-dollar bills?"

"No, sir. I didn't personally do that. Two assistants did that. One checked the numbers as they were read off, one as I wrote them down."

"The payrolls are for approximately a hundred thousand dollars, twice each month?"

"That's right. And ever since Mr. Bernal took charge, we have taken this means to identify payrolls. No attempt is made to list the bills in numerical order. The serial numbers are simply read off and written down. Unless a robbery occurs, there is no need to do anything further. In the event of a robbery, we can reclassify the numbers and list the bills in numerical order."

"These numbers are in your handwriting — every number?"

"Yes, sir. More than that, you will notice that at the bottom of each I have signed my initials."

"That's all," Mason said.

"I now offer once more to introduce this list in evidence," Flasher said.

"So ordered," Judge Haswell ruled.

"My next witness is Charles J. Oswald, the sheriff," the district attorney announced.

The sheriff, a long, lanky man with a quiet manner, took the stand. "You're acquainted with Harvey L. Corbin, the defendant in this case?" the district attorney asked.

"I am."

"Are you acquainted with his wife?"

"Yes, sir."

"Now, on the morning of the fifteenth of this month, the morning of the robbery at the Jebson Commercial Company, did you have any conversation with Mrs. Corbin?"

"I did. Yes, sir."

"Did you ask her about her husband's activities the night before?"

"Just a moment," Mason said. "I object to this on the ground that any conversation the sheriff had with Mrs. Corbin is not admissible against the defendant, Corbin; furthermore, that in this state a wife cannot testify against her husband. Therefore, any statement she might make would be an indirect violation of that rule. Furthermore, I object on the ground that the question calls for hearsay."

Judge Haswell looked ponderously thoughtful, then said, "It seems to me Mr. Mason is correct."

"I'll put it this way, Mr. Sheriff," the district attorney said. "Did you, on the morning of the fifteenth, take any money from Mrs. Corbin?"

"Objected to as incompetent, irrelevant, and immaterial," Mason said.

"Your Honor," Flasher said irritably, "that's the very gist of our case. We propose to show that two of the stolen twenty-dollar bills were in the possession of Mrs. Corbin."

Mason said, "Unless the prosecution can prove the bills were given Mrs. Corbin by her husband, the evidence is inadmissible."

"That's just the point," Flasher said. "Those bills *were* given to her by the defendant."

"How do you know?" Mason asked.

"She told the sheriff so."

"That's hearsay," Mason snapped.

Judge Haswell fidgeted on the bench. "It seems to me we're getting into a peculiar situation here. You can't call the wife as a witness, and I don't think her statement to the sheriff is admissible."

"Well," Flasher said desperately, "in this state, Your Honor, we have a community-property law. Mrs. Corbin had this money. Since she is the wife of the defendant, it was community property. Therefore, it's partially his property."

"Well now, there," Judge Haswell said, "I think I can agree wth you. You introduce the twenty-dollar bills. I'll overrule the objection made by the defense."

"Produce the twenty-dollar bills, Sheriff," Flasher said triumphantly.

The bills were produced and received in evidence.

"Cross-examine," Flasher said curtly.

"No questions of this witness," Mason said, "but I have a few questions to ask Mr. Bernal on cross-examination. You took him off the stand to lay the foundation for introducing the bank list, and I didn't have an opportunity to cross-examine him."

"I beg your pardon," Flasher said. "Resume the stand, Mr. Bernal."

His tone, now that he had the twenty-dollar bills safely introduced in evidence, had a gloating note to it.

Mason said, "This list which has been introduced in evidence is on the stationery of the Ivanhoe National Bank?"

"That's right. Yes, sir."

"It consists of several pages, and at the end there is the signature of the assistant cashier?"

"Yes, sir."

"And each page is initialed by the assistant cashier?"

"Yes, sir."

"This was the scheme which you thought of in order to safeguard the company against a payroll robbery?"

"Not to safeguard the company against a payroll robbery, Mr. Mason, but to assist us in recovering the money in the event there was a holdup."

"This was your plan to answer Mr. Nesbitt's objections that the vault was an outmoded model?"

"A part of my plan, yes. I may say that Mr. Nesbitt's objections had never been voiced until I took office. I felt he was trying to embarrass me by making my administration show less net returns than expected." Bernal tightened his lips and added, "Mr. Nesbitt had, I believe, been expecting to be appointed manager. He was disappointed. I believe he still expects to be manager."

In the spectators' section of the courtroom, Ralph Nesbitt glared at Bernal.

"You had a conversation with the defendant on the night of the fourteenth?" Mason asked Bernal.

"I did. Yes, sir."

"You told him that for reasons which you deemed sufficient you were discharging him immediately and wanted him to leave the premises at once?"

"Yes, sir. I did."

"And you paid him his wages in cash?"

"Mr. Nesbitt paid him in my presence, with money he took from the petty-cash drawer of the vault."

"Now, as part of the wages due him, wasn't Corbin given these two twenty-dollar bills which have been introduced in evidence?"

Bernal shook his head. "I had thought of that," he said, "but it would have been impossible. Those bills weren't available to us at that time. The payroll is received from the bank in a sealed package. Those two twenty-dollar bills were in that package."

"And the list of the numbers of the twenty-dollar bills?"

"That's in a sealed envelope. The money is placed in the vault. I lock the list of numbers in my desk."

"Are you prepared to swear that neither you nor Mr. Nesbitt had access to these two twenty-dollar bills on the night of the fourteenth?"

"That is correct."

"That's all," Mason said. "No further cross-examination."

"I now call Ralph Nesbitt to the stand," District Attorney Flasher said. "I want to fix the time of these events definitely, Your Honor."

"Very well," Judge Haswell said. "Mr. Nesbitt, come forward."

Ralph Nesbitt, after answering the usual preliminary questions, sat down in the witness chair.

"Were you present at a conversation which took place between the defendant, Harvey L. Corbin, and Frank Bernal on the fourteenth of this month?" the district attorney asked.

"I was. Yes, sir."

"What time did that conversation take place?"

"About 8 o'clock in the evening."

"And, without going into the details of that conversation, I will ask you if the general effect of it was that the defendant was discharged and ordered to leave the company's property?"

"Yes, sir."

"And he was paid the money that was due him?"

"In cash. Yes, sir. I took the cash from the safe myself."

"Where was the payroll then?"

"In the sealed package in a compartment in the safe. As cashier, I had the only key to that compartment. Earlier in the afternoon I had gone to Ivanhoe City and received the sealed package of money and the envelope containing the list of numbers. I personally locked the package of money in the vault."

"And the list of numbers?"

"Mr. Bernal locked that in his desk."

"Cross-examine," Flasher said.

"No questions," Mason said.

"That's our case, Your Honor," Flasher

275

observed.

"May we have a few minutes indulgence?" Mason asked Judge Haswell.

"Very well. Make it brief," the judge agreed.

Mason turned to Paul Drake and Della Street. "Well, there you are," Drake said. "You're confronted with the proof, Perry."

"Are you going to put the defendant on the stand?" Della Street asked.

Mason shook his head. "It would be suicidal. He has a record of a prior criminal conviction. Also, it's a rule of law that if one asks about any part of a conversation on direct examination, the other side can bring out all the conversation. That conversation, when Corbin was discharged, was to the effect that he had lied about his past record. And I guess there's no question that he did."

"And he's lying now," Drake said. "This is one case where you're licked. I think you'd better cop a plea, and see what kind of a deal you can make with Flasher."

"Probably not any," Mason said. "Flasher wants to have the reputation of having given me a licking — wait a minute, Paul. I have an idea."

Mason turned abruptly, walked away to where he could stand by himself, his back to the crowded courtroom.

"Are you ready?" the judge asked.

Mason turned. "I am quite ready, Your

Honor. I have one witness whom I wish to put on the stand. I wish a subpoena *duces tecum* issued for that witness. I want him to bring certain documents which are in his possession."

"Who is the witness, and what are the documents?" the judge asked.

Mason walked quickly over to Paul Drake. "What's the name of that character who has the garbage-collecting business," he said softly, "the one who has the first nickel he'd ever made?"

"George Addey."

The lawyer turned to the judge. "The witness that I want is George Addey, and the documents that I want him to bring to court with him are the twenty-dollar bills that he has received during the past sixty days."

"Your Honor," Flasher protested, "this is an outrage. This is making a travesty out of justice. It is exposing the court to ridicule."

Mason said, "I give Your Honor my assurance that I think this witness is material, and that the documents are material. I will make an affidavit to that effect if necessary. As attorney for the defendant, may I point out that if the court refuses to grant this subpoena, it will be denying the defendant due process of law."

"I'm going to issue the subpoena," Judge Haswell said, testily, "and for your own good, Mr. Mason, the testimony had better be relevant."

George Addey, unshaven and bristling with indignation, held up his right hand to be sworn. He glared at Perry Mason.

"Mr. Addey," Mason said, "you have the contract to collect garbage from Jebson City?"

"I do."

"How long have you been collecting garbage there?"

"For over five years, and I want to tell you —"

Judge Haswell banged his gavel. "The witness will answer questions and not interpolate any comments."

"I'll interpolate anything I dang please," Addey said.

"That'll do," the judge said. "Do you wish to be jailed for contempt of court, Mr. Addey?"

"I don't want to go to jail, but I —"

"Then you'll remember the respect that is due the court," the judge said. "Now you sit there and answer questions. This is a court of law. You're in this court as a citizen, and I'm here as a judge, and I propose to see that the respect due to the court is enforced." There was a moment's silence while the judge glared angrily at the witness. "All right, go ahead, Mr. Mason," Judge Haswell said.

Mason said, "During the thirty days prior

to the fifteenth of this month, did you deposit any money in any banking institution?"

"I did not."

"Do you have with you all the twenty-dollar bills that you received during the last sixty days?"

"I have, and I think making me bring them here is just like inviting some crook to come and rob me and —"

Judge Haswell banged with his gavel. "Any more comments of that sort from the witness and there will be a sentence imposed for contempt of court. Now you get out those twenty-dollar bills, Mr. Addey, and put them right up here on the clerk's desk."

Addey, mumbling under his breath, slammed a roll of twenty-dollar bills down on the desk in front of the clerk.

"Now," Mason said, "I'm going to need a little clerical assistance. I would like to have my secretary, Miss Street, and the clerk help me check through the numbers on these bills. I will select a few at ramdom."

Mason picked up three of the twenty-dollar bills and said, "I am going to ask my assistants to check the list of numbers introduced in evidence. In my hand is a twenty-dollar bill that has the number L 07083274 A. Is that bill on the list? The next bill that I pick up is number L 07579190 A. Are any of those bills on the list?"

The courtroom was silent. Suddenly, Della

Street said, "Yes, here's one that's on the list — bill number L 07579190 A. It's on the list, on page eight."

"What?" the prosecutor shouted.

"Exactly," Mason said smiling. "So, if a case is to be made against a person merely because he has possession of the money that was stolen on the fifteenth of this month, then your office should prefer charges against this witness, George Addey, Mr. District Attorney."

Addey jumped from the witness stand and shook his fist in Mason's face. "You're a cockeyed liar!" he screamed. "There ain't a one of those bills but what I didn't have it before the fifteenth. The company cashier changes my money into twenties, because I like big bills. I bury 'em in cans, and I put the date on the side of the can."

"Here's the list," Mason said. "Check it for yourself."

A tense silence gripped the courtoom as the judge and the spectators waited.

"I'm afraid I don't understand this, Mr. Mason," Judge Haswell said, after a moment.

"I think it's quite simple," Mason said. "And I now suggest the court take a recess for an hour and check these other bills against this list. I think the district attorney may be surprised."

And Mason sat down and proceeded to put papers in his briefcase.

Della Street, Paul Drake, and Perry Mason were sitting in the lobby of the Ivanhoe Hotel.

"When are you going to tell us?" Della Street asked fiercely. "Or do we tear you limb from limb? How could the garbage man have —?"

"Wait a minute," Mason said. "I think we're about to get results. Here comes the esteemed district attorney, Vernon Flasher, and he's accompanied by Judge Haswell."

The two strode over to Mason's group and bowed with cold formality.

Mason got up.

Judge Haswell began in his best courtroom voice. "A most deplorable situation has occurred. It seems that Mr. Frank Bernal has — well —"

"Been detained somewhere," Vernon Flasher said.

"Disappeared," Judge Haswell said. "He's gone."

"I expected as much," Mason said.

"Now will you kindly tell me just what sort of pressure you brought to bear on Mr. Bernal to —?"

"Just a moment, Judge," Mason said. "The only pressure I brought to bear on him was to cross-examine him."

"Did you know that there had been a mistake in the dates on those lists?"

"There was no mistake. When you find

Bernal, I'm sure you will discover there was a deliberate falsification. He was short in his accounts, and he knew he was about to be demoted. He had a desperate need for a hundred thousand dollars in ready cash. He had evidently been planning this burglary, or, rather, this embezzlement, for some time. He learned that Corbin had a criminal record. He arranged to have these lists furnished by the bank. He installed a burglar alarm, and, naturally, knew how to circumvent it. He employed a watchman he knew was addicted to drink. He only needed to stage his coup at the right time. He fired Corbin and paid him off with bills that had been recorded by the bank on page eight of the list of bills *in the payroll on the first of the month.*

"Then he removed page eight from the list of bills contained in the payroll *of the fifteenth,* before he showed it to the police, and substituted page eight of the list for the *first of the month* payroll. It was that simple.

"Then he drugged the watchman's whiskey, took an acetylene torch, burned through the vault doors, and took all the money."

"May I ask how you knew all this?" Judge Haswell demanded.

"Certainly," Mason said. "My client told me he received those bills from Nesbitt, who took them from the petty-cash drawer in the safe. He also told the sheriff that. I happened to be the only one who believed him. It sometimes pays, Your Honor, to have faith in a man, even if he has made a previous mistake. Assuming my client was innocent, I knew either Bernal or Nesbitt must be guilty. I then realized that only Bernal had custody of the *previous* lists of numbers.

"As an employee, Bernal had been paid on the first of the month. He looked at the numbers on the twenty-dollar bills in his pay envelope and found that they had been listed on page eight of the payroll for the first.

"Bernal only needed to abstract all twenty-dollar bills from the petty-cash drawer, substitute twenty-dollar bills from his own pay envelope, call in Corbin, and fire him. His trap was set.

"I let him know I knew what had been done by bringing Addey into court and proving my point. Then I asked for a recess. That was so Bernal would have a chance to skip out. You see, flight may be received as evidence of guilt. It was a professional courtesy to the district attorney. It will help him when Bernal is arrested."

Introducing Susan Dare

Mignon Eberhart

SUSAN DARE WATCHED a thin stream of blue smoke ascend without haste from the long throat of a tiger lily. Michela, then, had escaped also. She was not, however, on the long veranda, for the clear, broadening light of the rising moon revealed it wide and empty, and nothing moved against the silvered lawn which sloped gently toward the pine woods.

Susan listened a moment for the tap of Michela's heels, did not hear it or any other intrusive sound, and then pushed aside the bowl of lilies on the low window seat, let the velvet curtains fall behind her, and seated herself in the little niche thus formed. It was restful and soothing to be thus shut away from the house with its subtly warring elements and to make herself part of the silent night beyond the open windows.

A pity, thought Susan, to leave. But after tonight she could not stay. After all, a guest, any guest, ought to have sense enough to leave when a situation develops in the family of her hostess. The thin trail of smoke from the lily caught Susan's glance again and she wished Michela wouldn't amuse herself by putting cigarette ends in flowers.

A faint drift of voices came from somewhere, and Susan shrank farther into herself and into the tranquil night. It had been an unpleasant dinner, and there would be still an hour or so before she could gracefully extract herself and escape again. Nice of Christabel to give her the guest house — the small green cottage across the terrace at the other side of the house, and through the hedge and up the winding green path. Christabel Frame was a perfect hostess, and Susan had had a week of utter rest and content.

But then Randy Frame, Christabel's young brother, had returned.

And immediately Joe Bromfel and his wife Michela, guests also, had arrived, and with them something that had destroyed all content. The old house of the Frames, with its gracious pillars and long windows and generous dim spaces, was exactly the same — the lazy Southern air and the misty blue hills and the quiet pine woods and the boxed paths through the flowers — none of it had actually changed. But it was, all the same, a different place.

A voice beyond the green velvet curtains

called impatiently: "Michela — Michela ——"

It was Randy Frame. Susan did not move, and she was sure that the sweeping velvet curtains hid even her silver toes. He was probably at the door of the library, and she could see, without looking, his red hair and lithe young body and impatient, thin face. Impatient for Michela. Idiot, oh, idiot, thought Susan. Can't you see what you are doing to Christabel?

His feet made quick sounds upon the parquet floor of the hall and were gone, and Susan herself made a sharply impatient movement. Because the Frame men had been red-haired, gallant, quick-tempered, reckless, and (added Susan to the saga) abysmally stupid and selfish, Randy had accepted the mold without question. A few words from the dinner conversation floated back into Susan's memory. They'd been talking of fox hunting — a safe enough topic, one would have thought, in the Carolina hills. But talk had veered — through Michela, was it? — to a stableman who had been shot by one of the Frames and killed. It had happened a long time ago, had been all but forgotten, and had nothing at all to do with the present generation of Frames. But Christabel said hurriedly it had been an accident; dreadful. She had looked white. And Randy had laughed and said the Frames shot first and inquired afterwards and that there was always a revolver in the top buffet drawer.

"Here she is," said a voice. The curtains were pulled suddenly backward, and Randy, a little flushed, stood there. His face fell as he discovered Susan's fair, smooth hair and thin lace gown. "Oh," he said. "I thought you were Michela."

Others were trailing in from the hall, and a polite hour or so must be faced. Queer how suddenly and inexplicably things had become tight and strained and unpleasant!

Randy had turned away and vanished without more words, and Tryon Welles, strolling across the room with Christabel, was looking at Susan and smiling affably.

"Susan Dare," he said. "Watching the moonlight, quietly planning murder." He shook his head and turned to Christabel. "I simply don't believe you, Christabel. If this young woman writes anything, which I doubt, it's gentle little poems about roses and moonlight."

Christabel smiled faintly and sat down. Mars, his black face shining, was bringing in the coffee tray. In the doorway Joe Bromfel, dark and bulky and hot-looking in his dinner coat, lingered a moment to glance along the hall and then came into the room.

"If Susan writes poems," said Christabel lightly, "it is her secret. You are quite wrong, Tryon. She writes ——" Christabel's silver voice hesitated. Her slender hands were searching, hovering rather blindly over the tray, the large amethyst on one white finger full of trembling purple lights. It was a barely perceptible second before she took a fragile old cup and began to pour from the tall silver coffeepot. "She writes murders," said Christabel steadily. "Lovely, grisly ones, with sensible solutions. Sugar, Tryon? I've forgotten."

"One. But isn't that for Miss Susan?"

Tryon Welles was still smiling. He, the latest arrival, was a neat gray man with tight eyes, pink cheeks, and an affable manner. The only obvious thing about him was a rather finical regard for color, for he wore gray tweed with exactly the right shades of green — green tie, green shirt, a cautious green stripe in gray socks. He had reached the house on the heels of his telephoned message from town, saying he had to talk business with Christabel, and he had not had time to dress before dinner.

"Coffee, Joe?" asked Christabel. She was very deft with the delicate china. Very deft and very graceful, and Susan could not imagine how she knew that Christabel's hands were shaking.

Joe Bromfel stirred, turned his heavy dark face toward the hall again, saw no one, and took coffee from Christabel's lovely hand. Christabel avoided looking directly into his face, as, Susan had noticed, she frequently did.

"A sensible solution," Tryon Welles was saying thoughtfully. "Do murders have sensible solutions?"

His question hung in the air. Christabel did not reply, and Joe Bromfel did not appear to hear it. Susan said:

"They must have. After all, people don't murder just — well, just to murder."

"Just for the fun of it, you mean?" said Tryon Welles, tasting his coffee. "No, I suppose not. Well, at any rate," he went on, "it's nice to know your interest in murder is not a practical one."

He probably thought he was making light and pleasant conversation, reflected Susan. Strange that he did not know that every time he said the word "murder" it felt like a heavy stone in that silent room. She was about to wrench the conversation to another channel when Michela and Randy entered from the hall; Randy was laughing and Michela smiling.

At the sound of Randy's laugh, Joe Bromfel twisted bulkily around to watch their approach, and, except for Randy's laugh, it was entirely silent in the long book-lined room. Susan watched too. Randy was holding Michela's hand, swinging it as if to suggest a kind of frank camaraderie. Probably, thought Susan, he's been kissing her out in the darkness of the garden. Holding her very tight.

Michela's eyelids were white and heavy over unexpectedly shallow dark eyes. Her straight black hair was parted in the middle and pulled severely backward to a knot on her rather fat white neck. Her mouth was deeply crimson. She had been born, Susan knew, in rural New England, christened Michela by a romantic mother, and had striven to live up to the name ever since. Or down, thought Susan tersely, and wished she could take young Randy by his large and outstanding ears and shake him.

Michela had turned toward a chair, and her bare back presented itself to Susan, and she saw the thin red line with an angle that a man's cuff, pressing into the creamy flesh, had made. It was unmistakable. Joe Bromfel had seen it, too. He couldn't have helped seeing it. Susan looked into her coffee cup and wished fervently that Joe Bromfel hadn't seen the imprint of Randy's cuff, and then wondered why she wished it so fervently.

"Coffee, Michela?" said Christabel, and something in her voice was more, all at once, than Susan could endure. She rose and said rather breathlessly:

"Christabel darling, do you mind — I have some writing to do ——"

"Of course." Christabel hesitated. "But wait — I'll go along with you to the cottage."

"Don't let us keep you, Christabel," said

290

Michela lazily.

Christabel turned to Tryon Welles and neatly forestalled a motion on his part to accompany her and Susan.

"I won't be long, Tryon," she said definitely. "When I come back — we'll talk."

A clear little picture etched itself on Susan's mind: the long, lovely room, the mellow little areas of light under lamps here and there, one falling directly upon the chair she had just left, the pools of shadows surrounding them; Michela's yellow satin, and Randy's red head and slim black shoulders; Joe, a heavy, silent figure, watching them broodingly; Tryon Welles, neat and gray and affable, and Christabel with her gleaming red head held high on her slender neck, walking lightly and gracefully amid soft mauve chiffons. Halfway across the room she paused to accept a cigarette from Tryon and to bend to the small flare of a lighter he held for her, and the amethyst on her finger caught the flickering light of it and shone.

Then Susan and Christabel had crossed the empty flagstone veranda and turned toward the terrace.

Their slippered feet made no sound upon the velvet grass. Above the lily pool the flower fragrances were sweet and heavy on the night air.

"Did you hear the bullfrog last night?" asked Christabel. "He seems to have taken up a permanent residence in the pool. I don't know what to do about him. Randy says he'll shoot him, but I don't want that. He *is* a nuisance of course, bellowing away half the night. But after all — even bullfrogs — have a right to live."

"Christabel," said Susan, trying not to be abrupt, "I must go soon. I have — work to do ——"

Christabel stopped and turned to face her. They were at the gap in the laurel hedge where a path began and wound upward to the cottage.

"Don't make excuses, Susan honey," she said gently. "Is it the Bromfels?"

A sound checked Susan's reply — an unexpectedly eerie sound that was like a wail. It rose and swelled amid the moonlit hills, and Susan gasped and Christabel said quickly, though with a catch in her voice: "It's only the dogs howling at the moon."

"They are not," Susan said, "exactly cheerful. It emphasizes ——" She checked herself abruptly on the verge of saying that it emphasized their isolation.

Christabel had turned in at the path. It was darker there, and her cigarette made a tiny red glow. "If Michela drops another cigarette into a flower I'll kill her," said Christabel quiety.

"*What* ——"

"I said I'd kill her," said Christabel. "I

292

won't, of course. But she — oh, you've seen how things are, Susan. You can't have failed to see. She took Joe — years ago. Now she's taking Randy."

Susan was thankful that she couldn't see Christabel's face. She said something about infatuation and Randy's youth.

"He is twenty-one," said Christabel. "He's no younger than I was when Joe — when Joe and I were to be married. That was why Michela was here — to be a guest at the wedding and all the parties." They walked on for a few quiet steps before Christabel added: "It was the day before the wedding that they left together."

Susan said: "Has Joe changed?"

"In looks, you mean," said Christabel, understanding. "I don't know. Perhaps. He must have changed inside. But I don't want to know that."

"Can't you send them away?"

"Randy would follow."

"Tryon Welles," suggested Susan desperately. "Maybe he could help. I don't know how, though. Talk to Randy, maybe."

Christabel shook her head.

"Randy wouldn't listen. Opposition makes him stubborn. Besides, he doesn't like Tryon. He's had to borrow too much money from him."

It wasn't like Christabel to be bitter. One of the dogs howled again and was joined by others. Susan shivered.

"You are cold," said Christabel. "Run along inside, and thanks for listening. And — I think you'd better go, honey. I meant to keep you for comfort. But ——"

"No, no, I'll stay — I didn't know ——"

"Don't be nervous about being alone. The dogs would know it if a stranger put a foot on the place. Good-night," said Christabel firmly, and was gone.

The guest cottage was snug and warm and tranquil, but Susan was obliged finally to read herself to sleep and derived only a small and fleeting satisfaction from the fact that it was over a rival author's book that she finally grew drowsy. She didn't sleep well even then, and was glad suddenly that she'd asked for the guest cottage and was alone and safe in that tiny retreat.

Morning was misty and chill.

It was perhaps nine-thirty when Susan opened the cottage door, saw that mist lay thick and white, and went back to get her rubbers. Tryon Welles, she thought momentarily, catching a glimpse of herself in the mirror, would have nothing at all that was florid and complimentary to say this morning. And indeed, in her brown knitted suit, with her fair hair tight and smooth and her spectacles on, she looked not unlike a chill and aloof little owl.

The path was wet, and the laurel leaves

shining with moisture, and the hills were looming gray shapes. The house lay white and quiet, and she saw no one about.

It was just then that it came. A heavy concussion of sound, blanketed by mist.

Susan's first thought was that Randy had shot the bullfrog.

But the pool was just below her, and no one was there.

Besides, the sound came from the house. Her feet were heavy and slow in the drenched grass — the steps were slippery and the flagstones wet. Then she was inside.

The wide hall ran straight through the house, and away down at its end Susan saw Mars. He was running away from her, his black hands outflung, and she was vaguely conscious that he was shouting something. He vanished, and instinct drew Susan to the door at the left which led to the library.

She stopped, frozen, in the doorway.

Across the room, sagging bulkily over the arm of the green damask chair in which she'd sat the previous night, was a man. It was Joe Bromfel, and he'd been shot, and there was no doubt that he was dead.

A newspaper lay at his feet as if it had slipped there. The velvet curtains were pulled together across the window behind him.

Susan smoothed back her hair. She couldn't think at all, and she must have slipped down to the footstool near the door for she was there when Mars, his face drawn, and Randy, white as his pajamas, came running into the room. They were talking excitedly and were examining a revolver which Randy had picked up from the floor. Then Tryon Welles came from somewhere, stopped beside her, uttered an incredulous exclamation, and ran across the room too. Then Christabel came and stopped, too, on the threshold, and became under Susan's very eyes a different woman — a strange woman, shrunken and gray, who said in a dreadful voice:

"Joe — Joe ——"

Only Susan heard or saw her. It was Michela, hurrying from the hall, who first voiced the question.

"I heard something — what was it? What ——" She brushed past Christabel.

"Don't look, Michela!"

But Michela looked — steadily and long. Then her flat dark eyes went all around the room and she said: "Who shot him?"

For a moment there was utter shocked stillness.

Then Mars cleared his throat and spoke to Randy.

"I don' know who shot him, Mista Randy. But I saw him killed. An' I saw the han' that killed him ——"

"Hand!" screamed Michela.

"Hush, Michela." Tryon Welles was speaking. "What do you mean, Mars?"

296

"They ain't nothin' to tell except that, Mista Tryon. I was just comin' to dust the library and was right there at the door when I heard the shot, and there was just a han' stickin' out of them velvet curtains. And I saw the han' and I saw the revolver and I — I do' know what I did then." Mars wiped his forehead. "I guess I ran for help, Mista Tryon."

There was another silence.

"Whose hand was it, Mars?" said Tryon Welles gently.

Mars blinked and looked very old.

"Mista Tryon, God's truth is, I do' know. I do' know."

Randy thrust himself forward.

"Was it a man's hand?"

"I reckon it was maybe," said the old Negro slowly, looking at the floor. "But I do' know for sure, Mista Randy. All I saw was — was the red ring on it."

"A red *ring?*" cried Michela. "What do you mean ——"

Mars turned a bleak dark face toward Michela; a face that rejected her and all she had done to his house. "A red ring, Miz Bromfel," he said with a kind of dignity. "It sort of flashed. And it was red."

After a moment Randy uttered a curious laugh.

"But there's not a red ring in the house. None of us runs to rubies ——" He stopped abruptly. "I say, Tryon; hadn't we better —

well, carry him to the divan. It isn't decent to — just leave him — like that."

"I suppose so —" Tryon Welles moved toward the body. "Help me, Randy ——"

The boy shivered, and Susan quite suddenly found her voice.

"Oh, but you can't do that. You can't ——" She stopped. The two men were looking at her in astonishment. Michela, too, had turned toward her, although Christabel did not move. "But you can't do that," repeated Susan. "Not when it's — murder."

This time the word, falling into the long room, was weighted with its own significance. Tryon Welles's gray shoulders moved.

"She's perfectly right," he said. "I'd forgotten — if I ever knew. But that's the way of it. We'll have to send for people — doctor, sheriff, coroner, I suppose."

Afterward, Susan realized that but for Tryon Welles the confusion would have become mad. He took a quiet command of the situation, sending Randy, white and sick-looking, to dress, telephoning into town, seeing that the body was decently covered, and even telling Mars to bring them hot coffee. He was here, there, everywhere: upstairs, downstairs, seeing to them all, and finally outside to meet the sheriff . . . brisk, alert, efficient. In the interval Susan sat numbly beside Christabel on the love seat in the hall, with Michela restlessly prowling up and down the hall before their eyes, listening to the telephone calls, drinking hot coffee, watching everything with her sullen, flat black eyes. Her red-and-white sports suit, with its scarlet bracelets and earrings, looked garish and out of place in that house of violent death.

And Christabel. Still a frozen image of a woman who drank coffee automatically, she sat erect and still and did not speak. The glowing amethyst on her finger caught the light and was the only living thing about her.

Gradually the sense of numb shock and confusion was leaving Susan. Fright was still there and horror and a queer aching pity, but she saw Randy come running down the wide stairway again, his red hair smooth now above a sweater, and she realized clearly that he was no longer white and sick and frightened; he was instead alert and defiantly ready for what might come. And it would be, thought Susan, in all probability, plenty.

And it was.

Questions — questions. The doctor, who was kind, the coroner, who was not; the sheriff, who was merely observant — all of them questioning without end. No time to think. No time to comprehend. Time only to reply as best one might.

But gradually out of it all certain salient facts began to emerge. They were few, however, and brief.

The revolver was Randy's, and it had been taken from the top buffet drawer — when no one knew or, at least, would tell. "Everybody knew it was there," said Randy sulkily. The fingerprints on it would probably prove to be Randy's or Mars's, since they picked it up.

No one knew anything of the murder, and no one had an alibi, except Liz (the Negro second girl) and Minnie (the cook), who were together in the kitchen.

Christabel had been writing letters in her own room: she'd heard the shot, but thought it was only Randy shooting a bullfrog in the pool. But then she'd heard Randy and Mars running down the front stairway, so she'd come down too. Just to be sure that that was what it was.

"What else did you think it could be?" asked the sheriff. But Christabel said stiffly that she didn't know.

Randy had been asleep when Mars had awakened him. He had not heard the sound of the shot at all. He and Mars had hurried down to the library. (Mars, it developed, had gone upstairs by means of the small back stairway off the kitchen.)

Tryon Welles had walked down the hill in front of the house to the mail box and was returning when he heard the shot. But it was muffled, and he did not know what had happened until he reached the library. He created a mild sensation at that point by taking off a ring, holding it so they could all see it, and demanding of Mars if that was the ring he had seen on the murderer's hand. However, the sensation was only momentary, for the large clear stone was as green as his neat green tie.

"No, suh, Mista Tryon," said Mars. "The ring on the han' I saw was red. I could see it plain, an' it was red."

"This," said Tryon Welles, "is a flawed emerald. I asked because I seem to be about the only person here wearing a ring. But I suppose that, in justice to us, all our belongings should be searched."

Upon which the sheriff's gaze slid to the purple pool on Christabel's white hand. He said, however, gently, that that was being done, and would Mrs. Michela Bromfel tell what she knew of the murder.

But Mrs. Michela Bromfel somewhat spiritedly knew nothing of it. She'd been walking in the pine woods, she said defiantly, glancing obliquely at Randy, who suddenly flushed all over his thin face. She'd heard the shot but hadn't realized it was a gunshot. However, she was curious and came back to the house.

"The window behind the body opens toward the pine woods," said the sheriff. "Did you see anyone, Mrs. Bromfel?"

"No one at all," said Michela definitely.

Well, then, had she heard the dogs barking? The sheriff seemed to know that the kennels were just back of the pine woods.

But Michela had not heard the dogs.

Someone stirred restively at that, and the sheriff coughed and said unnecessarily that there was no tramp about, then, and the questioning continued. Continued wearily on and on and on, and still no one knew how Joe Bromfel had met his death. And as the sheriff was at last dismissing them and talking to the coroner of an inquest, one of his men came to report on the search. No one was in the house who didn't belong there; they could tell nothing of footprints; the French windows back of the body had been ajar, and there was no red ring anywhere in the house.

"Not, that is, that we can find," said the man.

"All right," said the sheriff. "That'll be all now, folks. But I'd take it kindly if you was to stay around here today."

All her life Susan was to remember that still, long day with a kind of sharp reality. It was, after those first moments when she'd felt so ill and shocked, weirdly natural, as if, one event having occurred, another was bound to follow, and then upon that one's heels another, and all of them quite in the logical order of things. Even the incident of the afternoon, so trivial in itself but later so significant, was as natural, as unsurprising as anything could be. And that was her meeting with Jim Byrne.

302

It happened at the end of the afternoon, long and painful, which Susan spent with Christabel, knowing somehow that, under her frozen surface, Christabel was grateful for Susan's presence. But there were nameless things in the air between them which could be neither spoken of nor ignored, and Susan was relieved when Christabel at last took a sedative and, eventually, fell into a sleep that was no more still than Christabel waking had been.

There was no one to be seen when Susan tiptoed out of Christabel's room and down the stairway, although she heard voices from the closed door of the library.

Out the wide door at last and walking along the terrace above the lily pool, Susan took a long breath of the mist-laden air.

So this was murder. This was murder, and it happened to people one knew, and it did indescribable and horrible things to them. Frightened them first, perhaps. Fear of murder itself came first — simple, primitive fear of the unleashing of the beast. And then on its heels came more civilized fear, and that was fear of the law, and a scramble for safety.

She turned at the hedge and glanced backward. The house lay white and stately amid its gardens as it had lain for generations. But it was no longer tranquil — it was charged now with violence. With murder. And it remained dignified and stately and would cling, as Christabel would cling and had clung all those years, to its protective ritual.

Christabel: Had she killed him? Was that why she was so stricken and gray? Or was it because she knew that Randy had killed him? Or was it something else?

Susan did not see the man till she was almost upon him, and then she cried out involuntarily, though she as a rule was not at all nervous. He was sitting on the small porch of the cottage, hunched up with his hat over his eyes and his coat collar turned up, furiously scribbling on a pad of paper. He jumped up as he heard her breathless little cry and whirled to face her and took off his hat all in one motion.

"May I use your typewriter?" he said.

His eyes were extremely clear and blue and lively. His face was agreeably irregular in feature, with a mouth that laughed a great deal, a chin that took insolence from no man, and generous width of forehead. His hair was thinning but not yet showing gray and his hands were unexpectedly fine and beautiful. "Hard on the surface," thought Susan. "Terribly sensitive, really. Irish. What's he doing here?"

Aloud she said: "Yes."

"Good. Can't write fast enough and want to get this story off tonight. I've been waiting for you, you know. They told me you wrote things. My name's Byrne. James Byrne. I'm a reporter. Cover special stories. I'm taking a busman's holiday. I'm actually on a Chicago paper and down here for a vacation. I didn't expect a murder story to break."

Susan opened the door upon the small living room.

"The typewriter's there. Do you need paper? There's a stack beside it."

He fell upon the typewriter absorbedly, like a dog upon a bone. She watched him for a while, amazed at his speed and fluency and utter lack of hesitancy.

Presently she lighted the fire already laid in the tiny fireplace and sat there quietly, letting herself be soothed by the glow of the flames and the steady rhythm of the type-writer keys. And for the first time that day its experiences, noted and stored away in whatever place observations are stored, began to arouse and assort and arrange themselves and march in some sort of order through her conscious thoughts. But it was a dark and macabre procession, and it frightened Susan. She was relieved when Jim Byrne spoke.

"I say," he said suddenly, over the clicking keys, "I've got your name Louise Dare. Is that right?"

"Susan."

He looked at her. The clicking stopped.

"Susan. Susan Dare," he repeated thoughtfully. "I say, you can't be the Susan Dare that writes murder stories!"

"Yes," said Susan guardedly, "I can be that Susan Dare."

There was an expression of definite incredulity in his face. "But you ——"

"If you say," observed Susan tensely, "that I don't look as if I wrote murder stories, you can't use my typewriter for your story."

"I suppose you are all tangled up in this mess," he said speculatively.

"Yes," said Susan, sober again. "And no," she added, looking at the fire.

"Don't commit yourself," said Jim Byrne dryly. "Don't say anything reckless."

"But I mean just that," said Susan. "I'm a guest here. A friend of Christabel Frame's. I didn't murder Joe Bromfel. And I don't care at all about the rest of the people here except that I wish I'd never seen them."

"But you do," said the reporter gently, "care a lot about Christabel Frame?"

"Yes," said Susan gravely.

"I've got all the dope, you know," said the reporter softly. "It wasn't hard to get. Everybody around here knows about the Frames. The thing I can't understand is why she shot Joe. It ought to have been Michela."

"*What* ——" Susan's fingers were digging into the wicker arms of her chair, and her eyes strove frantically to plumb the clear blue eyes above the typewriter.

"I say, it ought to have been Michela. She's the girl who's making the trouble."

"But it wasn't — it couldn't — Christabel wouldn't ——"

"Oh, yes, she could," said the reporter rather wearily. "All sorts of people could do the strangest things. Christabel could murder. But I can't see why she'd murder Joe and let Michela go scot-free."

"Michela," said Susan in a low voice, "would have a motive."

"Yes, she's got a motive. Get rid of a husband. But so had Randy Frame. Same one. And he's what the people around here call a Red Frame — impulsive, reckless, bred to a tradition of — violence."

"But Randy was asleep — upstairs ——"

He interrupted her.

"Oh, yes, I know all that. And you were approaching the house from the terrace, and Tryon Welles had gone down after the mail, and Miss Christabel was writing letters upstairs, and Michela was walking in the pine woods. Not a damn alibi among you. The way the house and grounds are laid out, neither you nor Tryon Welles nor Michela would be visible to each other. And anyone could have escaped readily from the window and turned up innocently a moment later from the hall. I know all that. Who was behind the curtains?"

"A tramp —" attempted Susan in a small voice. "A burglar ——"

"Burglar nothing," said Jim Byrne with

scorn. "The dogs would have had hysterics. It was one of you. *Who?*"

"I don't know," said Susan. *"I don't know!"* Her voice was uneven, and she knew it and tried to steady it and clutched the chair arms tighter. Jim Byrne knew it, too, and was suddenly alarmed.

"Oh, look here, now," he cried. "Don't look like that. Don't cry. Don't ——"

"I am not crying," said Susan. "But it wasn't Christabel."

"You mean," said the reporter kindly, "that you don't want it to be Christabel. Well ——" He glanced at his watch, said, "Golly," and flung his papers together and rose. "There's something I'll do. Not for you exactly — just for — oh, because. I'll let part of my story wait until tomorrow if you want the chance to try to prove your Christabel didn't murder him."

Susan was frowning perplexedly.

"You don't understand me," said the reporter cheerfully. "It's this. You write murder mysteries, and I've read one or two of them. They are not bad," he interpolated hastily, watching Susan. "Now, here's your chance to try a real murder mystery."

"But I don't want ——" began Susan.

He checked her imperatively.

"You do want to," he said. "In fact, you've got to. You see — your Christabel is in a spot. You know that ring she wears ——"

"When did you see it?"

"Oh, does it matter?" he cried impatiently. "Reporters see everything. The point is the ring."

"But it's an amethyst," said Susan defensively.

"Yes," he agreed grimly. "It's an amethyst. And Mars saw a red stone. He saw it, it has developed, on the right hand. And the hand holding the revolver. And Christabel wears her ring on her right hand."

"But," repeated Susan, "it *is* an amethyst."

"M-m," said the reporter. "It's an amethyst. And a little while ago I said to Mars: 'What's the name of that flowering vine over there?' And he said: 'That red flower, suh? That's wisteria.' "

He paused. Susan felt exactly as if something had clutched her heart and squeezed it.

"The flowers were purple, of course," said the reporter softly. "The color of a dark amethyst."

"But he would have recognized Christabel's ring," said Susan after a moment.

"Maybe," said the reporter. "And maybe he wishes he'd never said a word about the red ring. He was scared when he first mentioned it, probably; hadn't had a chance to think it over."

"But Mars — Mars would confess to murdering rather than ——"

"No," said Jim Byrne soberly. "He wouldn't. That theory sounds all right. But it doesn't happen that way. People don't murder or confess to having murdered for somebody else. When it is a deliberate, planned murder and not a crazy drunken brawl, when anything can happen, there's a motive. And it's a strong and urgent and deeply personal and selfish motive and don't you forget it. I've got to hurry. Now then, shall I send in my story about the wisteria ——"

"Don't," said Susan choking. "Oh, don't. Not yet."

He picked up his hat. "Thanks for the typewriter. Get your wits together and go to work. After all, you ought to know something of murders. I'll be seeing you."

The door closed, and the flames crackled. After a long time Susan moved to the writing table and drew a sheet of yellow manuscript paper toward her, and a pencil, and wrote: Characters; possible motives; clues; queries.

It was strange, she thought, not how different real life was to its written imitation, but how like. How terribly like!

She was still bent over the yellow paper when a peremptory knock at the door sent her pencil jabbing furiously on the paper and her heart into her throat. It proved to be, however, only Michela Bromfel, and she wanted help.

"It's my knees," said Michela irritably. "Christabel's asleep or something, and the three servants are all scared of their shadows." She paused to dig savagely at first one knee and then the other. "Have you got anything to put on my legs? I'm nearly going crazy. It's not mosquito bites. I don't know what it is. Look!"

She sat down, pulled back her white skirt and rolled down her thin stockings, disclosing just above each knee a scarlet blotchy rim around her fat white legs.

Susan looked and had to resist a wild desire to giggle. "It's n-nothing," she said, quivering. "That is, it's only jiggers — here, I'll get you something. Alcohol."

"Jiggers," said Michela blankly. "What's that?"

Susan went into the bathroom. "Little bugs," she called. Where was the alcohol? "They are thick in the pine woods. It'll be all right by morning." Here it was. She took the bottle in her hand and turned again through the bedroom into the tiny living room.

At the door she stopped abruptly. Michela was standing at the writing table. She looked up, saw Susan, and her flat dark eyes flickered.

"Oh," said Michela. "Writing a story?"

"No," said Susan. "It's not a story. Here's the alcohol."

Under Susan's straight look Michela had

311

the grace to depart rather hastily, yanking up her stockings and twisting them hurriedly, and clutching at the bottle of alcohol. Her red bracelets clanked, and her scarlet fingernails looked as if they'd been dipped in blood. Of the few people who might have killed Joe Bromfel, Susan reflected coolly, she would prefer it to be Michela.

It was just then that a curious vagrant memory began to tease Susan. Rather it was not so much a memory as a memory *of* a memory — something that sometime she had known and now could not remember. It was tantalizing. It was maddeningly elusive. It floated teasingly on the very edge of her consciousness.

Deliberately, at last, Susan pushed it away and went back to work. Christabel and the amethyst. Christabel and the wisteria. Christabel.

It was dark and still drizzly when Susan took her way down toward the big house.

At the laurel hedge she met Tryon Welles.

"Oh, hello," he said. "Where've you been?"

"At the cottage," said Susan. "There was nothing I could do. How's Christabel?"

"Liz says she is still asleep — thank heaven for that. God, what a day! You oughtn't to be prowling around alone at this time of night. I'll walk to the house with you."

"Have the sheriff and other men gone?"

"For the time being. They'll be back, I suppose."

"Do they know any more about — who killed him?"

"I don't know. You can't tell much. I don't know of any evidence they have unearthed. They asked me to stay on." He took a quick puff or two of his cigarette and then said irritably: "It puts me in a bad place. It's a business deal where time matters. I'm a broker — I ought to be going back to New York tonight——" He broke off abruptly and said: "Oh, Randy —" as young Randy's pale, thin face above a shining mackintosh emerged from the dusk — "let's just escort Miss Susan to the steps."

"Is she afraid of the famous tramp?" asked Randy and laughed unpleasantly. He'd been drinking, thought Susan, with a flicker of anxiety. Sober, Randy was incalculable enough; drinking, he might be dangerous. Could she do anything with him? No, better leave it to Tryon Welles. "The tramp," Randy was repeating loudly. "Don't be afraid of a tramp. It wasn't any tramp killed Joe. And everybody knows it. You're safe enough, Susan, unless you've got some evidence. Have you got any evidence, Susan?"

He took her elbow and joggled it urgently.

"She's the quiet kind, Tryon, that sees everything and says nothing. Bet she's got

313

evidence enough to hang us all. Evidence. That's what we need. Evidence."

"Randy, you're drunk," said Susan crisply. She shook off his clutch upon her arm and then, looking at his thin face, which was so white and tight-drawn in the dusk, was suddenly sorry for him. "Go on and take your walk," she said more kindly. "Things will be all right."

"Things will never be the same again," said Randy. "Never the same — do you know why, Susan?" He's very drunk, thought Susan; worse than I thought. "It's because Michela shot him. Yes, sir."

"Randy, shut up!"

"Don't bother me, Tryon, I know what I'm saying. And Michela," asserted Randy with simplicity, "makes me sick."

"Come on, Randy." This time Tryon Welles took Randy's arm. "I'll take care of him, Miss Susan."

The house was deserted and seemed cold. Christabel was still asleep, Michela nowhere to be seen, and Susan finally told Mars to send her dinner on a tray to the cottage and returned quietly like a small brown wraith through the moist twilight.

But she was an oddly frightened wraith.

She was alone on the silent terrace, she was alone on the dark path — strange that she felt as if someone else were there, too. Was the bare fact of murder like a presence hovering, beating dark wings, waiting to sweep downward again?

"Nonsense," said Susan aloud. "Nonsense ——" and ran the rest of the way.

She was not, however, to be alone in the cottage, for Michela sat there, composedly awaiting her.

"Do you mind," said Michela, "if I spend the night here? There's two beds in there. You see —" she hesitated, her flat dark eyes were furtive — "I'm — afraid."

"Of what?" said Susan, after a moment. "Of whom?"

"I don't know who," said Michela, "or what."

After a long, singularly still moment Susan forced herself to say evenly:

"Stay if you are nervous. It's safe here." Was it? Susan continued hurriedly: "Mars will send up dinner."

Michela's thick white hand made an impatient movement.

"Call it nerves — although I've not a nerve in my body. But when Mars comes with dinner — just be sure it *is* Mars before you open the door, will you? Although as to that — *I* don't know. But I brought my revolver — loaded." She reached into her pocket, and Susan sat upright, abruptly. Susan, whose knowledge of revolvers had such a wide and peculiar range that any policeman, learning of it, would arrest her on suspicion alone, was

nevertheless somewhat uneasy in their immediate vicinity.

"Afraid?" said Michela.

"Not at all," said Susan. "But I don't think
a revolver will be necessary."

"I hope not, I'm sure," said Michela
somberly and stared at the fire.

After that, as Susan later reflected, there
was not much to be said. The only interrup-
tion during the whole queer evening was the
arrival of Mars and dinner.

Later in the evening Michela spoke again,
abruptly. "I didn't kill Joe," she said. And
after another long silence she said unexpectedly: "Did Christabel ask you how to kill him
and get by with it?"

"No!"

"Oh." Michela looked at her queerly. "I
thought maybe she'd got you to plan it for
her. You — knowing so much about murders
and all."

"She didn't," said Susan forcefully. "And
I don't plan murders for my friends, I assure
you. I'm going to bed."

Michela, following her, put the revolver on
the small table between the two beds.

If the night before had been heavy with
apprehension, this night was an active nightmare. Susan tossed and turned and was
uneasily conscious that Michela was awake
and restless, too.

Susan must have slept at last, though, for

316

she waked up with a start and sat upright, instantly aware of some movement in the room. Then she saw a figure dimly outlined against the window. It was Michela.

Susan joined her. "What are you doing?"

"Hush," whispered Michela. Her face was pressed against the glass. Susan looked, too, but could see only blackness.

"There's someone out there," whispered Michela. "And if he moves again I'm going to shoot."

Susan was suddenly aware that the ice-cold thing against her arm was the revolver.

"You are not," said Susan and wrenched the thing out of Michela's hand. Michela gasped and whirled, and Susan said grimly: "Go back to bed. Nobody's out there."

"How do you know?" said Michela, her voice sulky.

"I don't," said Susan, very much astonished at herself, but clutching the revolver firmly. "But I do know that you aren't going to start shooting. If there's any shooting to be done," said Susan with aplomb, "I'll do it myself. Go to bed."

But long after Michela was quiet Susan still sat bolt upright, clutching the revolver and listening.

Along toward dawn, out of the *mêlée* of confused, unhappy thoughts, the vagrant little recollection of a recollection came back to tantalize her. Something she'd known and now did not know. This time she returned as completely as she could over the track her thoughts had taken in the hope of capturing it by association. She'd been thinking of the murder and of the possible suspects; that if Michela had not murdered Joe, then there were left Randy and Christabel and Tryon Welles. And she didn't want it to be Christabel; it must not be Christabel. And that left Randy and Tryon Welles. Randy had a motive, but Tryon Welles had not. Tryon Welles wore a ring habitually, and Randy did not. But the ring was an emerald. And Christabel's ring was what Mars called red. Red — then what would he have called Michela's scarlet bracelet? Pink? But that was a bracelet. She wrenched herself back to dig at the troublesome phantom of a memory. It was something trivial — but something she could not project into her conscious memory. And it was something that somehow she needed. Needed now.

She awoke and was horrified to discover her cheek pillowed cosily upon the revolver. She thrust it away. And realized with a sinking of her heart that day had come and, with it, urgent problems. Christabel, first.

Michela was still silent and sulky. Crossing the terrace, Susan looked at the wisteria winding upward over its trellis. It was heavy with purple blossoms — purple like dark amethysts.

Christabel was in her own room, holding a breakfast tray on her lap and looking out the window with a blank, unseeing gaze. She was years older; shrunken somehow inside. She was pathetically willing to answer the few questions that Susan asked, but added nothing to Susan's small store of knowledge. She left her finally, feeling that Christabel wanted only solitude. But she went away reluctantly. It would not be long before Jim Byrne returned, and she had nothing to tell him — nothing, that is, except surmise.

Randy was not at breakfast, and it was a dark and uncomfortable meal. Dark because Tryon Welles said something about a headache and turned out the electric light, and uncomfortable because it could not be otherwise. Michela had changed to a thin suit — red again. The teasing ghost of a memory drifted over Susan's mind and away again before she could grasp it.

As the meal ended Susan was called to the telephone. It was Jim Byrne saying that he would be there in an hour.

On the terrace Tryon Welles overtook her again and said: "How's Christabel?"

"I don't know," said Susan slowly. "She looks — stunned."

"I wish I could make it easier for her," he said. "But — I'm caught, too. There's nothing I can do, really. I mean about the house, of course. Didn't she tell you?"

"No."

He looked at her, considered, and went on slowly.

"She wouldn't mind your knowing. You see — oh, it's tragically simple. But I can't help myself. It's like this: Randy borrowed money of me — kept on borrowing it, spent it like water. Without Christabel knowing it, he put up the house and grounds as collateral. She knows now, of course. Now I'm in a pinch in business and have got to take the house over legally in order to borrow enough money on it myself to keep things going for a few months. Do you see?"

Susan nodded. Was it this knowledge, then, that had so stricken Christabel?

"I hate it," said Tryon Welles. "But what can I do? And now Joe's — death — on top of it —" He paused, reached absently for a cigarette case, extracted a cigarette, and the small flame from his lighter flared suddenly clear and bright. "It's — hell," he said, puffing, "for her. But what can I do? I've got my own business to save."

"I see," said Susan slowly.

And quite suddenly, looking at the lighter, she did see. It was as simple, as miraculously simple as that. She said, her voice to her own ears marvelously unshaken and calm: "May I have a cigarette?"

He was embarrassed at not having offered it to her: he fumbled for his cigarette case and then held the flame of the lighter for her. Susan was very deliberate about getting her cigarette lighted. Finally she did so, said, "Thank you," and added, quite as if she had the whole thing planned: "Will you wake Randy, Mr. Welles, and send him to me? Now?"

"Why, of course," he said. "You'll be in the cottage?"

"Yes," said Susan and fled.

She was bent over the yellow paper when Jim Byrne arrived.

He was fresh and alert and, Susan could see, prepared to be kind. He expected her, then, to fail.

"Well," he said gently, "have you discovered the murderer?"

"Yes," said Susan Dare.

Jim Byrne sat down quite suddenly.

"I know who killed him," she said simply, "but I don't know why."

Jim Byrne reached into his pocket for a handkerchief and dabbed it lightly to his forehead. "Suppose," he suggested in a hushed way, "you tell all."

"Randy will be here in a moment," said Susan. "But it's all very simple. You see, the final clue was only the proof. I knew Christabel couldn't have killed him, for two reasons: one is, she's inherently incapable of killing anything; the other is — she loved him still. And I knew it wasn't Michela, because she is, actually, cowardly; and then, too, Michela had an alibi.''

"Alibi?''

"She really *was* in the pine woods for a long time that morning. Waiting, I think, for Randy, who slept late. I know she was there, because she was simply chewed by jiggers, and they are only in the pine woods.''

"Maybe she was there the day before.''

Susan shook her head decidedly.

"No, I know jiggers. If it had been during the previous day they'd have stopped itching by the time she came to me. And it wasn't during the afternoon, for no one went in the pine woods then except the sheriff's men.''

"That would leave, then, Randy and Tryon Welles.''

"Yes,'' said Susan. Now that it had come to doing it, she felt ill and weak; would it be her evidence, her words, that would send a fellow creature over that long and ignominious road that ends so tragically?

Jim Byrne knew what she was thinking.

"Remember Christabel,'' he said quietly.

"Oh, I know,'' said Susan sadly. She locked her fingers together, and there were quick footsteps on the porch.

"You want me, Susan?'' said Randy.

"Yes, Randy,'' said Susan. "I want you to tell me if you owed Joe Bromfel anything. Money — or — or anything.''

"How did you know?'' said Randy.

322

"Did you give him a note — anything?"

"Yes."

"What was your collateral?"

"The house — it's all mine ——"

"When was it dated? Answer me, Randy."

He flung up his head.

"I suppose you've been talking to Tryon," he said defiantly. "Well, it was dated before Tryon got his note. I couldn't help it. I'd got some stocks on margin. I had to have ——"

"So the house actually belonged to Joe Bromfel?" Susan was curiously cold. Christabel's house. Christabel's brother.

"Well, yes — if you want to put it like that."

Jim Byrne had risen quietly.

"And after Joe Bromfel, to Michela, if she knows of this and claims it?" pressed Susan.

"I don't know," said Randy. "I never thought of that."

Jim Byrne started to speak, but Susan silenced him.

"No, he really didn't think of it," she said wearily. "And I knew it wasn't Randy who killed him because he didn't, really, care enough for Michela to do that. It was — Tryon Welles who killed Joe Bromfel. He had to. For he had to silence Joe and then secure the note and, probably, destroy it, in order to have a clear title to the house, himself. Randy — did Joe have the note here with him?"

"Yes."

"It was not found upon his body?"

It was Jim Byrne who answered: "Nothing of the kind was found anywhere."

"Then," said Susan, "after the murder was discovered and before the sheriff arrived and the search began, only you and Tryon Welles were upstairs and had the opportunity to search Joe's room and find the note and destroy it. Was it you who did that, Randy?"

"No — no!" The color rose in his face.

"Then it must have been then that Tryon Welles found and destroyed it." She frowned. "Somehow, he must have known it was there. I don't know how — perhaps he had had words with Joe about it before he shot him and Joe inadvertently told him where it was. There was no time for him to search the body. But he knew ——"

"Maybe," said Randy reluctantly, "I told him. You see — I knew Joe had it in his letter case. He — he told me. But I never thought of taking it."

"It was not on record?" asked Jim Byrne.

"No," said Randy, flushing. "I — asked him to keep it quiet."

"I wonder," said Susan, looking away from Randy's miserable young face, "just how Tryon Welles expected to silence you."

"Well," said Randy dully, after a moment, "it was not exactly to my credit. But you needn't rub it in. I never thought of this — I

324

was thinking of — Michela. That she did it. I've had my lesson. And if he destroyed the note, how are you going to prove all this?"

"By your testimony," said Susan. "And besides — there's the ring."

"Ring," said Randy. Jim Byrne leaned forward intently.

"Yes," said Susan. "I'd forgotten. But I remembered that Joe had been reading the newspaper when he was killed. The curtains were pulled together back of him, so, in order to see the paper, he must have had the light turned on above his chair. It wasn't burning when I entered the library, or I should have noted it. So the murderer had pulled the cord of the lamp before he escaped. And ever since then he has been very careful to avoid any artificial light."

"What are you talking about?" cried Randy.

"Yet he had to keep on wearing the ring," said Susan. "Fortunately for him he didn't have it on the first night — I suppose the color at night would have been wrong with his green tie. But this morning he lit a cigarette and I saw."

"Saw what, in God's name," said Randy burstingly.

"That the stone isn't an emerald at all," replied Susan. "It's an Alexandrite. It changed color under the flare of the lighter."

"Alexandrite!" cried Randy impatiently.

"What's that?"

"It's a stone that's a kind of red-purple under artificial light and green in daylight," said Jim Byrne shortly. "I had forgotten there was such a thing — I don't think I've ever happened to see one. They are rare — and costly. Costly," repeated Jim Byrne slowly. "This one has cost a life ——"

Randy interrupted: "But if Michela knows about the note, why, Tryon may kill her ——" He stopped abruptly, thought for a second or two, then got out a cigarette. "Let him," he said airily.

It had been Tryon Welles, then, prowling about during the night — if it had been anyone. He had been uncertain, perhaps, of the extent of Michela's knowledge — but certain of his ability to deal with her and with Randy, who was so heavily in his debt.

"Michela doesn't know now," said Susan slowly. "And when you tell her, Randy — she might settle for a cash consideration. And, Randy Frame, somehow you've got to recover this house for Christabel and do it honestly."

"But right now," said Jim Byrne cheerily, "for the sheriff. And my story."

At the doorway he paused to look at Susan. "May I come back later," he said, "and use your typewriter?"

"Yes," said Susan Dare.

A Man Called Spade

Dashiell Hammett

SAMUEL SPADE PUT his telephone aside and looked at his watch. It was not quite four o'clock. He called, "Yoo-hoo!"

Effie Perine came in from the outer office. She was eating a piece of chocolate cake.

"Tell Sid Wise I won't be able to keep that date this afternoon," he said.

She put the last of the cake into her mouth and licked the tips of forefinger and thumb. "That's the third time this week."

When he smiled, the v's of his chin, mouth, and brows grew longer. "I know, but I've got to go out and save a life." He nodded at the telephone. "Somebody's scaring Max Bliss."

She laughed. "Probably somebody named John D. Conscience."

He looked up at her from the cigarette he had begun to make. "Know anything I ought to know about him?"

"Nothing you don't know. I was just thinking about the time he let his brother go to San Quentin.''

Spade shrugged. "That's not the worst thing he's done." He lit his cigarette, stood up, and reached for his hat. "But he's all right now. All Samuel Spade clients are honest, God-fearing folk. If I'm not back at closing time just run along."

He went to a tall apartment building on Nob Hill, pressed a button set in the frame of a door marked *10K*. The door was opened immediately by a burly dark man in wrinkled dark clothes. He was nearly bald and carried a gray hat in one hand.

The burly man said, "Hello, Sam." He smiled, but his small eyes lost more of their shrewdness. "What are you doing here?"

Spade said, "Hello, Tom." His face was wooden, his voice expressionless. "Bliss in?"

"Is he!" Tom pulled down the corners of his thick-lipped mouth. "You don't have to worry about that."

Spade's brows came together. "Well?"

A man appeared in the vestibule behind Tom. He was smaller than either Spade or Tom, but compactly built. He had a ruddy, square face and a close-trimmed, grizzled mustache. His clothes were neat. He wore a black bowler perched on the back of his head.

Spade addressed this man over Tom's shoulder: "Hello, Dundy."

Dundy nodded briefly and came to the door. His blue eyes were hard and prying.

"What is it?" he asked Tom.

"B-l-i-s-s, M-a-x," Spade spelled patiently. "I want to see him. He wants to see me. Catch on?"

Tom laughed. Dundy did not. Tom said, "Only one of you gets your wish." Then he glanced sidewise at Dundy and abruptly stopped laughing. He seemed uncomfortable.

Spade scowled. "All right," he demanded irritably; "is he dead or has he killed somebody?"

Dundy thrust his square face up at Spade and seemed to push his words out with his lower lip. "What makes you think either?"

Spade said, "Oh, sure! I come calling on Mr. Bliss and I'm stopped at the door by a couple of men from the police Homicide Detail, and I'm supposed to think I'm just interrupting a game of rummy."

"Aw, stop it, Sam," Tom grumbled, looking at neither Spade nor Dundy. "He's dead."

"Killed?"

Tom wagged his head slowly up and down. He looked at Spade now. "What've you got on it?"

Spade replied in a deliberate monotone, "He called me up this afternoon — say at five minutes to four — I looked at my watch after he hung up and there was still a minute or so to go — and said somebody was after his scalp. He wanted me to come over. It seemed real enough to him — it was up in his neck all right." He made a small gesture with one hand. "Well, here I am."

"Didn't say who or how?" Dundy asked.

Spade shook his head. "No. Just somebody had offered to kill him and he believed them, and would I come over right away."

"Didn't he —?" Dundy began quickly.

"He didn't say anything else," Spade said. "Don't you people tell me anything?"

Dundy said curtly, "Come in and take a look at him."

Tom said, "It's a sight."

They went across the vestibule and through a door into a green and rose living room.

A man near the door stopped sprinkling white powder on the end of a glass-covered small table to say, "Hello, Sam."

Spade nodded, said, "How are you, Phels?" and then nodded at the two men who stood talking by a window.

The dead man lay with his mouth open. Some of his clothes had been taken off. His throat was puffy and dark. The end of his tongue showing in a corner of his mouth was bluish, swollen. On his bare chest, over the heart, a five-pointed star had been outlined in black ink and in the center of it a T.

Spade looked down at the dead man and stood for a moment silently studying him. Then he asked, "He was found like that?"

"About," Tom said. "We moved him

around a little." He jerked a thumb at the shirt, undershirt, vest, and coat lying on a table. "They were spread over the floor."

Spade rubbed his chin. His yellow-gray eyes were dreamy. "When?"

Tom said, "We got it at four twenty. His daughter gave it to us." He moved his head to indicate a closed door. "You'll see her."

"Know anything?"

"Heaven knows," Tom said wearily. "She's been kind of hard to get along with so far." He turned to Dundy. "Want to try her again now?"

Dundy nodded, then spoke to one of the men at the window. "Start sifting his papers, Mack. He's supposed to've been threatened."

Mack said, "Right." He pulled his hat down over his eyes and walked towards a green *secrétaire* in the far end of the room.

A man came in from the corridor, a heavy man of fifty with a deeply lined, grayish face under a broad-brimmed black hat. He said, "Hello, Sam," and then told Dundy, "He had company around half past two, stayed just about an hour. A big blond man in brown, maybe forty or forty-five. Didn't send his name up. I got it from the Filipino in the elevator that rode him both ways."

"Sure it was only an hour?" Dundy asked.

The gray-faced man shook his head. "But he's sure it wasn't more than half past three

331

when he left. He says the afternoon papers came in then, and this man had ridden down with him before they came." He pushed his hat back to scratch his head, then pointed a thick finger at the design inked on the dead man's breast and asked somewhat plaintively, "What the deuce do you suppose that thing is?"

Nobody replied. Dundy asked, "Can the elevator boy identify him?"

"He says he could, but that ain't always the same thing. Says he never saw him before." He stopped looking at the dead man. "The girl's getting me a list of his phone calls. How you been, Sam?"

Spade said he had been all right. Then he said slowly, "His brother's big and blond and maybe forty or forty-five."

Dundy's blue eyes were hard and bright. "So what?" he asked.

"You remember the Graystone Loan swindle. They were both in it, but Max eased the load over on Theodore and it turned out to be one to fourteen years in San Quentin."

Dundy was slowly wagging his head up and down. "I remember now. Where is he?"

Spade shrugged and began to make a cigarette.

Dundy nudged Tom with an elbow. "Find out."

Tom said, "Sure, but if he was out of here at half past three and this fellow was still alive at five to four —"

"And he broke his leg so he couldn't duck back in," the gray-faced man said jovially.

"Find out," Dundy repeated.

Tom said, "Sure, sure," and went to the telephone.

Dundy addressed the gray-faced man: "Check up on the newspapers; see what time they were actually delivered this afternoon."

The gray-faced man nodded and left the room.

The man who had been searching the *secrétaire* said, "Uh-huh," and turned around holding an envelope in one hand, a sheet of paper in the other.

Dundy held out his hand. "Something?"

The man said, "Uh-huh," again and gave Dundy the sheet of paper.

Spade was looking over Dundy's shoulder.

It was a small sheet of common white paper bearing a penciled message in neat, undistinguished handwriting:

When this reaches you I will be too close for you to escape — this time. We will balance our accounts — for good.

The signature was a five-pointed star enclosing a T, the design on the dead man's left breast.

Dundy held out his hand again and was given the envelope. Its stamp was French.

The address was typewritten:

MAX BLISS , ESQ.
AMSTERDAM APARTMENTS
SAN FRANCISCO, CALIF.
U.S.A.

"Postmarked Paris," he said, "the second of the month." He counted swiftly on his fingers. "That would get it here today, all right." He folded the message slowly, put it in the envelope, put the envelope in his coat pocket. "Keep digging," he told the man who had found the message.

The man nodded and returned to the *secrétaire*.

Dundy looked at Spade. "What do you think of it?"

Spade's brown cigarette wagged up and down with his words. "I don't like it. I don't like any of it."

Tom put down the telephone. "He got out the fifteenth of last month," he said. "I got them trying to locate him."

Spade went to the telephone, called a number, and asked for Mr. Darrell. Then: "Hello, Harry, this is Sam Spade. . . . Fine. How's Lil? . . . Yes. . . . Listen, Harry, what does a five-pointed star with a capital T in the middle mean? . . . What? How do you spell it? . . . Yes, I see. . . . And if you found it on a body? . . . Neither do I. . . .

334

Yes, and thanks. I'll tell you about it when I see you. . . . Yes, give me a ring. . . . Thanks. . . . 'By.''

Dundy and Tom were watching him closely when he turned from the telephone. He said, "That's a fellow who knows things sometimes. He says it's a pentagram with a Greek tau — t-a-u — in the middle; a sign magicians used to use. Maybe Rosicrucians still do."

"What's a Rosicrucian?" Tom asked.

"It could be Theodore's first initial, too," Dundy said.

Spade moved his shoulders, said carelessly, "Yes, but if he wanted to autograph the job it'd been just as easy for him to sign his name."

He then went on more thoughtfully, "There are Rosicrucians at both San Jose and Point Loma. I don't go much for this, but maybe we ought to look them up."

Dundy nodded.

Spade looked at the dead man's clothes on the table. "Anything in his pockets?"

"Only what you'd expect to find," Dundy replied. "It's on the table there."

Spade went to the table and looked down at the little pile of watch and chain, keys, wallet, address book, money, gold pencil, handkerchief, and spectacle case beside the clothing. He did not touch them, but slowly picked up, one at a time, the dead man's shirt, undershirt, vest, and coat. A blue necktie lay on the table beneath them. He scowled irritably at it. "It hasn't been worn," he complained.

Dundy, Tom, and the coroner's deputy, who had stood silent all this while by the window — he was a small man with a slim, dark, intelligent face — came together to stare down at the unwrinkled blue silk.

Tom groaned miserably. Dundy cursed under his breath. Spade lifted the necktie to look at its back. The label was a London haberdasher's.

Spade said cheerfully, "Swell. San Francisco, Point Loma, San Jose, Paris, London."

Dundy glowered at him.

The gray-faced man came in. "The papers got here at three thirty, all right," he said. His eyes widened a little. "What's up?" As he crossed the room towards them he said, "I can't find anybody that saw Blondy sneak back in here again." He looked uncomprehendingly at the necktie until Tom growled, "It's brand-new"; then he whistled softly.

Dundy turned to Spade. "The deuce with all this," he said bitterly. "He's got a brother with reasons for not liking him. The brother just got out of stir. Somebody who looks like his brother left here at half past three. Twenty-five minutes later he phoned you he'd been threatened. Less than half an hour after that his daughter came in and found him dead — strangled." He poked a finger at the small, dark-faced man's chest. "Right?"

"Strangled," the dark-faced man said precisely, "by a man. The hands were large."

"O.K." Dundy turned to Spade again. "We find a threatening letter. Maybe that's what he was telling you about, maybe it was something his brother said to him. Don't let's guess. Let's stick to what we know. We know he —"

The man at the *secrétaire* turned around and said, "Got another one." His mien was somewhat smug.

The eyes with which the five men at the table looked at him were identically cold, unsympathetic.

He, nowise disturbed by their hostility, read aloud:

"Dear Bliss:
I am writing this to tell you for the last time that I want my money back, and I want it back by the first of the month, all of it. If I don't get it I am going to do something about it, and you ought to be able to guess what I mean. And don't think I am kidding.
Yours truly,
DANIEL TALBOT"

He grinned. "That's another T for you." He picked up an envelope. "Postmarked San Diego, the twenty-fifth of last month." He grinned again. "And that's another city for you."

Spade shook his head. "Point Loma's down that way," he said.

He went over with Dundy to look at the letter. It was written in blue ink on white stationery of good quality, as was the address on the envelope, in a cramped, angular handwriting that seemed to have nothing in common with that of the penciled letter.

Spade said ironically, "Now we're getting somewhere."

Dundy made an impatient gesture. "Let's stick to what we know," he growled.

"Sure," Spade agreed. "What is it?"

There was no reply.

Spade took tobacco and cigarette papers from his pocket. "Didn't somebody say something about talking to a daughter?" he asked.

"We'll talk to her." Dundy turned on his heel, then suddenly frowned at the dead man on the floor. He jerked a thumb at the small, dark-faced man. "Through with it?"

"I'm through."

Dundy addressed Tom curtly: "Get rid of it." He addressed the gray-faced man: "I want to see both elevator boys when I'm finished with the girl."

He went to the closed door Tom had pointed out to Spade and knocked on it.

A slightly harsh female voice within asked, "What is it?"

"Lieutenant Dundy. I want to talk to Miss Bliss."

There was a pause; then the voice said, "Come in."

Dundy opened the door and Spade followed him into a black, gray, and silver room, where a big-boned and ugly middle-aged woman in black dress and white apron sat beside a bed on which a girl lay.

The girl lay, elbow on pillow, cheek on hand, facing the big-boned, ugly woman. She was apparently about eighteen years old. She wore a gray suit. Her hair was blond and short, her face firm-featured and remarkably symmetrical. She did not look at the two men coming into the room.

Dundy spoke to the big-boned woman, while Spade was lighting his cigarette: "We want to ask you a couple of questions, too, Mrs. Hooper. You're Bliss's housekeeper, aren't you?"

The woman said, "I am." Her slightly harsh voice, the level gaze of her deep-set gray eyes, the stillness and size of her hands lying in her lap, all contributed to the impression she gave of resting strength.

"What do you know about this?"

"I don't know anything about it. I was let off this morning to go over to Oakland to my nephew's funeral, and when I got back you and the other gentlemen were here and — and this had happened."

Dundy nodded, asked, "What do you think about it?"

"I don't know what to think," she replied simply.

"Didn't you know he expected it to happen?"

Now the girl suddenly stopped watching Mrs. Hooper. She sat up in bed, turning wide, excited eyes on Dundy, and asked, "What do you mean?"

"I mean what I said. He'd been threatened. He called up Mr. Spade" — he indicated Spade with a nod — "and told him so just a few minutes before he was killed."

"But who —?" she began.

"That's what we're asking you," Dundy said. "Who had that much against him?"

She stared at him in astonishment. "Nobody would —"

This time Spade interrupted her, speaking with a softness that made his words seem less brutal than they were. "Somebody did." When she turned her stare on him he asked, "You don't know of any threats?"

She shook her head from side to side with emphasis.

He looked at Mrs. Hooper. "You?"

"No, sir," she said.

He returned his attention to the girl. "Do you know Daniel Talbot?"

"Why, yes," she said. "He was here for dinner last night."

"Who is he?"

"I don't know, except that he lives in San Diego, and he and Father had some sort of business together. I'd never met him before."

"What sort of terms were they on?"

She frowned a little, said slowly, "Friendly."

Dundy spoke: "What business was your father in?"

"He was a financier."

"You mean a promoter?"

"Yes, I suppose you could call it that."

"Where is Talbot staying, or has he gone back to San Diego?"

"I don't know."

"What does he look like?"

She frowned again, thoughtfully. "He's kind of large, with a red face and white hair and a white mustache."

"Old?"

"I guess he must be sixty; fifty-five at least."

Dundy looked at Spade, who put the stub of his cigarette in a tray on the dressing table and took up the questioning. "How long since you've seen your uncle?"

Her face flushed. "You mean Uncle Ted?"

He nodded.

"Not since," she began, and bit her lip. Then she said, "Of course, you know. Not since he first got out of prison."

"He came here?"

"Yes."

"To see your father?"

"Of course."

"What sort of terms were they on?"

She opened her eyes wide. "Neither of them is very demonstrative," she said, "but they are brothers, and Father was giving him money to set him up in business again."

"Then they were on good terms?"

"Yes," she replied in the tone of one answering an unnecessary question.

"Where does he live?"

"On Post Street," she said, and gave a number.

"And you haven't seen him since?"

"No. He was shy, you know, about having been in prison —" She finished the sentence with a gesture of one hand.

Spade addressed Mrs. Hooper: "You've seen him since?"

"No, sir."

He pursed his lips, asked slowly, "Either of you know he was here this afternoon?"

They said, "No," together.

"Where did —?"

Someone knocked on the door.

Dundy said, "Come in."

Tom opened the door far enough to stick his head in. "His brother's here," he said.

The girl, leaning forward, called, "Oh, Uncle Ted!"

A big, blond man in brown appeared

behind Tom. He was sunburned to an extent that made his teeth seem whiter, his clear eyes bluer, than they were.

He asked, "What's the matter, Miriam?"

"Father's dead," she said, and began to cry.

Dundy nodded at Tom, who stepped out of Theodore Bliss's way and let him come into the room.

A woman came in behind him, slowly, hesitantly. She was a tall woman in her late twenties, blond, not quite plump. Her features were generous, her face pleasant and intelligent. She wore a small brown hat and a mink coat.

Bliss put an arm around his niece, kissed her forehead, sat on the bed beside her. "There, there," he said awkwardly.

She saw the blond woman, stared through her tears at her for a moment, then said, "Oh, how do you do, Miss Barrow?"

The blond woman said, "I'm awfully sorry to —"

Bliss cleared his throat, and said, "She's Mrs. Bliss now. We were married this afternoon."

Dundy looked angrily at Spade. Spade, making a cigarette, seemed about to laugh.

Miriam Bliss, after a moment's surprised silence, said, "Oh, I do wish you all the happiness in the world." She turned to her uncle while his wife was murmuring "Thank you" and said, "And you too, Uncle Ted."

He patted her shoulder and squeezed her to him. He was looking questioningly at Spade and Dundy.

"Your brother died this afternoon," Dundy said. "He was murdered."

Mrs. Bliss caught her breath. Bliss's arm tightened around his niece with a little jerk, but there was not yet any change in his face. "Murdered?" he repeated uncomprehendingly.

"Yes." Dundy put his hands in his coat pockets. "You were here this afternoon."

Theodore Bliss paled a little under his sunburn, but said, "I was," steadily enough.

"How long?"

"About an hour. I got here about half past two and —" He turned to his wife. "It was almost half past three when I phoned you, wasn't it?"

She said, "Yes."

"Well, I left right after that."

"Did you have a date with him?" Dundy asked.

"No. I phoned his office" — he nodded at his wife — "and was told he'd left for home, so I came on up. I wanted to see him before Elise and I left, of course, and I wanted him to come to the wedding, but he couldn't. He said he was expecting somebody. We sat here and talked longer than I had intended, so I had to phone Elise to meet me at the Municipal Building."

After a thoughtful pause, Dundy asked, "What time?"

"That we met there?" Bliss looked inquiringly at his wife, who said, "It was just quarter to four." She laughed a little. "I got there first and I kept looking at my watch."

Bliss said very deliberately, "It was a few minutes after four that we were married. We had to wait for Judge Whitfield — about ten minutes, and it was a few more before we got started — to get through with the case he was hearing. You can check it up — Superior Court, Part Two, I think."

Spade whirled around and pointed at Tom. "Maybe you'd better check it up."

Tom said, "Oke," and went away from the door.

"If that's so, you're all right, Mr. Bliss," Dundy said, "but I have to ask these things. Now, did your brother say who he was expecting?"

"No."

"Did he say anything about having been threatened?"

"No. He never talked much about his affairs to anybody, not even to me. Had he been threatened?"

Dundy's lips tightened a little. "Were you and he on intimate terms?"

"Friendly, if that's what you mean."

"Are you sure?" Dundy asked. "Are you sure neither of you held any grudge against the other?"

Theodore Bliss took his arm free from around his niece. Increasing pallor made his sunburned face yellowish. He said, "Everybody here knows about my having been in San Quentin. You can speak out, if that's what you're getting at."

"It is," Dundy said, and then, after a pause, "Well?"

Bliss stood up. "Well, what?" he asked impatiently. "Did I hold a grudge against him for that? No. Why should I? We were both in it. He could get out; I couldn't. I was sure of being convicted whether he was or not. Having him sent over with me wasn't going to make it any better for me. We talked it over and decided I'd go it alone, leaving him outside to pull things together. And he did. If you look up his bank account you'll see he gave me a check for twenty-five thousand dollars two days after I was discharged from San Quentin, and the registrar of the National Steel Corporation can tell you a thousand shares of stock have been transferred from his name to mine since then."

He smiled apologetically and sat down on the bed again. "I'm sorry. I know you have to ask things."

Dundy ignored the apology. "Do you know Daniel Talbot?" he asked.

Bliss said, "No."

His wife said, "I do; that is, I've seen him.

346

He was in the office yesterday."

Dundy looked her up and down carefully before asking, "What office?"

"I am — I was Mr. Bliss's secretary, and —"

"Max Bliss's?"

"Yes, and a Daniel Talbot came in to see him yesterday afternoon, if it's the same one."

"What happened?"

She looked at her husband, who said, "If you know anything, for heaven's sake tell them."

She said, "But nothing really happened. I thought they were angry with each other at first, but when they left together they were laughing and talking, and before they went Mr. Bliss rang for me and told me to have Trapper — he's the bookkeeper — make out a check to Mr. Talbot's order."

"Did he?"

"Oh, yes. I took it in to him. If was for seventy-five hundred and some dollars."

"What was it for?"

She shook her head. "I don't know."

"If you were Bliss's secretary," Dundy insisted, "you must have some idea of what his business with Talbot was."

"But I haven't," she said. "I'd never even heard of him before."

Dundy looked at Spade. Spade's face was wooden. Dundy glowered at him, then put a

347

question to the man on the bed: "What kind of necktie was your brother wearing when you saw him last?"

Bliss blinked, then stared distantly past Dundy, and finally shut his eyes. When he opened them he said, "It was green with — I'd know it if I saw it. Why?"

Mrs. Bliss said, "Narrow diagonal stripes of different shades of green. That's the one he had on at the office this morning."

"Where does he keep his neckties?" Dundy asked the housekeeper.

She rose, saying, "In a closet in his bedroom. I'll show you."

Dundy and the newly married Blisses followed her out.

Spade put his hat on the dressing table and asked Miriam Bliss, "What time did you go out?" He sat on the foot of her bed.

"Today? About one o'clock. I had a luncheon engagement for one and I was a little late, and then I went shopping and then —" She broke off with a shudder.

"And then you came home at what time?" His voice was friendly, matter-of-fact.

"Some time after four, I guess."

"And what happened?"

"I f-found Father lying there and I phoned — I don't know whether I phoned downstairs or the police, and then I don't know what I did. I fainted or had hysterics or something, and the first thing I remember is coming to and finding those men here and Mrs. Hooper." She looked him full in the face now.

"You didn't phone a doctor?"

She lowered her eyes again. "No, I don't think so."

"Of course you wouldn't, if you knew he was dead," he said casually.

She was silent.

"You knew he was dead?" he asked.

She raised her eyes and looked blankly at him. "But he *was* dead," she said.

He smiled. "Of course; but what I'm getting at is, did you make sure before you phoned?"

She put a hand to her throat. "I don't remember what I did," she said earnestly. "I think I just knew he was dead."

He nodded understandingly. "And if you phoned the police it was because you knew he had been murdered."

She worked her hands together and looked at them and said, "I suppose so. It was awful. I don't know what I thought or did."

Spade leaned forward and made his voice low and persuasive. "I'm not a police detective, Miss Bliss. I was engaged by your father — a few minutes too late to save him. I am, in a way, working for you now, so if there is anything I can do — maybe something the police wouldn't —" He broke off as Dundy, followed by the Blisses and the housekeeper, returned to the room. "What luck?"

Dundy said, "The green tie's not there."

His suspicious gaze darted from Spade to the girl. "Mrs. Hooper says the blue tie we found is one of half a dozen he just got from England."

Bliss asked, "What's the importance of the tie?"

Dundy scowled at him. "He was partly undressed when we found him. The tie with his clothes had never been worn."

"Couldn't he have been changing clothes when whoever killed him came, and was killed before he had finished dressing?"

Dundy's scowl deepened. "Yes, but what did he do with the green tie? Eat it?"

Spade said, "He wasn't changing clothes. If you'll look at the shirt collar you'll see he must've had it on when he was choked."

Tom came to the door. "Checks all right," he told Dundy. "The judge and a bailiff named Kittredge say they were there from about a quarter to four till five or ten minutes after. I told Kittredge to come over and take a look at them to make sure they're the same ones."

Dundy said, "Right," without turning his head and took the penciled threat signed with the T in a star from his pocket. He folded it so only the signature was visible. Then he asked, "Anybody know what this is?"

Miriam Bliss left the bed to join the others in looking at it. From it they looked at one another blankly.

"Anybody know anything about it?" Dundy asked.

Mrs. Hooper said, "It's like what was on poor Mr. Bliss's chest, but —" The others said, "No."

"Anybody ever seen anything like it before?"

They said they had not.

Dundy said, "All right. Wait here. Maybe I'll have something else to ask you after a while."

Spade said, "Just a minute. Mr. Bliss, how long have you known Mrs. Bliss?"

Bliss looked curiously at Spade. "Since I got out of prison," he replied somewhat cautiously. "Why?"

"Just since last month," Spade said as if to himself. "Meet her through your brother?"

"Of course — in his office. Why?"

"And at the Municipal Building this afternoon, were you together all the time?"

"Yes, certainly." Bliss spoke sharply. "What are you getting at?"

Spade smiled at him, a friendly smile. "I have to ask things," he said.

Bliss smiled too. "It's all right." His smile broadened. "As a matter of fact, I'm a liar. We weren't actually together all the time. I went out into the corridor to smoke a cigarette, but I assure you every time I looked through the glass of the door I could see her still sitting in the courtroom where I

351

had left her.''

Spade's smile was as light as Bliss's. Nevertheless, he asked, "And when you weren't looking through the glass you were in sight of the door? She couldn't've left the courtroom without your seeing her?''

Bliss's smile went away. "Of course she couldn't,'' he said, "and I wasn't out there more than five minutes.''

Spade said, "Thanks,'' and followed Dundy into the living room, shutting the door behind him.

Dundy looked sidewise at Spade. "Anything to it?''

Spade shrugged.

Max Bliss's body had been removed. Besides the man at the *secrétaire* and the gray-faced man, two Filipino boys in plum-colored uniforms were in the room. They sat close together on the sofa.

Dundy said, "Mack, I want to find a green necktie. I want this house taken apart, this block taken apart, and the whole neighborhood taken apart till you find it. Get what men you need.''

The man at the *secrétaire* rose, said "Right,'' pulled his hat down over his eyes, and went out.

Dundy scowled at the Filipinos. "Which of you saw the man in brown?''

The smaller stood up. "Me, sir.''

Dundy opened the bedroom door and

said, "Bliss."

Bliss came to the door.

The Filipino's face lighted up. "Yes, sir, him."

Dundy shut the door in Bliss's face. "Sit down."

The boy sat down hastily.

Dundy stared gloomily at the boys until they began to fidget. Then, "Who else did you bring up to this apartment this afternoon?"

They shook their heads in unison from side to side. "Nobody else, sir," the smaller one said. A desperately ingratiating smile stretched his mouth wide across his face.

Dundy took a threatening step towards them. "Nuts!" he snarled. "You brought up Miss Bliss."

The larger boy's head bobbed up and down. "Yes, sir. Yes, sir. I bring them up. I think you mean other people." He too tried a smile.

Dundy was glaring at him. "Never mind what you think I mean. Tell me what I ask. Now, what do you mean by 'them'?"

The boy's smile died under the glare. He looked at the floor between his feet and said, "Miss Bliss and the gentleman."

"What gentleman? The gentleman in there?" He jerked his head toward the door he had shut on Bliss.

"No, sir. Another gentleman, not an American gentleman." He had raised his head again and now brightness came back into his face. "I think he is Armenian."

"Why?"

"Because he not like us Americans, not talk like us."

Spade laughed; asked, "Ever seen an Armenian?"

"No, sir. That is why I think he —" He shut his mouth with a click as Dundy made a growling noise in his throat.

"What'd he look like?" Dundy asked.

The boy lifted his shoulders, spread his hands. "He tall, like this gentleman." He indicated Spade. "Got dark hair, dark mustache. Very" — he frowned earnestly — "very nice clothes. Very nice-looking man. Cane, gloves, spats, even, and —"

"Young?" Dundy asked.

The head went up and down again. "Young. Yes, sir."

"When did he leave?"

"Five minutes," the boy replied.

Dundy made a chewing motion with his jaws, then asked, "What time did they come in?"

The boy spread his hands, lifted his shoulders again. "Four o'clock — maybe ten minutes after."

"Did you bring anybody else up before we got here?"

The Filipinos shook their heads in unison once more.

Dundy spoke out the side of his mouth to Spade: "Get her."

Spade opened the bedroom door, bowed slightly, said, "Will you come out a moment, Miss Bliss?"

"What is it?" she asked warily.

"Just for a moment," he said, holding the door open. Then he suddenly added, "And you'd better come along, too, Mr. Bliss."

Miriam Bliss came slowly into the living room followed by her uncle, and Spade shut the door behind them. Miss Bliss's lower lip twitched a little when she saw the elevator boys. She looked apprehensively at Dundy.

He asked, "What's this fiddlededee about the man that came in with you?"

Her lower lip twitched again. "Wh-what?" She tried to put bewilderment on her face. Theodore Bliss hastily crossed the room, stood for a moment before her as if he intended to say something, and then, apparently changing his mind, took up a position behind her, his arms crossed over the back of a chair.

"The man who came in with you," Dundy said harshly, rapidly. "Who is he? Where is he? Why'd he leave? Why didn't you say anything about him?"

The girl put her hands over her face and began to cry. "He didn't have anything to do with it," she blubbered through her hands. "He didn't, and it would just make trouble

355

for him.''

"Nice boy," Dundy said. "So, to keep his name out of the newspapers, he runs off and leaves you alone with your murdered father."

She took her hands away from her face. "Oh, but he had to," she cried. "His wife is so jealous, and if she knew he had been with me again she'd certainly divorce him, and he hasn't a cent in the world of his own."

Dundy looked at Spade. Spade looked at the goggling Filipinos and jerked a thumb at the outer door. "Scram," he said. They went out quickly.

"And who is this gem?" Dundy asked the girl.

"But he didn't have any —"

"Who is he?"

Her shoulders drooped a little and she lowered her eyes. "His name is Boris Smekalov," she said wearily.

"Spell it."

She spelled it.

"Where does he live?"

"At the St. Mark Hotel."

"Does he do anything for a living except marry money?"

Anger came into her face as she raised it, but went away as quickly. "He doesn't do anything," she said.

Dundy wheeled to address the gray-faced man. "Get him."

The gray-faced man grunted and went out.

Dundy faced the girl again. "You and this Smekalov in love with each other?"

Her face became scornful. She looked at him with scornful eyes and said nothing.

He said, "Now your father's dead, will you have enough money for him to marry if his wife divorces him?"

She covered her face with her hands.

He said, "Now your father's dead, will —?"

Spade, leaning far over, caught her as she fell. He lifted her easily and carried her into the bedroom. When he came back he shut the door behind him and leaned against it. "Whatever the rest of it was," he said, "the faint's a phony."

"Everything's a phony," Dundy growled.

Spade grinned mockingly. "There ought to be a law making criminals give themselves up."

Mr. Bliss smiled and sat down at his brother's desk by the window.

Dundy's voice was disagreeable. "You got nothing to worry about," he said to Spade. "Even your client's dead and can't complain. But if I don't come across I've got to stand for riding from the captain, the chief, the newspapers, and heaven knows who all."

"Stay with it," Spade said soothingly; "you'll catch a murderer sooner or later yet." His face became serious except for the lights in his yellow-gray eyes. "I don't want to run this job up any more alleys than we have to, but don't you think we ought to check up on the funeral the housekeeper said she went to? There's something funny about that woman."

After looking suspiciously at Spade for a moment, Dundy nodded, and said, "Tom'll do it."

Spade turned about and, shaking his finger at Tom, said, "It's a ten-to-one bet there wasn't any funeral. Check on it . . . don't miss a trick."

Then he opened the bedroom door and called Mrs. Hooper. "Sergeant Polhaus wants some information from you," he told her.

While Tom was writing down names and addresses that the woman gave him, Spade sat on the sofa and made and smoked a cigarette, and Dundy walked the floor slowly, scowling at the rug. With Spade's approval, Theodore Bliss rose and rejoined his wife in the bedroom.

Presently Tom put his notebook in his pocket, said, "Thank you," to the housekeeper, "Be seeing you," to Spade and Dundy, and left the apartment.

The housekeeper stood where he had left her, ugly, strong, serene, patient.

Spade twisted himself around on the sofa until he was looking into her deep-set, steady eyes. "Don't worry about that," he said, flirting a hand toward the door Tom had gone through. "Just routine." He pursed his lips, asked, "What do you honestly think of this thing, Mrs. Hooper?"

She replied calmly, in her strong, somewhat harsh voice; "I think it's the judgment of God."

Dundy stopped pacing the floor.

Spade said, "What?"

There was certainty and no excitement in her voice: "The wages of sin is death."

Dundy began to advance towards Mrs. Hooper in the manner of one stalking game. Spade waved him back with a hand which the sofa hid from the woman. His face and voice showed interest, but were now as composed as the woman's. "Sin?" he asked.

She said, " 'Whosoever shall offend one of these little ones that believe in me, it were better for him that a millstone were hanged around his neck, and he were cast into the sea.' " She spoke, not as if quoting, but as if saying something she believed.

Dundy barked a question at her: "What little one?"

She turned her grave gray eyes on him, then looked past him at the bedroom door.

"Her," she said; "Miriam."

Dundy frowned at her. "His daughter?"

The woman said, "Yes, his own adopted daughter."

Angry blood mottled Dundy's square face. "What the heck is this?" he demanded. He shook his head as if to free it from some clinging thing. "She's not really his daughter?"

The woman's serenity was in no way disturbed by his anger. "No. His wife was an invalid most of her life. They didn't have any children."

Dundy moved his jaws as if chewing for a moment and when he spoke again his voice was cooler. "What did he do to her?"

"I don't know," she said, "but I truly believe that when the truth's found out you'll see that the money her father — I mean her real father — left her has been —"

Spade interrupted her, taking pains to speak very clearly, moving one hand in small circles with his words. "You mean you don't actually know he's been gypping her? You just suspect it?"

She put a hand over her heart. "I know it here," she replied calmly.

Dundy looked at Spade, Spade at Dundy, and Spade's eyes were shiny with not altogether pleasant merriment. Dundy cleared his throat and addressed the woman again. "And you think this" — he waved a hand at the floor where the dead man had lain — "was the judgment of God, huh?"

"I do."

He kept all but the barest trace of craftiness out of his eyes. "Then whoever did it was just acting as the hand of God?"

"It's not for me to say," she replied.

Red began to mottle his face again. "That'll

be all right now," he said in a choking voice, but by the time she had reached the bedroom door his eyes became alert again and he called, "Wait a minute." And when they were facing each other: "Listen, do you happen to be a Rosicrucian?"

"I wish to be nothing but a Christian."

He growled, "All right, all right," and turned his back on her. She went into the bedroom and shut the door. He wiped his forehead with the palm of his right hand and complained wearily, "Great Scott, what a family!"

Spade shrugged. "Try investigating your own some time."

Dundy's face whitened. His lips, almost colorless, came back tight over his teeth. He balled his fists and lunged towards Spade. "What do you —?" The pleasantly surprised look on Spade's face stopped him. He averted his eyes, wet his lips with the tip of his tongue, looked at Spade again and away, essayed an embarrassed smile, and mumbled, "You mean any family. Uh-huh, I guess so." He turned hastily towards the corridor door as the doorbell rang.

The amusement twitching Spade's face accentuated his likeness to a blond satan.

An amiable, drawling voice came in through the corridor door: "I'm Jim Kittredge, Superior Court. I was told to come over here."

Dundy's voice: "Yes, come in."

Kittredge was a roly-poly ruddy man in too-tight clothes with the shine of age on them. He nodded at Spade and said, "I remember you, Mr. Spade, from the Burke–Harris suit."

Spade said, "Sure," and stood up to shake hands with him.

Dundy had gone to the bedroom door to call Theodore Bliss and his wife. Kittredge looked at them, smiled at them amiably, said, "How do you do?" and turned to Dundy. "That's them, all right." He looked around as if for a place to spit, found none, and said, "It was just about ten minutes to four that the gentleman there came in the courtroom and asked me how long His Honor would be, and I told him about ten minutes, and they waited there; and right after court adjourned at four o'clock we married them."

Dundy said, "Thanks." He sent Kittredge away, the Blisses back to the bedroom, scowled with dissatisfaction at Spade, and said, "So what?"

Spade, sitting down again, replied, "So you couldn't get from here to the Municipal Building in less than fifteen minutes on a bet, so he couldn't've ducked back here while he was waiting for the judge, and he couldn't have hustled over here to do it after the wedding and before Miriam arrived."

The dissatisfaction in Dundy's face increased. He opened his mouth, but shut it

362

in silence when the gray-faced man came in with a tall, slender, pale young man who fitted the description the Filipino had given of Miriam Bliss's companion.

The gray-faced man said, "Lieutenant Dundy, Mr. Spade, Mr. Boris — uh — Smekalov."

Dundy nodded curtly.

Smekalov began to speak immediately. His accent was not heavy enough to trouble his hearers much, though his r's sounded more like w's. "Lieutenant, I must beg of you that you keep this confidential. If it should get out it will ruin me, Lieutenant, ruin me completely and most unjustly. I am most innocent, sir, I assure you, in heart, spirit, and deed, not only innocent, but in no way whatever connected with any part of the whole horrible matter. There is no —"

"Wait a minute." Dundy prodded Smekalov's chest with a blunt finger. "Nobody's said anything about you being mixed up in anything — but it'd looked better if you'd stuck around."

The young man spread his arms, his palms forward, in an expansive gesture. "But what can I do? I have a wife who —" He shook his head violently. "It is impossible. I cannot do it."

The gray-faced man said to Spade in an inadequately subdued voice, "Goofy, these Russians."

Dundy screwed up his eyes at Smekalov and made his voice judicial. "You've probably," he said, "put yourself in a pretty tough spot."

Smekalov seemed about to cry. "But only put yourself in my place," he begged, "and you —"

"Wouldn't want to." Dundy seemed, in his callous way, sorry for the young man. "Murder's nothing to play with in this country."

"Murder! But I tell you, Lieutenant, I happen' to enter into this situation by the merest mischance only. I am not —"

"You mean you came in here with Miss Bliss by accident?"

The young man looked as if he would like to say "Yes." He said, "No," slowly, then went on with increasing rapidity: "But that was nothing, sir, nothing at all. We had been to lunch. I escorted her home and she said, 'Will you come in for a cocktail?' and I would. That is all, I give you my word." He held out his hands, palms up. "Could it not have happened so to you?" He moved his hands in Spade's direction. "To you?"

Spade said, "A lot of things happen to me. Did Bliss know you were running around with his daughter?"

"He knew we were friends, yes."

"Did he know you had a wife?"

Smekalov said cautiously, "I do not

think so."

Dundy said, "You know he didn't."

Smekalov moistened his lips and did not contradict the lieutenant.

Dundy asked, "What do you think he'd've done if he found out?"

"I do not know, sir."

Dundy stepped close to the young man and spoke through his teeth in a harsh, deliberate voice: "What *did* he do when he found out?"

The young man retreated a step, his face white and frightened.

The bedroom door opened and Miriam Bliss came into the room. "Why don't you leave him alone?" she asked indignantly. "I told you he had nothing to do with it. I told you he didn't know anything about it." She was beside Smekalov now and had one of his hands in hers. "You're simply making trouble for him without doing a bit of good. I'm awfully sorry, Boris, I tried to keep them from bothering you."

The young man mumbled unintelligibly.

"You tried, all right," Dundy agreed. He addressed Spade: "Could it've been like this, Sam? Bliss found out about the wife, knew they had the lunch date, came home early to meet them when they came in, threatened to tell the wife, and was choked to stop him." He looked sidewise at the girl. "Now, if you want to fake another faint, hop to it."

The young man screamed and flung himself

at Dundy, clawing with both hands. Dundy grunted — "Uh!" — and struck him in the face with a heavy fist. The young man went backwards across the room until he collided with a chair. He and the chair went down on the floor together. Dundy said to the gray-faced man, "Take him down to the Hall — material witness."

The gray-faced man said, "Oke," picked up Smekalov's hat, and went over to help pick him up.

Theodore Bliss, his wife, and the house-keeper had come to the door Miriam Bliss had left open. Miriam Bliss was crying, stamping her foot, threatening Dundy: "I'll report you, you coward. You had no right to . . ." and so on. Nobody paid much attention to her; they watched the gray-faced man help Smekalov to his feet, take him away. Smekalov's nose and mouth were red smears.

Then Dundy said, "Hush," negligently to Miriam Bliss and took a slip of paper from his pocket. "I got a list of the calls from here today. Sing out when you recognize them."

He read a telephone number.

Mrs. Hooper said, "That is the butcher. I phoned him before I left this morning." She said the next number Dundy read was the grocer's.

He read another.

"That's the St. Mark," Miriam Bliss said. "I called up Boris." She identified two more numbers as those of friends she had called.

The sixth number, Bliss said, was his brother's office. "Probably my call to Elise to ask her to meet me."

Spade said, "Mine," to the seventh number, and Dundy said, "That last one's police emergency." He put the slip back in his pocket.

Spade said cheerfully, "And that gets us a lot of places."

The doorbell rang.

Dundy went to the door. He and another man could be heard talking in voices too low for their words to be recognized in the living room.

The telephone rang. Spade answered it. "Hello. . . . No, this is Spade. Wait a min — All right." He listened. "Right, I'll tell him. . . . I don't know. I'll have him call you. . . . Right."

When he turned from the telephone Dundy was standing, hands behind him, in the vestibule doorway. Spade said, "O'Gar says your Russian went completely nuts on the way to the Hall. They had to shove him into a strait-jacket."

"He ought to been there long ago," Dundy growled. "Come here."

Spade followed Dundy into the vestibule. A uniformed policeman stood in the outer doorway.

Dundy brought his hands from behind him.

In one was a necktie with narrow diagonal stripes in varying shades of green, in the other was a platinum scarfpin in the shape of a crescent set with small diamonds.

Spade bent over to look at three small, irregular spots on the tie. "Blood?"

"Or dirt," Dundy said. "He found them crumpled up in a newspaper in the rubbish can on the corner."

"Yes, sir," the uniformed man said proudly; "there I found them, all wadded up in —" He stopped because nobody was paying any attention to him.

"Blood's better," Spade was saying. "It gives a reason for taking the tie away. Let's go in and talk to people."

Dundy stuffed the tie in one pocket, thrust his hand holding the pin into another. "Right — and we'll call it blood."

They went into the living room. Dundy looked from Bliss to Bliss's wife, to Bliss's niece, to the housekeeper, as if he did not like any of them. He took his fist from his pocket, thrust it straight out in front of him, and opened it to show the crescent pin lying in his hand. "What's that?" he demanded.

Miriam Bliss was the first to speak. "Why, it's Father's pin," she said.

"So it is?" he said disagreeably. "And did he have it on today?"

"He always wore it." She turned to the others for confirmation.

Mrs. Bliss said, "Yes," while the others nodded.

"Where did you find it?" the girl asked.

Dundy was surveying them one by one again, as if he liked them less than ever. His face was red. "He always wore it," he said angrily, "but there wasn't one of you could say, 'Father always wore a pin. Where is it?' No, we got to wait till it turns up before we can get a word out of you about it."

Bliss said, "Be fair. How were we to know —?"

"Never mind what you were to know," Dundy said. "It's coming round to the point where I'm going to do some talking about what I know." He took the green necktie from his pocket. "This is his tie?"

Mrs. Hooper said, "Yes, sir."

Dundy said, "Well, it's got blood on it, and it's not his blood, because he didn't have a scratch on him that we could see." He looked narrow-eyed from one to another of them. "Now, suppose you were trying to choke a man that wore a scarfpin, and he was wrestling with you, and —"

He broke off to look at Spade.

Spade had crossed to where Mrs. Hooper was standing. Her big hands were clasped in front of her. He took her right hand, turned it over, took the wadded handkerchief from her palm, and there was a two-inch-long fresh scratch in the flesh.

She had passively allowed him to examine her hand. Her mien lost none of its tranquillity now. She said nothing.

"Well?" he asked.

"I scratched it on Miss Miriam's pin fixing her on the bed when she fainted," the housekeeper said calmly.

Dundy's laugh was brief, bitter. "It'll hang you just the same," he said.

There was no change in the woman's face. "The Lord's will be done," she replied.

Spade made a peculiar noise in his throat as he dropped her hand. "Well, let's see how we stand." He grinned at Dundy. "You don't like that star-T, do you?"

Dundy said, "Not by a long shot."

"Neither do I," Spade said. "The Talbot threat was probably on the level, but that debt seems to have been squared. Now — wait a minute!" He went to the telephone and called his office. "The tie thing looked pretty funny, too, for a while," he said while he waited, "but I guess the blood takes care of that."

He spoke into the telephone: "Hello, Effie. Listen: Within half an hour or so of the time Bliss called me, did you get any call that maybe wasn't on the level? Anything that could have been a stall? . . . Yes, before . . . Think now."

He put his hand over the mouthpiece and said to Dundy, "There's a lot of deviltry going on in this world."

He spoke into the telephone again: "Yes? . . . Yes . . . Kruger? . . . Yes. Man or woman? . . . Thanks. . . . No, I'll be through in half an hour. Wait for me and I'll buy your dinner. 'By."

He turned away from the telephone. "About half an hour before Bliss phoned, a man called my office and asked for Mr. Kruger."

Dundy frowned. "So what?"

"Kruger wasn't there."

Dundy's frown deepened. "Who's Kruger?"

"I don't know," Spade said blandly. "I never heard of him." He took tobacco and cigarette papers from his pockets. "All right, Bliss, where's your scratch?"

Theodore Bliss said, "What?" while the others stared blankly at Spade.

"Your scratch," Spade repeated in a consciously patient tone. His attention was on the cigarette he was making. "The place where your brother's pin gouged you when you were choking him."

"Are you crazy?" Bliss demanded. "I was —"

"Uh-huh, you were being married when he was killed. You were not." Spade moistened the edge of his cigarette paper and smoothed it with his forefinger.

Mrs. Bliss spoke now, stammering a little: "But he — but Max Bliss called —"

371

"Who says Max Bliss called me?" Spade asked. "I don't know that. I wouldn't know his voice. All I know is a man called me and said he was Max Bliss. Anybody could say that."

"But the telephone records here show the call came from here," she protested.

He shook his head and smiled. "They show I had *a* call from here, and I did, but not that one. I told you somebody called up half an hour or so before the supposed Max Bliss call and asked for Mr. Kruger." He nodded at Theodore Bliss. "He was smart enough to get a call from this apartment to my office on the record before he left to meet you."

She stared from Spade to her husband with dumbfounded blue eyes.

Her husband said lightly, "It's nonsense, my dear. You know —"

Spade did not let him finish that sentence. "You know he went out to smoke a cigarette in the corridor while waiting for the judge, and he knew there were telephone booths in the corridor. A minute would be all he needed." He lit his cigarette and returned his lighter to his pocket.

Bliss said, "Nonsense!" more sharply. "Why should I want to kill Max?" He smiled reassuringly into his wife's horrified eyes. "Don't let this disturb you, dear. Police methods are sometimes —"

"All right," Spade said, "let's look you over for scratches."

Bliss wheeled to face him more directly. "Damned if you will!" He put a hand behind him.

Spade, wooden-faced and dreamy-eyed, came forward.

Spade and Effie Perine sat at a small table in Julius's Castle on Telegraph Hill. Through the window beside them ferryboats could be seen carrying lights to and from the cities' lights on the other side of the bay.

" . . . hadn't gone there to kill him, chances are," Spade was saying; "just to shake him down for some more money; but when the fight started, once he got his hands on his throat, I guess, his grudge was too hot in him for him to let go till Max was dead. Understand, I'm just putting together what the evidence says, and what we got out of his wife, and the not much that we got out of him."

Effie nodded. "She's a nice, loyal wife."

Spade drank coffee, shrugged. "What for? She knows now that he made his play for her only because she was Max's secretary. She knows that when he took out the marriage license a couple of weeks ago it was only to string her along so she'd get him the photostatic copies of the records that tied Max up with the Graystone Loan swindle. She knows

— Well, she knows she wasn't just helping an injured innocent to clear his good name."

He took another sip of coffee. "So he calls on his brother this afternoon to hold San Quentin over his head for a price again, and there's a fight, and he kills him, and gets his wrist stratched by the pin while he's choking him. Blood on the tie, a scratch on his wrist — that won't do. He takes the tie off the corpse and hunts up another, because the absence of a tie will set the police to thinking. He gets a bad break there: Max's new ties are on the front of the rack, and he grabs the first one he comes to. All right. Now he's got to put it around the dead man's neck — or wait — he gets a better idea. Pull off some more clothes and puzzle the police. The tie'll be just as inconspicuous off as on, if the shirt's off too. Undressing him, he gets another idea. He'll give the police something else to worry about, so he draws a mystic sign he has seen somewhere on the dead man's chest."

Spade emptied his cup, set it down, and went on: "By now he's getting to be a regular master mind at bewildering the police. A threatening letter signed with the thing on Max's chest. The afternoon mail is on the desk. One envelope's as good as another so long as it's typewritten and has no return address, but the one from France adds a touch of the foreign, so out comes the original letter and in goes the threat. He's overdoing it now;

374

see? He's giving us so much that's wrong that we can't help suspecting things that seem all right — the phone call, for instance.

"Well, he's ready for the phone calls now — his alibi. He picks my name out of the private detectives in the phone book and does the Mr. Kruger trick; but that's after he calls the blond Elise and tells her that not only have the obstacles to their marriage been removed, but he's had an offer to go in business in New York and has to leave right away, and will she meet him in fifteen minutes and get married? There's more than just an alibi to that. He wants to make sure *she* is dead sure he didn't kill Max, because she knows he doesn't like Max, and he doesn't want her to think he was just stringing her along to get the dope on Max, because she might be able to put two and two together and get something like the right answer.

"With that taken care of, he's ready to leave. He goes out quite openly, with only one thing to worry about now — the tie and pin in his pocket. He takes the pin along because he's not sure the police mightn't find traces of blood around the setting of the stones, no matter how carefully he wipes it. On his way out he picks up a newspaper — buys one from the newsboy he meets at the street door — wads tie and pin up in a piece of it, and drops it in the rubbish can at the corner. That seems all right. No reason for the police to look for the tie. No reason for the street cleaner who empties the can to investigate a crumpled piece of newspaper, and if something does go wrong — what the deuce! — the murderer dropped it there, but he, Theodore, can't be the murderer, because he's going to have an alibi.

"Then he jumps in his car and drives to the Municipal Building. He knows there are plenty of phones there and he can always say he's got to wash his hands, but it turns out he doesn't have to. While they're waiting for the judge to get through with a case he goes out to smoke a cigarette, and there you are — 'Mr. Spade, this is Max Bliss and I've been threatened.' "

Effie Perine nodded, then asked, "Why do you suppose he picked on a private detective instead of the police?"

"Playing safe. If the body had been found, meanwhile, the police might've heard of it and trace the call. A private detective wouldn't be likely to hear about it till he read it in the papers."

She laughed, then said, "And that was your luck."

"Luck? I don't know." He looked gloomily at the back of his left hand. "I hurt a knuckle stopping him and the job only lasted an afternoon. Chances are whoever's handling the estate'll raise hobs if I send them a bill for any decent amount of money." He raised a hand to attract the waiter's attention. "Oh, well, better luck next time. Want to catch a movie or have you got something else to do?"

The Pencil

Raymond Chandler

HE WAS A slightly fat man with a dishonest smile that pulled the corners of his mouth out half an inch leaving the thick lips tight and his eyes bleak. For a fattish man he had a slow walk. Most fat men are brisk and light on their feet. He wore a gray herringbone suit and a handpainted tie with part of a diving girl visible on it. His shirt was clean, which comforted me, and his brown loafers, as wrong as the tie for his suit, shone from a recent polishing.

He sidled past me as I held the door between the waiting room and my thinking parlor. Once inside, he took a quick look around. I'd have placed him as a mobster, second grade, if I had been asked. For once I was right. If he carried a gun, it was inside his pants. His coat was too tight to hide the bulge of an underarm holster.

He sat down carefully and I sat opposite and we looked at each other. His face had a

378

sort of foxy eagerness. He was sweating a little. The expression on my face was meant to be interested but not clubby. I reached for a pipe and the leather humidor in which I kept my Pearce's tobacco. I pushed the cigarettes at him.

"I don't smoke." He had a rusty voice. I didn't like it any more than I liked his clothes, or his face. While I filled the pipe he reached inside his coat, prowled in a pocket, came out with a bill, glanced at it, and dropped it across the desk in front of me. It was a nice bill and clean and new. One thousand dollars.

"Ever save a guy's life?"

"Once in a while, maybe."

"Save mine."

"What goes?"

"I heard you leveled with the customers, Marlowe."

"That's why I stay poor."

"I still got two friends. You make it three and you'll be out of the red. You got five grand coming if you pry me loose."

"From what?"

"You're talkative as hell this morning. Don't you pipe who I am?"

"Nope."

"Never been east, huh?"

"Sure — but I wasn't in your set."

"What set would that be?"

I was getting tired of it. "Stop being so damn cagey or pick up your grand and be missing."

"I'm Ikky Rossen. I'll be missing but good unless you can figure something out. Guess."

"I've already guessed. You tell me and tell me quick. I don't have all day to watch you feeding me with an eye-dropper."

"I ran out on the Outfit. The high boys don't go for that. To them it means you got info you figure you can peddle, or you got independent ideas, or you lost your moxie. Me, I lost my moxie. I had it up to here." He touched his Adam's apple with the forefinger of a stretched hand. "I done bad things. I scared and hurt guys. I never killed nobody. That's nothing to the Outfit. I'm out of line. So they pick up the pencil and they draw a line. I got the word. The operators are on the way. I made a bad mistake. I tried to hole up in Vegas. I figured they'd never expect me to lie up in their own joint. They outfigured me. What I did's been done before, but I didn't know it. When I took the plane to L.A. there must have been somebody on it. They know where I live."

"Move."

"No good now. I'm covered."

I knew he was right.

"Why haven't they taken care of you already?"

"They don't do it that way. Always specialists. Don't you know how it works?"

"More or less. A guy with a nice hardware

store in Buffalo. A guy with a small dairy in K.C. Always a good front. They report back to New York or somewhere. When they mount the plane west or wherever they're going, they have guns in their brief cases. They're quiet and well-dressed and they don't sit together. They could be a couple of lawyers or income-tax sharpies — anything at all that's well-mannered and inconspicuous. All sorts of people carry brief cases. Including women."

"Correct as hell. And when they land they'll be steered to me, but not from the airfield. They got ways. If I go to the cops, somebody will know about me. They could have a couple Mafia boys right on the City Council for all I know. The cops will give me twenty-four hours to leave town. No use. Mexico? Worse than here. Canada? Better but still no good. Connections there too."

"Australia?"

"Can't get a passport. I been here twenty-five years — illegal. They can't deport me unless they can prove a crime on me. The Outfit would see they didn't. Suppose I got tossed into the freezer. I'm out on a writ in twenty-four hours. And my nice friends got a car waiting to take me home — only not home."

I had my pipe lit and going well. I frowned down at the one-grand note. I could use it very nicely. My checking account could kiss the sidewalk without stooping.

"Let's stop horsing," I said. "Suppose — just suppose — I could figure an out for you. What's your next move?"

"I know a place — if I could get there without bein' tailed. I'd leave my car here and take a rent car. I'd turn it in just short of the county line and buy a secondhand job. Halfway to where I'm going I trade it on a new last-year's model, a leftover — this is just the right time of year. Good discount, new models out soon. Not to save money — less show off. Where I'd go is a good-sized place but still pretty clean."

"Uh-huh," I said. "Wichita, last I heard. But it might have changed."

He scowled at me. "Get smart, Marlowe, but not too damn smart."

"I'll get as smart as I want to. Don't try to make rules for me. If I take this on, there aren't any rules. I take it for this grand and the rest if I bring it off. Don't cross me. I might leak information. If I get knocked off, put just one red rose on my grave. I don't like cut flowers. I like to see them growing. But I could take one, because you're such a sweet character. When's the plane in?"

"Sometime today. It's nine hours from New York. Probably come in about 5:30 p.m."

"Might come by San Diego and switch or by San Francisco and switch. A lot of planes from both places. I need a helper."

"Damn you, Marlowe —"

"Hold it. I know a girl. Daughter of a Chief of Police who got broken for honesty. She wouldn't leak under torture."

"You got no right to risk her," Ikky said angrily.

I was so astonished my jaw hung halfway to my waist. I closed it slowly and swallowed.

"Good God, the man's got a heart."

"Women ain't built for the rough stuff," he said grudgingly.

I picked up the thousand-dollar note and snapped it. "Sorry. No receipt," I said. "I can't have my name in your pocket. And there won't be any rough stuff if I'm lucky. They'd have me outclassed. There's only one way to work it. Now give me your address and all the dope you can think of — names, descriptions of any operators you have ever seen in the flesh."

He did. He was a pretty good observer. Trouble was, the Outfit would know what he had seen. The operators would be strangers to him.

He got up silently and put his hand out. I had to shake it, but what he had said about women made it easier. His hand was moist. Mine would have been in his spot. He nodded and went out silently.

It was a quiet street in Bay City, if there are any quiet streets in this beatnik generation when you can't get through a meal without some male or female stomach-singer belching out a kind of love that is as old-fashioned as a bustle or some Hammond organ jazzing it up in the customer's soup.

The little one-story house was as neat as a fresh pinafore. The front lawn was cut lovingly and very green. The smooth composition driveway was free of grease spots from standing cars, and the hedge that bordered it looked as though the barber came every day.

The white door had a knocker with a tiger's head, a go-to-hell window, and a dingus that let someone inside talk to someone outside without even opening the little window.

I'd have given a mortgage on my left leg to live in a house like that. I didn't think I ever would.

The bell chimed inside and after a while she opened the door in a pale-blue sports shirt and white shorts that were short enough to be friendly. She had gray-blue eyes, dark red hair, and fine bones in her face. There was usually a trace of bitterness in the gray-blue eyes. She couldn't forget that her father's life had been destroyed by the crooked power of a gambling-ship mobster, that her mother had died too.

She was able to suppress the bitterness when she wrote nonsense about young love for the shiny magazines, but this wasn't her life. She didn't really have a life. She had an existence without much pain and enough money to make it safe. But in a tight spot she was as cool and resourceful as a good cop. Her name was Anne Riordan.

She stood to one side and I passed her pretty close. But I have rules too. She shut the door and parked herself on a sofa and went through the cigarette routine, and here was one doll who had the strength to light her own cigarette.

I stood looking around. There were a few changes, not many.

"I need your help," I said.

"The only time I ever see you."

"I've got a client who is an ex-hood, used to be a troubleshooter for the Outfit, the Syndicate, the big mob, or whatever name you want to use for it. You know damn well it exists and is as rich as Midas. You can't beat it because not enough people want to, especially the million-a-year lawyers who work for it."

"My God, are you running for office somewhere? I never heard you sound so pure."

She moved her legs around, not provocatively — she wasn't the type — but it made it difficult for me to think straight just the same.

"Stop moving your legs around," I said. "Or put a pair of slacks on."

"Damn you, Marlowe. Can't you think of anything else?"

"I'll try. I like to think that I know at least one pretty and charming female who doesn't have round heels." I swallowed and went on. "The man's name is Ikky Rossen. He's not beautiful and he's not anything that I like — except one thing. He got mad when I said I needed a girl helper. He said women were not made for the rough stuff. That's why I took the job. To a real mobster, a woman means no more than a sack of flour. They use women in the usual way, but if it's advisable to get rid of them they do it without a second thought."

"So far you've told me a whole lot of nothing. Perhaps you need a cup of coffee or a drink."

"You're sweet but I don't in the morning — except sometimes, and this isn't one of them. Coffee later. Ikky has been penciled."

"Now what's that?"

"You have a list. You draw a line through a name with a pencil. The guy is as good as dead. The Outfit has reasons. They don't do it just for kicks any more. They don't get any kick. It's just bookkeeping to them."

"What on earth can I do? I might even have said, what can *you* do?"

"I can try. What you can do is help me spot their plane and see where they go — the operators assigned to the job."

"Yes, but how can you do anything?"

"I said I could try. If they took a night plane

they are already here. If they took a morning plane they can't be here before five or so. Plenty of time to get set. You know what they look like?"

"Oh, sure. I meet killers every day. I have them in for whiskey sours and caviar on hot toast." She grinned. While she was grinning I took four long steps across the tan-figured rug and lifted her and put a kiss on her mouth. She didn't fight me but she didn't go all trembly either. I went back and sat down.

"They'll look like anybody who's in a quiet well-run business or profession. They'll have quiet clothes and they'll be polite — when they want to be. They'll have brief cases with guns in them that have changed hands so often they can't possibly be traced. When and if they do the job, they'll drop the guns. They'll probably use revolvers, but they could use automatics. They won't use silencers because silencers can jam a gun and the weight makes it hard to shoot accurately. They won't sit together on the plane, but once off of it they may pretend to know each other and simply not have noticed during the flight. They may shake hands with appropriate smiles and walk away and get in the same taxi. I think they'll go in the same taxi. I think they'll go to a hotel first. But very soon they will move into something from which they can watch Ikky's movements and get used to his schedule. They won't be in a hurry unless

Ikky makes a move. That would tip them off that Ikky has been tipped off. He has a couple of friends left — he says."

"Will they shoot him from this room or apartment across the street — assuming there is one?"

"No. They'll shoot him from three feet away. They'll walk up behind and say 'Hello, Ikky.' He'll either freeze or turn. They'll fill him with lead, drop the guns, and hop into the car they have waiting. Then they'll follow the crash car off the scene."

"Who'll drive the crash car?"

"Some well-fixed and blameless citizen who hasn't been rapped. He'll drive his own car. He'll clear the way, even if he has to accidentally on purpose crash somebody, even a police car. He'll be so damn sorry he'll cry all the way down his monogrammed shirt. And the killers will be long gone."

"Good heavens," Anne said. "How can you stand your life? If you did bring it off, they'll send operators after you."

"I don't think so. They don't kill a legit. The blame will go to the operators. Remember, these top mobsters are businessmen. They want lots and lots of money. They only get really tough when they figure they have to get rid of somebody, and they don't crave that. There's always a chance of a slipup. Not much of a chance. No gang killing has ever been solved here or anywhere else except two or three times. The top mobster is awful big and awful tough. When he gets too big, too tough — pencil."

She shuddered a little. "I think I need a drink myself."

I grinned at her. "You're right in the atmosphere, darling. I'll weaken."

She brought a couple of Scotch highballs. When we were drinking them I said, "If you spot them or think you spot them, follow to where they go — if you can do it safely. Not otherwise. If it's a hotel — and ten to one it will be — check in and keep calling me until you get me."

She knew my office number and I was still on Yucca Avenue. She knew that too.

"You're the damndest guy," she said. "Women do anything you want them to. How come I'm still a virgin at twenty-eight?"

"We need a few like you. Why don't you get married?"

"To what? Some cynical chaser who has nothing left? I don't know any really nice men — except you. I'm no pushover for white teeth and a gaudy smile."

I went over and pulled her to her feet. I kissed her long and hard. "I'm honest," I almost whispered. "That's something. But I'm too shop-soiled for a girl like you. I've thought of you, I've wanted you, but that sweet clear look in your eyes tells me to lay off."

"Take me," she said softly. "I have dreams too."

"I couldn't. I've had too many women to deserve one like you. We have to save a man's life. I'm going."

She stood up and watched me leave with a grave face.

The women you get and the women you don't get — they live in different worlds. I don't sneer at either world. I live in both myself.

At Los Angeles International Airport you can't get close to the planes unless you're leaving on one. You see them land, if you happen to be in the right place, but you have to wait at a barrier to get a look at the passengers. The airport buildings don't make it any easier. They are strung out from here to breakfast time, and you can get calluses walking from TWA to American.

I copied an arrival schedule off the boards and prowled around like a dog that has forgotten where he put his bone. Planes came in, planes took off, porters carried luggage, passengers sweated and scurried, children whined, the loudspeaker overrode all the other noises.

I passed Anne a number of times. She took no notice of me.

At 5:45 they must have come. Anne disappeared. I gave it half an hour, just in case she had some other reason for fading. No. She was gone for good. I went out to my car and drove some long crowded miles to Hollywood and my office. I had a drink and sat. At 6:45 the phone rang.

"I think so," she said. "Beverly-Western Hotel. Room 410. I couldn't get any names. You know the clerks don't leave registration cards lying around these days. I didn't like to ask any questions. But I rode up in the elevator with them and spotted their room. I walked right on past them when the bellman put a key in their door, and went down to the mezzanine and then downstairs with a bunch of women from the tea room. I didn't bother to take a room."

"What were they like?"

"They came up the ramp together but I didn't hear them speak. Both had brief cases, both wore quiet suits, nothing flashy. White shirts, starched, one blue tie, one black striped with gray. Black shoes. A couple of businessmen from the East Coast. They could be publishers, lawyers, doctors, account executives — no, cut the last; they weren't gaudy enough. You wouldn't look at them twice."

"Faces?"

"Both medium-brown hair, one a bit darker than the other. Smooth faces, rather expressionless. One had gray eyes, the one with the lighter hair had blue eyes. Their eyes were interesting. Very quick to move, very observant, watching everything near them. That might have been wrong. They should have been a bit preoccupied with what they came out for or interested in California. They seemed more occupied with faces. It's a good thing I spotted them and not you. You don't look like a cop, but you don't look like a man who is not a cop. You have marks on you."

"Phooey. I'm a damn good-looking heart wrecker."

"Their features were strictly assembly line. Each picked up a flight suitcase. One suitcase was gray with two red and white stripes up and down, about six or seven inches from the ends, the other a blue and white tartan. I didn't know there was such a tartan."

"There is, but I forget the name of it."

"I thought you knew everything."

"Just almost everything. Run along home now."

"Do I get a dinner and maybe a kiss?"

"Later, and if you're not careful you'll get more than you want."

"You'll take over and follow them?"

"If they're the right men, they'll follow me. I already took an apartment across the street from Ikky — that block on Poynter with six lowlife apartment houses on the block. I'll bet the incidence of chippies is very high."

"It's high everywhere these days."

"So long, Anne. See you."

"When you need help."

She hung up. I hung up. She puzzles me. Too wise to be so nice. I guess all nice women are wise too.

I called Ikky. He was out. I had a drink from the office bottle, smoked for half an hour, and called again. This time I got him.

I told him the score up to then, and said I hoped Anne had picked the right men. I told him about the apartment I had taken.

"Do I get expenses?" I asked.

"Five grand ought to cover the lot."

"If I earn it and get it. I heard you had a quarter of a million," I said in a wild venture.

"Could be, pal, but how do I get at it? The high boys know where it is. It'll have to cool a long time."

I said that was all right. I had cooled a long time myself. Of course, I didn't expect to get the other four thousand, even if I brought the job off. Men like Ikky Rossen would steal their mother's gold teeth. There seemed to be a little good in him somewhere — but little was the operative word.

I spent the next half hour trying to think of a plan. I couldn't think of one that looked promising. It was almost eight o'clock and I needed food. I didn't think the boys would move that night. Next morning they would drive past Ikky's place and scout the neighborhood.

I was ready to leave the office when the buzzer sounded from the door of my waiting room. I opened the communicating door. A small tight-looking man was standing in the middle of the floor rocking on his heels with his hands behind his back. He smiled at me, but he wasn't good at it. He walked toward me.

"You Philip Marlowe?"

"Who else? What can I do for you?"

He was close now. He brought his right hand around fast with a gun in it. He stuck the gun in my stomach.

"You can lay off Ikky Rossen," he said in a voice that matched his face, "or you can get your belly full of lead."

He was an amateur. If he had stayed four feet away, he might have had something. I reached up and took the cigarette out of my mouth and held it carelessly.

"What makes you think I know any Ikky Rossen?"

He laughed and pushed his gun into my stomach.

"Wouldn't you like to know!" The cheap sneer, the empty triumph of that feeling of power when you hold a fat gun in a small hand.

"It would be fair to tell me."

As his mouth opened for another crack, I dropped the cigarette and swept a hand. I can be fast when I have to. There are boys that are faster, but they don't stick guns in your stomach.

I got my thumb behind the trigger and my hand over his. I kneed him in the groin. He bent over with a whimper. I twisted his arm to the right and I had his gun. I hooked a heel behind his heel and he was on the floor.

He lay there blinking with surprise and pain, his knees drawn up against his stomach. He rolled from side to side groaning. I reached down and grabbed his left hand and yanked him to his feet. I had six inches and forty pounds on him. They ought to have sent a bigger, better trained messenger.

"Let's go into my thinking parlor," I said. "We could have a chat and you could have a drink to pick you up. Next time don't get near enough to a prospect for him to get your gun hand. I'll just see if you have any more iron on you."

He hadn't. I pushed him through the door and into a chair. His breath wasn't quite so rasping. He grabbed out a handkerchief and mopped his face.

"Next time," he said between his teeth. "Next time."

"Don't be an optimist. You don't look the part."

I poured him a drink of Scotch in a paper cup, set it down in front of him. I broke his .38 and dumped the cartridges into the desk drawer. I clicked the chamber back and laid the gun down.

"You can have it when you leave — if you leave."

"That's a dirty way to fight," he said, still gasping.

"Sure. Shooting a man is so much cleaner. Now, how did you get here?"

"Nuts."

"Don't be a fool. I have friends. Not many, but some. I can get you for armed assault, and you know what would happen then. You'd be out on a writ or on bail and that's the last anyone would hear of you. The biggies don't go for failures. Now who sent you and how did you know where to come?"

"Ikky was covered," he said sullenly. "He's dumb. I trailed him here without no trouble at all. Why would he go see a private eye? People want to know."

"More."

"Go to hell."

"Come to think of it, I don't have to get you for armed assault. I can smash it out of you right here and now."

I got up from the chair and he put out a flat hand.

"If I get knocked about, a couple of real tough monkeys will drop around. If I don't report back, same thing. You ain't holding no real high cards. They just look high," he said.

"You haven't anything to tell. If this Ikky came to see me, you don't know why, nor whether I took him on. If he's a mobster, he's not my type of client."

"He come to get you to try and save his hide."

"Who from?"

"That'd be talking."

"Go right ahead. Your mouth seems to work fine. And tell the boys any time I front for a hood, that will be the day."

You have to lie a little once in a while in my business. I was lying a little. "What's Ikky done to get himself disliked? Or would that be talking?"

"You think you're a lot of man," he sneered, rubbing the place where I had kneed him. "In my league you wouldn't make pinch runner."

I laughed in his face. Then I grabbed his right wrist and twisted it behind his back. He began to squawk. I reached into his breast pocket with my left hand and hauled out a wallet. I let him go. He reached for his gun on the desk and I bisected his upper arm with a hard cut. He fell into the customer's chair and grunted.

"You can have your gun," I told him. "When I give it to you. Now be good or I'll have to bounce you just to amuse myself."

In the wallet I found a driver's license made out to Charles Hickon. It did me no good at all. Punks of his type always have slangy aliases. They probably called him Tiny, or

397

Slim, or Marbles, or even just "you." I tossed the wallet back to him. It fell to the floor. He couldn't even catch it.

"Hell," I said, "there must be an economy campaign on, if they send you to do more than pick up cigarette butts."

"Nuts."

"All right, mug. Beat it back to the laundry. Here's your gun."

He took it, made a business of shoving it into his waistband, stood up, gave me as dirty a look as he had in stock, and strolled to the door, nonchalant as a hustler with a new mink stole.

He turned at the door and gave me the beady eye. "Stay clean, tinhorn. Tin bends easy."

With this blinding piece of repartee he opened the door and drifted out.

After a little while I locked my other door, cut the buzzer, made the office dark, and left. I saw no one who looked like a lifetaker. I drove to my house, packed a suitcase, drove to a service station where they were almost fond of me, stored my car, and picked up a rental Chevrolet.

I drove this to Poynter Street, dumping my suitcase in the sleazy apartment I had rented early in the afternoon, and went to dinner at Victor's. It was nine o'clock, too late to drive to Bay City and take Anne to dinner.

I ordered a double Gibson with fresh limes

and drank it, and I was as hungry as a schoolboy.

On the way back to Poynter Street I did a good deal of weaving in and out and circling blocks and stopping, with a gun on the seat beside me. As far as I could tell, no one was trying to tail me.

I stopped on Sunset at a service station and made two calls from the box. I caught Bernie Ohls just as he was leaving to go home.

"This is Marlowe, Bernie. We haven't had a fight in years. I'm getting lonely."

"Well, get married. I'm chief investigator for the Sheriff's Office now. I rank acting captain until I pass the exam. I don't hardly speak to private eyes."

"Speak to this one. I need help. I'm on a ticklish job where I could get killed."

"And you expect me to interfere with the course of nature?"

"Come off it, Bernie. I haven't been a bad guy. I'm trying to save an ex-mobster from a couple of executioners."

"The more they mow each other down, the better I like it."

"Yeah. If I call you, come running or send a couple of good boys. You'll have had time to teach them."

We exchanged a couple of mild insults and hung up. I dialed Ikky Rossen's number. His rather unpleasant voice said, "Okay, talk."

"Marlowe. Be ready to move out about

midnight. We've spotted your boy friends and they are holed up at the Beverly-Western. They won't move to your street tonight. Remember, they don't know you've been tipped."

"Sounds chancy."

"Good God, it wasn't meant to be a Sunday School picnic. You've been careless, Ikky. You were followed to my office. That cuts the time we have."

He was silent for a moment. I heard him breathing. "Who by?" he asked.

"Some little tweezer who stuck a gun in my belly and gave me the trouble of taking it away from him. I can only figure they sent a punk on the theory they don't want me to know too much, in case I don't know it already."

"You're in for trouble, friend."

"When not? I'll come over to your place about midnight. Be ready. Where's your car?"

"Out front."

"Get it on a side street and make a business of locking it up. Where's the back door to your flop?"

"In back. Where would it be? On the alley."

"Leave your suitcase there. We walk out together and go to your car. We drive by the alley and pick up the suitcase or cases."

"Suppose some guy steals them?"

"Yeah. Suppose you get dead. Which do you like better?"

"Okay," he grunted. "I'm waiting. But we're taking big chances."

"So do race drivers. Does that stop them? There's no way to get out but fast. Douse your lights about ten and rumple the bed well. It would be good if you could leave some baggage behind. Wouldn't look so planned."

He grunted okay and I hung up. The telephone box was well lighted outside. They usually are in service stations. I took a good long gander around while I pawed over the collection of giveaway maps inside the station. I saw nothing to worry me. I took a map of San Diego just for the hell of it and got into my rented car.

On Poynter I parked around the corner and went up to my second-floor sleazy apartment and sat in the dark watching from my window. I saw nothing to worry about. A couple of medium-class chippies came out of Ikky's apartment house and were picked up in a late-model car. A man about Ikky's height and build went into the apartment house. Various other people came and went. The street was fairly quiet. Since they put in the Hollywood Freeway nobody uses the off-the-boulevard streets unless they live in the neighborhood.

It was a nice fall night — or as nice as they get in Los Angeles' climate — clearish but not even crisp. I don't know what's happened

401

to the weather in our overcrowded city, but it's not the weather I knew when I came to it.

It seemed like a long time to midnight. I couldn't spot anybody watching anything, and no couple of quiet-suited men paged any of the six apartment houses available. I was pretty sure they'd try mine first when they came, but I wasn't sure if Anne had picked the right men, and if the tweezer's message back to his bosses had done me any good or otherwise.

In spite of the hundred ways Anne could be wrong, I had a hunch she was right. The killers had no reason to be cagey if they didn't know Ikky had been warned. No reason but one. He had come to my office and been tailed there. But the Outfit, with all its arrogance of power, might laugh at the idea he had been tipped off or come to me for help. I was so small they would hardly be able to see me.

At midnight I left the apartment, walked two blocks watching for a tail, crossed the street, and went into Ikky's dive. There was no locked door, and no elevator. I climbed steps to the third floor and looked for his apartment. I knocked lightly. He opened the door with a gun in his hand. He probably looked scared.

There were two suitcases by the door and another against the far wall. I went over a lifted it. It was heavy enough. I opened it —

it was unlocked.

"You don't have to worry," he said. "It's got everything a guy could need for three-four nights, and nothing except some clothes that I couldn't glom off in any ready-to-wear place."

I picked up one of the other suitcases. "Let's stash this by the back door."

"We can leave by the alley too."

"We leave by the front door. Just in case we're covered — though I don't think so — we're just two guys going out together. Just one thing. Keep both hands in your coat pockets and the gun in your right. If anybody calls out your name behind you turn fast and shoot. Nobody but a lifetaker will do it. I'll do the same."

"I'm scared," he said in his rusty voice.

"Me too, if it helps any. But we have to do it. If you're braced they'll have guns in their hands. Don't bother asking them questions. They wouldn't answer in words. If it's just my small friend, we'll cool him and dump him inside the door. Got it?"

He nodded, licking his lips. We carried the suitcases down and put them outside the back door. I looked along the alley. Nobody, and only a short distance to the side street. We went back in and along the hall to the front. We walked out on Poynter Street with all the casualness of a wife buying her husband a birthday tie.

Nobody made a move. The street was empty.

We walked around the corner to Ikky's rented car. He unlocked it. I went back with him for the suitcases. Not a stir. We put the suitcases in the car and started up and drove to the next street.

A traffic light not working, a boulevard stop or two, the entrance to the Freeway. There was plenty of traffic on it even at midnight. California is loaded with people going places and making speed to get there. If you don't drive eighty miles an hour, everybody passes you. If you do, you have to watch the rear-view mirror for highway patrol cars. It's the rat race of rat races.

Ikky did a quiet seventy. We reached the junction to Route 66 and he took it. So far nothing. I stayed with him to Pomona.

"This is far enough for me," I said. "I'll grab a bus back if there is one, or park myself in a motel. Drive to a service station and we'll ask for the bus stop. It should be close to the Freeway."

He did that and stopped midway on a block. He reached for his pocketbook and held out four thousand-dollar bills.

"I don't really feel I've earned all that. It was too easy."

He laughed with a kind of wry amusement on his pudgy face. "Don't be a sap. I have it made. You didn't know what you was walking into. What's more, your troubles are just beginning. The Outfit has eyes and ears everywhere. Perhaps I'm safe if I'm damn careful. Perhaps I ain't as safe as I think I am. Either way, you did what I asked. Take the dough. I got plenty."

I took it and put it away. He drove to an all-night service station and we were told where to find the bus stop. "There's a cross-country Greyhound at 2:25 a.m.," the attendant said, looking at a schedule. "They'll take you, if they got room."

Ikky drove to the bus stop. We shook hands and he went gunning down the road toward the Freeway. I looked at my watch and found a liquor store still open and bought a pint of Scotch. Then I found a bar and ordered a double with water.

My troubles were just beginning, Ikky had said. He was so right.

I got off at the Hollywood bus station, grabbed a taxi, and drove to my office. I asked the driver to wait a few moments. At that time of night he was glad to. The night man let me into the building.

"You work late, Mr. Marlowe. But you always did, didn't you?"

"It's that sort of business," I said. "Thanks, Jimmy."

Up in my office I pawed the floor for mail and found nothing but a longish narrowish box, Special Delivery, with a Glendale postmark.

It contained nothing at all but a freshly sharpened pencil — the mobster's mark of death.

I didn't take it too hard. When they mean it, they don't send it to you. I took it as a sharp warning to lay off. There might be a beating arranged. From their point of view, that would be good discipline. "When we pencil a guy, any guy that tries to help him is in for a smashing." That could be the message.

I thought of going to my house on Yucca Avenue. Too lonely. I thought of going to Anne's place in Bay City. Worse. If they got wise to her, real hoods would think nothing of beating her up too.

It was the Poynter Street flop for me — easily the safest place now. I went down to the waiting taxi and had him drive me to within three blocks of the so-called apartment house. I went upstairs, undressed, and slept raw. Nothing bothered me but a broken spring — that bothered my back.

I lay until 3:30 pondering the situation with my massive brain. I went to sleep with a gun under the pillow, which is a bad place to keep a gun when you have one pillow as thick and soft as a typewriter pad. It bothered me, so I transferred it to my right hand. Practice had taught me to keep it there even in sleep.

I woke up with the sun shining. I felt like

a piece of spoiled meat. I struggled into the bathroom and doused myself with cold water and wiped off with a towel you couldn't have seen if you held it sideways. This was a really gorgeous apartment. All it needed was a set of Chippendale furniture to be graduated into the slum class.

There was nothing to eat and if I went out, Miss-Nothing Marlowe might miss something. I had a pint of whiskey. I looked at it and smelled it, but I couldn't take it for breakfast on an empty stomach, even if I could reach my stomach, which was floating around near the ceiling.

I looked into the closets in case a previous tenant might have left a crust of bread in a hasty departure. Nope. I wouldn't have liked it anyhow, not even with whiskey on it. So I sat at the window. An hour of that and I was ready to bite a piece off a bellhop's arm.

I dressed and went around the corner to the rented car and drove to an eatery. The waitress was sore too. She swept a cloth over the counter in front of me and let me have the last customer's crumbs in my lap.

"Look, sweetness," I said, "don't be so generous. Save the crumbs for a rainy day. All I want is two eggs three minutes — no more — a slice of your famous concrete toast, a tall glass of tomato juice with a dash of Lee and Perrins, a big happy smile, and don't give anybody else any coffee. I might need it all."

"I got a cold," she said. "Don't push me around. I might crack you one on the kisser."

"Let's be pals. I had a rough night too."

She gave me a half smile and went through the swing door sideways. It showed more of her curves, which were ample, even excessive. But I got the eggs the way I liked them. The toast had been painted with melted butter past its bloom.

"No Lee and Perrins," she said, putting down the tomato juice. "How about a little Tabasco? We're fresh out of arsenic too."

I used two drops of Tabasco, swallowed the eggs, drank two cups of coffee, and was about to leave the toast for a tip, but I went soft and left a quarter instead. That really brightened her. It was a joint where you left a dime or nothing. Mostly nothing.

Back on Poynter Street nothing had changed. I got to my window again and sat. At about 8:30 the man I had seen go into the apartment house across the way — the one about the same height and build as Ikky — came out with a small brief case and turned east. Two men got out of a dark-blue sedan. They were of the same height and very quietly dressed and had soft hats pulled low over their foreheads. Each jerked out a revolver.

"Hey, Ikky!" one of them called out.

The man turned. "So long, Ikky," the other man said.

Gunfire racketed between the houses. The

408

man crumpled and lay motionless. The two men rushed for their car and were off, going west. Halfway down the block I saw a limousine pull out and start ahead of them.

In no time at all they were completely gone.

It was a nice swift clean job. The only thing wrong with it was that they hadn't given it enough time for preparation.

They had shot the wrong man.

I got out of there fast, almost as fast as the two killers. There was a smallish crowd grouped around the dead man. I didn't have to look at him to know he was dead — the boys were pros. Where he lay on the sidewalk on the other side of the street I couldn't see him — people were in the way. But I knew just how he would look and I already heard sirens in the distance. It could have been just the routine shrieking from Sunset, but it wasn't. So somebody had telephoned. It was too early for the cops to be going to lunch.

I strolled around the corner with my suitcase and jammed into the rented car and beat it away from there. The neighborhood was not my piece of shortcake any more. I could imagine the questions.

"Just what took you over there, Marlowe? You got a flop of your own, ain't you?"

"I was hired by an ex-mobster in trouble with the Outfit. They'd sent killers after him!"

"Don't tell us he was trying to go straight."

"I don't know. But I liked his money."

"Didn't do much to earn it, did you?"

"I got him away last night. I don't know where he is now, and I don't want to know."

"You got him away?"

"That's what I said."

"Yeah — only he's in the morgue with multiple bullet wounds. Try something better. Or somebody's in the morgue."

And on and on. Policeman's dialogue. It comes out of an old shoebox. What they say doesn't mean anything, what they ask doesn't mean anything. They just keep boring in until you are so exhausted you flip on some detail. Then they smile happily and rub their hands, and say, "Kind of careless there, weren't you? Let's start all over again."

The less I had of that, the better. I parked in my usual parking slot and went up to the office. It was full of nothing but stale air. Every time I went into the dump I felt more and more tired. Why the hell hadn't I got myself a government job ten years ago? Make it fifteen years. I had brains enough to get a mail-order law degree. The country's full of lawyers who couldn't write a complaint without the book.

So I sat in my office chair and disadmired myself. After a while I remembered the pencil. I made certain arrangements with a .45 gun, more gun that I ever carry — too much weight. I dialed the Sheriff's Office and asked for Bernie Ohls. I got him. His voice was sour.

"Marlowe. I'm in trouble — real trouble," I said.

"Why tell me?" he growled. "You must be used to it by now."

"This kind of trouble you don't get used to. I'd like to come over and tell you."

"You in the same office?"

"The same."

"Have to go over that way. I'll drop in."

He hung up. I opened two windows. The gentle breeze wafted a smell of coffee and stale fat to me from Joe's Eats next door. I hated it, I hated myself, I hated everything.

Ohls didn't bother with my elegant waiting room. He rapped on my own door and I let him in. He scowled his way to the customer's chair.

"Okay. Give."

"Ever hear of a character named Ikky Rossen?"

"Why would I? Record?"

"An ex-mobster who got disliked by the mob. They put a pencil through his name and sent the usual two tough boys on a plane. He got tipped and hired me to help him get away."

"Nice clean work."

"Cut it out, Bernie." I lit a cigarette and blew smoke in his face. In retaliation he began to chew a cigarette. He never lit one, but he certainly mangled them.

"Look," I went on. "Suppose the man wants to go straight and suppose he doesn't. He's entitled to his life as long as he hasn't killed anyone. He told me he hadn't."

"And you believed the hood, huh? When do you start teaching Sunday School?"

"I neither believed him nor disbelieved him. I took him on. There was no reason not to. A girl I know and I watched the planes yesterday. She spotted the boys and tailed them to a hotel. She was sure of what they were. They looked it right down to their black shoes. This girl —"

"Would she have a name?"

"Only for you."

"I'll buy, if she hasn't cracked any laws."

"Her name is Anne Riordan. She lives in Bay City. Her father was once Chief of Police there. And don't say that makes him a crook, because he wasn't."

"Uh-huh. Let's have the rest. Make a little time too."

"I took an apartment opposite Ikky. The killers were still at the hotel. At midnight I got Ikky out and drove with him as far as Pomona. He went on in his rented car and I came back by Greyhound. I moved into the apartment on Poynter Street, right across from his dump."

"Why — if he was already gone?"

I opened the middle desk drawer and took

out the nice sharp pencil. I wrote my name on a piece of paper and ran the pencil through it.

"Because someone sent me this. I didn't think they'd kill me, but I thought they planned to give me enough of a beating to warn me off any more pranks."

"They knew you were in on it?"

"Ikky was tailed here by a little squirt who later came around and stuck a gun in my stomach. I knocked him around a bit, but I had to let him go. I thought Poynter Street was safer after that. I live lonely."

"I get around," Bernie Ohls said. "I hear reports. So they gunned the wrong guy."

"Same height, same build, same general appearance. I saw them gun him. I couldn't tell if it was the two guys from the Beverly-Western. I'd never seen them. It was just two guys in dark suits with hats pulled down. They jumped into a blue Pontiac sedan, about two years old, and lammed off, with a big Caddy running crash for them."

Bernie stood up and stared at me for a long moment. "I don't think they'll bother with you now," he said. "They've hit the wrong guy. The mob will be very quiet for a while. You know something? This town is getting to be almost as lousy as New York, Brooklyn, and Chicago. We could end up real corrupt."

"We've made a hell of a good start."

"You haven't told me anything that makes

me take action, Phil. I'll talk to the city homicide boys. I don't guess you're in any trouble. But you saw the shooting. They'll want that."

"I couldn't identify anybody, Bernie. I didn't know the man who was shot. How did *you* know it was the wrong man?"

"You told me, stupid."

"I thought perhaps the city boys had a make on him."

"They wouldn't tell me, if they had. Besides, they ain't hardly had time to go out for breakfast. He's just a stiff in the morgue to them until the ID comes up with something. But they'll want to talk to you, Phil. They just love their tape recorders."

He went out and the door whooshed shut behind him. I sat there wondering if I had been a dope to talk to him. Or to take on Ikky's troubles. Five thousand green men said no. But they can be wrong too.

Somebody banged on my door. It was a uniform holding a telegram. I receipted for it and tore it loose.

It said: ON MY WAY TO FLAGSTAFF. MIRADOR MOTOR COURT. THINK I'VE BEEN SPOTTED. COME FAST.

I tore the wire into small pieces and burned them in my big ashtray.

I called Anne Riordan.

"Funny thing happened," I told her, and told her about the funny thing.

414

"I don't like the pencil," she said. "And I don't like the wrong man being killed — probably some poor bookkeeper in a cheap business or he wouldn't be living in that neighborhood. You should never have touched it, Phil."

"Ikky had a life. Where he's going he might make himself decent. He can change his name. He must be loaded or he wouldn't have paid me so much."

"I said I didn't like the pencil. You'd better come down here for a while. You can have your mail readdressed — if you get any mail. You don't have to work right away anyhow. And L.A. is oozing with private eyes."

"You don't get the point. I'm not through with the job. The city dicks have to know where I am, and if they do, all the crime reporters will know too. The cops might even decide to make me a suspect. Nobody who saw the shooting is going to put out a description that means anything. The American people know better than to be witnesses to gang killings."

"All right, but my offer stands."

The buzzer sounded in the outside room. I told Anne I had to hang up. I opened the communicating door and a well-dressed — I might say elegantly dressed — middle-aged man stood six feet inside the outer door. He had a pleasantly dishonest smile on his face. He wore a white Stetson and one of those

415

narrow ties that go through an ornamental buckle. His cream-colored flannel suit was beautifully tailored.

He lit a cigarette with a gold lighter and looked at me over the first puff of smoke.

"Mr. Philip Marlowe?"

I nodded.

"I'm Foster Grimes from Las Vegas. I run the Rancho Esperanza on South Fifth. I hear you got a little involved with a man named Ikky Rossen."

"Won't you come in?"

He strolled past me into my office. His appearance told me nothing — a prosperous man who liked or felt it good business to look a bit western. You see them by the dozen in the Palm Springs winter season. His accent told me he was an easterner, but not New England. New York or Baltimore, likely. Long Island, the Berkshires — no, too far from the city.

I showed him the customer's chair with a flick of the wrist and sat down in my antique swivelsqueaker. I waited.

"Where is Ikky now, if you know?"

"I don't know, Mr. Grimes."

"How come you messed with him?"

"Money."

"A damned good reason," he smiled. "How far did it go?"

"I helped him leave town. I'm telling you this, although I don't know who the hell you are, because I've already told an old friend-enemy of mine, a top man in the Sheriff's Office."

"What's a friend-enemy?"

"Law men don't go around kissing me, but I've known him for years, and we are as much friends as a private star can be with a law man."

"I told you who I was. We have a unique set-up in Vegas. We own the place except for one lousy newspaper editor who keeps climbing our backs and the backs of our friends. We let him live because letting him live makes us look better than knocking him off. Killings are not good business any more."

"Like Ikky Rossen."

"That's not a killing. It's an execution. Ikky got out of line."

"So your gun boys had to rub the wrong guy. They could have hung around a little to make sure."

"They would have, if you'd kept your nose where it belonged. They hurried. We don't appreciate that. We want cool efficiency."

"Who's this great big fat 'we' you keep talking about?"

"Don't go juvenile on me, Marlowe."

"Okay. Let's say I know."

"Here's what we want." He reached into his pocket and drew out a loose bill. He put it on the desk on his side. "Find Ikky and tell him to get back in line and everything is okay.

417

With an innocent bystander gunned, we don't want any trouble or any extra publicity. It's that simple. You get this now," he nodded at the bill. It was a grand. Probably the smallest bill they had. "And another when you find Ikky and give him the message. If he holds out — curtains."

"Suppose I say take your grand and blow your nose with it?"

"That would be unwise." He flipped out a Colt Woodsman with a short silencer on it. A Colt Woodsman will take one without jamming. He was fast too, fast and smooth. The genial expression on his face didn't change.

"I never left Vegas," he said calmly. "I can prove it. You're dead in your office chair and nobody knows anything. Just another private eye that tried the wrong pitch. Put your hands on the desk and think a little. Incidentally, I'm a crack shot even with this damned silencer."

I flipped the nicely sharpened pencil across to him. He grabbed for it after a swift change of the gun to his left hand — very swift. He held the pencil up so that he could look at it without taking his eyes off me.

I said, "It came to me by Special Delivery mail. No message, no return address. Just the pencil. Think I've never heard about the pencil, Mr. Grimes?"

He frowned and tossed the pencil down.

Before he could shift his long lithe gun back to his right hand I dropped mine under the desk and grabbed the butt of the .45 and put my finger hard on the trigger.

"Look under the desk, Mr. Grimes. You'll see a .45 in an open-end holster. It's fixed there and it's pointing at your belly. Even if you could shoot me through the heart, the .45 would still go off from a convulsive movement of my hand. And your belly would be hanging by a shred and you would be knocked out of that chair. A .45 slug can throw you back six feet. Even the movies learned that at last."

"Looks like a Mexican stand-off," he said quietly. He holstered his gun. He grinned. "Nice work, Marlowe. We could use a man like you. I suggest that you find Ikky and don't be a drip. He'll listen to reason. He doesn't really want to be on the run for the rest of his life."

"Tell me something, Mr. Grimes. Why pick on me? Apart from Ikky, what did I ever do to make you dislike me?"

Not moving, he thought a moment, or pretended to. "The Larsen case. You helped send one of our boys to the gas chamber. That we don't forget. We had you in mind as a fall guy for Ikky. You'll always be a fall guy, unless you play it our way. Something will hit you when you least expect it."

"A man in my business is always a fall guy,

Mr. Grimes. Pick up your grand and drift out quietly. I might decide to do it your way, but I have to think about it. As for the Larsen case, the cops did all the work. I just happened to know where he was. I don't guess you miss him terribly."

"We don't like interference." He stood up. He put the grand note casually back in his pocket. While he was doing it I let go of the .45 and jerked out my Smith and Wesson five-inch .38.

He looked at it contemptuously. "I'll be in Vegas, Marlowe — in fact, I never left Vegas. You can catch me at the Esperanza. No, we don't give a damn about Larsen personally. Just another gun handler. They come in gross lots. We *do* give a damn that some punk private eye fingered him."

He nodded and went out by my office door.

I did some pondering. I knew Ikky wouldn't go back to the Outfit. He wouldn't trust them enough even if he got the chance. But there was another reason now. I called Anne Riordan again.

"I'm going to look for Ikky. I have to. If I don't call you in three days, get hold of Bernie Ohls. I'm going to Flagstaff, Arizona. Ikky says he will be there."

"You're a fool," she wailed. "It's some sort of trap."

"A Mr. Grimes of Vegas visited me with a silenced gun. I beat him to the punch, but I won't always be that lucky. If I find Ikky and report to Grimes, the mob will let me alone."

"You'd condemn a man to death?" Her voice was sharp and incredulous.

"No. He won't be there when I report. He'll have to hop a plane to Montreal, buy forged papers, and plane to Europe. He may be fairly safe there. But the Outfit has long arms and Ikky won't have a dull life staying alive. He hasn't any choice. For him it's either hide or get the pencil."

"So clever of you, darling. What about your own pencil?"

"If they meant it, they wouldn't have sent it. Just a bit of scare technique."

"And you don't scare, you wonderful handsome brute."

"I scare. But it doesn't paralyze me. So long. Don't take any lovers until I get back."

"Damn you, Marlowe!"

She hung up on me. I hung up on myself.

Saying the wrong thing is one of my specialties.

I beat it out of town before the homicide boys could hear about me. It would take them quite a while to get a lead. And Bernie Ohls wouldn't give a city dick a used paper bag. The Sheriff's men and the City Police cooperate about as much as two tomcats on a fence.

I made Phoenix by evening and parked myself

in a motor court on the outskirts. Phoenix was damned hot. The motor court had a dining room, so I had dinner. I collected some quarters and dimes from the cashier and shut myself in a phone booth and started to call the Mirador in Flagstaff.

How silly could I get? Ikky might be registered under any name from Cohen to Cordileone, from Watson to Woichehovski. I called anyway and got nothing but as much of a smile as you can get on the phone.

So I asked for a room the following night. Not a chance unless someone checked out, but they would put me down for a cancellation or something. Flagstaff is too near the Grand Canyon. Ikky must have arranged in advance. That was something to ponder too.

I bought a paperback and read it. I set my alarm watch for 6:30. The paperback scared me so badly that I put two guns under my pillow. It was about a guy who bucked the hoodlum boss of Milwaukee and got beaten up every fifteen minutes. I figured that his head and face would be nothing but a piece of bone with a strip of skin hanging from it. But in the next chapter he was as gay as a meadow lark.

Then I asked myself why I was reading this drivel when I could have been memorizing *The Brothers Karamazov*. Not knowing any good answers, I turned the light out and went to sleep.

At 6:30 I shaved, showered, had breakfast, and took off for Flagstaff. I got there by lunchtime, and there was Ikky in the restaurant eating mountain trout. I sat down across from him. He looked surprised to see me.

I ordered mountain trout and ate it from the outside in, which is the proper way. Boning spoils it a little.

"What gives?" he asked me with his mouth full. A delicate eater.

"You read the papers?"

"Just the sports section."

"Let's go to your room and talk about it."

We paid for our lunches and went along to a nice double. The motor courts are getting so good that they make a lot of hotels look cheap. We sat down and lit cigarettes.

"The two hoods got up too early and went over to Poynter Street. They parked outside your apartment house. They hadn't been briefed carefully enough. They shot a guy who looked a little like you."

"That's a hot one," he grinned. "But the cops will find out, and the Outfit will find out. So the tag for me stays on."

"You must think I'm dumb," I said. "I am."

"I thought you did a first-class job, Marlowe. What's dumb about that?"

"What job did I do?"

"You got me out of there pretty slick."

"Anything about it you couldn't have done yourself?"

423

"With luck — no. But it's nice to have a helper."

"You mean sucker."

His face tightened. And his rusty voice growled. "I don't catch. And give me back some of that five grand, will you? I'm shorter than I thought."

"I'll give it back to you when you find a hummingbird in a salt shaker."

"Don't be like that." He almost sighed, and flicked a gun into his hand. I didn't have a flick. I was holding one in my side pocket.

"I oughtn't to have boobed off," I said. "Put the heater away. It doesn't pay any more than a Vegas slot machine."

"Wrong. Them machines pay the jackpot every so often. Otherwise — no customers."

"Every so seldom, you mean. Listen, and listen good."

He grinned. His dentist was tired waiting for him.

"The set-up intrigued me," I went on, debonair as Philo Vance in an S.S. Van Dine story and a lot brighter in the head. "First off, could it be done? Second, if it could be done, where would I be? But gradually I saw the little touches that flawed the picture. Why would you come to me at all? The Outfit isn't naive. Why would they send a little punk like this Charles Hickon or whatever name he uses on Thursdays? Why would an old hand like you let anybody trail you to a dangerous connection?"

"You slay me, Marlowe. You're so bright I could find you in the dark. You're so dumb you couldn't see a red, white, and blue giraffe. I bet you were back there in your unbrain emporium playing with that five grand like a cat with a bag of catnip. I bet you were kissing the notes."

"Not after you handled them. Then why the pencil that was sent to me? Big dangerous threat. It reinforced the rest. But like I told your choir boy from Vegas, they don't send them when they mean them. By the way, he had a gun too. A Woodsman .22 with a silencer. I had to make him put it away. He was nice about that. He started waving grands at me to find out where you were and tell him. A well-dressed, nice-looking front man for a pack of dirty rats. The Women's Christian Temperance Association and some bootlicking politicians gave them the money to be big, and they learned how to use it and make it grow. Now they're pretty well unstoppable. But they're still a pack of dirty rats. And they're always where they can't make a mistake. That's inhuman. Any man has a right to a few mistakes. Not the rats. They have to be perfect all the time. Or else they get stuck with *you*."

"I don't know what the hell you're talking about. I just know it's too long."

"Well, allow me to put it in English. Some

poor jerk from the East Side gets involved with the lower echelons of a mob. You know what an echelon is, Ikky?"

"I been in the Army," he sneered.

"He grows up in the mob, but he's not all rotten. He's not rotten enough. So he tries to break loose. He comes out here and gets himself a cheap job of some sort and changes his name or names and lives quietly in a cheap apartment house. But the mob by now has agents in many places. Somebody spots him and recognizes him. It might be a pusher, a front man for a bookie joint, a night girl. So the mob, or call them the Outfit, says through their cigar smoke: 'Ikky can't do this to us. It's a small operation because he's small. But it annoys us. Bad for discipline. Call a couple of boys and have them pencil him.' But what boys do they call? A couple they're tired of. Been around too long. Might make a mistake or get chilly toes. Perhaps they like killing. That's bad too. That makes for recklessness. The best boys are the ones that don't care either way. So although they don't know it, the boys they call are on their way out. But it would be kind of cute to frame a guy they already don't like, for fingering a hood named Larsen. One of these puny little jokes the Outfit takes big. 'Look, guys, we even got time to play footsie with a private eye.' So they send a ringer."

"The Torrence brothers ain't ringers.

They're real hard boys. They proved it — even if they did make a mistake."

"Mistake nothing. They got Ikky Rossen. You're just a singing commercial in this deal. And as of now you're under arrest for murder. You're worse off than that. The Outfit will habeas corpus you out of the clink and blow you down. You've served your purpose and you failed to finger me into a patsy."

His finger tightened on the trigger. I shot the gun out of his hand. The gun in my coat pocket was small, but at that distance accurate. And it was one of my days to be accurate.

He made a faint moaning sound and sucked at his hand. I went over and kicked him hard in the chest. Being nice to killers is not part of my repertoire. He went over backward and stumbled four or five steps. I picked up his gun and held it on him while a tapped all the places — not just pockets or holsters — where a man could stash a second gun. He was clean — that way anyhow.

"What are you trying to do to me?" he whined. "I paid you. You're clear. I paid you damn well."

"We both have problems there. Yours is to stay alive." I took a pair of cuffs out of my pocket and wrestled his hands behind him and snapped them on. His hand was bleeding. I tied his show handkerchief around it and then went to the telephone and called the police.

I had to stick around for a few days, but I didn't mind that as long as I could have trout caught eight or nine thousand feet up. I called Annie and Bernie Ohls. I called my answering service. The Arizona D.A. was a young keen-eyed man and the Chief of Police was one of the biggest men I ever saw.

I got back to L.A. in time and took Anne to Romanoff's for dinner and champagne.

"What I can't see," she said over a third glass of bubbly, "is why they dragged you into it, why they set up the fake Ikky Rossen. Why didn't they just let the two lifetakers do their job?"

"I couldn't really say. Unless the big boys feel so safe they're developing a sense of humor. And unless this Larsen guy who went to the gas chamber was bigger than he seemed to be. Only three or four important mobsters have made the electric chair or the rope or the gas chamber. None that I know of in the life-imprisonment states like Michigan. If Larsen was bigger than anyone thought, they might have had my name on a waiting list."

"But why wait?" she asked me. "They'd go after you quickly."

"They can afford to wait. Who's going to bother them? Except when they make a mistake."

"Income tax rap?"

"Yeah, like Capone. Capone may have had

428

several hundred men killed, and killed a few of them himself, personally. But it took the Internal Revenue boys to get him. But the Outfit won't make that mistake often."

"What I like about you, apart from your enormous personal charm, is that when you don't know an answer you make one up."

"The money worries me," I said. "Five grand of their dirty money. What do I do with it?"

"Don't be a jerk all your life. You earned the money and you risked your life for it. You can buy Series E Bonds — they'll make the money clean. And to me that would be part of the joke."

"*You* tell *me* one good sound reason why they pulled the switch."

"You have more of a reputation than you realize. And suppose it was the false Ikky who pulled the switch? He sounds like one of these over-clever types that can't do anything simple."

"The Outfit will get him for making his own plans — if you're right."

"If the D.A. doesn't. And I couldn't care less about what happens to him. More champagne, please."

They extradited "Ikky" and he broke under pressure and named the two gunmen — after I had already named them, the Torrence brothers. But nobody could find them. They never went home. And you can't prove conspiracy on one man. The law couldn't even get him for accessory after the fact. They couldn't prove he knew the real Ikky had been gunned.

They could have got him for some trifle, but they had a better idea. They left him to his friends. They just turned him loose.

Where is he now? My hunch says nowhere.

Anne Riordan was glad it was all over and I was safe. Safe — that isn't a word you use in my trade.

The Zero Clue

Rex Stout

IT BEGAN WITH a combination of circumstances, but what doesn't? To mention just one, if there hadn't been a couple of checks to deposit that morning I might not have been in that neighborhood at all.

But I was, and, approving of the bright sun and the sharp, clear air, I turned east off of Lexington Avenue into 37th Street and walked some forty paces to the number. It was a five-story yellow brick. The lobby, not much bigger than my bedroom, had a fancy rug, a fireplace without a fire, some greenery, and a watchdog in uniform who looked at me suspiciously.

As I opened my mouth to meet his challenge, circumstances combined. A big guy in a dark-blue top-coat and a gray Homburg, entering from the street, breezed past me, heading for the elevator, and as he did so the elevator door opened and a dark-haired girl with a fur jacket over her arm emerged.

431

Four of us in that undersized lobby made a crowd, and we had to maneuver. Meanwhile, I was speaking to the watchdog, "My name's Goodwin and I'm calling on Leo Heller."

His expression changing, he blurted at me, "You the Archie Goodwin who works for Nero Wolfe?"

The girl stopped short and turned, and the big guy, inside the elevator, blocked the door from closing and stuck his head out, while the watchdog was going on, "I've saw your picture in the paper, and, look, I want Nero Wolfe's autograph."

It would have been more to the point if he had wanted mine, but I'm not petty. The man in the elevator, which was self-service, was letting the door close, but the girl was standing by, and I hated to disappoint her by denying I was me, as of course I would have had to do if I had been there on an operation that needed cover.

I was actually not on an operation at all. Chiefly, I was satisfying my curiosity. At five in the afternoon the day before, in Nero Wolfe's office on the ground floor of his old brownstone house on West 35th Street, there had been a phone call. After taking it I had gone to the kitchen to get a glass of water. Fritz Brenner, the chef and housekeeper, was boning a pig's head for what he calls *fromage de cochon*. I told him I was going upstairs to do a little yapping.

"He is so happy up there," Fritz protested, but there was a gleam in his eye. He knows darned well that if I quit yapping, the day would come when there would be no money in the bank to meet the payroll, including him.

I went up three flights to the roof, where ten thousand square feet of glass in aluminum frames make a home for ten thousand orchid plants. The riot of color doesn't take my breath any more, but it is unquestionably a show, and as I went through that day, I kept my eyes straight ahead to preserve my mood for yapping intact. However, it was wasted. In the intermediate room Wolfe was glaring at a box of *Odontoglossum* seedlings in his hand, while Theodore Horstmann, the orchid nurse, stood nearby with his lips tightened to a thin line.

As I approached, Wolfe transferred the glare to me and barked savagely, "Thrips!"

I did some fast mood-shifting. There's a time to yap and a time not to yap. But I walked up to him.

"What do you want?" he rasped.

"I realize," I said politely but firmly, "that this is ill-timed, but I told Mr. Heller I would speak to you. He phoned —"

"Speak to me later! If at all!"

"I'm to call him back. It's Leo Heller, the probability wizard. He says that calculations have led him to suspect that a client of his may have committed a serious crime, but it's only a suspicion. He doesn't want to tell the police until it has been investigated, and he wants us to investigate. I asked for details but he wouldn't give them on the phone. I thought I might as well run over there now — it's over on East Thirty-seventy Street — and find out if it looks like a job. He wouldn't —"

"No!"

"My eardrums are not insured. No what?"

"Get out!" He shook the thrips-infested seedlings at me. "That man couldn't hire me for any conceivable job on any imaginable terms! Get out!"

I turned, prompt but dignified, and went. But on my way back down to the office I was wearing a grin. Even without the thrips, Wolfe's reaction to my message would have been substantially the same, which was why I had been prepared to yap. The thrips had merely keyed it up.

Leo Heller had been tagged by fame, with articles about him in magazines and Sunday newspapers. While making a living as a professor of mathematics at Underhill College, he had begun, for amusement, to apply the laws of probability, through highly complicated mathematical formulas, to various current events, ranging from ball games and horse races to farm crops and elections. Checking back on his records after a couple of years, he had been startled and pleased to find that the answers he had got from his formulas had been 86.3 per cent correct, and he had written a piece about it for a magazine.

Naturally, requests had started coming, from all kinds of people for all kinds of calculations. Heller had granted some of them to be obliging, but when he had tried telling a woman in Yonkers where to look for $31,000 in currency she had lost, and she had followed instructions and found it, and had insisted on giving him two grand, he resigned his professorship.

That had been three years ago, and now he was sitting pretty. It was said that his annual take was in six figures, that he returned all his mail unanswered, accepting only clients who called in person, and that there was nothing on earth he wouldn't try to dope a formula for, provided he was furnished with enough factors to make it feasible.

It had been suggested that he should be hauled in for fortune-telling, but the cops and the D.A.'s office let it lay, as well they might, since he had a college degree and there were at least a thousand fortune-tellers operating in New York who had never made it through high school.

It wasn't known whether Heller was keeping his percentage up to 86.3, but I happened to know it wasn't goose eggs. Some months earlier a president of a big corporation had hired Wolfe to find out which member of his staff was giving trade secrets to a competitor. I had been busy on another case at the time, and Wolfe had put Orrie Cather on the collection of details.

Orrie had made a long job of it, and the first we knew we were told by the corporation president that he had got impatient and gone to Leo Heller with the problem. Heller cooked up a formula and came out with an answer: the name of one of the junior vice-presidents, and the junior VP had confessed!

Our client freely admitted that most of the facts he had given Heller for the ingredients of his formula had been supplied by us, gathered by Orrie Cather. He offered no objection to paying our bill, but Wolfe was so sore he actually told me to send no bill — an instruction I disregarded, knowing how he would regret it after he had cooled off. However, he still had it in for Leo Heller. Taking on any kind of job for him would have been absolutely off the program that day or any other day, even if there had been no thrips within a mile of 35th Street.

Back downstairs in the office, I phoned Heller and told him nothing doing. "He's extremely sensitive," I explained, "and this is an insult. As you know, he's the greatest detective that ever lived, and — do you know that?"

"I'm willing to postulate it," Heller conceded, in a thin voice that tended to squeak. "Why an insult?"

"Because you want to hire Nero Wolfe, meaning me really, to collect facts on which you can base a decision whether your suspicion about your client is justified. You might as well try to hire Stan Musial as bat boy for a rookie outfielder. Mr. Wolfe doesn't sell the raw material for answers, he sells answers."

"I'm quite willing to pay him for an answer — any amount short of exorbitance, and in cash. I'm gravely concerned about this situation, and my data are insufficient. I shall be delighted if, with the data, I get an answer from Mr. Wolfe, and —"

"And," I put in, "if his answer is that your client has committed a serious crime, as you suspect, he decides whether and when to call a cop, not you. Yes?"

"Certainly." Heller was eager to oblige. "I do not intend or desire to shield a criminal — on the contrary."

"Okay. Then it's like this: It wouldn't do any good for me to take it up with Mr. Wolfe again today, because his feelings have been hurt. But tomorrow morning I have to go to our bank on Lexington Avenue, not far from your place, and I could drop in to see you. Frankly, I doubt if Mr. Wolfe will take this case on, but we can always use money and

I'll try to sell him. Shall I come?"

"What time?"

"Say a quarter past ten."

"Come ahead. My business begins at eleven. Take the elevator to the fifth floor. An arrow points right, to the waiting room, but go left, to the door at the end of the hall and push the button, and I'll let you in. If you're on time we'll have more than half an hour."

"I'm always on time."

That morning I was a little early. It was nine minutes past ten when I entered the lobby on 37th Street and gave the watchdog my name.

I told the watchdog I would try to get Nero Wolfe's autograph for him, and wrote his name in my notebook: Nils Lamm. Meanwhile, the girl stood there, frowning at us. She was twenty-three or four, and without the deep frown her face would probably have deserved attention. Since she showed no trace of embarrassment at staring fixedly at a stranger, I saw no reason why I should, but something had to be said, so I asked her, "Do you want one?"

She cocked her head. "One what?"

"Autograph. Either Mr. Wolfe's or mine, take your pick."

"Oh. You are Archie Goodwin, aren't you? I've seen your picture, too."

"Then I'm it."

"I . . ." She hesitated, then made up her mind. "I want to ask you something."

"Shoot."

Someone trotted in from the street, a brisk female in mink, executive type, between twenty and sixty, and the girl and I moved aside to clear the lane to the elevator. The newcomer told Nils Lamm she was seeing Leo Heller and refused to give her name, but when Lamm insisted, she coughed it up: Agatha Abbey, she said, and he let her take the elevator.

The girl told me she had been working all night and was tired, so we went to a bench by the fireplace. Close up, I would still have said twenty-three or -four, but someone or something had certainly been harrassing her. Naturally, there was a question in my mind about the night work.

She answered it: "My name's Susan Maturo, registered nurse."

"Thanks. You know mine and I'm a registered detective."

She nodded. "That's why I want to ask you something. If I hired Nero Wolfe to investigate a — a matter, how much would it cost?"

I raised my shoulders half an inch and let them down. "It all depends. The kind of matter, the amount of time taken, the wear and tear on his brain, the state of your finances."

I paused, letting it hang, to return a rude

stare that was being aimed at us by another arrival, a thin, tall, bony specimen in a brown suit that badly needed pressing, with a bulging brief case under his arm. When my gaze met his he called it off and strode to the elevator, without any exchange with Nils Lamm.

I resumed to Susan Maturo: "Have you got a matter, or are you just researching?"

"Oh, I've got a matter." She set her teeth on her lip, nice teeth and not a bad lip, and kept them that way a while, regarding me. Then she went on, "It hit me hard, and it's been getting worse instead of better. I decided to come to this Leo Heller and see what he could do, so I came this morning. I was sitting up there in his waiting room — two people were already there, a man and a woman — and I felt suddenly that I was just being bitter and vindictive, and I don't think I'm like that."

Apparently, she needed some cooperation, so I assured her, "You don't look vindictive."

She touched my sleeve with her fingertips to thank me. "So I got up and left. Then, as I was leaving the elevator, I heard that man saying your name and who you are, and it popped into my head to ask you. I asked how much it would cost to have Nero Wolfe investigate, but that was premature, because what I really want is to tell him about it and to get his advice about investigating."

She was dead-serious, so I arranged my face and voice to fit. "It's like this," I told her. "For that kind of approach to Mr. Wolfe, with no big fee in prospect, some expert preparation is required, and I'm the only expert in the field." I glanced at my wrist and saw 10:19. "I've got a date, but I can spare five minutes if you want to brief me on the essentials, and then I'll tell you how it strikes me. What was it that hit you?"

She looked at me, shot a glance at Nils Lamm, who couldn't have moved out of earshot in that lobby if he had wanted to, and came back to me. "When I start to talk about it," she said, "it sticks in my throat and chokes me, and five minutes wouldn't be enough. Anyway, I need someone old and wise like Nero Wolfe. Won't you let me see him?"

I promised to try, but I told her it would be a waste of time and effort for me to take her in to Wolfe cold. Though I was neither old nor wise she would have to give me at least a full outline before I could furnish either an opinion or help.

She agreed that that was reasonable and gave me her address and phone number, and we arranged to communicate later in the day. She slipped into her jacket and I went and opened the door for her, and she departed.

On the way up in the elevator my watch said 10:28, so I wasn't on time, after all, but we would still have half an hour before

Heller's business day began. On the fifth floor a plaque on the wall facing the elevator was lettered LEO HELLER, WAITING ROOM, with an arrow pointing right, and at the end of the narrow hall a door bore the invitation, WALK IN.

I turned left, toward the other end, where I pushed a button beside a door, noticing as I did so that the door was ajar a scanty inch. When my ring brought no response, and a second one, more prolonged, didn't, either, I shoved the door open, crossed the sill, and called Heller's name.

No reply. There was no one in sight.

Thinking that he had probably stepped into the waiting room and would soon return, I glanced around to see what the lair of a probability wizard looked like, and was impressed by some outstanding features. The door, of metal, was a good three inches thick, either for security or for sound-proofing, or maybe both. If there were any windows they were behind the heavy draperies; the artificial light came indirectly from channels in the walls just beneath the ceiling. The room was air-conditioned. There were locks on all the units of a vast assembly of filing cabinets that lined the rear wall. The floor, with no rugs, was tiled with some velvety material on which a footfall was barely audible.

The thick door was for sound-proofing. I had closed it, nearly, on entering, and the silence was complete. Not a sound of the city could be heard, though the clang and clatter of Lexington Avenue was almost next door one way and of Third Avenue the other.

I crossed for a look at the desk, but there was nothing remarkable about it except that it was twice the usual size. Among other items it held a vase of flowers, a rack of books with titles that were not tempting, an abacus of ivory or a good imitation, and a stack of legal-size working pads. Stray sheets of paper were scattered about, and a single pad had on its top sheet some scribbled formulas that looked like doodles by Einstein. Also, a jar of sharpened lead pencils had been overturned, and some of them were in a sort of pattern near the edge of the desk.

I had been in there ten minutes and no Heller, and when, at eleven o'clock by schedule, Wolfe came down to the office from his morning session with the orchids, it was desirable that I should be present. So I went, leaving the door ajar as I found it, walked down the hall to the door of the waiting room at the other end, and entered.

This room was neither air-conditioned nor sound-proofed. Someone had opened a window a couple of inches and the din was jangling in. Five people were here and there on chairs, three of whom I had seen before: the big guy in the dark-blue topcoat and Homburg, the brisk female in mink who called herself Agatha Abbey, and the tall, thin specimen with a brief case.

Neither of the other two was Leo Heller. One was a swarthy little article, slick and sly, with his hair pasted to his scalp, and the other was a big blob of an overfed matron with a spare chin.

I addressed the gathering: "Has Mr. Heller been in here?"

A couple of them shook their heads, and the swarthy article said hoarsely, "Not visible till eleven o'clock, and you take your turn."

I thanked him, left, and went back to the other room. Still no Heller. I didn't bother to call his name again, since even if it had flushed him I would have had to leave immediately. So I departed.

Down in the lobby I told Nils Lamm I'd see what I could do about an autograph. Outside, deciding there wasn't time to walk it, I flagged a taxi. Home again, I hadn't been in the office more than twenty seconds when the sound came of Wolfe's elevator descending.

That was funny thing. I'm strong on hunches, and I've had some beauts during the years I've been with Wolfe; but that day there wasn't the slightest glimmer of something impending.

I was absolutely blithe as I asked Wolfe how the anti-thrips campaign was doing, and later, after lunch, as I dialed the number Susan Maturo had given me. I admit I was a little dampened when I got no answer, since I had the idea of finding out some day how she would look with the frown gone.

But still later, shortly after six o'clock, I went to answer the doorbell, and through the one-way glass panel, saw Inspector Cramer of Manhattan Homicide there on the stoop. There was an instant reaction on the lower third of my spine, but I claim no credit for a hunch, since, after all, a homicide Inspector does not go around ringing doorbells to sell tickets to the policemen's annual ball.

I took him to the office, where Wolfe was scowling at the three United States senators on television.

Cramer, bulky and burly, with a big red face and sharp gray eyes, sat in the red-leather chair near the end of Wolfe's desk. "I dropped in on the way down and I haven't got long." He was gruff, which was normal. "I'd appreciate some quick information. What are you doing for Leo Heller?"

"Nothing." Wolfe was brusque, which was also normal.

"You're not working for him?"

"No."

"Then why did Goodwin go to see him this morning?"

"He didn't."

"Hold it," I put in. "I went on my own, just exploring. Mr. Wolfe didn't know I was going. This is the first he's heard of it."

There were two simultaneous looks of exasperation — Cramer's at Wolfe, and Wolfe's at me.

Cramer backed his up with words: "For Pete's sake! This is the rawest one you ever tried to pull! Been rehearsing it all afternoon?"

Wolfe let me go temporarily, to cope with Cramer. "Pfui! Suppose we have. Justify your marching into my house to demand an accounting of Mr. Goodwin's movements. What if he did call on Mr. Heller? Has Mr. Heller been found dead?"

"Yes."

"Indeed." Wolfe's brows went up a little. "Violence?"

"Murdered. Shot through the heart."

"On his premises?"

"Yeah. I'd like to hear from Goodwin."

Wolfe's eyes darted to me. "Did you kill Mr. Heller, Archie?"

"No, sir."

"Then oblige Mr. Cramer, please. He's in a hurry."

I obliged. First telling about the phone call the day before, and Wolfe's refusal to take on anything for Heller, and my calling Heller back. I then reported on my morning visit at 37th Street, supplying all details. I did soft-pedal Susan Maturo's state of harassment, putting it merely that she asked me to arrange for her to see Wolfe and didn't tell me what about.

When I had finished, Cramer had a few questions. Among them: "So you didn't see Heller at all?"

"Nope."

He grunted. "I know only too well how nosy you are, Goodwin. There were three doors in the walls of that room beside the one you entered by. You didn't open any of them?"

"Nope."

"One of them is the door to the closet in which Heller's body was found by a caller, a friend, at three o'clock this afternoon. The Medical Examiner says that the breakfast Heller ate at nine thirty hadn't been in him more than an hour when he died, so it's practically certain that the body was in the closet while you were there in the room. As nosy as you are, you're telling me that you didn't open the door and see the body?"

"Yep. I apologize. Next time I'll open every door in sight."

"A gun had been fired. You didn't smell it?"

"No. The room is air-conditioned."

"You didn't look through the desk drawers?"

"No. I apologize again."

"We did." Cramer took something from his breast pocket. "In one drawer we found this envelope, sealed. On it was written in pencil, in Heller's hand, *Mr. Nero Wolfe.* In it were five one-hundred-dollar bills."

"I'm sorry I missed that," I said with feeling.

Wolfe stirred. "I assume that has been examined for fingerprints."

"Certainly."

"May I see it, please?"

Wolfe extended a hand. Cramer hesitated a moment, then tossed it across to the desk, and Wolfe picked it up. He took out the bills, crisp new ones, counted them, and looked inside the envelope.

"This was sealed," he observed dryly, "with my name written on it, and you opened it."

"We sure did." Cramer came forward in his chair with a hand stretched. "Let me have it."

It was a demand, not a request, and Wolfe reacted impulsively. If he had taken a second to think he would have realized that if he claimed it he would have to earn it, or at least pretend to, but Cramer's tone of voice was the kind of provocation he would not take.

He returned the bills to the envelope and put it in his pocket. "It's mine," he stated.

"It's evidence," Cramer growled, "and I want it."

Wolfe shook his head. "Evidence of what?" He tapped his pocket with a fingertip. "My property. Connect it, or connect me, with a crime."

Cramer was controlling himself, which

wasn't easy in the circumstances. "I might have known," he said bitterly. "You want to be connected with a crime? Okay. I don't know how many times I've sat in this chair and listened to you making assumptions. Now I've got some of my own to offer, but first here are a few facts: In that building on Thirty-seventh Street, Heller lived on the fourth floor and worked on the fifth, the top floor. At five minutes to ten this morning, on good evidence, he left his living quarters to go up to his office. Goodwin says he entered that office at ten twenty-eighty, so if the body was in the closet when Goodwin was there, and it almost certainly was, Heller was killed between nine fifty-five and ten twenty-eight. We can't find anyone who heard the shot, and the way that room is sound-proofed we probably never will. We've tested it."

Cramer squeezed his eyes shut and opened them again, a trick of his. "Very well. The doorman always demanded the name of anyone he didn't recognize. We've got a list from him of everyone who entered the place during that period. Most of these callers have been collected and we're getting the others. There were six of them. The nurse, Susan Maturo, left before Goodwin went up, and the other five left later, at intervals, when they got tired waiting for Heller to show up — according to them. As it stands now, and I don't see what could change it, one of them

449

killed Heller. Any of them, on leaving the elevator at the fifth floor, could have gone to Heller's office and shot him, and then gone on to the waiting room."

Wolfe muttered, "Putting the body in the closet?"

"Of course, to postpone its discovery. If someone happened to see the murderer leaving the office, he had to be able to say he had gone in to look for Heller and Heller wasn't there. He couldn't say that if the body was there in sight. There are marks on the floor where the body — and Heller was a featherweight — was dragged to the closet. In leaving, the murderer left the door ajar, to make it more plausible, if someone saw him, that he had found it that way. Also —"

"Fallacy."

"I'll tell him you said so the first chance I get. Also, of course he couldn't leave the building. Knowing that Heller started to see callers at eleven o'clock, those people had all come early so as not to have a long wait. Including the murderer. He had to go to the waiting room and wait with the others. One of them did leave, the nurse, and she made a point of telling Goodwin why she was going. It's up to her to make it stick under questioning."

"You were going to connect me with a crime."

"Right." Cramer was positive. "First, one

450

more fact. The gun was in the closet with the body, under it on the floor. It's a nasty little short-nose revolver, and there's not a chance in a thousand of tracing it, though we're trying. Now, here are my assumptions: The murderer went armed to kill, pushed the button at the door of Heller's office, and was admitted. Since Heller went to his desk and sat, he couldn't —"

"Established?"

"Yes. He couldn't have been in fear of a mortal attack. But after some conversation, which couldn't have been more than a few minutes on account of the timetable as verified, he was not only in fear, he felt that death was upon him, and in that super-sound-proofed room he was helpless. The gun had been drawn and was aimed at him. He talked, trying to stall, not because he had any hope of living, but because he wanted to leave a message to be read after he was dead.

"Shaking with nervousness, with a trembling hand, perhaps a pleading one, he upset the jar of pencils on his desk, and then he nervously fumbled with them, moving them around on the desk in front of him, all the while talking. Then the gun went off and he wasn't nervous any more. The murderer circled the desk, made sure his victim was dead, and dragged the body to the closet. It didn't occur to him that the scattered pencils had been arranged to convey a dying message.

If it had, one sweep of the hand would have taken care of it."

Cramer stood up. "If you'll let me have eight pencils I'll show you how they were."

Wolfe opened his desk drawer, but I got there first, with a handful taken from my tray. Inspector Cramer moved around to Wolfe's side, and Wolfe, making a face, moved his chair over to make room.

"I'm in Heller's place at his desk," Cramer said, "and I'm putting them as he did from where he sat. Getting the eight pencils arranged to his satisfaction, he stepped aside. "There it is; take a look."

Wolfe inspected it from his side, and I from mine. It was like this from Wolfe's side.

"You say," Wolfe inquired, "that was a message?"

"Yes," Cramer asserted. "It has to be."

"By mandate? Yours?"

"Blah. You know there's not one chance in a million those pencils took that pattern by accident. Goodwin, you saw them. Were they like that?"

"Approximately," I conceded. "I didn't know there was a corpse in the closet at the time, so I wasn't as interested in it as you were. But since you ask me, the pencil points were all in the same direction, and an eraser from one of them was there in the middle." I put a fingertip on the spot. "Right there."

"Fix it as you saw it."

I went around to Wolfe's side of the desk and did as requested, removing an eraser from one of the pencils and placing it as I had indicated. Then it was like this:

"Of course," I said, "you had the photographer shoot it. I don't say that's exact, but they were pointing in the same direction, and the eraser was there."

"Didn't you realize it was a message?"

"Sure I thought it was Heller's way of telling me he had gone to the bathroom and would be back in eight minutes. Eight pencils, see? Pretty clever. Isn't that how you read it?"

"It is not." Cramer was emphatic. "I think Heller turned it sideways to make it less likely that his attacker would see what it was. Move around here, please? Both of you. Look at it from here."

Wolfe and I joined him at the left end of the desk and looked as requested. One glance was enough. You can see what we saw by turning the page a quarter-turn counterclockwise.

Cramer spoke: "Could you ask for a plainer NW?"

"I could," I objected. "Why the extra pencil on the left of the W?"

"He put it there deliberately, for camouflage, to make it less obvious, or it rolled there accidentally. I don't care which. It is unmistakably NW." He focused on Wolfe. "I promised to connect you with a crime."

Wolfe, back in his chair, interlaced his fingers. "You're not serious."

"Who says I'm not." Cramer returned to the red-leather chair. "That's why I came here, and came alone. You deny you sent Goodwin there, but I don't believe you. He admits he was in Heller's office ten minutes. He has to admit it, since the doorman saw him go up and five people saw him enter the waiting room. In a drawer in Heller's desk is an envelope addressed to you, containing five hundred dollars in cash.

"But the clincher is that message. Heller, seated at his desk, sure that he is going to be killed in a matter of second, uses those seconds to leave a message. Can there be any question what the message was about? Not for me. It was about the person or persons responsible for his death. I am assuming that its purpose was to identify that person or persons. Do you reject that assumption?''

"No. I think it quite likely. Highly probable.''

"You admit it?''

"I don't admit it, I state it.''

"Then I ask you to suggest any person or persons other than you whom the initials NW might identify. Unless you can do that here and now I'm going to take you and Goodwin downtown as material witnesses. I've got men in cars outside. If I didn't do it the D.A. would.''

Wolfe straightened up and sighed. "You are being uncommonly obnoxious, Mr. Cramer.'' He got to his feet. "Excuse me a moment.''

Detouring around Cramer's feet, he crossed to the other side of the room, to the bookshelves back of the big globe, and took a book down. He was too far away for me to see what it was. He turned first to the back of the book, where the index would be if it had one, and then to a page near the middle of it.

He went on to another page, and another, while Cramer, containing his emotions under pressure, got a cigar from a pocket, stuck it in his mouth, and sank his teeth in it. He never lit one.

Finally Wolfe returned to his desk, opened a drawer and put the book in it, and closed and locked the drawer.

Cramer was speaking: "I'm not being fantastic. You didn't kill him; you weren't there. I'm not even assuming Goodwin killed him, though he could have. I'm saying that Heller left a message that would give a lead to the killer. The message says NW, and that stands for Nero Wolfe. Therefore, you know something, and I want to know what. I want a yes or no to this: Do you or do you not know something that may indicate who murdered Leo Heller?"

Wolfe, settled in his chair again, nodded. "Yes."

"Ah. You do. What?"

"The message he left."

"The message only says NW. Go on from there."

"I need more information. I need to know — are the pencils still there on the desk as you found them?"

"Yes. They haven't been disturbed."

"You have a man there, of course. Get him on the phone and let me talk to him. You will hear us."

Cramer hesitated; then, deciding he might as well string along, he came to my desk, dialed a number, got his man, and told him Wolfe would speak to him. Wolfe took it with his phone while Cramer stayed at mine. I picked up the third phone on the table.

Wolfe was courteous but crisp: "I understand those pencils are there on the desk as they were found, that all but one of them have erasers in their ends, and that an eraser is there on the desk, between the two groups of pencils. Is that correct?"

"Right." The dick sounded bored.

"Take the eraser and insert it in the end of the pencil that hasn't one in it. I want to know if the eraser was loose enough to slip out accidentally."

"Inspector, are you on? You said not to disturb —"

"Go ahead," Cramer growled. "I'm right here."

"Yes, sir. Hold it, please."

There was a long wait, and then he was back on: "The eraser couldn't have slipped out accidentally. Part of it is still clamped in the pencil. It had to be torn out, and the torn surfaces are bright and fresh. I can pull one out of another pencil and tell you how much force it takes."

"No thank you, that's all I need. But, for the record, I suggest that you send the pencil and eraser to the laboratory to check that the torn surfaces fit."

"Do I do that, Inspector?"

"Yeah, you might as well. Mark them properly."

"Yes, sir."

457

Cramer returned to the red-leather chair, and I went to mine. He tilted the cigar upward from the corner of his mouth and demanded, "So what?"

"You know quite well what," Wolfe declared. " The eraser was yanked out and placed purposely. It was a part of the message. No doubt as a dot after the N to show it was an initial? And he was interrupted, permanently, before he could put one after the W?"

"Sarcasm don't change it any. It's still NW."

"No. It isn't. It never was."

"For me and the District Attorney it is. I guess we'd better get on down to his office."

Wolfe upturned a palm. "There you are. You're not hare-brained, but you are pigheaded. I warn you, sir, that if you proceed on the assumption that Mr. Heller's message says NW you are doomed; the best you can expect is to be tagged a jackass."

"I suppose you know what it does say."

"Yes."

"I'm waiting."

"You'll continue to wait. If I thought I could earn this money" — Nero Wolfe tapped his pocket — "by deciphering that message for you, that would be simple, but in your present state of mind you would only think I was contriving a humbug."

"Try me."

"No, sir." Wolfe half closed his eyes. "An alternative. You can go on as you have started and see where it lands you, understanding that Mr. Goodwin and I will persistently deny any knowledge of the affair or those concerned in it except what has been given you, and I'll pursue my own course; or you can bring the murderer here and let me at him — with you present."

"I'll be glad to. Name him."

"When I find him. I need all six of them, to learn which one Heller's message identifies. Since I can translate the message and you can't, you need me more than I need you, but you can save me much time and trouble and expense."

Cramer's level gaze had no trace whatever of sympathy. "If you can translate that message and refuse to disclose it, you're withholding evidence."

"Nonsense. A conjecture is not evidence. Heaven knows your conjecture that it says NW isn't. Nor is mine, but it should lead to some if I do the leading." Wolfe flung a hand impatiently and his voice rose: "Confound it, do you think I welcome an invasion of my premises by platoons of policemen herding a drove of scared citizens?"

Cramer took the cigar from his mouth and regarded it as if trying to decide exactly what it was. That accomplished, he glanced at Wolfe and then looked at me, by no means

459

as a bosom friend.

"I'll use the phone," he said, and got up and came to my desk . . . With three of the six scared citizens, it was a good thing that Wolfe didn't have to start from scratch. They had been absolutely determined not to tell why they had gone to see Leo Heller, and, as we learned from the transcripts of interviews and copies of statements they had signed, the cops had had a time dragging it out of them.

By the time the first one was brought to us in the office, a little after eight o'clock, Wolfe had sort of resigned himself to personal misery. Not only had he had to devour his dinner in one-fourth the usual time, also, he had been compelled to break one of his strictest rules and read documents while eating — and all that in the company of Inspector Cramer, who had accepted an invitation to have a bite.

Of course, Cramer returned to the office with us, and called in, from the assemblage in the front room, a police stenographer, who settled himself in a chair at the end of my desk. Sergeant Purley Stebbins, who once in a spasm of generosity admitted that he couldn't prove I was a hoodlum, after bringing the citizen in and seating him facing Wolfe and Cramer, took a chair against the wall.

The citizen, whose name was John R. Winslow as furnished by the documents, was

460

the big guy in a dark-blue topcoat and Homburg who had stuck his head out of the elevator for a look at Archie Goodwin. He was one of the three who had tried to refuse to tell what he had gone to Heller for; and considering what it was I couldn't blame him much.

He started in complaining: "This is unconstitutional! Nero Wolfe is a private detective and I don't have to submit to questioning by him."

"I'm here," Cramer said. "I can repeat Wolfe's questions if you insist, but it will take more time."

"Suppose," Wolfe suggested, "we start and see how it goes. I've read your statement, Mr. John Winslow, and I —"

"They had no right to let you! They promised me it would be confidential unless it had to be used as evidence!"

"Please, Mr. Winslow, don't bounce up like that. A hysterical woman is bad enough, but a hysterical man is insufferable. I assure you I am as discreet as any policeman. According to your statement, today was your third visit to Mr. Heller's office. You were trying to supply him with enough information for him to devise a formula for determining how much longer your aunt will live. You expect to inherit a considerable fortune from her, and you wanted to make plans intelligently based on expectations. So you say, but reports are

461

being received which indicate that you are deeply in debt and are hard pressed. Do you deny that?"

"No." Winslow's jaw worked. "I don't deny it."

"Are your debts, or any part of them, connected with any violation of the law? Any criminal act?"

"No!"

"Granted that Mr. Heller could furnish a valid calculation on your aunt's life, how would that help you any?"

Winslow looked at Cramer, and met only a stony stare. He went back to Wolfe: "I was negotiating to borrow a very large sum against my — expectations. There was to be a certain percentage added for each month that passed before repayment was made, and I had to know what my chances were. It was a question of probabilities, and I went to an expert."

"What data had you given Heller as a basis for his calculations?"

"I couldn't . . . all kinds of things."

"For instance?" Wolfe insisted.

Winslow looked at the police stenographer and me, but we couldn't help. He returned to Wolfe. "Hundreds of things. My aunt's age, her habits — eating, sleeping — the ages of her parents and grandparents when they died, her weight and build — I gave him photographs — her activities and interests, her temperament, her attitude to doctors, her politics —"

"Politics?"

"Yes. Heller said her pleasure or pain at the election of Eisenhower was a longevity factor."

Wolfe grunted. "The claptrap of the charlatan. Did he also consider as a longevity factor the possibility that you might intervene by dispatching your aunt?"

That struck Winslow as funny. He did not guffaw, but he tittered, and it did not suit his build.

Wolfe insisted, "Did he?"

"I really don't know, really," Winslow tittered again.

"From whom did your aunt inherit her fortune?"

"Her husband, my uncle Norton."

"When did he die?"

"Six years ago. He was shot accidentally while hunting. Hunting deer."

"Were you present?"

"Not present, no. I was more than a mile away at the time."

"Did you get a legacy from him?"

"No." Some emotion was moblizing Winslow's blood and turning his face pink. "He left me six cents in his will. He didn't like me."

Wolfe turned to speak to Cramer, but the Inspector forestalled him: "Two men are already on it. The shooting accident was up in Maine."

"There was no mystery about my uncle's death," Winslow said. "My aunt would be amused, as I am, at the idea of my having killed him, and she would be amused at the idea that I might try to kill her. As a matter of fact, I wouldn't mind a bit having her know about that, but if she finds out what I went to Leo Heller for — heaven help me." He gestured in appeal. "I was promised, absolutely promised."

"We disclose people's private affairs," Cramer rumbled, "only when it is unavoidable."

Wolfe was pouring beer. When the foam was at the rim he put the bottle down and resumed: "I have promised nothing, Mr. Winslow, but I have no time for tattle. Here's a suggestion: You're in this pickle only because of your association with Mr. Heller, and the question is, was there anything in that association to justify this badgering? Suppose you tell us. Start at the beginning, and recall as well as you can every word that passed between you. Go right through it. I'll interrupt as little as possible."

"You've already seen it," Cramer objected. "The transcript, the statement. Why, have you got a lead or haven't you?"

Wolfe nodded. "We have a night for it," he said, not happily. "Mr. Winslow doesn't know what the lead is, and it's Greek to you."

464

He went to Winslow, "Go ahead, sir. Everything that you said to Mr. Heller, and everything he said to you."

It took more than an hour, including interruptions. The interruptions came from various city employees who were scattered around the house working on other scared citizens, and from the telephone. Two of the phone calls were from homicide dicks who were trying to locate a citizen who had got mislaid — one named Henrietta Tillotson, Mrs. Albert Tillotson, the overfed matron whom I had seen in Heller's waiting room.

When Purley Stebbins got up to escort Winslow from the room, Wolfe's lead was still apparently Greek to Cramer, as it was to me. As the door closed behind them Cramer spoke emphatically, "It's a farce. I think that message was NW, meaning you, and you're stalling for some kind of a play."

"And if so?" Wolfe was testy. "Why are you tolerating this? Because if the message did mean me I'm the crux, and your only alternative is to cart me downtown, and that would merely make me mum and you know it."

He drank beer and put the glass down. "However, maybe we can expedite it without too great a risk. Tell your men who are now interviewing these people to be alert for something connected with the figure six. They must give no hint of it, they must them-

465

selves not mention it, but if the figure six appears in any segment of the interview they should concentrate on that segment until it is exhausted. They all know, I presume, of Heller's suspicion that one of his clients had committed a serious crime?"

"They know that Goodwin says so. What's this about six?"

Wolfe shook his head. "That will have to do. Even that may be foolhardy, since they're your men, not mine."

"Winslow's uncle died six years ago and left him six cents."

"I'm quite aware of it. You say that is being investigated. Do you want Mr. Goodwin to pass this word?"

Cramer said no thanks, he would, and left the room.

By the time he returned, citizen number two had been brought in by Stebbins, introduced to Wolfe, and seated where Winslow had been. It was Susan Maturo. She looked fully as harassed as she had that morning, but I wouldn't say much more so. There was now, of course, a new aspect to the matter: Did she looked harassed, or guilty?

If Heller had been killed by the client whom he suspected of having committed a crime, it must have been a client he had seen previously at least once, or how could he have got ground for suspicion? According to Susan Maturo, she had never called on Heller before and had never seen him.

Actually, that eliminated neither her nor Agatha Abbey, who also claimed that that morning had been her first visit. It was known that Heller had sometimes made engagements by telephone to meet prospective clients elsewhere, and Miss Maturo and Miss Abbey might well have been among that number.

Opening up on her, Wolfe was not too belligerent, probably because she had accepted an offer of beer and, after drinking some, had licked her lips. It pleases him when people share his joys.

"You are aware, Miss Maturo," he told her, "that you are in a class by yourself. The evidence indicates that Mr. Heller was killed by one of the six people who entered that building this morning to call on him, and you are the only one of the six who departed before eleven o'clock, Mr. Heller's appointment hour. Your explanation of your departure as given in your statement is close to incoherent. Can't you improve on it?"

She looked at me. "I've reported what you told me," I assured her. "Exactly as you said it."

She nodded at me vaguely and turned to Wolfe: "Do I have to go through it again?"

"You will probably," Wolfe advised her, "have to go through it again a dozen times. Why did you leave?"

She gulped, started to speak, found no sound was coming out, and had to start over again. "You know about the explosion and fire at the Montrose Hospital a month ago?"

"Certainly. I read newspapers."

"You know that three hundred and two people died there that night. I was there working, in Ward G on the sixth floor. In addition to those who died many were injured, but I went all through it and I didn't get a scratch or a burn. My dearest friend was killed, burned to death trying to save the patients. Another dear friend is crippled for life, and a young doctor I was engaged to marry — he was killed in the explosion. I don't know how I came out of it without a mark, because I tried to help, I'm positively sure of that — but I did. That's one trouble, I guess, because I couldn't be glad about it — how could I?"

She seemed to expect an answer, so Wolfe muttered, "No. Not to be expected."

"I am not," she said, "the kind of person who hates people."

She stopped, so Wolfe said, "No?"

"No, I'm not. I never have been. But I began to hate the man, or the woman, who put the bomb there. I can't say I went out of my mind, because I don't think I did, but I felt as if I had. After two weeks I tried to go back to work at another hospital, but I couldn't. I read all there was in the newspa-

468

pers, hoping they would catch him. I couldn't think of anything else. I even dreamed about it every night. I went to the police and wanted to help, but of course they had already questioned me and I had told them everything I knew. The days went by and it looked as if they never would catch him. I had read about that Leo Heller, and I decided to go to him and get him to do it."

Wolfe made a noise, and her head jerked up. "I said I hated him!"

Wolfe nodded. "So you did. Go on."

"And I went, that's all. I had some money saved and I could borrow some, to pay him. But while I was sitting there in the waiting room, with that man and woman there, I suddenly thought I must be crazy. I must have got so bitter and vindictive I didn't realize what I was doing. I wanted to think about it, so I got up and left.

"Going down in the elevator I felt as if a crisis had passed — that's a feeling a nurse often has about other people — and then as I left the elevator I heard the names Archie Goodwin and Nero Wolfe. The idea came to me — why not get them to find the person who planted the bomb? So I spoke to Mr. Goodwin, but I couldn't make myself tell him about it. I just told him I wanted to see Nero Wolfe to ask his advice. Mr. Goodwin said he would try to arrange it, and he would phone me or I could phone him."

She fluttered a hand. "That's how it was."

Wolfe regarded her. "It's not incoherent, but neither is it sapient. Do you consider yourself intelligent?"

"Why — yes. Enough to get along. I'm a good nurse, and a good nurse has to be intelligent."

"Yet you thought that by some hocus-pocus that quack could expose the man who planted the bomb in the hospital?"

"I thought he did it scientifically. I knew he had a great reputation, just as you have."

"Good heavens!" Wolfe opened his eyes wide at her. "Well, what were you going to ask my advice about?"

"Whether you thought there was any chance — whether you thought the police were going to find him."

Wolfe's eyes were back to normal, half shut again. "This performance I'm engaged in, Miss Maturo — this inquisition of a person involved by circumstance in a murder — is a hubbub in a jungle; at least, in its preliminary stage. Blind, I grope, and proceed by feel. You say you never saw Mr. Heller, but you can't prove it. I am free to assume that you had seen him, not at his office, and talked with him; that you were convinced, no matter how, that *he* had planted the bomb in the hospital and caused the holocaust; and that, moved by an obsessive rancor, you went to his place and killed him. One ad —"

470

She broke in: "Why on earth would I think he had planted the bomb?"

"I have no idea. As I said, I'm groping. One advantage of that assumption would be that you have confessed to a hatred so overpowering that surely it might have impelled you to kill if and when you identified its object. It is Mr. Cramer, not I, who is deploying the hosts of justice in this enterprise, but no doubt two or three men are calling on your friends and acquaintances to learn if you have ever hinted a suspicion of Leo Heller in connection with the hospital disaster. Also, they are probably asking whether you had any grudge against the hospital that might have provoked you to plant the bomb yourself."

A muscle at the side of her neck was twitching. "Me? Is that what it's like?"

"It is, indeed. That wouldn't be incongruous. Your proclaimed abhorrence of the perpetrator could be simply the screeching of your remorse."

"Well, it isn't." Suddenly she was out of her chair, and a bound took her to Wolfe's desk and her palms did a tattoo on the desk as she leaned forward at him. "Don't you dare say a thing like that! The six people I care for most in the world — they all died that night! How would you feel?" More tattoo. "How would anybody feel?"

I was up and at her elbow, but no bodily

471

discipline was required. She straightened and for a moment stood trembling all over. Then she got her control back and went to her chair and sat.

"I'm sorry," she said in a tight little voice.

"You should be," Wolfe said grimly. A woman cutting loose is always too much for him. "Pounding the top of my desk settles nothing. What were the names of these six people who died?"

She told him, and he wanted to know more about them. I was beginning to suspect that actually he had no more of a lead than I did, that he had given Cramer a runaround to jostle him loose from the NW he had fixed on, and that, having impulsively impounded the five hundred bucks, he had decided to spend the night trying to earn it.

The line he now took with Susan Maturo bore me out. It was merely the old grab-bag game: Keep her talking, about anything and anybody, in the hope that she would spill something that would faintly resemble a straw. I had known Wolfe, when the pickings had been slim, to play that game for hours on end.

He was still at it with Susan Maturo when an individual entered with a message for Cramer which he delivered in a whisper. Cramer got up and started for the door, then thought better of it and turned.

"You might as well be in on this," he told

Wolfe. "They've got Mrs. Tillotson and she's here."

That was a break for Susan Maturo, since Wolfe might have kept her going another hour or so. As she arose to go she favored me with a glance. It looked as if she intended it for a smile to show that were no hard feelings, but if so it was the poorest excuse for a smile I had ever seen. If it hadn't been unprofessional I would have gone and given her a pat on the shoulder.

The newcomer who was ushered in was not Mrs. Tillotson but an officer of the law, not in uniform. He was one of the new acquisitions on Homicide and I had never seen him before, but I admired his manly stride as he approached and his snappy stance when he halted and faced Cramer.

"Who did you leave over there?" Cramer asked him.

"Murphy, sir. Timothy Murphy."

"Okay. You tell it. Hold it." Cramer turned to Wolfe: "This man's name is Roca. He was on post at Heller's place. It was him you asked about the pencils and the eraser. Go on, Roca."

"Yes, sir. The doorman in the lobby phoned up that there was a woman down there that wanted to come up, and I told him to let her come. I thought that was compatible."

"Go ahead." Wolfe grimaced.

"She came up in the elevator. She wouldn't tell me her name. She asked me questions about how much longer would I be there and did I expect anybody else to come and so on. We bantered back and forth, my objective being to find out who she was, and then she came right out with it. She took a roll of bills from her bag. She offered me three hundred dollars, and then four hundred, and finally five hundred, if I would unlock the cabinets in Heller's office and let her be in there alone for an hour. That put me in a quandary."

"How did you get out?"

"If I had had keys to the cabinets I would have accepted her offer. I would have unlocked them and left her in there. When she was ready to go I would have arrested her and taken her to be searched, and we would have known what she had taken from the cabinet. That would have broken the case. But I had no keys to the cabinets."

"Uh-huh. If you had had keys and had unlocked the cabinets and left her in there, and she had taken something from a cabinet and burned it up, you would have collected the ashes and sent them to the laboratory for examination by modern scientific methods."

Roca swallowed. "I admit I didn't think about burning. But if I had had keys I would have thought harder."

"I bet you would. Did you take her money for evidence?"

"No, sir. I thought that might be instigation. I took her into custody. I phoned in. When a relief came, I brought her here to you. I am staying here to face her."

"You've faced her enough for tonight. Plenty. We'll have a talk later. Go tell Burger to bring her in."

Although my stay in Heller's waiting room that morning had been brief, I had long been trained to see what I look at and to remember what I see, and I would hardly have recognized Mrs. Albert Tillotson. She had lost five pounds and gained twice that many wrinkles, and the contrast between her lipstick and her drained-out skin made her look more like a woman-hater's pin-up than an overfed matron.

"I wish to speak with you privately," she told Inspector Cramer.

She was one of those. Her husband was president of something, and therefore it was absurd to suppose that she was not to expect privileges. It took Cramer a good five minutes to get it into her head that she was just one of the girls. It was a shock that she had to take time out to decide how to react to it.

She decided on a barefaced lie. She demanded to know if the man who had brought her there was a member of the police force. Cramer replied that he was.

"Well," she declared, "he shouldn't be. You may know that late this afternoon a police officer called at my residence to see me. He told me that Leo Heller had been murdered, and wanted to know for what purpose I had gone to his office this morning. Naturally, I didn't want to be involved in an ugly thing like that, so I told him I hadn't gone to see Leo Heller, but he convinced me that that wouldn't do, so I said I had gone to see him, but on an intimate personal matter that I wouldn't tell . . . Is that man putting down what I'm saying?"

"Yes. That's his job."

"I wouldn't want it. Nor yours, either . . . The officer insisted that I must tell why I had gone to see Heller, and I refused. When he said he would have to take me to the District Attorney's office, under arrest if necessary, and I saw that he meant it, I told him. I told him that my husband and I have been having some difficulty with our son, especially his schooling, and I went to Heller to ask what college would be best for him. I answered the officer's questions within reason, and finally he left. Perhaps you knew all this."

Cramer nodded. "Yes."

"Well, after the officer had gone I began to worry, and I went to see a friend and ask her advice. The trouble was that I had given Heller many details about my son, some of them very intimate and confidential, and since he had been murdered, the police would probably go through all his papers. Those details were private and I wanted to keep them private. I knew that Heller had made all his notes in a personal shorthand that no one else could read; anyhow, he had said so, but I couldn't be sure. After I had discussed it with my friend a long time, I decided to go to Heller's place and ask whoever was in charge to let me have any papers relating to my family affair, since they were not connected with the murder."

"I see," Cramer assured her.

"And that's what I did. The officer there pretended to listen to me, he pretended to be agreeing with me, and then suddenly he arrested me for trying to bribe an officer. When I indignantly denied it, as of course I did, and started to leave, he detained me by force. He actually was going to put handcuffs on me! So I came with him, and here I am. I hope you realize I have a complaint to make and I am making it!"

Cramer was eyeing her. "Did you try to bribe him?"

"No, I didn't!"

"You didn't offer him money?"

"No!"

Purley Stebbins permitted a low sound, half growl and half snort, to escape him. Cramer, ignoring that impertinence from a subordinate, took a deep breath and let it out again.

"Shall I take it?" Wolfe inquired.

"No, thank you," Cramer said acidly. He

was keeping his eyes on Mrs. Tillotson. "You're making a mistake, madam," he told her. "All these lies don't do you any good. They just made it harder for you. Try telling the truth for a change."

She drew herself up, but it wasn't very impressive because she was pretty well fagged after her hard day. "You're calling me a liar," she accused Cramer, "and in front of witnesses." She pointed a finger at the police stenographer. "You get that down just the way he said it!"

"He will," Cramer assured her. "Look, Mrs. Tillotson. You admit you lied about going to see Heller until you realized that the doorman would swear that you were there not only this morning but also previously. Now, about your trying to bribe an officer. That's a felony. If we charge you with it, and you go to trial, I can't say who the jury will believe, you or the officer, but I know who I believe. I believe him, and you're lying about it."

"Get him in here," she challenged. "I want to face him."

"He wants to face you, too, but that wouldn't help any. I'm satisfied that you're lying, and also that you're lying about what you wanted to get from Heller's files. He made his notes in a private code that it will take a squad of experts to decipher, and you knew that. I do not believe that you took the risk of going there and trying to bribe an officer just to get his notes about you and your family.

"I believe there is something in his files that can easily be recognized as pertaining to you or your family, and that's what you were after. In the morning we'll have men going through the contents of the files, item by item, and if anything like that is there they'll spot it. Meanwhile, I'm holding you for further questioning about your attempt to bribe an officer. If you want to telephone a lawyer, you may. One phone call, with an officer present."

Cramer's head swiveled. "Stebbins, take her to Lieutenant Rowcliff, and tell him how it stands."

Purley arose. Mrs. Tillotson was shrinking, looking less overfed every second. "Will you wait a minute?" she demanded.

"Two minutes, madam. But don't try cooking up any more lies. You're no good at it."

"That man misunderstood me. I wasn't trying to bribe him."

"I said you may phone a lawyer —"

"I don't want a lawyer." She was sure about that. "If they go through those files they'll find what I was after, so I might as well tell you. It's some letters in envelopes addressed to me. They're not signed, they're anonymous, and I wanted that Heller to find out who sent them."

"Are they about your son?"

"No. They're about me. They threatened me with something, and I was sure it was leading up to blackmail."

"How many letters?"

"Six."

"What do they threaten you with?"

"They — they don't exactly threaten. They're quotations from things. One of them says, 'He that cannot pay let him pray.' Another one says, 'So comes a reckoning when the banquet's o'er." The others are longer, but that's what they're like."

"What made you think they were leading up to blackmail?"

"Wouldn't you? 'He that cannot pay let him pray.' "

"And you wanted Heller to identify the sender. How many times had you seen him?"

"Twice."

"Of course you had given him all the information you could. We'll get the letters in the morning, but you can tell us now what you told Heller. As far as possible, everything that was said by both of you."

I permitted myself to grin, and glanced at Wolfe to see if he was properly appreciative of Cramer's adopting his approach, but he was just sitting there looking patient.

It was hard to tell, for me at least, how much Mrs. Tillotson was giving and how much she was covering. If there was something in her past that someone might have felt she should pay for or give a reckoning of, either she didn't know what it was, or she had kept it from Heller. Or if she had told him she certainly didn't intended to let us in on it.

Cramer played her back and forth until she was so tied up in contradictions that it would have taken a dozen mathematical wizards to make head or tail of it.

Wolfe finally intervened. He glanced up at the wall clock and announced, "It's after midnight. Thank heaven, you have an army to start sorting this out and checking it. If Lieutenant Rowcliff is still here, let him have her and let's have some cheese. I'm hungry."

Cramer, as ready for a recess as anybody, had no objection. Purley Stebbins removed Mrs. Tillotson and I went to the kitchen to give Fritz a hand, knowing that he was running himself ragged furnishing trays of sandwiches to flocks of homicide personnel distributed all over the premises.

When I returned to the office with a supply of provender, Cramer was riding Wolfe, pouring it on, and Wolfe was leaning back in his chair with his eyes shut. I passed around plates of Fritz's *il pesto* and crackers, with beer for Wolfe and the stenographer, coffee for Cramer and Stebbins, and milk for me.

In four minutes Cramer inquired, "What is this stuff?"

Wolfe told him. *"Il pesto."*

"What's in it?"

"Canestrato cheese, anchovies, pig liver, black walnuts, chives, sweet basil, garlic, and olive oil."

"For Pete's sake!"

In another four minutes Cramer addressed me in the tone of one doing a gracious favor. "I'll take some more of that, Goodwin."

But while I was gathering the empty plates he started in on Wolfe again. Wolfe didn't bother to counter. He wanted until Inspector Cramer halted for breath and then growled, "It's now nearly one o'clock and we have three more."

Cramer sent Purley for another scared citizen. This time it was the thin, tall, bony specimen who, entering the lobby on 37th Street that morning, had stopped to aim a rude stare at Susan Maturo and me. Having read his statement, I now knew that his name was Jack Ennis, that he was an expert diemaker, at present unemployed, that he was unmarried, that he lived in Queens, and that he was a born inventor who had not yet cashed in. His brown suit had not been pressed.

When Cramer told him that questions from Wolfe were to be considered a part of the official inquiry into Leo Heller's death, Ennis cocked his head to appraise Wolfe as if deciding whether or not such a procedure deserved his okay.

"You're a self-made man," he told Wolfe. "I've read about you. How old are you?"

Wolfe returned his gaze. "Some other time, Mr. Ennis. Tonight you're the target, not me. You're thirty-eight, aren't you?"

Ennis smiled. He had a wide mouth with thin, colorless lips, and his smile wasn't especially attractive. "Excuse me if you thought I was being fresh asking how old you are. I know you're right at the top of your racket, and I wondered how long it took you to get started up. I'm going to the top too, before I'm through, but it's taking me a long time to get a start. How old were you when you first got your name in the paper?"

"Two days. A notice of my birth . . . I understand that your call on Leo Heller was connected with your determination to get a start as an inventor?"

"That's right." Ennis smiled again. "Look. The cops have been at me now for seven hours, and where are they? What's the sense in going on with it? Why would I want to kill that guy?"

"That's what I'd like to know."

"Well, search me. I've got patents on six inventions, and none of them is on the market. One of them is not perfect — I know it's not, but it needs only one more trick to make it an absolute whiz. I can't find the trick. I've read about this Heller, and it seemed to me that if I gave him all the dope, all the stuff he needed for one of his formulas, there was a good chance he would come up with the answer.

"So I went to him. I spent three long sessions with him. He finally thought he had enough to try to work up a formula, and he was taking a crack at it. I had a date to see him this morning and find out how it was going."

Ennis stopped for emphasis. "So I'm hoping. After all the sweating I've done and the dough I've spent, maybe I'm going to get it at last. So I go. I go upstairs to his office and shoot him dead, and then go to the waiting room and sit down and wait." He smiled. "Listen. If you want to say there are smarter men than me, I won't argue. Maybe you're smarter, yourself. But I'm not a lunatic, am I?"

Wolfe's lips were pursed. "I won't commit myself on that, Mr. Ennis. But you have by no means demonstrated that it is fatuous to suppose you might have killed Heller. What if he devised a formula from the data you supplied, discovered the trick that would transform your faulty contraption into a whiz, as you expressed it, and refused to divulge it except on intolerable terms? That would be a motive for murder."

"It sure would," Ennis agreed without reservation. "I would have killed him with pleasure." He leaned forward and was suddenly intense. "Look. I'm headed for the top. I've got what I need in here" — he tapped his forehead — "and nothing and nobody is going to stop me. If Heller had done what you said I might have killed him, I don't deny it, but he didn't."

He jerked to Cramer: "And I'm glad of a chance to tell you what I've told those bozos that have been grilling me: I want to go through Heller's papers to see if I can find the formula he worked up for me. Maybe I can't recognize it, and if I do I doubt if I can figure it out, but I want to look for it, and not next year, either."

"We're doing the looking," Cramer said dryly. "If we find anything that can be identified as relating to you, you'll see it, and eventually you may get it."

"I don't want it eventually, I want it now. Do you know how long I've been working on that thing? Four years! It's mine, you understand that; it's mine!" He was getting upset.

"Calm down, bud," Cramer advised him. "We're right with you in seeing to it that you get what's yours."

"Meanwhile," Wolfe said, "There's a point or two: When you entered that building this morning, why did you stop and gape at Mr. Goodwin and Miss Maturo?"

Ennis' chin went up. "Who says I did?"

"I do, on information . . . Archie.

Did he?"

"Yes," I stated. "Rudely."

"Well," Ennis told Wolfe, "He's bigger than I am. Maybe I did, at that."

"Why? Any special reason?"

"It depends on what you call special. I thought I recognized her, a girl I knew once, and then saw I was wrong. She was much too young."

"Very well. I would like to explore my suggestions, which you reject, that Heller was trying to do you out of your invention as perfected by his calculations. I want you to describe the invention as you described it to him, particularly the flaw which you had tried to rectify."

"I won't attempt to report what followed, and I couldn't anyhow, since I understood less than a tenth of it. I did gather that it was a gadget intended to supersede all existing X-ray machines, but beyond that I got lost in a wilderness of cathodes and atomicity and coulombs.

If talking like a character out of space-science fiction proves you're an inventor, that bird was certainly one. He stood up to make motions to illustrate, and grabbed a pad and pencil from Wolfe's desk to explain with drawings. After a while it began to look as if it would be impossible to stop him. They finally managed it, with Sergeant Stebbins lending a hand by marching over and taking his elbow.

On his way out he turned at the door to call back: "I want that formula, and don't you forget it!"

The female of an executive type was still in mink, or, rather, she had it with her, but she was not so brisk. As I said before, that morning I would have classified her as between twenty and sixty, but the day's experiences had worn her down closer to reality, and I would now have put her at forty-seven. However, she was game. With all she had gone through, at that late hour, she still let us know, as she deposited the mink on a chair, sat on another, crossed her legs, that she was cool and composed and in command.

My typing her as an executive had been justified by the transcripts. Her name really was Agatha Abbey, and she was executive editor of a magazine, *Mode,* which I did not read regularly.

After Cramer had explained the nature of the session, including Wolfe's status, Wolfe took aim and went for the center of the target: "Miss Abbey. I presume you'd like to get to bed — I know I would — so we won't waste time flouncing around. Three things about you."

He held up a finger. "First: You claim that you never saw Leo Heller. It is corroborated that you had not visited his place before today, but whether you had seen him else-

487

where will be thoroughly investigated by men armed with pictures. They will ask people at your place of business, at your residence, and at other likely spots. If it is found that you had, in fact, met him and conferred with him, you won't like it."

He raised two fingers. "Second: You refused to tell why you went to see Heller. That does not brand you as a miscreant, since most people have private matters which they innocently and jealously guard; but you clung to your refusal beyond reason, even after it was explained that the information had to be given by all six persons who called on Heller this morning, and you were assured that it would be revealed to no one unless it proved to be an item of evidence in a murder case. You finally did give the information, but only when you perceived that if you didn't there would be a painstaking investigation into your affairs and movements."

He raised three fingers. "Third: When the information was wormed out of you, it was almost certainly flummery. You said that you wanted to engage Heller to find out who had stolen a ring from a drawer of your desk some three months ago. That was childish nonsense. I grant that even though the ring was insured, you may have been intent on disclosing the culprit, but if you have enough sense to hold a well-paid job in a highly competitive field, as you have, surely you would have known that it was stupid to suppose Heller could help you. Singling out a sneak thief from among a hundred possibilities was plainly an operation utterly unsuited to his technique, and even to his pretensions."

Wolfe moved his head an inch to the left and back again. "No, Miss Abbey, it won't do. I want to know whether you saw Leo Heller before today, and in any case what you wanted of him."

She answered in a controlled, thin, steely voice. "You make it sound overwhelming, Mr. Wolfe."

"Not I. It *is* overwhelming."

Her sharp, dark eyes went to Cramer. "You're an Inspector, in charge of this business?"

"That's right."

"Do the police share Mr. Wolfe's — skepticism?"

"You can take what he said as coming from me."

"Then, no matter what I tell you about why I went to see Heller, you'll check it?"

"Not necessarily. If it fits all right, and if we can't connect it with the murder, and if it's a private, confidential matter, we'll let it go at that. If we do check any, we'll be careful. There are enough innocent citizens sore at us already."

Her eyes darted back to Wolfe. "What

about you, Mr. Wolfe? Will you have to check?"

"I sincerely hope not. Let Mr. Cramer's assurance include me."

Her eyes went around. "What about these men?"

"They are trained confidential assistants. They hold their tongues or they lose their jobs."

The tip of her tongue came out and went in. "I'm not satisfied, but what can I do? If my only choice is between this and the whole New York detective force pawing at me, I take this. I phoned Leo Heller ten days ago, and he came to my office and spent two hours there. It was a business matter, not a personal one. I'm going to tell you exactly what it was, because I'm no good at ad-libbing a phony."

She was hating it, but she went on: "You said I have sense enough to hold a well-paid job in a highly competitive field, but if you only knew. It's not a field, it's a corral of wild beasts. There are six female tigers trying to get their claws on my job right now, and if they all died tonight there would be six others tomorrow. If it came out what I went to Leo Heller for, that would be the finish of me."

The top of her tongue flashed out and in. "So that's what this means to me. A magazine like *Mode* has two main functions, reporting and predicting. American women want to know what is being made and worn in Paris and New York, but even more they want to know what is going to be made and worn next season. *Mode*'s reporting has been good enough, I've been all right on that, but for the past year our predictions have been utterly rotten. We've got the contacts, but something has gone haywire, and our biggest rival has made monkeys of us. Another year like that, even another season, and good-bye."

Wolfe grunted. "To the magazine?"

"No, to me. So I decided to try Leo Heller. We had carried a piece about him, and I had met him. The idea was to give him everything we had, and we had plenty, about styles and colors and trends for the past ten years, and have him figure the probabilities six months ahead. He thought it was feasible, and I don't think he was a faker. He had to come to the office to go through our stuff. Of course, I had to camouflage what he was there for, but that wasn't hard. Do you want to know what I told them he was doing?"

"I think not," Wolfe muttered.

"So he came. I phoned him the next day, and he said it would take him at least a week to determine whether he had sufficient information to make up a probability formula. Yesterday I phoned again, and he said he had something to discuss and asked me to call at his place this morning. I went. You know the rest of it."

She stopped. Wolfe and Inspector Cramer exchanged glances. "I would like," Wolfe said, "to have the names of the six female tigers who are after your job."

She turned white. I have never seen color leave a face faster. "Darn you!" she said in bitter fury. "So you're a rat, like everybody else!"

Wolfe showed her a palm. "Please, madam. I have no desire to betray you to your enemies. I merely want —"

He saved his breath because his audience was leaving. She got up and headed for the door. Stebbins looked at Wolfe, Wolfe shook his head, and Stebbins trailed after her.

As he left the room at her heels Cramer called to him, "Bring Busch!" Then he turned to Wolfe to protest: "You had her open. Why give her a breather?"

Wolfe made a face. "The miserable wretch. She was dumb with rage and it would have been futile to keep at her. But you're keeping her?"

"You're right we are. For what?" He was out of his chair, glaring down at Wolfe. "Tell me for what! Except for dragging that out of that woman, there's not one single —"

He was off again. I miss no opportunity of resenting Inspector Cramer; I enjoy it and it's good for my appetite, but I must admit that on that occasion he seemed to me to have a point. I still had seen or heard no indication whatever that Wolfe's statement that he had a lead was anything but a stall.

So as Cramer yapped at my employer, I had a private feeling that some of the sentiments he expressed were not positively preposterous. He was still at it when the door opened to admit Stebbins with the sixth customer.

The sergeant, after conducting this one to the seat the others had occupied, facing Wolfe and Cramer, did not go to the chair against the wall, which he had favored throughout the evening. Instead, he lowered his bulk onto one at Cramer's left, only two arms' lengths from the subject.

That was interesting, because it meant that he was voting for Karl Busch as his pick of the lot, and while Stebbins had often been wrong, I had known him, more than once, to be right.

Karl Busch was the slick, sly, swarthy little article with his hair pasted to his scalp. In the specifications on his transcript I had noted the key NVMS, meaning No Visible Means of Support, but that was just a nod to routine. The details of the report on him left no real doubt as to the sources he tapped for jack.

He was a Broadway smoothie, third grade. He was not in the theater, or sports, or the flicks, or any of the tough rackets, but he knew everyone who was, and as the engraved lettuce swirled around the midtown corners and got trapped in the nets of the collectors, legitimate and otherwise, he had a hundred little dodges for fastening onto a specimen for himself.

To him Cramer's tone was noticeably different. "This is Nero Wolfe," he rasped. "Answer his questions. You hear, Busch?"

Busch said he did.

Wolfe, who was frowning, studying him, spoke, "Nothing is to be gained, Mr. Busch, by my starting the usual rigmarole with you. I've read your statement, and I doubt if it would be worthwhile to try to pester you into a contradiction. But you had three conversations with Leo Heller, and in your statement they are not reported, merely summarized. I want the details of those conversations, as completely as your memory will furnish. Start with the first one, two months ago. Exactly what was said?"

Busch slowly shook his head. "Impossible, mister."

"You won't try?"

"It's this way: If I took you to the pier and ast you to try to jump across to Brooklyn, what would you do? You'd say it was impossible and why get your feet wet. That's me."

"I told you," Cramer snapped, "to answer his questions."

Busch extended a dramatic hand in appeal.

"What do you want me to do — make it up?"

"I want you to do what you were told to the best of your ability."

"Okay. This will be good. I said to him, Mr. Heller, my name's Busch and I'm a broker. He said broker of what, and I said of anything people want broken, just for a gag, but he had no sense of humor, so I dropped that and explained. I told him there was a great demand among all kinds of people to know what horse was going to win a race the day before the race was run or even an hour before. I had read about his line of work and thought that he could help to meet that demand.

"He said that he had thought several times about using his method on horse races, but he didn't care himself to use the method for personal bets because he wasn't a betting man. He said for him to make up one of his formulas for just one race would take an awful lot of research. It would cost so much it wouldn't be worth it for any one person unless that person made a high-bracket plunge."

"You're paraphrasing it," Wolfe objected. "I'd prefer the words that were used."

"This is the best of my ability, mister."

"Very well. Go on."

"I said I wasn't a high-bracket boy myself, but anyway that wasn't here or there or under the rug, because what I had in mind was a wholesale setup. I had figgers to show him. Say he did ten races a week. I could round up at least twenty customers right off the bat. All he had to do was crack a percentage of forty or better and it would start a fire you couldn't put out if you ran a river down it. We could have a million customers if we wanted 'em. We would hand-pick a hundred and no more, and each one would ante one C per week, which, if I can add at all, would make ten grand every seven days."

"Go on."

"Well, that would make half a million per year, and Heller and me would split. Out of my half I would expense the operating, and out of his half he would expense the dope. He would have to walk on his nose to cut under a hundred grand all clear, and I wouldn't do so bad. We didn't sign no papers, but he could smell it, and after two more talks he agreed to do a dry run on three races.

"The first one he worked on his answer was the favorite, a horse named White Water, and it won, but it was just exercise for that rabbit. The next one it was heads or tails between two sweethearts. Heller had the winner all right, a horse named Short Order, but on a fifty-fifty call you don't exactly panic. But get this next one."

Busch gestured dramatically for emphasis.

"Now, get it. This animal was forty to one, but it might as well have been four hundred. It was a muscle-bound, sore-jointed hyena named Zero. That alone, a horse named Zero, was enough to put the curse of six saints on it, but also it was the kind of looking horse which, if you looked at it, would make you think promptly of canned dog food.

"When Heller came up with that horse, I thought, oh-oh, he's a loon after all, and watch me run. Well, you ast me to tell you the words we used, me and Heller. If I told you some I used when that Zero horse won that race, you would lock me up. Not only was Heller batting a thousand, but he had kicked through with the most — What are you doing, taking a nap?"

We all looked at Wolfe. He was leaning back with his eyes shut tight, and was motionless except for his lips, which were pushing out and in, and out and in, and again out and in. Cramer and Stebbins and I knew what that meant: something had hit his hook, and he had yanked and had a fish on.

A tingle ran up my spine. Stebbins arose and took a step to stand at Busch's elbow. Cramer just sat with his eyes on Wolfe.

Busch asked, "Is he having a fit?"

Wolfe's eyes opened and he came forward in his chair. "No, I'm not," he snapped, "but I've been having one all evening . . . Mr. Cramer. Will you please have Mr. Busch

497

removed? Temporarily.''

Cramer, with no hesitation, nodded at Purley, and Purley touched Busch's shoulder and they went. The door closed behind them, but it wasn't more than five seconds before it opened again and Purley was back with us. He wanted as quick a look at the fish as his boss and me.

''Have you ever,'' Wolfe was asking Cramer, ''called me, point-blank, a dolt and a dotard?''

''Those aren't my words, but I've certainly called you.''

''You may do so now. Your opinion of me at its lowest was far above my present opinion of myself.'' He looked up at the clock, which said five past three. ''We now need a proper setting. How many of your staff are in my house?''

''Fourteen.''

''We want them all in here, for the effect of their presence. Half of them should bring chairs. Also, of course, the six persons we have interviewed. This shouldn't take to long — possibly an hour, though I doubt it. I certainly won't prolong it.''

Cramer was looking contrary. ''You've already prolonged it plenty. You mean you prolonged it plenty. You mean you're prepared to name him?''

''I am not. I haven't the slightest notion who it is. But I am prepared to make an attack that will expose him — or her — and if it doesn't, I'll have no opinion of myself at all." Wolfe flattened his palms on his desk, for him a violent gesture. "Confound it, don't you know me well enough to realize when I'm ready to strike?"

"I know you too darn' well." Cramer looked at his sergeant. "Okay, Purley. Collect the audience."

The office is a good-sized room, but there wasn't much unoccupied space left when that gathering was fully assembled. The biggest assortment of homicide employees I had ever gazed on extended from wall to wall in the rear of the six subjects. Cramer was planted in the red-leather chair with Stebbins on his left, and the stenographer was hanging on at the end of my desk.

The six citizens were in a row up front, and none of them looked merry.

Wolfe's eyes went from right to left and back again, taking them in. He spoke: "I'll have to make this somewhat elaborate, so that all of you will clearly understand the situation. I could not at the moment hazard even a venturesome guess as to which of you killed Leo Heller, but I now know how to find out and I propose to do so."

Wolfe interlaced his fingers in front of his middle mound. "We have from the first had a hint that has not been imparted to you.

499

Yesterday — Tuesday, that is — Heller telephoned here to say that he suspected that one of his clients had committed a serious crime and to hire me to investigate. I declined, for reasons we needn't go into, but Mr. Goodwin took it upon himself to call on Heller this morning to discuss the matter."

He shot me a glance and I met it. Merely an incivility. He went on to them: "He entercd Heller's office but found it unoccupied. Tarrying there for some minutes, and meanwhile exercising his highly trained talent for observation, he noticed, among other details, that some pencils and an eraser from an overturned jar were arranged on the desk in a sort of pattern. Later on that same detail was, of course, noted by the police. It was a feature of that detail which led Mr. Cramer to come to see me. He assumed that Heller, seated at his desk and threatened with a gun, knowing or thinking he was about to die, had made the pencil pattern to leave a message, and that the purpose of the message was to give a clue to the identity of the murderer. On that point I agreed with Mr. Cramer. Will you all approach, please, and look at this arrangement on my desk? These pencils and the eraser are placed approximately the same as those on Heller's desk. From your side you are seeing them as Heller intended them to be seen."

The six did as requested, and they had company. Not only did most of the homicide subordinates leave their chairs and come forward for a view, but Cramer himself got up and took a glance — maybe just curiosity, but I wouldn't put it past him to suspect Wolfe of a shenanigan. However, the pencils and eraser were properly placed, as I ascertained by arising and stretching to peer over shoulders.

When they were all seated again Wolfe resumed: "Mr. Cramer had a notion about the message which I rejected and will not bother to expound. My own notion of it, conceived almost immediately, came merely as a stirring of memory. It reminded me vaguely of something I had seen somewhere. The vagueness disappeared when I reflected that Heller had been a mathematician, academically qualified and trained. The memory was old, and I checked it by going to my shelves for a book I had read some ten years ago. Its title is *Mathematics for the Million*, by Lancelot Hogben. After verifying my recollection, I locked the book in a drawer, because it seemed to me it would be a pity for Mr. Cramer to waste time leafing through it."

"Let's get on," Cramer growled.

Wolfe did so. "As told in Mr. Hogben's book, more than two thousand years ago what he calls a matchstick number script was being used in India. Three horizontal lines stood for two, and so on. That was indeed primitive, but it had greater possibilities than the clumsy devices of the Hebrews and Greeks and Romans. Around the time of the birth of Christ some brilliant Hindu improved it by connecting the horizontal lines with diagonals, making the units unmistakable."

He pointed to the arrangement on his desk. "These five pencils on your left form a 3 exactly as the Hindus formed a 3, and the three pencils on your right form a 2. These Hindu symbols are one of the great landmarks in the history of number language. You will note, by the way, that our own forms of the figure 3 and of the figure 2 are taken directly from these Hindu symbols."

A couple of them got up to look, and Wolfe politely waited until they were seated again. "So, since Heller had been a mathematician, and since those were famous patterns in the history of mathematics, I assumed that the message was a 3 and a 2. But evidence indicated that the eraser was also a part of the message and must be included. That was simple. It is the custom of an academic mathematician, if he wants to scribble 4 times 6, or 7 times 9, to use for the 'times' not an X, as we laymen do, but a dot. It is so well known a custom that Mr. Hogben uses it in his book without thinking it necessary to explain it, and therefore I confidently assumed that the eraser was meant for a dot, and that the message was 3 times 2, or 6.''

Wolfe compressed his lips and shook his head. ''That was an impetuous imbecility. During the whole seven hours that I sat here poking at you people, I was trying to find some connection with the figure 6 that would either set one of you clearly apart, or relate you to the commission of some crime, or both. Preferably both, of course, but either would serve. In the interviews the figure 6 did turn up with persistent monotony, but with no promising application, and I could only ascribe it to the mischief of coincidence.

''So at three o'clock in the morning I was precisely where I had been when I started. Without a fortuitous nudge I can't say how long it would have taken me to become aware of my egregious blunder, but I got the nudge, and I can at least say that I responded promptly and effectively. The nudge came from Mr. Busch when he mentioned the name of a horse, Zero.''

He upturned a palm. ''Of course. Zero! I

had been a witless ass. The use of the dot as a symbol for 'times' is a strictly modern device. Since the rest of the message, the figures 3 and 2, were in Hindu number script, surely the dot was, too — provided that the Hindus had made any use of the dot. And what made my blunder so unforgivable was that the Hindus had indeed used a dot; they had used it, as explained in Hogben's book, for the most brilliant and imaginative invention in the whole history of the language of numbers. For when you have once decided how to write 3 and how to write 2, how are you going to distinguish among 32 and 302 and 3002 and 30002?

"That was the crucial problem in number language, and the Greeks and Romans, for all their intellectual eminence, never succeeded in solving it. Some Hindu genius did, twenty centuries ago. He saw that the secret was position. Today we use our zero exactly as he did, to show position, but instead of a zero he used a dot. That's what the dot was in the early Hindu number language; it was used like our zero. So Heller's message was not 3 times 2, or 6; it was 3 zero 2, or 302."

Susan Maturo started, jerking her head up. Wolfe rested his eyes on her.

"Yes, Miss Maturo. Three hundred and two people died in the explosion and fire at the Montrose Hospital a month ago. You

504

mentioned that figure when you were talking with me, but even if you hadn't when I realized that Heller's message was the figure 302, I would certainly have eventually connected it with that disaster."

"But it's —" She was staring. "You mean it is connected?"

"I'm proceeding on that obvious assumption. I am assuming that through the information one of you six people furnished Leo Heller as factors for a formula, he formed a suspicion that one of you had committed a serious crime, and that his message, the figure 302, indicates that the crime was the planting of a bomb in the Montrose Hospital which caused the deaths of three hundred and two people — or at least involvement in that crime."

It seemed as if I could see or feel muscles tightening all over the room. Most of those dicks, maybe all of them, had, of course, been working on the Montrose thing. Cramer pulled his feet back, and his hands were fists. Purley Stebbins took his gun from his holster and rested it on his knee.

"So," Wolfe continued, "Heller's message identified not the person who was about to kill him, not the criminal, but the crime. That was superbly ingenious and, considering the situation he was in, he deserves our deepest admiration. He has mine, and I retract any derogation of him. It would seem natural to concentrate on Miss Maturo, since she was certainly connected with that disaster, but first let's clarify the matter. I'm going to ask the rest of you if you have at any time visited the Montrose Hospital, or been connected with it in any way, or had dealings with any of its personnel. Take the question just as I have stated it." His eyes went to the end of the row, at the left. "Mrs. Tillotson? Answer, please. Have you?"

"No." It was barely audible.

His eyes moved. "Mr. Ennis?"

"I have not. Never."

"We'll skip you, Miss Maturo. Mr. Busch?"

"I've never been in a hopsital."

"That answers only a third of the question. Answer all of it."

"The answer is no, mister."

"Miss Abbey?"

"I went there once about two years ago, to visit a patient, a friend. That was all." The tip of her tongue came out and in. "Except for that one visit I have never been connected with it in any way or dealt with any of its personnel."

"That is explicit. Mr. Winslow?"

"No to the whole question. An unqualified no."

"Well." Wolfe did not look frustrated. "That would seem to isolate Miss Maturo, but it is not conclusive." His head turned. "Mr. Cramer. If the person who not only killed Leo Heller but also bombed that hospital is among these six, I'm sure you won't want to take the slightest risk of losing him. I have a suggestion."

"I'm listening," Cramer growled.

"Take them in as material witnesses, and hold them without bail if possible. Starting immediately, collect as many as you can of the former staff of that hospital. There were scores who survived, and other scores who were not on duty at the time. Get all of them if possible, spare no effort, and have them look at these people and say if they have ever seen any of them.

"Meanwhile, of course, you will be working on Miss Maturo, but you have heard the denials of the other five, and if you get reliable evidence that one of them has lied I'm sure you will need no further suggestion from me. Indeed, if one of them had lied and leaves this room, in custody, with that lie undeclared, that alone will be half the battle. I'm sorry —"

"Wait a minute."

All eyes went to one spot. It was Jack Ennis, the inventor. His thin, colorless lips were twisted, but not in a smile. The look in his eyes showed that he had no idea of smiling.

"I didn't tell an exact lie," he said.

Wolfe's eyes were slits. "Then an inexact lie, Mr. Ennis?"

"I mean I didn't visit that hospital as a

hospital. And I didn't have dealings with them; I was just trying to. I wanted them to give my X-ray machine a trial. One of them was willing to, but the other two talked him down."

"When was this?"

"I was there three times, twice in December and once in January."

"I thought your X-ray machine had a flaw."

"It wasn't perfect, but it would work. It would have been better than anything they had. I was sure I was going to get it in, because he was for it — his name is Halsey — and I saw him first, and he wanted to try it. But the other two talked him out of it, and one of them was very — he —" He petered out.

Wolfe prodded him. "Very what, Mr. Ennis?"

"He didn't understand me! He hated me!"

"There are people like that. There are all kinds of people. Have you ever invented a bomb?"

"A bomb?" Ennis's lips worked and this time I thought he actually was trying to smile. "Why would I invent a bomb?"

"I don't know. Inventors invent many things. If you have never tried your hand at a bomb, of course you have never had occasion to get hold of the necessary materials — for instance, explosives. It's only fair to tell you what I now regard as a reasonable hypothesis: that you placed the bomb in the hospital in revenge for an injury, real or fancied; that included in the data you gave Leo Heller was an item or items which led him to suspect you of that crime; that something he said led you, in turn, to suspect that he suspected; that when you went to his place this morning you went armed, prepared for action if your suspicion was verified; that when you entered the building you recognized Mr. Goodwin as my assistant; that you went up to Heller's office and asked him if Mr. Goodwin was there for an appointment with him, and his answer heightened or confirmed your suspicion and you produced the gun; that —"

"Hold it," Inspector Cramer snapped. "I'll take it from here. Purley, get him out and —"

Purley was a little slow. He was up, but Ennis was up faster and off in a flying dive for Wolfe. I dived too, and got an arm, and jerked. He tore loose, but by then a whole squad was there, swarming into him, and since I wasn't needed I backed off.

As I did so, someone dived at me, and Susan Maturo was up against me, gripping my lapels. "Tell me!" she demanded. "Tell me! Was it him?"

I told her promptly and positively, to keep her from ripping my lapels off. "Yes," I said.

Two months later a jury of eight men and four women agreed with me.

I Can Find My Way Out

Ngaio Marsh

AT HALF-PAST SIX on the night in question, Anthony Gill, unable to eat, keep still, think, speak or act coherently, walked from his rooms to the Jupiter Theatre. He knew that there would be nobody backstage, that there was nothing for him to do in the theatre, that he ought to stay quietly in his rooms and presently dress, dine and arrive at, say, a quarter to eight. But it was as if something shoved him into his clothes, thrust him into the street and compelled him to hurry through the West End to the Jupiter. His mind was overlaid with a thin film of inertia. Odd lines from the play occurred to him, but without any particular significance. He found himself busily reiterating a completely irrelevant sentence: "She has a way of laughing that would make a man's heart turn over."

Piccadilly, Shaftesbury Avenue. "Here I go," he thought, turning into Hawke Street, "towards my play. It's one hour and twenty-

510

nine minutes away. A step a second. It's rushing towards me. Tony's first play. Poor young Tony Gill. Never mind. Try again."

The Jupiter. Neon lights: I CAN FIND MY WAY OUT — *by Anthony Gill.* And in the entrance the bills and photographs. *Coralie Bourne with H. J. Bannington, Barry George and Canning Cumberland.*

Canning Cumberland. The film across his mind split and there was the Thing itself and he would have to think about it. How bad would Canning Cumberland be if he came down drunk? Brilliantly bad, they said. He would bring out all the tricks. Clever actor stuff, scoring off everybody, making a fool of the dramatic balance. "In Mr. Canning Cumberland's hands indifferent dialogue and unconvincing situations seemed almost real." What can you do with a drunken actor?

He stood in the entrance feeling his heart pound and his inside deflate and sicken.

Because, of course, it was a bad play. He was at this moment and for the first time really convinced of it. It was terrible. Only one virtue in it and that was not his doing. It had been suggested to him by Coralie Bourne: "I don't think the play you have sent me will do as it is but it has occurred to me —" It was a brilliant idea. He had rewritten the play round it and almost immediately and quite innocently he had begun to think of it as his own although he had said shyly to Coralie

Bourne: "You should appear as joint author." She had quickly, over-emphatically, refused. "It was nothing at all," she said. "If you're to become a dramatist you will learn to get ideas from everywhere. A single situation is nothing. Think of Shakespeare," she added lightly. "Entire plots! Don't be silly." She had said later, and still with the same hurried, nervous air: "Don't go talking to everyone about it. They will think there is more, instead of less, than meets the eye in my small suggestion. Please promise." He promised, thinking he'd made an error in taste when he suggested that Coralie Bourne, so famous an actress, should appear as joint author with an unknown youth. And how right she was, he thought, because, of course, it's going to be a ghastly flop. She'll be sorry she consented to play in it.

Standing in front of the theatre he contemplated nightmare possibilities. What did audiences do when a first play flopped? Did they clap a little, enough to let the curtain rise and quickly fall again on a discomforted group of players? How scanty must the applause be for them to let him off his own appearance? And they were to go on to the Chelsea Arts Ball. A hideous prospect. Thinking he would give anything in the world if he could stop his play, he turned into the foyer. There were lights in the offices and he paused, irresolute, before a board of photo-

512

graphs. Among them, much smaller than the leading players, was Dendra Gay with the eyes looking straight into his. *She had a way of laughing that would make a man's heart turn over.* "Well," he thought, "so I'm in love with her." He turned away from the photograph. A man came out of the office. "Mr. Gill? Telegrams for you."

Anthony took them and as he went out he heard the man call after him: "Very good luck for tonight, sir."

There were queues of people waiting in the side street for the early doors.

At six-thirty Coralie Bourne dialled Canning Cumberland's number and waited.

She heard his voice. "It's me," she said.

"O, God! darling, I've been thinking about you." He spoke rapidly, too loudly. "Coral, I've been thinking about Ben. You oughtn't to have given that situation to the boy."

"We've been over it a dozen times, Cann. Why not give it to Tony? Ben will never know." She waited and then said nervously, "Ben's gone, Cann. We'll never see him again."

"I've got a 'Thing' about it. After all, he's your husband."

"No, Cann, no."

"Suppose he turns up. It'd be like him to turn up."

"He won't turn up."

She heard him laugh. "I'm sick of all this," she thought suddenly. "I've had it once too often. I can't stand any more. . . . Cann," she said into the telephone. But he had hung up.

At twenty to seven, Barry George looked at himself in his bathroom mirror. "I've got a better appearance," he thought, "than Cann Cumberland. My head's a good shape, my eyes are bigger and my jaw line's cleaner. I never let a show down. I don't drink. I'm a better actor." He turned his head a little, slewing his eyes to watch the effect. "In the big scene," he thought, "I'm the star. He's the feed. That's the way it's been produced and that's what the author wants. I ought to get the notices."

Past notices came up in his memory. He saw the print, the size of the paragraphs; a long paragraph about Canning Cumberland, a line tacked on the end of it. "Is it unkind to add that Mr. Barry George trotted in the wake of Mr. Cumberland's virtuosity with an air of breathless dependability?" And again: "It is a little hard on Mr. Barry George that he should be obliged to act as foil to this brilliant performance." Worst of all: "Mr. Barry George succeeded in looking tolerably unlike a stooge, an achievement that evidently exhausted his resources."

"Monstrous!" he said loudly to his own image, watching the fine glow of indignation in the eyes. Alcohol, he told himself, did two things to Cann Cumberland. He raised his finger. Nice, expressive hand. An actor's hand. Alcohol destroyed Cumberland's artistic integrity. It also invested him with devilish cunning. Drunk, he would burst the seams of a play, destroy its balance, ruin its form and himself emerge blazing with a showmanship that the audience mistook for genius. "While I," he said aloud, "merely pay my author the compliment of faithful interpretation. Psha!"

He returned to his bedroom, completed his dressing and pulled his hat to the right angle. Once more he thrust his face close to the mirror and looked searchingly at its image. "By God!" he told himself, "he's done it once too often, old boy. Tonight we'll even the score, won't we? By God, we will."

Partly satisfied, and partly ashamed, for the scene, after all, had smacked a little of ham, he took his stick in one hand and a case holding his costume for the Arts Ball in the other, and went down to the theatre.

At ten minutes to seven, H. J. Bannington passed through the gallery queue on his way to the stage door alley, raising his hat and saying: "Thanks so much," to the gratified ladies who let him through. He heard them murmur his name. He walked briskly along the alley, greeted the stage-doorkeeper,

515

passed under a dingy lamp, through an entry and so to the stage. Only working lights were up. The walls of an interior set rose dimly into shadow. Bob Reynolds, the stage-manager, came out through the prompt-entrance. "Hello, old boy," he said, "I've changed the dressing-rooms. You're third on the right: they've moved your things in. Suit you?"

"Better, at least, than a black-hole the size of a W.C. but without its appointments," H.J. said acidly. "I suppose the great Mr. Cumberland still has the star-room?"

"Well, yes, old boy."

"And who pray, is next to him? In the room with the other gas fire?"

"We've put Barry George there, old boy. You know what he's like."

"Only too well, old boy, and the public, I fear, is beginning to find out." H.J. turned into the dressing-room passage. The stage-manager returned to the set where he encountered his assistant. "What's biting *him?*" asked the assistant. "He wanted a dressing-room with a fire." "Only natural," said the A.S.M. nastily. "He started life reading gas meters."

On the right and left of the passage, nearest the stage end, were two doors, each with its star in tarnished paint. The door on the left was open. H.J. looked in and was greeted with the smell of greasepaint, powder, wet-

516

white, and flowers. A gas fire droned comfortably. Coralie Bourne's dresser was spreading out towels. "Good evening, Katie, my jewel," said H.J. "La Belle not down yet?" "We're on our way," she said.

H.J. hummed stylishly: *"Bella filia del amore,"* and returned to the passage. The star-room on the right was closed but he could hear Cumberland's dresser moving about inside. He went on to the next door, paused, read the card, "Mr. Barry George," warbled a high derisive note, turned in at the third door and switched on the light.

Definitely not a second lead's room. No fire. A wash-basin, however, and opposite mirrors. A stack of telegrams had been placed on the dressing-table. Still singing he reached for them, disclosing a number of bills that had been tactfully laid underneath and a letter, addressed in a flamboyant script.

His voice might have been mechanically produced and arbitrarily switched off, so abruptly did his song end in the middle of a roulade. He let the telegrams fall on the table, took up the letter and tore it open. His face, wretchedly pale, was reflected and endlessly re-reflected in the mirrors.

At nine o'clock the telephone rang. Roderick Alleyn answered it. "This is Sloane 84405. No, you're on the wrong number. *No.*" He hung up and returned to his wife and guest.

"That's the fifth time in two hours."

"Do let's ask for a new number."

"We might get next door to something worse."

The telephone rang again. "This is not 84406," Alleyn warned it. "No, I cannot take three large trunks to Victoria Station. No, I am not the Instant All Night Delivery. No."

"They're 84406," Mrs. Alleyn explained to Lord Michael Lamprey. "I suppose it's just faulty dialing, but you can't imagine how angry everyone gets. Why do you want to be a policeman?"

"It's a dull hard job, you know —" Alleyn began.

"Oh," Lord Mike said, stretching his legs and looking critically at his shoes, "I don't for a moment imagine I'll leap immediately into false whiskers and plainclothes. No, no. But I'm revoltingly healthy, sir. Strong as a horse. And I don't think I'm as stupid as you might feel inclined to imagine —"

The telephone rang.

"I say, do let me answer it," Mike suggested and did so.

"Hullo?" he said winningly. He listened, smiling at his hostess. "I'm afraid —" he began. "Here, wait a bit — Yes, but —" His expression became blank and complacent. "May I," he said presently, "repeat your order, sir? Can't be too sure, can we? Call at 11 Harrow Gardens, Sloan Square, for one

518

suitcase to be delivered immediately at the Jupiter Theatre to Mr. Anthony Gill. Very good, sir. Collect. Quite."

He replaced the receiver and beamed at the Alleyns.

"What the devil have you been up to?" Alleyn said.

"He just simply would't listen to reason. I tried to tell him."

"But it may be urgent," Mrs. Alleyn ejaculated.

"It couldn't be more urgent, really. It's a suitcase for Tony Gill at the Jupiter."

"Well, then —"

"I was at Eton with the chap," said Mike reminiscently. "He's four years older than I am so of course he was madly important while I was less than the dust. This'll learn him."

"I think you'd better put that order through at once," said Alleyn firmly.

"I rather thought of executing it myself, do you know, sir. It'd be a frightfully neat way of gate-crashing the show, wouldn't it? I did try to get a ticket but the house was sold out."

"If you're going to deliver this case you'd better get a bend on."

"It's clearly an occasion for dressing up though, isn't it? I say," said Mike modestly, "would you think it most frightful cheek if I — well I'd promise to come back and return everything. I mean —"

"Are you suggesting that my clothes look more like a vanman's than yours?"

"I thought you'd have things —"

"For Heaven's sake, Rory," said Mrs. Alleyn, "dress him up and let him go. The great thing is to get that wretched man's suitcase to him."

"I know," said Mike earnestly. "It's most frightfully sweet of you. That's how I feel about it."

Alleyn took him away and shoved him into an old and begrimed raincoat, a cloth cap and a muffler. "You wouldn't deceive a village idiot in a total eclipse," he said, "but out you go."

He watched Mike drive away and returned to his wife.

"What'll happen?" she asked.

"Knowing Mike, I should say he will end up in the front stalls and go on to supper with the leading lady. She, by the way, is Coralie Bourne. Very lovely and twenty years his senior so he'll probably fall in love with her." Alleyn reached for his tobacco jar and paused. "I wonder what's happened to her husband," he said.

"Who was he?"

"An extraordinary chap. Benjamin Vlasnoff. Violent temper. Looked like a bandit. Wrote two very good plays and got run in three times for common assault. She tried to divorce him but it didn't go through. I think he afterwards lit off to Russia.'' Alleyn yawned. "I believe she had a hell of a time with him," he said.

"All Night Delivery," said Mike in a hoarse voice, touching his cap. "Suitcase. One." "Here you are," said the woman who had answered the door. "Carry it carefully, now, it's not locked and the catch springs out."

''Fanks,'' said Mike. "Much obliged. Chilly, ain't it?''

He took the suitcase out to the car.

It was a fresh spring night. Sloane Square was threaded with mist and all the lamps had halos round them. It was the kind of night when individual sounds separate themselves from the conglomerate voice of London; hollow sirens spoke imperatively down on the river and a bugle rang out over in Chelsea Barracks; a night, Mike thought, for adventure.

He opened the rear door of the car and heaved the case in. The catch flew open, the lid dropped back and the contents fell out. "Damn!" said Mike and switched on the inside light.

Lying on the floor of the car was a false beard.

It was flaming red and bushy and was mounted on a chin-piece. With it was incorporated a stiffened mustache. There were wire hooks to attach the whole thing behind the ears. Mike laid it carefully on the seat. Next he picked up a wide black hat, then a vast overcoat with a fur collar, finally a pair of black gloves.

Mike whistled meditatively and thrust his hands into the pockets of Alleyn's mackintosh. His right-hand fingers closed on a card. He pulled it out. "Chief Detective-Inspector Alleyn," he read, "C.I.D. New Scotland Yard."

"Honestly," thought Mike exultantly, "this is a gift."

Ten minutes later a car pulled into the curb at the nearest parking place to the Jupiter Theatre. From it emerged a figure carrying a suitcase. It strode rapidly along Hawke Stret and turned into the stage-door alley. As it passed under the dirty lamp it paused, and thus murkily lit, resembled an illustration from some Edwardian spy-story. The face was completely shadowed, a black cavern from which these projected a square of scarlet beard, which was the only note of color.

The doorkeeper who was taking the air with a member of stage-staff, moved forward, peering at the stranger.

"Was you wanting something?"

"I'm taking this case in for Mr. Gill."

"He's in front. You can leave it with me."

"I'm so sorry," said the voice behind the beard, "but I promised I'd leave it backstage myself."

"So you will be leaving it. Sorry, sir, but no one's admitted be'ind without a card."

"A card? Very well. Here is a card."

He held it out in his black-gloved hand. The stage-doorkeeper, unwillingly removing his gaze from the beard, took the card and examined it under the light. "Coo!" he said, "what's up, governor?"

"No matter. Say nothing of this."

The figure waved its hand and passed through the door. " 'Ere!" said the door-keeper excitedly to the stage-hand, "take a slant at this. That's a plain-clothes flattie, that was."

"*Plain* clothes!" said the stage-hand. "Them!"

" 'E's disguised," said the doorkeeper. "That's what it is. 'E's disguised 'isself."

" 'E's bloody well lorst 'isself be'ind them whiskers if you arst me."

Out on the stage someone was saying in a pitched and beautifully articulate voice: *"I've always loathed the view from these windows. However if that's the sort of thing you admire. Turn off the lights, damn you. Look at it."*

"Watch it, now, watch it," whispered a voice so close to Mike that he jumped. "O.K.," said a second voice somewhere above his head. The lights on the set turned blue. "Kill that working light." "Working light gone."

Curtains in the set were wrenched aside and

a window flung open. An actor appeared, leaning out quite close to Mike, seeming to look into his face and saying very distinctly: "God: it's frightful!" Mike backed away towards a passage, lit only from an open door. A great volume of sound broke out beyond the stage. "House lights," said the sharp voice. Mike turned into the passage. As he did so, someone came through the door. He found himself face to face with Coralie Bourne, beautifully dressed and heavily painted.

For a moment she stood quite still; then she made a curious gesture with her right hand, gave a small breathy sound and fell forward at his feet.

Anthony was tearing his program into long strips and dropped them on the floor of the O.P. box. On his right hand, above and below, was the audience; sometimes laughing, sometimes still, sometimes as one corporate being, raising its hand and striking them together. As now; when down on the stage, Canning Cumberland, using a stage voice, and inspired by some inward devil, flung back the window and said: "God: it's frightful!"

"Wrong! Wrong!" Anthony cried inwardly, hating Cumberland, hating Barry George because he let one speech of three words over-ride him, hating the audience because they liked it. The curtain descended with a long sigh on the second act and a sound like heavy rain filled the theatre, swelled prodigiously and continued after the house lights welled up.

"They seem," said a voice behind him, "to be liking your play."

It was Gosset, who owned the Jupiter and had backed the show. Anthony turned on him stammering: "He's destroying it. It should be the other man's scene. He's stealing."

"My boy," said Gosset, "he's an actor."

"He's drunk. It's intolerable."

He felt Gosset's hand on his shoulder.

"People are watching us. You're on show. This is a big thing for you; a first play, and going enormously. Come and have a drink, old boy. I want to introduce you —"

Anthony got up and Gosset, with his arm across his shoulders, flashing smiles, patting him, led him to the back of the box.

"I'm sorry," Anthony said, "I can't. Please let me off. I'm going backstage."

"Much better not, old son." The hand tightened on his shoulder. "Listen, old son —" But Anthony had freed himself and slipped through the pass-door from the box to the stage.

At the foot of the breakneck stairs Dendra Gay stood waiting. "I thought you'd come," she said.

Anthony said: "He's drunk. He's murdering the play."

"It's only one scene, Tony. He finishes early in the next act. It's going colossally."

"But don't you understand —"

"I do. You *know* I do. But your success, Tony darling! You can hear it and smell it and feel it in your bones."

"Dendra —" he said uncertainly.

Someone came up and shook his hand and went on shaking it. Flats were being laced together with a slap of rope on canvas. A chandelier ascended into darkness. "Lights," said the stage-manager, and the set was flooded with them. A distant voice began chanting. "Last act, please. Last act."

"Miss Bourne all right?" the stage-manager suddenly demanded.

"She'll be all right. She's not on for ten minutes," said a woman's voice.

"What's the matter with Miss Bourne?" Anthony asked.

"Tony, I must go and so must you. Tony, it's going to be grand. *Please* think so. *Please.*"

"Dendra —" Tony began, but she had gone.

Beyond the curtain, horns and flutes announced the last act.

"Clear please."

The stage hands came off.

"House lights."

"House lights gone."

"Stand by."

And while Anthony still hesitated in the O.P. corner, the curtain rose. Canning Cumberland and H. J. Bannington opened the last act.

As Mike knelt by Coralie Bourne he heard someone enter the passage behind him. He turned and saw, silhouetted against the lighted stage, the actor who had looked at him through a window in the set. The silhouette seemed to repeat the gesture Coralie Bourne had used, and to flatten itself against the wall.

A woman in an apron came out of the open door.

"I say — here!" Mike said.

Three things happened almost simultaneously. The woman cried out and knelt beside him. The man disappeared through a door on the right.

The woman, holding Coralie Bourne in her arms, said violently: "Why have you come back?" Then the passage lights came on. Mike said: "Look here, I'm most frightfully sorry," and took off the broad black hat. The dresser gaped at him, Coralie Bourne made a crescendo sound in her throat and opened her eyes. "Katie?" she said.

"It's all right, my lamb. It's not him, dear. You're all right." The dressed jerked her head at Mike: "Get out of it," she said.

"Yes, of course, I'm most frightfully —"

He backed out of the passage, colliding with a youth who said: "Five minutes, please." The dresser called out: "Tell them she's not well. Tell them to hold the curtain."

"No," said Coralie Bourne strongly. "I'm all right, Katie. Don't say anything, Katie, what was it?"

They disappeared into the room on the left.

Mike stood in the shadow of a stack of scenic flats by the entry into the passage. There was great activity on the stage. He caught a glimpse of Anthony Gill on the far side talking to a girl. The call-boy was speaking to the stage-manager who now shouted into space: "Miss Bourne all right?" The dresser came into the passage and called: "She'll be all right. She's not on for ten minutes." The youth began chanting: "Last act, please." The stage-manager gave a series of orders. A man with an eyeglass and a florid beard came from further down the passage and stood outside the set, bracing his figure and giving little tweaks to his clothes. There was a sound of horns and flutes. Canning Cumberland emerged from the room on the right and on his way to the stage, passed close to Mike, leaving a strong smell of alcohol behind him. The curtain rose.

Behind his shelter, Mike stealthily removed his beard and stuffed it into the pocket of his overcoat.

A group of stage-hands stood nearby. One

of them said in a hoarse whisper: " 'E's squiffy." "Garn, 'e's going good." "So 'e may be going good. And for why? *Becos* 'e's squiffy."

Ten minutes passed. Mike thought: "This affair has definitely not gone according to plan." He listened. Some kind of tension seemed to be building up on the stage. Canning Cumberland's voice rose on a loud but blurred note. A door in the set opened. "Don't bother to come," Cumberland said. "Good-bye. I can find my way out." The door slammed. Cumberland was standing near Mike. Then, very close, there was a loud explosion. The scenic flats vibrated, Mike's flesh leapt on his bones and Cumberland went into his dressing-rooms. Mike heard the key turn in the door. The smell of alcohol mingled with the smell of gunpowder. A stage-hand moved to a trestle table and laid a pistol on it. The actor with the eyeglass made an exit. He spoke for a moment to the stage-manager, passed Mike and disappeared in the passage.

Smells. There were all sorts of smells. Subconsciously, still listening to the play, he began to sort them out. Glue. Canvas. Greasepaint. The call-boy tapped on doors. "Mr. George, please." "Miss Bourne, please." They came out, Coralie Bourne with her dresser. Mike heard her turn a door handle and say something. An indistinguishable voice answered her. Then she and her dresser passed him. The others spoke to her and she nodded and then seemed to withdraw into herself, waiting with her head bent, ready to make her entrance. Presently she drew back, walked swiftly to the door in the set, flung it open and swept on, followed a minute later by Barry George.

Smells. Dust, stale paint, cloth. Gas. Increasingly, the smell of gas.

The group of stage-hands moved away behind the set to the side of the stage. Mike edged out of cover. He could see the prompt-corner. The stage-manager stood there with folded arms, watching the action. Behind him were grouped the players who were not on. Two dressers stood apart, watching. The light from the set caught their faces. Coralie Bourne's voice sent phrases flying like birds into the auditorium.

Mike began peering at the floor. Had he kicked some gas fitting adrift? The call-boy passed him, stared at him over his shoulder and went down the passage, tapping. "Five minutes to the curtain, please. Five minutes." The actor with the elderly make-up followed the call-boy out. "God, what a stink of gas," he whispered. "Chronic, ain't it?" said the call-boy. They stared at Mike and then crossed to the waiting group. The man said something to the stage-manager who tipped his head up, sniffing. He made an impatient gesture and turned back to the prompt-box, reaching over the prompter's head. A bell rang somewhere up in the flies and Mike saw a stage-hand climb to the curtain platform.

The little group near the prompt-corner was agitated. They looked back towards the passage entrance. The call-boy nodded and came running back. He knocked on the first door on the right. *"Mr. Cumberland! Mr. Cumberland!* You're on for the call." He rattled the door handle. *"Mr. Cumberland! You're on."*

Mike ran into the passage. The call-boy coughed retchingly and jerked his hand at the door. "Gas!" he said, "Gas!"

"Break it in."

"I'll get Mr. Reynolds."

He was gone. It was a narrow passage. From halfway across the opposite room Mike took a run, head down, shoulder forward, at the door. It gave a little and a sickening increase in the smell caught him in the lungs. A vast storm of noise had broken out and as he took another run he thought: "It's hailing outside."

"Just a minute if *you* please sir."

It was a stage-hand. He'd got a hammer and screwdriver. He wedged the point of the screwdriver between the lock and the door-post, drove it home and wrenched. The screws squeaked, the wood splintered and gas poured into the passage. "No winders," coughed the stage-hand.

531

Mike wound Alleyn's scarf over his mouth and nose. Half-forgotten instructions from anti-gas drill occurred to him. The room looked queer but he could see the man slumped down in the chair quite clearly. He stooped low and ran in.

He was knocking against things as he backed out, lugging the dead weight. His arms tingled. A high insistent voice hummed in his brain. He floated a short distance and came to earth on a concrete floor among several pairs of legs. A long way off, someone said loudly: "I can only thank you for being so kind to what I know, too well, is a very imperfect play." Then the sound of hail began again. There was a heavenly stream of clear air flowing into his mouth and nostrils. "I could eat it," he thought and sat up.

The telephone rang. "Suppose," Mrs. Alleyn suggested, "that this time you ignore it."

"It might be the Yard," Alleyn said, and answered it.

"Is that Chief Detective-Inspector Alleyn's flat? I'm speaking from the Jupiter Theatre. I've rung up to say that the Chief Inspector is here and that he's had a slight mishap. He's all right, but I think it might be as well for someone to drive him home. No need to worry."

"What sort of mishap?" Alleyn asked.

"Er — well — er, he's been a bit gassed."

"Gassed! All right. Thanks, I'll come."

"What a bore for you, darling," said Mrs. Alleyn. "What sort of case is it? Suicide?"

"Masquerading within the meaning of the act, by the sound of it. Mike's in trouble."

"What trouble, for Heaven's sake?"

"Got himself gassed. He's all right. Good-night darling. Don't wait up."

When he reached the theatre, the front of the house was in darkness. He made his way down the side alley to the stage-door where he was held up.

"Yard," he said, and produced his official card.

" 'Ere," said the stage-doorkeeper. " 'Ow many more of you?"

"The man inside was working for me," said Alleyn and walked in. The doorkeeper followed, protesting.

To the right of the entrance was a large scenic dock from which the double doors had been rolled back. Here Mike was sitting in an armchair, very white about the lips. Three men and two women, all with painted faces, stood near him and behind them a group of stage-hands with Reynolds, the stage-manager, and, apart from these, three men in evening dress. The men looked woodenly shocked. The women had been weeping.

"I'm most frightfully sorry, sir," Mike said. "I've tried to explain. This," he added generally, "is Inspector Alleyn."

533

"I can't understand all this," said the oldest of the men in evening dress irritably. He turned on the doorkeeper. "You said —"

"I seen 'is card —"

"I know," said Mike, "but you see —"

"This is Lord Michael Lamprey," Alleyn said. "A recruit to the Police Department. What's happened here?"

"Doctor Rankin, would you —"

The second of the men in evening dress came forward. "All right, Gosset. It's a bad business, Inspector. I've just been saying the police would have to be informed. If you'll come with me —"

Alleyn followed him through a door onto the stage proper. It was dimly lit. A trestle table had been set up in the centre and on it, covered with a sheet, was an unmistakable shape. The smell of gas, strong everywhere, hung heavily about the table.

"Who is it?"

"Canning Cumberland. He'd locked the door of his dressing-room. There's a gas fire. Your young friend dragged him out, very pluckily, but it was no go. I was in front. Gosset, the manager, had asked me to supper. It's a perfectly clear case of suicide as you'll see."

"I'd better look at the room. Anybody been in?"

"God, no. It was a job to clear it. They turned the gas off at the main. There's no

534

window. They had to open the double doors at the back of the stage and a small outside door at the end of the passage. It may be possible to get in now."

He led the way to the dressing-room passage. "Pretty thick, still," he said. "It's the first room on the right. They burst the lock. You'd better keep down near the floor."

The powerful lights over the mirror were on and the room still had its look of occupation. The gas fire was against the left hand wall. Alleyn squatted down by it. The tap was still turned on, its face lying parallel with the floor. The top of the heater, the tap itself, and the carpet near it, were covered with a creamish powder. On the end of the dressing-table shelf nearest to the stove was a box of this powder. Further along the shelf, grease-paints were set out in a row beneath the mirror. Then came a wash basin and in front of this an overturned chair. Alleyn could see the track of heels, across the pile of the carpet, to the door immediately opposite. Beside the wash basin was a quart bottle of whiskey, three parts empty, and a tumbler. Alleyn had had about enough and returned to the passage.

"Perfectly clear," the hovering doctor said again, "isn't it?"

"I'll see the other rooms, I think."

The one next to Cumberland's was like his

in reverse, but smaller. The heater was back to back with Cumberland's. The dressing-shelf was set out with much the same assortment of greasepaints. The tap of this heater, too, was turned on. It was of precisely the same make as the other and Alleyn, less embarrassed here by fumes, was able to make a longer examination. It was a common enough type of gas fire. The lead-in was from a pipe through a flexible metallic tube with a rubber connection. There were two taps, one in the pipe and one at the junction of the tube with the heater itself. Alleyn disconnected the tube and examined the connection. It was perfectly sound, a close fit and stained red at the end. Alleyn noticed a wiry thread of some reddish stuff resembling packing that still clung to it. The nozzle and tap were brass, the tap pulling over when it was turned on, to lie in a parallel plane with the floor. No powder had been scattered about here.

He glanced round the room, returned to the door and read the card: "Mr. Barry George."

The doctor followed him into the rooms opposite these, on the left-hand side of the passage. They were a repetition in design of the two he had already seen but were hung with women's clothes and had a more elaborate assortment of greasepaint and cosmetics.

There were a mass of flowers in the star-

room. Alleyn read the cards. One in particular caught his eye: "From Anthony Gill to
say a most inadequate 'thank you' for the
great idea." A vase of red roses stood before
the mirror: "To your greatest triumph,
Coralie darling. C.C." In Miss Gay's room
there were only two bouquets, one from the
management and one "from Anthony, with
love."

Again in each room he pulled off the lead-
in to the heater and looked at the connection.

"All right, aren't they?" said the doctor.

"Quite all right. Tight fit. Good solid grey
rubber."

"Well, then —"

Next on the left was an unused room, and
opposite it, "Mr. H.J. Bannington." Neither
of these rooms had gas fires. Mr. Bannington's dressing-table was littered with the usual
array of greasepaint, the materials for his
beard, a number of telegrams and letters, and
several bills.

"About the body," the doctor began.

"We'll get a mortuary van from the Yard."

"But — Surely in a case of suicide —"

"I don't think this is suicide."

"But, good God! — D'you mean there's
been an accident?"

"No accident," said Alleyn.

At midnight, the dressing-room lights in the
Jupiter Theatre were brilliant, and men were

busy there with the tools of their trade. A constable stood at the stage-door and a van waited in the yard. The front of the house was dimly lit and there, among the shrouded stalls, sat Coralie Bourne, Basil Gosset, H.J. Bannington, Dendra Gay, Anthony Gill, Reynolds, Katie the dresser, and the call-boy. A constable sat behind them and another stood by the doors into the foyer. The stared across the backs of seats at the fire curtain. Spirals of smoke rose from their cigarettes and about their feet were discarded programs. "Basil Gosset presents I CAN FIND MY WAY OUT by Anthony Gill."

In the manager's office Alleyn said: "You're sure of your facts, Mike?"

"Yes, sir. Honestly. I was right up against the entrance into the passage. They didn't see me because I was in the shadow. It was very dark off-stage."

"You'll have to swear to it."

"I know."

"Good. All right, Thompson. Miss Gay and Mr. Gosset may go home. Ask Miss Bourne to come in."

When Sergeant Thompson had gone Mike said: "I haven't had a chance to say I know I've made a perfect fool of myself. Using your card and everything."

"Irresponsible gaiety doesn't go down very well in the service, Mike. You behaved like a clown."

"I *am* a fool," said Mike wretchedly.

The red beard was lying in front of Alleyn on Gosset's desk. He picked it up and held it out. "Put it on," he said.

"She might do another faint."

"I think not. Now the hat: yes — yes, I see. Come in."

Sergeant Thompson showed Coralie Bourne in and then sat at the end of the desk with his notebook.

Tears had traced their course through the powder on her face, carrying black cosmetic with them and leaving the greasepaint shining like snail-tracks. She stood near the doorway looking dully at Michael. "Is he back in England?" she said. "Did he tell you to do this?" She made an impatient movement. "Do take it off," she said, "it's a very bad beard. If Cann had only looked —" Her lips trembled. "Who told you to do it?"

"Nobody," Mike stammered, pocketing the beard. "I mean — As a matter of fact, Tony Gill —"

"*Tony?* But *he* didn't know. Tony wouldn't do it. Unless —"

"Unless?" Alleyn said.

She said frowning: "Tony didn't want Cann to play the part that way. He was furious."

"He says it was his dress for the Chelsea Arts Ball," Mike mumbled. "I brought it here. I just thought I'd put it on — it was idiotic, I know — for fun. I'd no idea you and

Mr. Cumberland would mind."

"Ask Mr. Gill to come in," Alleyn said.

Anthony was white and seemed bewildered and helpless. "I've told Mike," he said. "It was my dress for the ball. They sent it round from the costume-hiring place this afternoon but I forgot it. Dendra reminded me and rang up the Delivery people — or Mike, as it turns out — in the interval."

"Why," Alleyn asked, "did you choose that particular disguise?"

"I didn't. I didn't know what to wear and I was too rattled to think. They said they were hiring things for themselves and would get something for me. They said we'd all be characters out of a Russian melodrama."

"Who said this?"

"Well — well, it was Barry George, actually."

"*Barry,*" Coralie Bourne said. "*It was Barry.*"

"I don't understand," Anthony said. "Why should a fancy dress upset everybody?"

"It happened," Alleyn said, "to be a replica of the dress usually worn by Miss Bourne's husband who also had a red beard. That was it, wasn't it, Miss Bourne? I remember seeing him —"

"Oh, yes," she said, "you would. He was known to the police." Suddenly she broke down completely. She was in an armchair near the desk but out of the range of its shaded

540

lamp. She twisted and writhed, beating her hand against the padded arm of the chair. Sergeant Thompson sat with his head bent and his hand over his notes. Mike, after an agonized glance at Alleyn, turned his back. Anthony Gill leant over her: "Don't," he said violently. "Don't! For God's sake, stop."

She twisted away from him and gripping the edge of the desk, began to speak to Alleyn; little by little gaining mastery of herself. "I want to tell you. I want you to understand. Listen." Her husband had been fantastically cruel, she said. "It was a kind of slavery." But when she sued for divorce he brought evidence of adultery with Cumberland. They had thought he knew nothing. "There was an abominable scene. He told us he was going away. He said he'd keep track of us and if I tried again for divorce, he'd come home. He was very friendly with Barry in those days." He had left behind him the first draft of a play he had meant to write for her and Cumberland. It had a wonderful scene for them. "And now you will never have it," he had said, "because there is no other playwright who could make this play for you but I." He was, she said, a melodramatic man but he was never ridiculous. He returned to the Ukraine where he was born and they had heard no more of him. In a little while she would have been able to presume death. But years of waiting did not agree with Canning

541

Cumberland. He drank consistently and at his worst used to imagine her husband was about to return. "He was really terrified of Ben," she said. "He seemed like a creature in a nightmare."

Anthony Gill said: "This play — was it —?"

"Yes. There was an extraordinary similarity between your play and his. I saw at once that Ben's central scene would enormously strengthen your piece. Cann didn't want me to give it to you. Barry knew. He said: 'Why not?' He wanted Cann's part and was furious when he didn't get it. So you see, when he suggested you should dress and make-up like Ben —" She turned to Alleyn. "You see?"

"What did Cumberland do when he saw you?" Alleyn asked Mike.

"He made a queer movement with his hands as if — well, as if he expected me to go for him. Then he just bolted into his room."

"He thought Ben had come back," she said.

"Were you alone at any time after you fainted?" Alleyn asked.

"I? No. No, I wasn't. Katie took me into my dressing-room and stayed with me until I went on for the last scene."

"One other question. Can you, by any chance, remember of the heater in your room behaved at all oddly?"

She looked wearily at him. "Yes, it did give

a sort of plop, I think. It made me jump. I was nervy."

"You went straight from your room to the stage?"

"Yes. With Katie. I wanted to go to Cann. I tried the door when we came out. It was locked. He said: 'Don't come in.' I said: 'It's all right. It wasn't Ben,' and went on to the stage."

"I heard Miss Bourne," Mike said.

"He must have made up his mind by then. He was terribly drunk when he played his last scene." She pushed her hair back from her forehead. "May I go?" she asked Alleyn.

"I've sent for a taxi. Mr. Gill, will you see if it's there? In the meantime, Miss Bourne, would you like to wait in the foyer?"

"May I take Katie home with me?"

"Certainly. Thompson will find her. Is there anyone else we can get?"

"No, thank you. Just old Katie."

Alleyn opened the door for her and watched her walk into the foyer. "Check up with the dresser, Thompson," he murmured, "and get Mr. H.J. Bannington."

He saw Coralie Bourne sit on the lower step of the dress-circle stairway and lean her head against the wall. Nearby, on a gilt easel, a huge photograph of Canning Cumberland smiled handsomely at her.

H.J. Bannington looked pretty ghastly. He

543

had rubbed his hand across his face and smeared his make-up. Florid red paint from his lips had stained the crêpe hair that had been gummed on and shaped into a beard. His monocle was still in his left eye and gave him an extraordinarily rakish look. "See here," he complained, "I've about *had* this party. When do we go home?"

Alleyn uttered placatory phrases and got him to sit down. He checked over H.J.'s movements after Cumberland left the stage and found that his account tallied with Mike's. He asked if H.J. had visited any of the other dressing-rooms and was told acidly that H.J. knew his place in the company. "I remained in my unheated and squalid kennel, thank you very much."

"Do you know if Mr. Barry George followed your example?"

"Couldn't say, old boy. He didn't come near *me.*"

"Have you any theories at all about this unhappy business, Mr. Bannington?"

"Do you mean, why did Cann do it? Well, speak no ill of the dead, but I'd have thought it was pretty obvious he was morbid-drunk. Tight as an owl when we finished the second act. Ask the great Mr. Barry George. Cann took the big scene away from Barry with both hands and left him looking pathetic. All wrong artistically, but that's how Cann was in his cups." H.J.'s wicked little eyes narrowed. "The great Mr. George," he said, "must be feeling very unpleasant by now. You might say he'd got a suicide on his mind, mightn't you? Or don't you know about that?"

"It was not suicide."

The glass dropped from H.J.'s eye. "God!" he said. "God, I told Bob Reynolds! I told him the whole plant wanted overhauling."

"The gas plant, you mean?"

"Certainly. I was in the gas business years ago. Might say I'm in it still with a difference, ha-ha!"

"Ha-ha!" Alleyn agreed politely. He leaned forward. "Look here," he said: "We can't dig up a gas man at this time of night and may very likely need an expert opinion. You can help us."

"Well, old boy, I was rather pining for a spot of shut-eye. But, of course —"

"I shan't keep you very long."

"God, I hope not!" said H.J. earnestly.

Barry George had been made up pale for the last act. Colorless lips and shadows under his cheek bones and eyes had skillfully underlined his character as a repatriated but broken prisoner-of-war. Now, in the glare of the office lamp, he looked like a grossly exaggerated figure of mourning. He began at once to tell Alleyn how grieved and horrified he was. Everybody, he said, had their faults, and poor old Cann was no exception but wasn't it terrible to think what could happen to a man who let himself go downhill? He, Barry George, was abnormally sensitive and he didn't think he'd every really get over the awful shock this had been to him. What, he wondered, could be at the bottom of it? Why had poor old Cann decided to end it all?

"Miss Bourne's theory," Alleyn began. Mr. George laughed. "Coralie?" he said. "So she's got a theory! Oh, well. Never mind."

"Her theory is this. Cumberland saw a man whom he mistook for her husband and, having a morbid dread of his return, drank the greater part of a bottle of whiskey and gassed himself. The clothes and beard that deceived him had, I understand, been ordered by you for Mr. Anthony Gill."

This statement produced startling results. Barry George broke into a spate of expostulation and apology. There had been no thought in his mind of resurrecting poor old Ben, who was no doubt dead but had been, mind you, in many ways one of the best. They were all to go to the Ball as exaggerated characters from melodrama. Not for the world — He gesticulated and protested. A line of sweat broke out along the margin of his hair. "I don't know what you're getting at," he shouted. "What are you suggesting?"

"I'm suggesting, among other things, that Cumberland was murdered."

"You're mad! He'd locked himself in. They had to break down the door. There's no window. You're crazy!"

"Don't," Alleyn said wearily, "let us have any nonsense about sealed rooms. Now, Mr. George, you knew Benjamin Vlasnoff pretty well. Are you going to tell us that when you suggested Mr. Gill should wear a coat with a fur collar, a black sombrero, black gloves and a red beard, it never occurred to you that his appearance might be a shock to Miss Bourne and to Cumberland?"

"I wasn't the only one," he blustered. "H.J. knew. And if it had scared him off, *she* wouldn't have been so sorry. She'd had about enough of him. Anyway if this is murder, the costume's got nothing to do with it."

"That," Alleyn said, getting up, "is what we hope to find out."

In Barry George's room, Detective-Sergeant Bailey, a fingerprint expert, stood by the gas heater. Sergeant Gibson, a police photographer, and a uniformed constable were near the door. In the centre of the room stood Barry George, looking from one man to another and picking at his lips.

"I don't know why he wants me to watch all this," he said. "I'm exhausted. I'm emotionally used up. What's he doing?" Where is he?"

Alleyn was next door in Cumberland's

dressing-room, with H.J., Mike and Sergeant Thompson. It was pretty clear now of fumes and the gas fire was burning comfortably. Segeant Thompson sprawled in the armchair near the heater, his head sunk and his eyes shut.

"This is the theory, Mr. Bannington," Alleyn said. "You and Cumberland have made your final exits; Miss Bourne and Mr. George and Miss Gay are all on the stage. Lord Michael is standing just outside the entrance to the passage. The dressers and stage-staff are watching the play from the side. Cumberland has locked himself in this room. There he is, dead drunk and sound asleep. The gas fire is burning, full pressure. Earlier in the evening he powdered himself and a thick layer of the powder lies undisturbed on the tap. Now."

He tapped on the wall.

The fire blew out with a sharp explosion. This was followed by the hiss of escaping gas. Alleyn turned the taps off. "You see," he said, "I've left an excellent print on the powdered surface. Now, come next door."

Next door, Barry George appealed to him stammering: "But I didn't know. I don't know anything about it. I don't *know*."

"Just show Mr. Bannington, will you, Bailey?"

Bailey knelt down. The lead-in was disconnected from the tap on the heater. He turned on the tap in the pipe and blew down the tube.

"An air lock, you see. It works perfectly."

H.J. was staring at Barry George. "But I don't know about gas, H.J. H.J., tell them —"

"One moment." Alleyn removed the towels that had been spread over the dressing-shelf, revealing a sheet of clean paper on which lay the rubber push-on connection.

"Will you take this lens, Bannington, and look at it. You'll see that it's stained a florid red. It's a very slight stain but it's unmistakably greasepaint. And just above the stain you'll see a wiry hair. Rather like some sort of packing material, but it's not that. It's crêpe hair, isn't it?"

The lens wavered above the paper.

"Let me hold it for you," Alleyn said. He put his hand over H.J.'s shoulder and, with a swift movement, plucked a tuft from his false moustache and dropped it on the paper. "Identical, you see. Ginger. It seems to be stuck to the connection with spirit-gum."

The lens fell. H.J. twisted round, faced Alleyn for a second, and then struck him full in the face. He was a small man but it took three of them to hold him.

"In a way, sir, it's handy when they have a smack at you," said Detective-Sergeant Thompson half an hour later. "You can pull them in nice and straightforward without any 'will you come to the station and make a statement' business."

"Quite," said Alleyn, nursing his jaw.

Mike said: "He must have gone to the room after Barry George and Miss Bourne were called."

"That's it. He had to be quick. The call-boy would be round in a minute and he had to be back in his own room."

"But look here — what about motive?"

"That, my good Mike, is precisely why, at half-past one in the morning, we're still in this miserable theatre. You're getting a view of the duller aspect of homicide. Want to go home?"

"No. Give me another job."

"Very well. About ten feet from the prompt-entrance, there's a sort of garbage tin. Go through it."

At seventeen minutes to two, when the dressing-rooms and passages had been combed clean and Alleyn had called a spell, Mike came to him with filthy hands. *"Eureka,"* he said, "I hope."

They all went into Bannington's room. Alleyn spread out on the dressing-table the fragments of paper that Mike had given him.

"They'd been pushed down to the bottom of the tin," Mike said.

Alleyn moved the fragments about. Thompson whistled through his teeth. Bailey and Gibson mumbled together.

"There you are," Alleyn said at last.

They collected round him. The letter that H. J. Bannington had opened at this same table six hours and forty-five minutes earlier, was pieced together like a jig-saw puzzle.

"Dear H.J.

Having seen the monthly statement of my account, I called at my bank this morning and was shown a check that is undoubtedly a forgery. Your histrionic versatility, my dear H.J., is only equalled by your audacity as a calligraphist. But fame has its disadvantages. The teller recognized you. I propose to take action."

"Unsigned," said Bailey.

"Look at the card on the red roses in Miss Bourne's room, signed C.C. It's a very distinctive hand." Alleyn turned to Mike. "Do you still want to be a policeman?"

"Yes."

"Lord help you. Come and talk to me at the office tomorrow."

"Thank you, sir."

They went out, leaving a constable on duty. It was a cold morning. Mike looked up at the façade of the Jupiter. He could just make out the shape of the neon sign: I CAN FIND MY WAY OUT — *by Anthony Gill.*

551

Rear Window

William Irish
(Cornell Woolrich)

I DIDN'T KNOW their names. I'd never heard their voices. I didn't even know them by sight, strictly speaking, for their faces were too small to fill in with identifiable features at that distance. Yet I could have constructed a timetable of their comings and goings, their daily habits and activities. They were the rear-window dwellers around me.

Sure, I suppose it *was* a little bit like prying, could even have been mistaken for the fevered concentration of a Peeping Tom. That wasn't my fault, that wasn't the idea. The idea was, my movements were strictly limited just around this time. I could get from the window to the bed, and from the bed to the window, and that was all. The bay window was about the best feature my rear bedroom had in the warm weather. It was unscreened, so I had to sit with the light out or I would have had every insect in the vicinity in on me. I couldn't

552

sleep, because I was used to getting plenty of exercise. I'd never acquired the habit of reading books to ward off boredom, so I hadn't that to turn to. Well, what should I do, sit there with my eyes tightly shuttered?

Just to pick a few at random: Straight over, and the windows square, there was a young jitter-couple, kids in their teens, only just married. It would have killed them to stay home one night. They were always in such a hurry to go, wherever it was they went, they never remembered to turn out the lights. I don't think it missed once in all the time I was watching. But they never forgot altogether, either. I was to learn to call this delayed action, as you will see. He'd always come skittering madly back in about five minutes, probably from all the way down in the street, and rush around killing the switches. Then fall over something in the dark on his way out. They gave me an inward chuckle, those two.

The next house down, the windows already narrowed a little with perspective. There was a certain light in that one that always went out each night too. Something about it, it used to make me a little sad. There was a woman living there with her child, a young widow I suppose. I'd see her put the child to bed, and then bend over and kiss her in a wistful sort of way. She'd shade the light off her and sit there painting her eyes and mouth. Then she'd go out. She'd never come back till the night was nearly spent. Once I was still up, and I looked and she was sitting there motionless with her head buried in her arms. Something about it, it used to make me a little sad.

The third one down no longer offered any insight, the windows were just slits like in a medieval battlement, due to foreshortening. That brings us around to the one on the end. In that one, frontal vision came back full-depth again, since it stood at right angles to the rest, my own included, sealing up the inner hollow all these houses backed on. I could see into it, from the rounded projection of my bay window, as freely as into a doll house with its rear wall sliced away. And scaled down to about the same size.

It was a flat building. Unlike all the rest it had been constructed originally as such, not just cut up into furnished rooms. It topped them by two stories and had rear fire escapes, to show for this distinction. But it was old, evidently hadn't shown a profit. It was in the process of being modernized. Instead of clearing the entire building while the work was going on, they were doing it a flat at a time, in order to lose as little rental income as possible. Of the six rearward flats it offered to view, the topmost one had already been completed, but not yet rented. They were working on the fifth-floor one now, disturbing the peace of everyone all up and down the "inside" of the block with their hammering and sawing.

I felt sorry for the couple in the flat below. I used to wonder how they stood it with that bedlam going on above their heads. To make it worse the wife was in chronic poor health, too; I could tell that even at a distance by the listless way she moved about over there, and remained in her bathrobe without dressing. Sometimes I'd see her sitting by the window, holding her head. I used to wonder why he didn't have a doctor in to look her over, but maybe they couldn't afford it. He seemed to be out of work. Often their bedroom light was on late at night behind the drawn shade, as though she were unwell and he was sitting up with her. And one night in particular he must have had to sit up with her all night, it remained on until nearly daybreak. Not that I sat watching all that time. But the light was still burning at three in the morning, when I finally transferred from chair to bed to see if I could get a little sleep myself. And when I failed to, and hopscotched back again around dawn, it was still peering wanly out behind the tan shade.

Moments later, with the first brightening of day, it suddenly dimmed around the edges of the shade, and then shortly afterward, not that one, but a shade in one of the other rooms — for all of them alike had been down

— went up, and I saw him standing there looking out.

He was holding a cigarette in his hand. I couldn't see it, but I could tell it was that by the quick, nervous little jerks with which he kept putting his hand to his mouth, and the haze I saw rising around his head. Worried about her, I guess. I didn't blame him for that. Any husband would have been. She must have only just dropped off to sleep, after night-long suffering. And then in another hour or so, at the most, that sawing of wood and clattering of buckets was going to start in over them again. Well, it wasn't any of my business, I said to myself, but he really ought to get her out of there. If I had an ill wife on my hands. . . .

He was leaning slightly out, maybe an inch past the window frame, carefully scanning the back faces of all the houses abutting on the hollow square that lay before him. You can tell, even at a distance, when a person is looking fixedly. There's something about the way the head is held. And yet his scrutiny wasn't held fixedly to any one point, it was a slow, sweeping one, moving along the houses on the opposite side from me first. When it got to the end of them, I knew it would cross over to my side and come back along there. Before it did, I withdrew several yards inside my room, to let it go safely by. I didn't want him to think I was sitting there prying into his affairs. There was still enough blue night-shade in my room to keep my slight with-drawal from catching his eye.

When I returned to my original position a moment or two later, he was gone. He had raised two more of the shades. The bedroom one was still down. I wondered vaguely why he had given that peculiar, comprehensive, semicircular stare at all the rear windows around him. There wasn't anyone at any of them, at such an hour. It wasn't important, of course. It was just a little oddity, it failed to blend in with his being worried or disturbed about his wife. When you're worried or disturbed, that's an internal preoccupation, you stare vacantly at nothing at all. When you stare around you in a great sweeping arc at windows, that betrays external preoccupation, outward interest. One doesn't quite jibe with the other. To call such a discrepancy trifling is to add to its importance. Only someone like me, stewing in a vaccum of total idleness, would have noticed it at all.

The flat remained lifeless after that, as far as could be judged by its windows. He must have either gone out or gone to bed himself. Three of the shades remained at normal height, the one masking the bedroom remained down. Sam, my day houseman, came in not long after with my eggs and morning paper, and I had that to kill time with for awhile. I stopped thinking about other people's windows and staring at them.

The sun slanted down on one side of the hollow oblong all morning long, then it shifted over to the other side for the afternoon. Then it started to slip off both alike, and it was evening again – another day gone.

The lights started to come on around the quadrangle. Here and there a wall played back, like a sounding board, a snatch of radio program that was coming in too loud. If you listened carefully you could hear an occasional clink of dishes mixed in, faint, far off. The chain of little habits that were their lives unreeled themselves. They were all bound in them tighter than the tightest straitjacket any jailer ever devised, though they all thought themselves free. The jitterbugs made their nightly dash for the great open spaces, forgot their lights, he came careening back, thumbed them out, and their place was dark until the early morning hours. The woman put her child to bed, leaned mournfully over its cot, then sat down with heavy despair to redden her mouth.

In the fourth-floor flat at right angles to the long, interior "street" the three shades had remained up, and the fourth shade had remained at full length, all day long. I hadn't been conscious of that because I hadn't particularly been looking at it, or thinking of it, until now. My eyes may have rested on those windows at times, during the day, but my thoughts had been elsewhere. It was only when a light suddenly went up in the end room behind one of the raised shades, which was their kitchen, that I realized that the shades had been untouched like that all day. That also brought something else to my mind that hadn't been in it until now: I hadn't seen the woman all day. I hadn't seen any sign of life within those windows until now.

He'd come in from outside. The entrance was at the opposite side of their kitchen, away from the window. He'd left his hat on, so I knew he'd just come in from the outside.

He didn't remove his hat. As though there was no one there to remove it for any more. Instead, he pushed it farther to the back of his head by pronging a hand to the roots of his hair. That gesture didn't denote removal of perspiration, I knew. To do that a person makes a sidewise sweep — this was up over his forehead. It indicated some sort of harassment or uncertainty. Besides, if he'd been suffering from excess warmth, the first thing he would have done would be to take off his hat altogether.

She didn't come out to greet him. The first link, of the so-strong chain of habit, of custom, that binds us all, had snapped wide open.

She must be so ill she had remained in bed, in the room behind the lowered shade, all day. I watched. He remained where he was, two rooms away from there. Expectancy became surprise, surprise incomprehension. Funny, I thought, that he doesn't go in to her. Or at least go as far as the doorway, look in to see how she is.

Maybe she was asleep, and he didn't want to disturb her. Then immediately: but how can he know for sure that she's asleep, without at least looking in at her? He just came in himself.

He came forward and stood there by the window, as he had at dawn. Sam had carried out my tray quite some time before, and my lights were out. I held my ground, I knew he couldn't see me within the darkness of the bay window. He stood there motionless for several minutes. And now his attitude was the proper one for inner preoccupation. He stood there looking downward at nothing, lost in thought.

He's worried about her, I said to myself, as any man would be. It's the most natural thing in the world. Funny, though, he should leave her in the dark like that, without going near her. If he's worried, then why didn't he at least look in on her on returning? Here was another of those trivial discrepancies, between inward motivation and outward indication. And just as I was thinking that, the original one, that I had noted at daybreak, repeated itself. His head went up with renewed alertness, and I could see it start to give that slow circular sweep of interrogation around the panorama of rearward windows again. True, the light was behind him this time, but there was enough of it falling on him to show me the microscopic but continuous shift of direction his head made in the process. I remained carefully immobile until the distant glance had passed me safely by. Motion attracts.

Why is he so interested in other people's windows, I wondered detachedly. And of course an effective brake to dwelling on that thought too lingeringly clamped down almost at once: Look who's talking. What about you yourself?

An important difference escaped me. I wasn't worried about anything. He, presumably, was.

Down came the shades again. The lights stayed on behind their beige opaqueness. But behind the one that had remained down all along, the room remained dark.

Time went by. Hard to say how much – a quarter of an hour, twenty minutes. A cricket chirped in one of the back yards. Sam came in to see if I wanted anything before he went home for the night. I told him no, I didn't – it was all right, run along. He stood there for a minute, head down. Then I saw him shake it slightly, as if at something he didn't like. "What's the matter?" I asked.

"You know what that means? My old

mammy told it to me, and she never told me a lie in her life. I never once seen it to miss, either."

"What, the cricket?"

"Any time you hear one of them things, that's a sign of death – someplace close around."

I swept the back of my hand at him. "Well, it isn't in here, so don't let it worry you."

He went out, muttering stubbornly: "It's somewhere close by, though. Somewhere not very far off. Got to be."

The door closed after him, and I stayed there alone in the dark.

It was a stifling night, much closer than the one before. I could hardly get a breath of air even by the open window at which I sat. I wondered how he – that unknown over there – could stand it behind those drawn shades.

Then suddenly, just as idle speculation about this whole matter was about to alight on some fixed point in my mind, crystallize into something like suspicion, up came the shades again, and off it flitted, as formless as ever and without having had a chance to come to rest on anything.

He was in the middle windows, the living room. He'd taken off his coat and shirt, was bare-armed in his undershirt. He hadn't been able to stand it himself, I guess – the sultriness.

I couldn't make out what he was doing at

first. He seemed to be busy in a perpendicular, up-and-down way rather than lengthwise. He remained in one place, but he kept dipping down out of sight and then straightening up into view again, at irregular intervals. It was almost like some sort of calisthenic exercise, except that the dips and rises weren't evenly timed enough for that. Sometimes he'd stay down a long time, sometimes he'd bob right up again, sometimes he'd go down two or three times in rapid succession. There was some sort of a widespread black V railing him off from the window. Whatever it was, there was just a sliver of it showing above the upward inclination to which the window sill deflected my line of vision. All it did was strike off the bottom of his undershirt, to the extent of a sixteenth of an inch maybe. But I hadn't seen it there at other times, and I couldn't tell what it was.

Suddenly he left it for the first time since the shades had gone up, came out around it to the outside, stooped down into another part of the room, and straightened again with an armful of what looked like varicolored pennants at the distance at which I was . He went back behind the V and allowed them to fall across the top of it for a moment, and stay that way. He made one of his dips down out of sight and stayed that way a good while.

The "pennants" slung across the V kept changing color right in front of my eyes. I have very good sight. One moment they were white, the next red, the next blue.

Then I got it. They were a woman's dresses, and he was pulling them down to him one by one, taking the topmost one each time. Suddenly they were all gone, the V was black and bare again, and his torso had reappeared. I knew what it was now, and what he was doing. The dresses had told me. He confirmed it for me. He spread his arms to the ends of the V, I could see him heave and hitch, as if exerting pressure, and suddenly the V had folded up, become a cubed wedge. Then he made rolling motions with his whole upper body, and the wedge disappeared off to one side.

He'd been packing a trunk, packing his wife's things into a large upright trunk.

He reappeared at the kitchen window presently, stood still for a moment. I saw him draw his arm across his forehead, not once but several times, and then whip the end of it off into space. Sure, it was hot work for such a night. Then he reached up along the wall and took something down. Since it was the kitchen he was in, my imagination had to supply a cabinet and a bottle.

I could see the two or three quick passes his hand made to his mouth after that. I said to myself tolerantly: That's what nine men out of ten would do after packing a trunk — take a good stiff drink. And if the tenth didn't, it would only be because he didn't have any liquor at hand.

Then he came closer to the window again, and standing edgewise to the side of it, so that only a thin paring of his head and shoulder showed, peered watchfully out into the dark quadrilateral, along the line of windows, most of them unlighted by now, once more. He always started on the left-hand side, the side opposite mine, and made his circuit of inspection from there on around.

That was the second time in one evening I'd seen him do that. And once at daybreak, maybe three times altogether. I smiled mentally. You'd almost think he felt guilty about something. It was probably nothing, just an odd little habit, a quirk, that he didn't know he had himself. I had them myself, everyone does.

He withdrew into the room again, and it blacked out. His figure passed into the one that was still lighted next to it, the living room. That blacked next. It didn't surprise me that the third room, the bedroom with the drawn shade, didn't light up on his entering there. He wouldn't want to disturb her, of course — particularly if she was going away tomorrow for her health, as his packing of her trunk showed. She needed all the rest she could get, before making the trip. Simple enough for him to slip into bed in the dark.

It did surprise me, though, when a match-flare winked some time later, to have it still come from the darkened living room. He must be lying down in there, trying to sleep on a sofa or something for the night. He hadn't gone near the bedroom at all, was staying out of it altogether. That puzzled me, frankly. That was carrying solicitude almost too far.

Ten minutes or so later, there was another match-wink, still from that same living room window. He couldn't sleep.

The night brooded down on both of us alike, the curiosity-monger in the bay window, the chain-smoker in the fourth-floor flat, without giving any answer. The only sound was that interminable cricket.

I was back at the window again with the first sun of morning. Not because of him. My mattress was like a bed of hot coals. Sam found me there when he came in to get things ready for me. "You're going to be a wreck, Mr. Jeff," was all he said.

First, for awhile, there was no sign of life over there. Then suddenly I saw his head bob up from somewhere down out of sight in the living room, so I knew I'd been right; he'd spent the night on a sofa or easy chair in there. Now, of course, he'd look in at her, to see how she was, find out if she felt any better. That was only common ordinary humanity. He hadn't been near her, so far as I could make out, since two nights before.

He didn't. He dressed, and he went in the

opposite direction, into the kitchen, and wolfed something in there, standing up and using both hands. Then he suddenly turned and moved off side, in the direction in which I knew the flat-entrance to be, as if he had just heard some summons, like the doorbell.

Sure enough, in a moment he came back, and there were two men with him in leather aprons. Expressmen. I saw him standing by while they laboriously maneuvered that cubed black wedge out between them, in the direction they'd just come from. He did more than just stand by. He practically hovered over them, kept shifting from side to side, he was so anxious to see that it was done right.

Then he came back alone, and I saw him swipe his arm across his head, as though it was he, not they, who was all heated up from the effort.

So he was forwarding her trunk, to wherever it was she was going. That was all.

He reached up along the wall again and took something down. He was taking another drink. Two. Three. I said to myself, a little at a loss: Yes, but he hasn't just packed a trunk this time. That trunk has been standing packed and ready since last night. Where does the hard work come in? The sweat and the need for a bracer?

Now, at last, after all those hours, he finally did go in to her. I saw his form pass through the living room and go beyond, into the bedroom. Up went the shade, that had been down all this time. Then he turned his head and looked around behind him. In a certain way, a way that was unmistakable, even from where I was. Not in one certain direction, as one looks at a person. But from side to side, and up and down, and all around, as one looks at — *an empty room.*

He stepped back, bent a little, gave a fling of his arms, and an unoccupied mattress and bedding upended over the foot of a bed, stayed that way, emptily curved. A second one followed a moment later.

She wasn't in there.

They use the expression "delayed action." I found out then what it meant. For two days a sort of formless uneasiness, a disembodied suspicion, I don't know what to call it, had been flitting and volplaning around in my mind, like an insect looking for a landing place. More than once, just as it had been ready to settle, some slight thing, some slight reassuring thing, such as the raising of the shades after they had been down unnaturally long, had been enough to keep it winging aimlessly, prevent it from staying still long enough for me to recognize it. The point of contact had been there all along, waiting to receive it. Now, for some reason, within a split second after he tossed over the empty mattresses, it landed — *zoom!* And the point of contact expanded — or exploded, whatever you care to call it — into a certainty of murder.

In other words, the rational part of my mind was far behind the instinctive, subconscious part. Delayed action. Now the one had caught up to the other. The thought-message that sparked from the synchronization was: He's done something to her!

I looked down and my hand was bunching the goods over my kneecap, it was knotted so tight. I forced it open. I said to myself, steadyingly: Now wait a minute, be careful, go slow. You've seen nothing. You know nothing. You only have the negative proof that you don't see her any more.

Sam was standing there looking over at me from the pantry way. He said accusingly: "You ain't touched a thing. And your face looks like a sheet."

It felt like one. It had that needling feeling, when the blood has left it involuntarily. It was more to get him out of the way and give myself some elbow room for undisturbed thinking, than anything else, that I said: "Sam, what's the street address of that building down there? Don't stick your head too far out and gape at it."

"Somep'n or other Benedict Avenue." He scratched his neck helpfully.

"I know that. Chase around the corner a minute and get me the exact number on it, will you?"

"Why you want to know that for?" he asked

as he turned to go.

"None of your business," I said with the good-natured firmness that was all that was necessary to take care of that once and for all. I called after him just as he was closing the door: "And while you're about it, step into the entrance an see if you can tell from the mailboxes who has the fourth-floor rear. Don't get me the wrong one now. And try not to let anyone catch you at it."

He went out mumbling something that sounded like, "When a man ain't got nothing to do but just sit all day, he sure can think up the blamest things ——" The door closed and I settled down to some good constructive thinking.

I said to myself: What are you really building up this monstrous supposition on? Let's see what you've got. Only that there were several little things wrong with the mechanism, the chain-belt, of their recurrent daily habits over there. 1. The lights were on all night the first night. 2. He came in later than usual the second night. 3. He left his hat on. 4. She didn't come out to greet him — she hasn't appeared since the evening before the lights were on all night. 5. He took a drink after he finished packing her trunk. But he took three stiff drinks the next morning, immediately after her trunk went out. 6. He was inwardly disturbed and worried, yet superimposed upon this was an unnatural external concern about the surrounding rear windows that was off-key. 7. He slept in the living room, didn't go near the bedroom, during the night before the departure of the trunk.

Very well. If she had been ill that first night, and he had sent her away for her health, that automatically canceled out points 1, 2, 3, 4. It left points 5 and 6 totally unimportant and unincriminating. But when it came up against 7, it hit a stumbling block.

If she went away immediately after being ill that first night, why didn't he want to sleep in their bedroom *last night?* Sentiment? Hardly. Two perfectly good beds in one room, only a sofa or uncomfortable easy chair in the other. Why should he stay out of there if she was already gone? Just because he missed her, was lonely? A grown man doesn't act that way. All right, then she was still in there.

Sam came back parenthetically at this point and said: "That house is Number 525 Benedict Avenue. The fourth-floor rear, it got the name of Mr. and Mrs. Lars Thorwald up."

"Sh-h," I silenced, and motioned him backhand out of my ken.

"First he want it, then he don't," he grumbled philosophically, and retired to his duties.

I went ahead digging at it. But if she was still there, in that bedroom last night, then she couldn't have gone away to the country, because I never saw her leave today. She could have left without my seeing her in the early hours of yesterday morning. I'd missed a few hours, been asleep. But this morning I had been up before he was himself, I only saw his head rear up from that sofa after I'd been at the window for some time.

To go at all she would have had to go yesterday morning. Then why had he left the bedroom shade down, left the mattresses undisturbed, until today? Above all, why had he stayed out of that room last night? That was evidence that she hadn't gone, was still in there. Then today, immediately after the trunk had been dispatched, he went in, pulled up the shade, tossed over the mattresses, and showed that she hadn't been in there. The thing was like a crazy spiral.

No, it wasn't either. *Immediately after the trunk had been dispatched* ——

The trunk.

That did it.

I looked around to make sure the door was safely closed between Sam and me. My hand hovered uncertainly over the telephone dial a minute. Boyne, he'd be the one to tell about it. He was on Homicide. He had been, anyway, when I'd last seen him. I didn't want to get a flock of strange dicks and cops into my hair. I didn't want to be involved any more than I had to. Or at all, if possible.

They switched my call to the right place

572

after a couple of wrong tries, and I got him finally.

"Look, Boyne? This is Hal Jeffries ——"

"Well, where've you been the last sixty-two years?" he started to enthuse.

"We can take that up later. What I want you to do now is take down a name and address. Ready? Lars Thorwald. Five twenty-five Benedict Avenue. Fourth-floor rear. Got it?"

"Fourth-floor rear. Got it. What's it for?"

"Investigation. I've got a firm belief you'll uncover a murder there if you start digging at it. Don't call on me for anything more than that — just a conviction. There's been a man and wife living there until now. Now there's just the man. Her trunk went out early this morning. If you can find someone who saw *her* leave herself ——"

Marshaled aloud like that and conveyed to somebody else, a lieutenant of detectives above all, it did sound flimsy, even to me. He said hesitantly, "Well, but ——" Then he accepted it as was. Because I was the source. I even left my window out of it completely. I could do that with him and get away with it because he'd known me years, he didn't question my reliability. I didn't want my room all cluttered up with dicks and cops taking turns nosing out of the window in this hot weather. Let them tackle it from the front.

"Well, we'll see what we see," he said. "I'll

keep you posted."

I hung up and sat back to watch and wait events. I had a grandstand seat. Or rather a grandstand seat in reverse. I could only see from behind the scenes, but not from the front. I couldn't watch Boyne go to work. I could only see the results, when and if there were any.

Nothing happened for the next few hours. The police work that I knew must be going on was as invisible as police work should be. The figure in the fourth-floor windows over there remained in sight, alone and undisturbed. He didn't go out. He was restless, roamed from room to room without staying in one place very long, but he stayed in. Once I saw him eating again — sitting down this time — and once he shaved, and once he even tried to read the paper, but he didn't stay with it long.

Little unseen wheels were in motion around him. Small and harmless as yet, preliminaries. If he knew, I wondered to myself, would he remain there quiescent like that, or would he try to bolt out and flee? That mightn't depend so much upon his guilt as upon his sense of immunity, his feeling that he could outwit them. Of his guilt I myself was already convinced, or I wouldn't have taken the step I had.

At three my phone rang. Boyne calling back. "Jeffries? Well, I don't know. Can't you give me a little more than just a bald statement like that?"

"Why?" I fenced. "Why do I have to?"

"I've had a man over there making inquiries. I've just had his report. The building superintendent and several of the neighbors all agree she left for the country, to try and regain her health, early yesterday morning."

"Wait a minute. Did any of them *see* her leave, according to your man?"

"No."

"Then all you've gotten is a second-hand version of an unsupported statement by him. Not an eyewitness account."

"He was met returning from the depot, after he'd bought her ticket and seen her off on the train."

"That's still an unsupported statement, once removed."

"I've sent a man down there to the station to try and check with the ticket agent if possible. After all, he should have been fairly conspicuous at that early hour. And we're keeping him under observation, of course, in the meantime, watching all his movements. The first chance we get we're going to jump in and search the place."

I had a feeling that they wouldn't find anything, even if they did.

"Don't expect anything more from me. I've dropped it in your lap. I've given you all I have to give. A name, an address, and an opinion."

"Yes, and I've always valued your opinion highly before now, Jeff ——"

"But now you don't, that it?"

"Not at all. The thing is, we haven't turned up anything that seems to bear out your impression so far."

"You haven't gotten very far along, so far."

He went back to his previous cliché. "Well, we'll see what we see. Let you know later."

Another hour or so went by, and sunset came on. I saw him start to get ready to go out, over there. He put on his hat, put his hand in his pocket and stood still looking at it for a minute. Counting change, I guess. It gave me a peculiar sense of suppressed excitement, knowing they were going to come in the minute he left. I thought grimly, as I saw him take a last look around: If you've got anything to hide, brother, now's the time to hide it.

He left. A breath-holding interval of misleading emptiness descended on the flat. A three-alarm fire couldn't have pulled my eyes off those windows. Suddenly the door by which he had just left parted slightly and two men insinuated themselves, one behind the other. There they were now. They closed it behind them, separated at once, and got busy. One took the bedroom, one the kitchen, and they started to work their way toward one another again from those extremes of the flat. They were thorough. I could see them going over everything from top to bottom. They took the living room together. One cased one side, the other man the other.

They'd already finished before the warning caught them. I could tell that by the way they straightened up and stood facing one another frustratedly for a minute. Then both their heads turned sharply, as at a tip-off by door-bell that he was coming back. They got out fast.

I wasn't unduly disheartened, I'd expected that. My own feeling all along had been that they wouldn't find anything incriminating around. The trunk had gone.

He came in with a mountainous brown-paper bag sitting in the curve of one arm. I watched him closely to see if he'd discover that someone had been there in his absence. Apparently he didn't. They'd been adroit about it.

He stayed in the rest of the night. Sat tight, safe and sound. He did some desultory drinking, I could see him sitting there by the window and his hand would hoist every once in awhile, but not to excess. Apparently everything was under control, the tension had eased, now that — the trunk was out.

Watching him across the night, I specu-lated: Why doesn't he get out? If I'm right about him, and I am, why does he stick around — after it? That brought its own answer: Because he doesn't know anyone's on to him yet. He doesn't think there's any hurry. To go too soon, right after she has, would be more dangerous than to stay awhile.

The night wore on. I sat there waiting for Boyne's call. It came later than I thought it would. I picked the phone up in the dark. He was getting ready to go to bed, over there, now. He'd risen from where he'd been sitting drinking in the kitchen, and put the light out. He went into the living room, lit that. He started to pull his shirt-tail up out of his belt. Boyne's voice was in my ear as my eyes were on him, over there. Three-cornered arrangement.

"Hello, Jeff? Listen, absolutely nothing. We searched the place while he was out ——"

I nearly said, "I know you did, I saw it," but checked myself in time.

"— and didn't turn up a thing. But ——" He stopped as though this was going to be important. I waited impatiently for him to go ahead.

"Downstairs in his letter box we found a post card waiting for him. We fished it up out of the slot with bent pins ——"

"And?"

"And it was from his wife, written only yesterday from some farm upcountry. Here's the message we copied: 'Arrived O.K.

Already feeling a little better. Love, Anna.' "

I said, faintly but stubbornly: "You say, written only yesterday. Have you proof of that? What was the postmark-date on it?"

He made a disgusted sound down in his tonsils. At me, not it. "The post-mark was blurred. A corner of it got wet, and the ink smudged."

"All of it blurred?"

"The year-date," he admitted. "The hour and the month came out O.K. August. And seven thirty P.M., it was mailed at."

This time I made the disgusted sound, in my larynx. "August, seven thirty P.M. — 1937 or 1939 or 1942. You have no proof how it got into that mail box, whether it came from a letter carrier's pouch or from the back of some bureau drawer!"

"Give up, Jeff," he said. "There's such a thing as going too far."

I don't know what I would have said. That is, if I hadn't happened to have my eyes on the Thorwald flat living room windows just then. Probably very little. The post card *had* shaken me, whether I admitted it or not. But I was looking over there. The light had gone out as soon as he'd taken his shirt off. But the bedroom didn't light up. A match-flare winked from the living room, low down, as from an easy chair or sofa. With two unused beds in the bedroom, he was *still staying out of there.*

"Boyne," I said in a glassy voice, "I don't care what post cards from the other world you've turned up, I say that man has done away with his wife! Trace that trunk he shipped out. Open it up when you've located it — and I think you'll find her!"

And I hung up without waiting to hear what he was going to do about it. He didn't ring back, so I suspected he was going to give my suggestion a spin after all, in spite of his loudly proclaimed skepticism.

I stayed there by the window all night, keeping a sort of deathwatch. There were two more match-flares after the first, at about half-hour intervals. Nothing more after that. So possibly he was asleep over there. Possibly not. I had to sleep some time myself, and I finally succumbed in the flaming light of the early sun. Anything that he was going to do, he would have done under cover of darkness and not waited for broad daylight. There wouldn't be anything much to watch, for a while now. And what was there that he needed to do any more, anyway? Nothing, just sit tight and let a little disarming time slip by.

It seemed like five minutes later that Sam came over and touched me, but it was already high noon. I said irritably: "Didn't you lamp that note I pinned up, for you to let me sleep?"

He said: "Yeah, but it's your old friend Inspector Boyne. I figured you'd sure want to ——"

It was a personal visit this time. Boyne came into the room behind him without waiting, and without much cordiality.

I said to get rid of Sam: "Go inside and smack a couple of eggs together."

Boyne began in a galvanized-iron voice: "Jeff, what do you mean by doing anything like this to me? I've made a fool out of myself, thanks to you. Sending my men out right and left on wild-goose chases. Thank God, I didn't put my foot in it any worse than I did, and have this guy picked up and brought in for questioning."

"Oh, then you don't think that's necessary?" I suggested, drily.

The look he gave me took care of that. "I'm not alone in the department, you know. There are men over me I'm accountable to for my actions. That looks great, don't it, sending one of my fellows one-half-a-day's train ride up into the sticks to some God-forsaken whistle-stop or other at departmental expense ——"

"Then you located the trunk?"

"We traced it through the express agency," he said flintily.

"And you opened it?"

"We did better than that. We got in touch with the various farmhouses in the immediate locality, and Mrs. Thorwald came down to the junction in a produce-truck from one of them and opened it for him herself, with her own keys!"

Very few men have ever gotten a look from an old friend such as I got from him. At the door he said, stiff as a rifle barrel: "Just let's forget all about it, shall we? That's about the kindest thing either one of us can do for the other. You're not yourself, and I'm out a little of my own pocket money, time and temper. Let's let it go at that. If you want to telephone me in future I'll be glad to give you my home number."

The door went *whopp!* behind him.

For about ten minutes after he stormed out my numbed mind was in a sort of straitjacket. Then it started to wriggle its way free. The hell with the police. I can't prove it to them, but I can prove it to myself, one way or the other, once and for all. Either I'm wrong or I'm right. He's got his armor on against them. But his back is naked and unprotected against me.

I called Sam in. "Whatever became of that spyglass we used to have, when we were bumming around on that cabin-cruiser that season?"

He found it some place downstairs and came in with it, blowing on it and rubbing it along his sleeve. I let it lie idle in my lap first. I took a piece of paper and a pencil and wrote six words on it: *What have you done with her?*

I sealed it in an envelope and left the envelope blank. I said to Sam: "Now here's what I want you to do, and I want you to be slick about it. You take this, go in that building 525, climb the stairs to the fourth-floor rear, and ease it under the door. You're fast, at least you used to be. Let's see if you're fast enough to keep from being caught at it. Then when you get safely down again, give the outside doorbell a little poke, to attract attention."

His mouth started to open.

"And don't ask me any questions, you understand? I'm not fooling."

He went, and I got the spyglass ready.

I got him in the right focus after a minute or two. A face leaped up, and I was really seeing him for the first time. Dark-haired, but unmistakable Scandinavian ancestry. Looked like a sinewy customer, although he didn't run to much bulk.

About five minutes went by. His head turned sharply, profilewards. That was the bell-poke, right there. The note must be in already.

He gave me the back of his head as he went back toward the flat-door. The lens could follow him all the way to the rear, where my unaided eyes hadn't been able to before.

He opened the door first, missed seeing it, looked out on a level. He closed it. Then he

583

dipped, straightened up. He had it. I could see him turning it this way and that.

He shifted in, away from the door, nearer the window. He thought danger lay near the door, safety away from it. He didn't know it was the other way around, the deeper into his own rooms he retreated the greater the danger.

He'd torn it open, he was reading it. God, how I watched his expression. My eyes clung to it like leeches. There was a sudden widening, a pulling — the whole skin of his face seemed to stretch back behind the ears, narrowing his eyes to Mongoloids. Shock. Panic. His hand pushed out and found the wall, and he braced himself with it. Then he went back toward the door again slowly. I could see him creeping up on it, stalking it as though it were something alive. He opened it so slenderly you couldn't see it at all, peered fearfully through the crack. Then he closed it, and he came back, zigzag, off balance from sheer reflex dismay. He toppled into a chair and snatched up a drink. Out of the bottle neck itself this time. And even while he was holding it to his lips, his head was turned looking over his shoulder at the door that had suddenly thrown his secret in his face.

I put the glass down.

Guilty! Guilty as all hell, and the police be damned!

My hand started toward the phone, came

back again. What was the use? They wouldn't listen now any more than they had before. "You should have seen his face, etc." And I could hear Boyne's answer: "Anyone gets a jolt from an anonymous letter, true or false. You would yourself." They had a real live Mrs. Thorwald to show me — or thought they had. I'd have to show them the dead one, to prove that they both weren't one and the same. I, from my window, had to show them a body.

Well, he'd have to show me first.

It took hours before I got it. I kept pegging away at it, pegging away at it, while the afternoon wore away. Meanwhile he was pacing back and forth there like a caged panther. Two minds with but one thought, turned inside-out in my case. How to keep it hidden, how to see that it wasn't kept hidden.

I was afraid he might try to light out, but if he intended doing that he was going to wait until after dark, apparently, so I had a little time yet. Possibly he didn't want to himself, unless he was driven to it — still felt that it was more dangerous than to stay.

The customary sights and sounds around me went on unnoticed, while the main stream of my thoughts pounded like a torrent against that one obstacle stubbornly damming them up: how to get him to give the location away to me, so that I could give it away in turn to the police.

I was dimly conscious, I remember, of the landlord or somebody bringing in a prospective tenant to look at the sixth-floor apartment, the one that had already been finished. This was two over Thorwald's; they were still at work on the in-between one. At one point an odd little bit of synchronization, completely accidental of course, cropped up. Landlord and tenant both happened to be near the living room windows on the sixth at the same moment that Thorwald was near those on the fourth. Both parties moved onward simultaneously into the kitchen from there, and, passing the blind spot of the wall, appeared next at the kitchen windows. It was uncanny, they were almost like precision-strollers or puppets manipulated on one and the same string. It probably wouldn't have happened again just like that in another fifty years. Immediately afterwards they digressed, never to repeat themselves like that again.

The thing was, something about it had disturbed me. There had been some slight flaw or hitch to mar its smoothness. I tried for a moment or two to figure out what it had been, and couldn't. The landlord and tenant had gone now, and only Thorwald was in sight. My unaided memory wasn't enough to recapture it for me. My eyesight might have if it had been repeated, but it wasn't.

It sank into my subconscious, to ferment there like yeast, while I went back to the main problem at hand.

I got it finally. It was well after dark, but I finally hit on a way. It mightn't work, it was cumbersome and roundabout, but it was the only way I could think of. An alarmed turn of the head, a quick precautionary step in one certain direction, was all I needed. And to get this brief, flickering, transitory give-away, I need two phone calls and an absence of about half an hour on his part between them.

I leafed a directory by matchlight until I'd found what I wanted: *Thorwald, Lars. 525 Bndct. . . . SWansea 5-2114.*

I blew out the match, picked up the phone in the dark. It was like television. I could see to the other end of my call, only not along the wire but by a direct channel of vision from window to window.

He said "Hullo?" gruffly.

I thought: How strange this is. I've been accusing him of murder for three days straight, and only now I'm hearing his voice for the first time.

I didn't try to disguise my own voice. After all, he'd never see me and I'd never see him. I said: "You got my note?"

He said guardedly: "Who is this?"

"Just somebody who happens to know."

He said craftily: "Know what?"

"Know what you know. You and I, we're the only ones."

He controlled himself well. I didn't hear a

sound. But he didn't know he was open another way too. I had the glass balanced there at proper height on two large books on the sill. Through the window I saw him pull open the collar of his shirt as though its stricture was intolerable. Then he backed his hand over his eyes like you do when there's a light blinding you.

His voice came back firmly. "I don't know what you're talking about."

"Business, that's what I'm talking about. It should be worth something to me, shouldn't it? To keep it from going any further." I wanted to keep him from catching on that it was the windows. I still needed them, I needed them now more than ever. "You weren't very careful about your door the other night. Or maybe the draft swung it open a little."

That hit him where he lived. Even the stomach-heave reached me over the wire. "You didn't see anything. There wasn't anything to see."

"That's up to you. Why should I go to the police?" I coughed a little. "If it would pay me not to."

"Oh," he said. And there was relief of a sort in it. "D'you want to — see me? Is that it?"

"That would be the best way, wouldn't it? How much can you bring with you for now?"

"I've only got about seventy dollars

around here."

"All right, then we can arrange the rest for later. Do you know where Lakeside Park is? I'm near there now. Suppose we make it there." That was about thirty minutes away. Fifteen there and fifteen back. "There's a little pavilion as you go in."

"How many of you are there?" he asked cautiously.

"Just me. It pays to keep things to yourself. That way you don't have to divvy up."

He seemed to like that too. "I'll take a run out," he said, "just to see what it's all about."

I watched him more closely then ever, after he'd hung up. He flitted straight through to the end room, the bedroom, that he didn't go near any more. He disappeared into a clothes-closet in there, stayed a minute, came out again. He must have taken something out of a hidden cranny or niche in there that even the dicks had missed. I could tell by the piston-like motion of his hand, just before it disappeared inside his coat, what it was. A gun.

It's a good thing, I thought, I'm not out there in Lakeside Park waiting for my seventy dollars.

The place blacked and he was on his way.

I called Sam in. "I want you to do something for me that's a little risky. In fact, damn risky. You might break a leg, or you might get shot, or you might even get pinched. We've been together ten years, and I wouldn't ask you anything like that if I could do it myself. But I can't, and it's got to be done." Then I told him. "Go out the back way, cross the backyard fences, and see if you can get into that fourth-floor flat up the fire escape. He's left one of the windows down a little from the top."

"What do you want me to look for?"

"Nothing." The police had been there already, so what was the good of that? "There are three rooms over there. I want you to disturb everything just a little bit, in all three, to show someone's been in there. Turn up the edge of each rug a little, shift every chair and table around a little, leave the closet doors standing out. Don't pass up a thing. Here, keep your eyes on this." I took off my own wrist watch, strapped it on him. "You've got twenty-five minutes, starting from now. If you stay within those twenty-five minutes, nothing will happen to you. When you see they're up, don't wait any longer, get out and get out fast."

"Climb back down?"

"No." He wouldn't remember, in his excitement, if he'd left the windows up or not. And I didn't want him to connect danger with the back of his place, but with the front. I wanted to keep my own window out of it. "Latch the window down tight, let yourself out the door, and beat it out of the building the front way, for your life!"

"I'm just an easy mark for you," he said ruefully, but he went.

He came out through our own basement door below me, and scrambled over the fences. If anyone had challenged him from one of the surrounding windows, I was going to backstop for him, explain I'd sent him down to look for something. But no one did. He made it pretty good for anyone his age. He isn't so young any more. Even the fire escape backing the flat, which was drawn up short, he managed to contact by standing up on something. He got in, lit the light, looked over at me. I motioned him to go ahead, not weaken.

I watched him at it. There wasn't any way I could protect him, now that he was in there. Even Thorwald would be within his rights in shooting him down — this was break and entry. I had to stay in back behind the scenes, like I had been all along. I couldn't get out in front of him as a lookout and shield him. Even the dicks had had a lookout posted.

He must have been tense, doing it. I was twice as tense, watching him do it. The twenty-five minutes took fifty to go by. Finally he came over to the window, latched it fast. The lights went, and he was out. He'd made it. I blew out a bellyful of breath that was twenty-five minutes old.

I heard him keying the street door, and when he came up I said warningly: "Leave the light out in there. Go and build yourself a great big two-story whiskey punch; you're as close to white as you'll ever be."

Thorwald came back twenty-nine minutes after he'd left for Lakeside Park. A pretty slim margin to hang a man's life on. So now for the finale of the long-winded business, and here was hoping. It got my second phone call in before he had time to notice anything amiss. It was tricky timing but I'd been sitting there with the receiver ready in my hand, dialing the number over and over, then killing it each time. He came on the 2 of 5-2114, and I saved that much time. The ring started before his hand came away from the light switch.

This was the one that was going to tell the story.

"You were supposed to bring money, not a gun; that's why I didn't show up." I saw the jolt that threw into him. The window still had to stay out of it. "I saw you tap the inside of your coat, where you had it, as you came out on the street." Maybe he hadn't, but he wouldn't remember by now whether he had or not. You usually do when you're packing a gun and aren't an habitual carrier.

"Too bad you had your trip out and back for nothing. I didn't waste my time while you were gone, though. I know more now than I

592

knew before." This was the important part. I had the glass up and I was practically fluoroscoping him. "I've found out where — it is. You know what I mean. I know now where you've got — it. I was there while you were out."

Not a word. Just quick breathing.

"Don't you believe me? Look around. Put the receiver down and take a look for yourself. I found it."

He put it down, moved as far as the living room entrance, and touched off the lights. He just looked around him once, in a sweeping, all-embracing stare, that didn't come to a head on any one fixed point, didn't center at all.

He was smiling grimly when he came back to the phone. All he said, softly and with malignant satisfaction, was: "You're a liar."

Then I saw him lay the receiver down and take his hand off it. I hung up at my end.

The test had failed. And yet it hadn't. He hadn't given the location away as I'd hoped he would. And yet that "You're a liar" was a tacit admission that it was there to be found, somewhere around him, somewhere on those premises. In such a good place that he didn't have to worry about it, didn't even have to look to make sure.

So there was a kind of sterile victory in my defeat. But it wasn't worth a damn to me.

He was standing there with his back to me,

and I couldn't see what he was doing. I knew the phone was somewhere in front of him, but I thought he was just standing there pensive behind it. His head was slightly lowered, that was all. I'd hung up at my end. I didn't even see his elbow move. And if his index finger did, I couldn't see it.

He stood like that for a moment or two, then finally he moved aside. The lights went out over there; I lost him. He was careful not even to strike matches, like he sometimes did in the dark.

My mind no longer distracted by having him to look at, I turned to trying to recapture something else — that troublesome little hitch in synchronization that had occurred this afternoon, when the renting agent and he both moved simultaneously from window to the next. The closest I could get was this: it was like when you're looking at someone through a pane of imperfect glass, and a flaw in the glass distorts the symmetry of the reflected image for a second, until it has gone on past that point. Yet that wouldn't do, that was not it. The windows had been open and there had been no glass between. And I hadn't been using the lens at the time.

My phone rang. Boyne, I supposed. It wouldn't be anyone else at this hour. Maybe, after reflecting on the way he'd jumped all over me — I said "Hello" unguardedly, in my own normal voice.

There wasn't any answer.

I said: "Hello? Hello? Hello?" I kept giving away samples of my voice.

There wasn't a sound from first to last.

I hung up finally. It was still dark over there, I noticed.

Sam looked in to check out. He was a bit thick-tongued from his restorative drink. He said something about "Awri' if I go now?" I half heard him. I was trying to figure out another way of trapping *him* over there into giving away the right spot. I motioned my consent absently.

He went a little unsteadily down the stairs to the ground floor and after a delaying moment or two I heard the street door close after him. Poor Sam, he wasn't much used to liquor.

I was left alone in the house, one chair the limit of my freedom of movement.

Suddenly a light went on over there again, just momentarily, to go right out again afterwards. He must have needed it for something, to locate something that he had already been looking for and found he wasn't able to put his hands on readily without it. He found it, whatever it was, almost immediately, and moved back at once to put the lights out again. As he turned to do so, I saw him give a glance out the window. He didn't come to the window to do it, he just shot it out in passing.

Something about it struck me as different from any of the others I'd seen him give in all the time I'd been watching him. If you can qualify such an elusive thing as a glance, I would have termed it a glance with a purpose. It was certainly anything but vacant or random, it had a bright spark of fixity in it. It wasn't one of those precautionary sweeps I'd seen him give, either. It hadn't started over on the other side and worked its way around to my side, the right. It had hit dead-center at my bay window, for just a split second while it lasted, and then was gone again. And the lights were gone, and he was gone.

Sometimes your senses take things in without your mind translating them into their proper meaning. My eyes saw that look. My mind refused to smelter it properly. "It was meaningless," I thought. "An unintentional bull's-eye, that just happened to hit square over here, as he went toward the lights on his way out."

Delayed action. A wordless ring of the phone. To test a voice? A period of bated darkness following that, in which two could have played at the same game — stalking one another's window-squares, unseen. A last-moment flicker of the lights, that was bad strategy but unavoidable. A parting glance, radioactive with malignant intention. All these things sank in without fusing. My eyes did their job, it was my mind that didn't — or at least took its time about it.

Seconds went by in packages of sixty. It was very still around the familiar quadrangle formed by the back of the houses. Sort of a breathless stillness. And then a sound came into it, starting up from nowhere, nothing. The unmistakable, spaced clicking a cricket makes in the silence of the night. I thought of Sam's superstition about them, that he claimed had never failed to fulfill itself yet. If that was the case, it looked bad for somebody in one of these slumbering houses around here ——

Sam had been gone only about ten minutes. And how he was back again, he must have forgotten something. That drink was responsible. Maybe his hat, or maybe even the key to his own quarters uptown. He knew I couldn't come down and let him in, and he was trying to be quiet about it, thinking perhaps I'd dozed off. All I could hear was this faint jiggling down at the lock of the front door. It was one of those old-fashioned stoop houses, with an outer pair of storm doors that were allowed to swing free all night, and then a small vestibule, and then the inner door, worked by a simple iron key. The liquor had made his hand a little unreliable, although he'd had this difficulty once or twice before, even without it. A match would have helped him find the keyhole quicker, but then, Sam doesn't smoke. I knew he wasn't likely to have one on him.

The sound had stopped now. He must have given up, gone away again, decided to let whatever it was go until tomorrow. He hadn't gotten in, because I knew his noisy way of letting doors coast shut by themselves too well, and there hadn't been any sound of that sort, that loose slap he always made.

Then suddenly it exploded. Why at this particular moment, I don't know. That was some mystery of the inner workings of my own mind. It flashed like waiting gunpowder which a spark has finally reached along a slow train. Drove all thoughts of Sam, and the front door, and this and that completely out of my head. It had been waiting there since midafternoon today, and only now —— More of that delayed action. Damn that delayed action.

The renting agent and Thorwald had both started even from the living room window. An intervening gap of blind wall, and both had reappeared at the kitchen window, still one above the other. But some sort of a hitch or flaw or jump had taken place, right there, that bothered me. The eye is a reliable surveyor. There wasn't anything the matter with their timing, it was with their parallelness, or whatever the word is. The hitch had been vertical, not horizontal. There had been an upward "jump."

Now I had it, now I knew. And it couldn't wait. It was too good. They wanted a body? Now I had one for them.

Sore or not, Boyne would *have* to listen to me now. I didn't waste any time, I dialed his precinct-house then and there in the dark, working the slots in my lap by memory alone. They didn't make much noise going around, just a light click. Not even as distinct as that cricket out there ——

"He went home long ago," the desk sergeant said.

This couldn't wait. "All right, give me his home phone number."

He took a minute, came back again. "Trafalgar," he said. Then nothing more.

"Well? Trafalgar what?" Not a sound.

"Hello? Hello?" I tapped it. "Operator, I've been cut off. Give me that party again." I couldn't get her either.

I hadn't been cut off. My wire had been cut. That had been too sudden, right in the middle of —— And to be cut like that it would have to be done somewhere right here inside the house with me. Outside it went underground.

Delayed action. This time final, fatal, altogether too late. A voiceless ring of the phone. A direction-finder of a look from over there. "Sam" seemingly trying to get back in a while ago.

Surely, death was somewhere inside the

house here with me. And I couldn't move, I couldn't get up out of this chair. Even if I had gotten through to Boyne just now, that would have been too late. There wasn't time enough now for one of those camera-finishes in this. I could have shouted out the window to that gallery of sleeping rear-window neighbors around me, I supposed. It would have brought them to the windows. It couldn't have brought them over here in time. By the time they had even figured which particular house it was coming from, it would stop again, be over with. I didn't open my mouth. Not because I was brave, but because it was so obviously useless.

He'd be up in a minute. He must be on the stairs now, although I couldn't hear him. Not even a creak. A creak would have been a relief, would have placed him. This was like being shut up in the dark with the silence of a gliding, coiling cobra somewhere around you.

There wasn't a weapon in the place with me. There were books there on the wall, in the dark, within reach. Me, who never read. The former owner's books. There was a bust of Rousseau or Montesquieu, I'd never been able to decide which, one of those gents with flowing manes, topping them. It was a monstrosity, bisque clay, but it too dated from before my occupancy.

I arched my middle upward from the chair

seat and clawed desperately up at it. Twice my fingertips slipped off it, then at the third raking I got it to teeter, and the fourth brought it down into my lap, pushing me down into the chair. There was a steamer rug under me. I didn't need it around me in this weather, I'd been using it to soften the seat of the chair. I tugged it out from under and mantled it around me like an Indian brave's blanket. Then I squirmed far down in the chair, let my head and one shoulder dangle out over the arm, on the side next to the wall. I hoisted the bust to my other, upward shoulder, balanced it there precariously for a second head, blanket tucked around its ears. From the back, in the dark, it would look — I hoped ——

I proceeded to breathe adenoidally, like someone in heavy upright sleep. It wasn't hard. My own breath was coming nearly that labored anyway, from tension.

He was good with knobs and hinges and things. I never heard the door open, and this one, unlike the one downstairs, was right behind me. A little eddy of air puffed through the dark at me. I could feel it because my scalp, the real one, was all wet at the roots of the hair right then.

If it was going to be a knife or head-blow, the dodge might give me a second chance, that was the most I could hope for, I knew. My arms and shoulders are hefty. I'd

601

bring him down on me in a bear-hug after the first slash or drive, and break his neck or collarbone against me. If it was going to be a gun, he'd get me anyway in the end. A difference of a few seconds. He had a gun, I knew, that he was going to use on me in the open, over at Lakeside Park. I was hoping that here, indoors, in order to make his own escape more practicable ——

Time was up.

The flash of the shot lit up the room for a second, it was so dark. Or at least the corners of it, like flickering, weak lightning. The bust bounced on my shoulder and disintegrated into chunks.

I thought he was jumping up and down on the floor for a minute with frustrated rage. Then when I saw him dart by me and lean over the window sill to look for a way out, the sound transferred itself rearwards and downwards, because a pummeling with hoof and hip at the street door. The camera-finish after all. But he still could have killed me five times.

I flung my body down into the narrow crevice between chair arm and wall, but my legs were still up, and so was my head and that one shoulder.

He whirled, fired at me so close that it was looking a sunrise in the face. I didn't feel it, so — it hadn't hit.

"You ——" I heard him grunt to himself.

I think it was the last thing he said. The rest of his life was all action, not verbal.

He flung over the sill on one arm and dropped into the yard. Two-story drop. He made it because he missed the cement, landed on the sod-strip in the middle. I jacked myself up over the chair arm and flung myself bodily forward at the window, nearly hitting it chin first.

He went all right. When life depends on it, you go. He took the first fence, rolled over that bellywards. He went over the second like a cat, hands and feet pointed together in a spring. Then he was back in the rear yard of his own building. He got up on something, just about like Sam had —— The rest was all footwork, with quick little corkscrew twists at each landing stage. Sam had latched his windows down when he was over there, but he'd reopened one of them for ventilation on his return. His whole life depended now on that casual, unthinking little act ——

Second, third. He was up to his own windows. He'd made it. Something went wrong. He veered out away from them in another pretzel-twist, flashed up toward the fifth, the one above. Something sparked in the darkness of one of his own windows where he'd been just now, and a shot thudded heavily out around the quadrangle-enclosure like a big bass drum.

He passed the fifth, the sixth, got up to the

roof. He'd made it a second time. Gee, he loved life! The guys in his own windows couldn't get him, he was over them in a straight line and there was too much fire escape interlacing in the way.

I was too busy watching him to watch what was going on around me. Suddenly Boyne was next to me, sighting. I heard him mutter: "I almost hate to do this, he's got to fall so far."

He was balanced on the roof parapet up there, with a star right over his head. An unlucky star. He stayed a minute too long, trying to kill before he was killed. Or maybe he was killed, and knew it.

A shot cracked, high up against the sky, the window pane flew apart all over the two of us, and one of the books snapped right behind me.

Boyne didn't say anything more about hating to do it. My face was pressing outward against his arm. The recoil of his elbow jarred my teeth. I blew a clearing through the smoke to watch him go.

It was pretty horrible. He took a minute to show anything, standing up there on the parapet. Then he let his gun go, as if to say: "I won't need this any more." Then he went after it. He missed the fire escape entirely, came all the way down on the outside. He landed so far out he hit one the projecting planks, down there out of sight. It bounced his body up, like a springboard. Then it landed again — for good. And that was all.

I said to Boyne: "I got it. I got it finally. The fifth-floor flat, the one over his, that they're still working on. The cement kitchen floor, raised above the level of the other rooms. They wanted to comply with the fire laws and also obtain a dropped living room effect, as cheaply as possible. Dig it up ——"

He went right over then and there, down through the basement and over the fences, to save time. The electricity wasn't turned on yet in that one, they had to use their torches. It didn't take them long at that, once they'd got started. In about half an hour he came to the window and wigwagged over for my benefit. It meant yes.

He didn't come over until nearly eight in the morning; after they'd tidied up and taken them away. Both away, the hot dead and the cold dead. He said: "Jeff, I take it all back. That damn fool that I sent up there about the trunk — well, it wasn't my fault, in a way. I'm to blame. He didn't have orders to check on the woman's description, only on the contents of the trunk. He came back and touched on it in a general way. I go home and I'm in bed already, and suddenly pop! into my brain — one of the tenants I questioned two whole days ago had given us a few details and they didn't tally with his on several important points. Talk about being slow to catch on!"

"I've had that all the way through this damn thing," I admitted ruefully. "I call it delayed action. It nearly killed me."

"I'm a police officer and you're not."

"That how you happened to shine at the right time?"

"Sure. We came over to pick him up for questioning. I left them planted there when we saw he wasn't in, and came on over here by myself to square it up with you while we were waiting. How did you happen to hit on that cement floor?"

I told him about the freak synchronization. "The renting agent showed up taller at the kitchen window in proportion to Thorwald, than he had been a moment before when both were at the living room windows together. It was no secret that they were putting in cement floors, topped by a cork composition, and raising them considerably. But it took on new meaning. Since the top floor one has been finished for some time, it had to be the fifth. Here's the way I have it lined up, just in theory. She's been in ill health for years, and he's been out of work, and he got sick of that and of her both. Met this other ——"

"She'll be here later today, they're bringing her down under arrest."

"He probably insured her for all he could get, and then started to poison her slowly, trying not to leave any trace. I imagine — and remember, this is pure conjecture — she

606

caught him at it that night the light was on all night. Caught on in some way, or caught him in the act. He lost his head, and did the very thing he had wanted all along to avoid doing. Killed her by violence — strangulation or a blow. The rest had to be hastily improvised. He got a better break than he deserved at that. He thought of the apartment upstairs, went up and looked around. They'd just finished laying the floor, the cement hadn't hardened yet, and the materials were still around. He gouged a trough out of it just wide enough to take her body, put her in it, mixed fresh cement and recemented over her, possibly raising the general level of the flooring an inch or two so that she'd be safely covered. A permanent, odorless coffin. Next day the workmen came back, laid down the cork surfacing on top of it without noticing anything, I suppose he'd used one of their own trowels to smooth it. Then he sent his accessory upstate fast, where his wife had been several summers before, but to a different farmhouse where she wouldn't be recognized, along with the trunk keys. Sent the trunk up after her, and dropped himself an already used post card into his mailbox, with the year-date blurred. In a week or two she would have probably committed 'suicide' up there as Mrs. Anna Thorwald. Despondency due to ill health. Written him a farewell note and left her clothes beside some body of deep water. It was risky, but they might have succeeded in collecting the insurance at that."

By nine Boyne and the rest had gone. I was still there in the chair, too keyed up to sleep. Sam came in and said: "Here's Doc Preston."

He showed up rubbing his hands, in that way he has. "Guess we can take that cast off your leg now. You must be tired of sitting there all day doing nothing."

Midnight Blue

Ross Macdonald

IT HAD RAINED in the canyon during the night. The world had the colored freshness of a butterfly just emerged from the chrysalis stage and trembling in the sun. Actual butterflies danced in flight across free spaces of air or played a game of tag without any rules among the tree branches. At this height there were giant pines among the eucalyptus trees.

I parked my car where I usually parked it, in the shadow of the stone building just inside the gates of the old estate. Just inside the posts, that is — the gates had long since fallen from their rusted hinges. The owner of the country house had died in Europe, and the place had stood empty since the war. It was one reason I came here on the occasional Sunday when I wanted to get away from the Hollywood rat race. Nobody lived within two miles.

Until now, anyway. The window of the gatehouse overlooking the drive had been broken the last time that I'd noticed it. Now it was patched up with a piece of cardboard. Through a hole punched in the middle of the cardboard, bright emptiness watched me — human eye's bright emptiness.

"Hello," I said.

A grudging voice answered, "Hello."

The gatehouse door creaked open, and a white-haired man came out. A smile sat strangely on his ravaged face. He walked mechanically, shuffling in the leaves, as if his body was not at home in the world. He wore faded denims through which his clumsy muscles bulged like animals in a sack. His feet were bare.

I saw when he came up to me that he was a huge old man, a head taller than I was and a foot wider. His smile was not a greeting or any kind of smile that I could respond to. It was the stretched, blind grimace of a man who lived in a world of his own, a world that didn't include me.

"Get out of here. I don't want trouble. I don't want nobody messing around."

"No trouble," I said. "I came up to do a little target shooting. I probably have as much right here as you have."

His eyes widened. They were as blue and empty as holes in his head through which I could see the sky.

"Nobody has the rights here that I have. I lifted up mine eyes unto the hills and the voice spoke and I found sanctuary. Nobody's going to force me out of my sanctuary."

I could feel the short hairs bristling on the back of my neck. Though my instincts didn't say so, he was probably a harmless nut. I tried to keep my instincts out of my voice.

"I won't bother you. You don't bother me. That should be fair enough."

"You bother me just *being* here. I can't stand people. I can't stand cars. And this is twice in two days you come up harrying me and harassing me."

"I haven't been here for a month."

"You're an Ananias liar." His voice whined like a rising wind. He clenched his knobbed fists and shuddered on the verge of violence.

"Calm down, old man," I said. "There's room in the world for both of us."

He looked around at the high green world as if my words had snapped him out of a dream.

"You're right," he said in a different voice. "I have been blessed, and I must remember to be joyful. Creation belongs to all of us poor creatures." His smiling teeth were as long and yellow as an old horse's. His roving glance fell on my car. "And it wasn't you who come up here last night. It was a different automobile. I remember."

He turned away, muttering something about washing his socks, and dragged his horny feet back into the gatehouse. I got my

611

targets, pistol, and ammunition out of the trunk, and locked the car up tight. The old man watched me through his peephole, but he didn't come out again.

Below the road, in the wild canyon, there was an open meadow backed by a sheer bank which was topped by the crumbling wall of the estate. It was my shooting gallery. I slid down the wet grass of the bank and tacked a target to an oak tree, using the butt of my heavy-framed .22 as a hammer.

While I was loading it, something caught my eye — something that glinted red, like a ruby among the leaves. I stooped to pick it up and found that it was attached. It was a red-enameled fingernail at the tip of a white hand. The hand was cold and stiff.

I let out a sound that must have been loud in the stillness. A jaybird erupted from a manzanita, sailed up to a high limb of the oak, and yelled down curses at me. A dozen chickadees flew out of the oak and settled in another at the far end of the meadow.

Panting like a dog, I scraped away the dirt and wet leaves that had been loosely piled over the body. It was the body of a girl wearing a midnight-blue sweater and skirt. She was a blonde, about 17. The blood that congested her face made her look old and dark. The white rope with which she had been garroted was sunk almost out of sight in the flesh of her neck. The rope was tied at the nape in what is called a granny's knot, the kind of knot that any child can tie.

I left her where she lay and climbed back up to the road on trembling knees. The grass showed traces of the track her body had made where someone had dragged it down the bank. I looked for tire marks on the shoulder and in the rutted, impacted gravel of the road. If there had been any, the rain had washed them out.

I trudged up the road to the gatehouse and knocked on the door. It creaked inward under my hand. Inside there was nothing alive but the spiders that had webbed the low black beams. A dustless rectangle in front of the stone fireplace showed where a bedroll had lain. Several blackened tin cans had evidently been used as cooking utensils. Gray embers lay on the cavernous hearth. Suspended above it from a spike in the mantel was a pair of white cotton work socks. The socks were wet. Their owner had left in a hurry.

It wasn't my job to hunt him. I drove down the canyon to the highway and along it for a few miles to the outskirts of the nearest town. There a drab green box of a building with a flag in front of it housed the Highway Patrol. Across the highway was a lumberyard deserted on Sunday.

"Too bad about Ginnie," the dispatcher said when she had radioed the local sheriff. She was a thirtyish brunette with fine black eyes and dirty fingernails. She had on a plain white blouse, which was full of her.

"Do you know Ginnie?"

"My young sister knows her. They go — they went to high school together. It's an awful thing when it happens to a young person like that. I knew she was missing — I got the report when I came on at eight — but I kept hoping that she was just off on a lost weekend, like. Now there's nothing to hope for, is there?" Her eyes were liquid with feeling. "Poor Ginnie. And poor Mr. Green."

"Her father?"

"That's right. He was in here with her high school counselor not more than an hour ago. I hope he doesn't come back right away. I don't want to be the one that has to tell him."

"How long has the girl been missing?"

"Just since last night. We got the report here about three a.m., I think. Apparently she wandered away from a party at Cavern Beach. Down the pike a ways." She pointed south toward the canyon mouth.

"What kind of party was it?"

"Some of the kids from the Union High School — they took some wienies down and had a fire. The party was part of graduation week. I happen to know about it because my young sister Alice went. I didn't want her to go, even if it was supervised. That can be a dangerous beach at night. All sorts of bums

614

and scroungers hang out in the caves. Why, one night when I was a kid I saw a naked man down there in the moonlight. He didn't have a woman with him, either."

She caught the drift of her words, did a slow blush, and checked her loquacity. I leaned on the plywood counter between us.

"What sort of girl was Ginnie Green?"

"I wouldn't know. I never really knew her."

"Your sister does."

"I don't let my sister run around with girls like Ginnie Green. Does that answer your question?"

"Not in any detail."

"It seems to me you ask a lot of questions."

"I'm naturally interested, since I found her. Also I'm a private detective."

"Looking for a job?"

"I can always use a job."

"So can I, and I've got one and I don't intend to lose it." She softened the words with a smile. "Excuse me; I have work to do."

She turned to her short-wave and sent out a message to the patrol cars that Virginia Green had been found. Virginia Green's father heard it as he came in the door. He was a puffy gray-faced man with red-rimmed eyes. Striped pajama bottoms showed below the cuffs of his trousers. His shoes were muddy, and he walked as if he had been walking all night.

He supported himself on the edge of the

counter, opening and shutting his mouth like a beached fish. Words came out, half strangled by shock.

"I heard you say she was dead, Anita."

The woman raised her eyes to his. "Yes. I'm awfully sorry, Mr. Green."

He put his face down on the counter and stayed there like a penitent, perfectly still. I could hear a clock somewhere, snipping off seconds, and in the back of the room the L.A. police signals like muttering voices coming in from another planet. Another planet very much like this one, where violence measured out the hours.

"It's my fault," Green said to the bare wood under his face. "I didn't bring her up properly. I haven't been a good father."

The woman watched him with dark and glistening eyes ready to spill. She stretched out an unconscious hand to touch him, pulled her hand back in embarrassment when a second man came into the station. He was a young man with crew-cut brown hair, tanned and fit-looking in a Hawaiian shirt. Fit-looking except for the glare of sleeplessness in his eyes and the anxious lines around them.

"What is it, Miss Brocco? What's the word?"

"The word is bad." She sounded angry. "Somebody murdered Ginnie Green. This man here is a detective and he just found her body up in Trumbull Canyon."

The young man ran his fingers through his short hair and failed to get a grip on it, or on himself. "My God! That's terrible!"

"Yes," the woman said. "You were supposed to be looking after her, weren't you?"

They glared at each other across the counter. The tips of her breasts pointed at him through her blouse like accusing fingers. The young man lost the glaring match. He turned to me with a wilted look.

"My name is Connor, Franklin Connor, and I'm afraid I'm very much to blame in this. I'm a counselor at the high school, and I was supposed to be looking after the party, as Miss Brocco said."

"Why didn't you?"

"I didn't realize. I mean, I thought they were all perfectly happy and safe. The boys and girls had pretty well paired off around the fire. Frankly, I felt rather out of place. They aren't children, you know. They were all seniors, they had cars. So I said good night and walked home along the beach. As a matter of fact, I was hoping for a phone call from my wife."

"What time did you leave the party?"

"It must have been nearly eleven. The ones who hadn't paired off had gone home."

"Who did Ginnie pair off with?"

"I don't know. I'm afraid I wasn't paying too much attention to the kids. It's graduation week, and I've had a lot of problems —"

The father, Green, had been listening with a changing face. In a sudden yammering rage his impulsive grief and guilt exploded outward.

"It's your business to know! By God, I'll have your job for this. I'll make it *my* business to run you out of town."

Connor hung his head and looked at the stained tile floor. There was a thin spot in his short brown hair, and his scalp gleamed through it like bare white bone. It was turning into a bad day for everybody, and I felt the dull old nagging pull of other people's trouble, like a toothache you can't leave alone.

The sheriff arrived, flanked by several deputies and an HP sergeant. He wore a Western hat and a rawhide tie and a blue gabardine business suit which together produced a kind of gunsmog effect. His name was Pearsall.

I rode back up the canyon in the right front seat of Pearsall's black Buick, filling him in on the way. The deputies' Ford and an HP car followed us, and Green's new Oldsmobile convertible brought up the rear.

The sheriff said, "The old guy sounds like a loony to me."

"He's a loner, anyway."

"You never can tell about them hoboes. That's why I give my boys instructions to roust 'em. Well, it looks like an open-and-shut case.''

''Maybe. Let's keep our minds open anyway, Sheriff.''

''Sure. Sure. But the old guy went on the run. That shows consciousness of guilt. Don't worry, we'll hunt him down. I got men that know these hills like you know your wife's geography.''

''I'm not married.''

''Your girl friend, then.'' He gave me a sideways leer that was no gift. ''And if we can't find him on foot, we'll use the air squadron.''

''You have an air squadron?''

''Volunteers, mostly local ranchers. We'll get him.'' His tires squealed on a curve. ''Was the girl raped?''

''I didn't try to find out. I'm not a doctor. I left her as she was.''

The sheriff grunted. ''You did the right thing at that.''

Nothing had changed in the high meadow. The girl lay waiting to have her picture taken. It was taken many times, from several angles. All the birds flew away. Her father leaned on a tree and watched them go. Later he was sitting on the ground.

I volunteered to drive him home. It wasn't pure altruism. I'm incapable of it. I said when I had turned his Oldsmobile, ''Why did you say it was your fault, Mr. Green?''

He wasn't listening. Below the road four uniformed men were wrestling a heavy covered aluminum stretcher up the steep bank. Green watched them as he had watched the departing birds, until they were out of sight around a curve.

"She was so young," he said to the back seat.

I waited, and tried again. "Why did you blame yourself for her death?"

He roused himself from his daze. "Did I say that?"

"In the Highway Patrol office you said something of the sort."

He touched my arm. "I didn't mean I killed her."

"I didn't think you meant that. I'm interested in finding out who did."

"Are you a cop — a policeman?"

"I have been."

"You're not with the locals."

"No. I happen to be a private detective from Los Angeles. The name is Archer."

He sat and pondered this information. Below and ahead the summer sea brimmed up in the mouth of the canyon.

"You don't think the old tramp did her in?" Green said.

"It's hard to figure out how he could have. He's a strong looking old buzzard, but he couldn't have carried her all the way up from the beach. And she wouldn't have come along with him of her own accord."

It was a question, in a way.

"I don't know," her father said. "Ginnie was a little wild — she'd do a thing *because* it was wrong, *because* it was dangerous. She hated to turn down a dare, especially from a man."

"There were men in her life?"

"She was attractive to men. You saw her, even as she is." He gulped. "Don't get me wrong. Ginnie was never a *bad* girl. She was a little headstrong, and I made mistakes. That's why I blame myself."

"What sort of mistakes, Mr. Green?"

"All the usual ones, and some I made up on my own." His voice was bitter. "Ginnie didn't have a mother, you see. Her mother left me years ago, and it was as much my fault as hers. I tried to bring her up myself. I didn't give her proper supervision. I run a restaurant in town, and I don't get home nights till after midnight. Ginnie was pretty much on her own since she was in grade school. We got along fine when I was there, but I usually wasn't there.

"The worst mistake I made was letting her work in the restaurant over the weekends. That started about a year ago. She wanted the money for clothes, and I thought the discipline would be good for her. I thought I could keep an eye on her, you know. But it didn't work out. She grew up too fast, and the night work played hell with her studies.

"I finally got the word from the school authorities. I fired her a couple of months ago, but I guess it was too late. We haven't been getting along too well since then. Mr. Connor said she resented my indecision, that I gave her too much responsibility and then took it away again."

"You've talked her over with Connor?"

"More than once, including last night. He was her academic counselor, and he was concerned about her grades. We both were. Ginnie finally pulled through, after all, thanks to him. She was going to graduate. Not that it matters now, of course."

Green was silent for a time. The sea expanded below us like a second blue dawn. I could hear the roar of the highway. Green touched my elbow again, as if he needed human contact.

"I oughtn't to've blown my top at Connor. He's a decent boy, he means well. He gave my daughter hours of free tutoring this last month. And he's got troubles of his own, like he said."

"What troubles?"

"I happen to know his wife left him, same as mine. I shouldn't have borne down so hard on him. I have a lousy temper, always have had." He hesitated, then blurted out as if he had found a confessor, "I said a terrible thing to Ginnie at supper last night. She always has supper with me at the restaurant. I said if she wasn't home when I got home last night that I'd wring her neck."

"And she wasn't home," I said. And somebody wrung her neck, I didn't say.

The light at the highway was red. I glanced at Green. Tear tracks glistened like snail tracks on his face.

"Tell me what happened last night."

"There isn't anything much to tell," he said. "I got to the house about twelve thirty, and, like you said, she wasn't home. So I called Al Brocco's house. He's my night cook, and I knew his youngest daughter Alice was at the moonlight party on the beach. Alice was home all right."

"Did you talk to Alice?"

"She was in bed asleep. Al woke her up, but I didn't talk to her. She told him she didn't know where Ginnie was. I went to bed, but I couldn't sleep. Finally I got up and called Mr. Connor. That was about one thirty. I thought I should get in touch with the authorities, but he said no, Ginnie had enough black marks against her already. He came over to the house and we waited for a while and then we went down to Cavern Beach.

"There was no trace of her. I said it was time to call in the authorities, and he agreed. We went to his beach house, because it was nearer, and called the sheriff's office from

623

there. We went back to the beach with a couple of flashlights and went through the caves. He stayed with me all night. I give him that."

"Where are these caves?"

"We'll pass them in a minute. I'll show you if you want. But there's nothing in any of the three of them."

Nothing but shadows and empty beer cans, the odor of rotting kelp. I got sand in my shoes and sweat under my collar. The sun dazzled my eyes when I half walked, half crawled, from the last cave.

Green was waiting beside a heap of ashes.

"This is where they had the wienie roast," he said.

I kicked the ashes. A half-burned sausage rolled along the sand. Sand fleas hopped in the sun like fat on a griddle. Green and I faced each other over the dead fire. He looked out to sea. A seal's face floated like a small black nose cone beyond the breakers. Farther out a water skier slid between unfolding wings of spray.

Away up the beach two people were walking towards us. They were small and lonely and distant as Chirico figures in the long white distance.

Green squinted against the sun. Red-rimmed or not, his eyes were good. "I believe that's Mr. Connor. I wonder who the woman is with him."

They were walking as close as lovers, just above the white margin of the surf. They pulled apart when they noticed us, but they were still holding hands as they approached.

"It's Mrs. Connor," Green said in a low voice.

"I thought you said she left him."

"That's what he told me last night. She took off on him a couple of weeks ago, couldn't stand a high school teacher's hours. She must have changed her mind."

She looked as though she had a mind to change. She was a hard-faced blonde who walked like a man. A certain amount of style took the curse off her stiff angularity. She had on a madras shirt, mannishly cut, and a pair of Capri pants that hugged her long slim legs.

Connor looked at us in complex embarrassment. "I thought it was you from a distance, Mr. Green. I don't believe you know my wife."

"I've seen her in my place of business." He explained to the woman, "I run the Highway Restaurant in town."

"How do you do," she said aloofly, then added in an entirely different voice, "You're Virginia's father, aren't you? I'm so sorry."

The words sounded queer. Perhaps it was the surroundings; the ashes on the beach, the entrances to the caves, the sea, and the empty sky which dwarfed us all. Green answered her solemnly.

"Thank you, ma'am. Mr. Connor was a strong right arm to me last night, I can tell you." He was apologizing. And Connor responded, "Why don't you come to our place for a drink? It's just down the beach. You look as if you could use one, Mr. Green. You too," he said to me. "I don't believe I know your name."

"Archer. Lew Archer."

He gave me a hard hand. His wife interposed, "I'm sure Mr. Green and his friend won't want to be bothered with us on a day like this. Besides, it isn't even noon yet, Frank."

She was the one who didn't want to be bothered. We stood around for a minute, exchanging grim, nonsensical comments on the beauty of the day. Then she led Connor back in the direction they had come from. Private Property, her attitude seemed to say: Trespassers will be fresh-frozen.

I drove Green to the Highway Patrol station. He said that he was feeling better, and could make it home from there by himself. He thanked me profusely for being a friend in need to him, as he put it. He followed me to the door of the station, thanking me.

The dispatcher was cleaning her fingernails with an ivory-handled file. She glanced up.

"Did they catch him yet?"

"I was going to ask you the same question, Miss Brocco."

"No such luck. But they'll get him," she said with female vindictiveness. "The sheriff called out his air squadron, and he sent to Ventura for bloodhounds."

"Big deal."

She bridled. "What do you mean by that?"

"I don't think the old man of the mountain killed her. If he had, he wouldn't have waited till this morning to go on the lam. He'd have taken off right away."

"Then why did he go on the lam at all?" The word sounded strange in her prim mouth.

"I think he saw me discover the body, and realized he'd be blamed."

She considered this, bending the long nail file between her fingers. "If the old tramp didn't do it, who did?"

"You may be able to help me answer that question."

"Me help you? How?"

"You know Frank Connor, for one thing."

"I know him. I've seen him about my sister's grades a few times."

"You don't seem to like him much."

"I don't like him, I don't dislike him. He's just blah to me."

"Why? What's the matter with him?"

Her tight mouth quivered, and let out words. "I don't know what's the matter with him. He can't keep his hands off of

627

young girls."

"How do you know that?"

"I heard it."

"From your sister Alice?"

"Yes. The rumor was going around the school, she said."

"Did the rumor involve Ginnie Green?"

She nodded. Her eyes were as black as fingerprint ink.

"Is that why Connor's wife left him?"

"I wouldn't know about that. I never even laid eyes on Mrs. Connor."

"You haven't been missing much."

There was a yell outside, a kind of choked ululation. It sounded as much like an animal as a man. It was Green. When I reached the door, he was climbing out of his convertible with a heavy blue revolver in his hand.

"I saw the killer," he cried out exultantly.

"Where?"

He waved the revolver toward the lumber-yard across the road. "He poked his head up behind that pile of white pine. When he saw me, he ran like a deer. I'm going to get him."

"No. Give me the gun."

"Why? I got a license to carry it. And use it."

He started across the four-lane highway, dodging through the moving patterns of the Sunday traffic as if he were playing parcheesi on the kitchen table at home. The sounds of brakes and curses split the air. He had scrambled over the locked gate of the yard before I got to it. I went over after him.

Green disappeared behind a pile of lumber. I turned the corner and saw him running halfway down a long aisle walled with stacked wood and floored with beaten earth. The old man of the mountain was running ahead of him. His white hair blew in the wind of his own movement. A burlap sack bounced on his shoulders like a load of sorrow and shame.

"Stop or I'll shoot!" Green cried.

The old man ran on as if the devil himself were after him. He came to a cyclone fence, discarded his sack, and tried to climb it. He almost got over. Three strands of barbed wire along the top of the fence caught and held him struggling.

I heard a tearing sound, and then the sound of a shot. The huge old body espaliered on the fence twitched and went limp, fell heavily to the earth. Green stood over him breathing through his teeth.

I pushed him out of the way. The old man was alive, though there was blood in his mouth. He spat it onto his chin when I lifted his head.

"You shouldn't ought to of done it. I come to turn myself in. Then I got ascairt."

"Why were you scared?"

"I watched you uncover the little girl in the leaves. I knew I'd be blamed. I'm one of the chosen. They always blame the chosen. I been in trouble before."

"Trouble with girls?" At my shoulder Green was grinning terribly.

"Trouble with cops."

"For killing people?" Green said.

"For preaching on the street without a license. The voice told me to preach to the tribes of the wicked. And the voice told me this morning to come in and give my testimony."

"What voice?"

"The great voice." His voice was little and weak. He coughed red.

"He's as crazy as a bedbug," Green said.

"Shut up." I turned back to the dying man. "What testimony do you have to give?"

"About the car I seen. It woke me up in the middle of the night, stopped in the road below my sanctuary."

"What kind of car?"

"I don't know cars. I think it was one of them foreign cars. It made a noise to wake the dead."

"Did you see who was driving it?"

"No. I didn't go near. I was ascairt."

"What time was this car in the road?"

"I don't keep track of time. The moon was down behind the trees."

Those were his final words. He looked up at the sky with his sky-colored eyes, straight into the sun. His eyes changed color.

Green said, "Don't tell them. If you do, I'll make a liar out of you. I'm a respected citizen in this town. I got a business to lose. And they'll believe me ahead of you, mister."

"Shut up."

He couldn't. "The old fellow was lying, anyway. You know that. You heard him say yourself that he heard voices. That proves he's a psycho. He's a psycho killer. I shot him down like you would a mad dog, and I did right."

He waved the revolver.

"You did wrong, Green, and you know it. Give me that gun before it kills somebody else."

He thrust it into my hand suddenly. I unloaded it, breaking my fingernails in the process, and handed it back to him empty. He nudged up against me.

"Listen, maybe I did do wrong. I had provocation. It doesn't have to get out. I got a business to lose."

He fumbled in his hip pocket and brought out a thick sharkskin wallet. "Here. I can pay you good money. You say that you're a private eye; you know how to keep your lip buttoned."

I walked away and left him blabbering beside the body of the man he had killed. They were both vicious, in a sense, but only one of them had blood on his hands.

Miss Brocco was in the HP parking lot. Her

631

bosom was jumping with excitement.

"I heard a shot."

"Green shot the old man. Dead. You better send in for the meat wagon and call off your bloody dogs."

The words hit her like slaps. She raised her hand to her face, defensively. "Are you mad at me? Why are you mad at me?"

"I'm mad at everybody."

"You still don't think he did it."

"I know damned well he didn't. I want to talk to your sister."

"Alice? What for?"

"Information. She was on the beach with Ginnie Green last night. She may be able to tell me something."

"You leave Alice alone."

"I'll treat her gently. Where do you live?"

"I don't want my little sister dragged into this filthy mess."

"All I want to know is who Ginnie paired off with."

"I'll ask Alice. I'll tell you."

"Come on, Miss Brocco, we're wasting time. I don't need your permission to talk to your sister, after all. I can get the address out of the phone book if I have to."

She flared up then and then flared down.

"You win. We live on Orlando Street, 224. That's on the other side of town. You will be nice to Alice, won't you? She's bothered enough as it is about Ginnie's death."

"She really was a friend of Ginnie's, then?"

"Yes. I tried to break it up. But you know how kids are — two motherless girls, they stick together. I tried to be like a mother to Alice."

"What happened to your own mother?"

"Father — I mean, she died." A greenish pallor invaded her face and turned it to old bronze. "Please. I don't want to talk about it. I was only a kid when she died."

She went back to her muttering radios. She was quite a woman, I thought as I drove away. Nubile but unmarried, probably full of untapped Mediterranean passions. If she worked an eight-hour shift and started at eight, she'd be getting off about four.

It wasn't a large town, and it wasn't far across it. The highway doubled as its main street. I passed the Union High School. On the green playing field beside it a lot of kids in mortarboards and gowns were rehearsing their graduation exercises. A kind of pall seemed to hang over the field. Perhaps it was in my mind.

Farther along the street I passed Green's Highway Restaurant. A dozen cars stood in its parking space. A couple of white-uniformed waitresses were scooting around behind the plate glass windows.

Orlando Street was a lower-middle-class residential street bisected by the highway. Jacaranda trees bloomed like low small purple clouds among its stucco and frame cottages. Fallen purple petals carpeted the narrow lawn in front of the Brocco house.

A thin dark man, wiry under his T-shirt, was washing a small red Fiat in the driveway beside the front porch. He must have been over fifty, but his long hair was as black as an Indian's. His Sicilian nose was humped in the middle by an old break.

"Mr. Brocco?"

"That's me."

"Is Alice home?"

"She's home."

"I'd like to speak to her."

He turned off his hose, pointing its dripping nozzle at me like a gun.

"You're a little old for her, ain't you?"

"I am a detective investigating the death of Ginnie Green."

"Alice don't know nothing about that."

"I've just been talking to your older daughter at the Highway Patrol office. She thinks Alice may know something."

He shifted on his feet. "Well, if Anita says it's all right."

"It's okay, Dad," a girl said from the front door. "Anita just called me on the telephone. Come in, Mister — Archer, isn't it?"

"Archer."

She opened the screen door for me. It opened directly into a small square living room containing worn green frieze furniture and a television set which the girl switched off. She was a handsome, serious-looking girl, a younger version of her sister with ten years and ten pounds subtracted and a pony tail added. She sat down gravely on the edge of a chair, waving her hand at the chesterfield. Her movements were languid. There were blue depressions under her eyes. Her face was sallow.

"What kind of questions do you want to ask me? My sister didn't say."

"Who was Ginnie with last night?"

"Nobody. I mean, she was with me. She didn't make out with any of the boys." She glanced from me to the blind television set, as if she felt caught between. "It was on the television that she was with a man, that there was medical evidence to prove it. But I didn't see her with no man. Any man."

"Did Ginnie go with men?"

She shook her head. Her pony tail switched and hung limp. She was close to tears.

"You told Anita she did."

"I did not!"

"Your sister wouldn't lie. You passed on a rumor to her — a high school rumor that Ginnie had had something to do with one man in particular."

The girl was watching my face in fascination. Her eyes were like a bird's eyes, bright and shallow and fearful.

"Was the rumor true?"

She shrugged her thin shoulders. "How would I know?"

"You were good friends with Ginnie."

"Yes. I was." Her voice broke on the past tense. "She was a real nice kid, even if she was kind of boy crazy."

"She was boy crazy, but she didn't make out with any of the boys last night?"

"Not while I was there."

"Did she make out with Mr. Connor?"

"No. He wasn't there. He went away. He said he was going home. He lives up the beach."

"What did Ginnie do?"

"I don't know. I didn't notice."

"You said she was with you. Was she with you all evening?"

"Yes." Her face was agonized. "I mean no."

"Did Ginnie go away, too?"

She nodded.

"In the same direction Mr. Connor took? The direction of his house?"

Her head moved almost imperceptibly downward.

"What time was that, Alice?"

"About eleven o'clock, I guess."

"And Ginnie never came back from Mr. Connor's house?"

"I don't know. I don't know for certain that she went there."

"But Ginnie and Mr. Connor were good

friends?"

"I guess so."

"How good? Like a boy friend and a girl friend?"

She sat mute, her birdlike stare unblinking.

"Tell me, Alice."

"I'm afraid."

"Afraid of Mr. Connor?"

"No. Not him."

"Has someone threatened you — told you not to talk?"

Her head moved in another barely perceptible nod.

"Who threatened you, Alice? You'd better tell me for your own protection. Whoever did threaten you is probably a murderer."

She burst into frantic tears. Brocco came to the door.

"What goes on in here?"

"Your daughter is upset. I'm sorry."

"Yeah, and I know who upset her. You better get out of here or you'll be sorrier."

He opened the screen door and held it open, his head poised like a dark and broken ax. I went out past him. He spat after me. The Broccos were a very emotional family.

I started back toward Connor's beach house on the south side of town but ran into a diversion on the way. Green's car was parked in the lot beside his restaurant. I went in.

The place smelled of grease. It was almost full of late Sunday lunchers seated in booths

637

and at the U-shaped breakfast bar in the middle. Green himself was sitting on a stool behind the cash register counting money. He was counting it as if his life and his hope of heaven depended on the colored paper in his hands.

He looked up, smiling loosely and vaguely. "Yes, sir?" Then he recognized me. His face went through a quick series of transformations and settled for a kind of boozy shame. "I know I shouldn't be here working on a day like this. But it keeps my mind off my troubles. Besides, they steal you blind if you don't watch 'em. And I'll be needing the money."

"What for, Mr. Green?"

"The trial." He spoke the word as if it gave him a bitter satisfaction.

"Whose trial?"

"Mine. I told the sheriff what the old guy said. And what I did. I know what I did. I shot him down like a dog, and I had no right to. I was crazy with my sorrow, you might say."

He was less crazy now. The shame in his eyes was clearing. But the sorrow was still there in their depths, like stone at the bottom of a well.

"I'm glad you told the truth, Mr. Green."

"So am I. It doesn't help him, and it doesn't bring Ginnie back. But at least I can live with myself."

"Speaking of Ginnie," I said. "Was she

seeing quite a lot of Frank Connor?"

"Yeah. I guess you could say so. He came over to help her with her studies quite a few times. At the house, and at the library. He didn't charge me, either."

"That was nice of him. Was Ginnie fond of Connor?"

"Sure she was. She thought very highly of Mr. Connor."

"Was she in love with him?"

"In love? Hell, I never thought of anything like that. Why?"

"Did she have dates with Connor?"

"Not to my knowledge," he said. "If she did, she must have done it behind my back." His eyes narrowed to two red swollen slits. "You think Frank Connor had something to do with her death?"

"It's a possibility. Don't go into a sweat now. You know where that gets you."

"Don't worry. But what about this Connor? Did you get something on him? I thought he was acting queer last night."

"Queer in what way?"

"Well, he was pretty tight when he came to the house. I gave him a stiff snort, and that straightened him out for a while. But later on, down on the beach, he got almost hysterical. He was running around like a rooster with his head chopped off."

"Is he a heavy drinker?"

"I wouldn't know. I never saw him drink

before last night at my house." Green narrowed his eyes. "But he tossed down a triple bourbon like it was water. And remember this morning, he offered us a drink on the beach. A drink in the morning, that isn't the usual thing, especially for a high school teacher."

"I noticed that."

"What else have you been noticing?"

"We won't go into it now," I said. "I don't want to ruin a man unless and until I'm sure he's got it coming."

He sat on his stool with his head down. Thought moved murkily under his knitted brows. His glance fell on the money in his hands. He was counting tens.

"Listen, Mr. Archer. You're working on this case on your own, aren't you? For free?"

"So far."

"So go to work for me. Nail Connor for me and I'll pay you whatever you ask."

"Not so fast," I said. "We don't know that Connor is guilty. There are other possibilities."

"Such as?"

"If I tell you, can I trust you not to go on a shooting spree?"

"Don't worry," he repeated. "I've had that."

"Where's your revolver?"

"I turned it in to Sheriff Pearsall. He asked for it."

We were interrupted by a family group getting up from one of the booths. They gave Green their money and their sympathy. When they were out of hearing, I said, "You mentioned that your daughter worked here in the restaurant for a while. Was Al Brocco working here at the same time?"

"Yeah. He's been my night cook for six-seven years. Al is a darned good cook. He trained as a chef on the Italian line." His slow mind, punchy with grief, did a double-take. "You wouldn't be saying that he messed around with Ginnie?"

"I'm asking you."

"Shucks, Al is old enough to be her father. He's all wrapped up in his own girls, Anita in particular. He worships the ground she walks on. She's the mainspring of that family."

"How did he get on with Ginnie?"

"Very well. They kidded back and forth. She was the only one who could ever make him smile. Al is a sad man, you know. He had a tragedy in his life."

"His wife's death?"

"It was worse than that," Green said. "Al Brocco killed his wife with his own hand. He caught her with another man and put a knife in her."

"And he's walking around loose?"

"The other man was a Mex," Green said in an explanatory way. "A wetback. He couldn't even talk the English language. The town hardly blamed Al, the jury gave him manslaughter. But when he got out of the pen, the people at the Pink Flamingo wouldn't give him his old job back — he used to be chef there. So I took him on. I felt sorry for the girls, I guess, and Al's been a good worker. A man doesn't do a thing like that twice, you know."

He did another slow mental double-take. His mouth hung open.

"Let's hope not."

"Listen here," he said. "You go to work for me, eh? You nail the guy, whoever he is. I'll pay you. I'll pay you now. How much do you want?"

I took a hundred dollars of his money and left him trying to comfort himself with the rest of it. The smell of grease stayed in my nostrils.

Connor's house clung to the edge of a low bluff about halfway between the HP station and the mouth of the canyon where the thing had begun: a semi-cantilevered redwood cottage with a closed double garage fronting the highway. From the grape-stake-fenced patio in the angle between the garage and the front door a flight of wooden steps climbed to the flat roof which was railed as a sun deck. A second set of steps descended the fifteen or twenty feet to the beach.

I tripped on a pair of garden shears crossing

the patio to the garage window. I peered into the interior twilight. Two things inside interested me: a dismasted flattie sitting on a trailer, and a car. The sailboat interested me because its cordage resembled the white rope that had strangled Ginnie. The car interested me because it was an imported model, a low-slung Triumph two-seater.

I was planning to have a closer look at it when a woman's voice screeched overhead like a gull's, "What do you think you're doing?"

Mrs. Connor was leaning over the railing on the roof. Her hair was in curlers. She looked like a blonde Gorgon. I smiled up at her, the way that Greek whose name I don't remember must have smiled.

"Your husband invited me for a drink, remember? I don't know whether he gave me a rain check or not."

"He did not! Go away! My husband is sleeping!"

"Shh. You'll wake him up. You'll wake up the people in Forest Lawn."

She put her hand to her mouth. From the expression on her face she seemed to be biting her hand. She disappeared for a moment, and then came down the steps with a multicolored silk scarf over her curlers. The rest of her was sheathed in a white satin bathing suit. Against it her flesh looked like brown wood.

"You get out of here," she said. "Or I shall

643

call the police."

"Fine. Call them. I've got nothing to hide."

"Are you implying that we have?"

"We'll see. Why did you leave your husband?"

"That's none of your business."

"I'm making it my business, Mrs. Connor. I'm a detective investigating the murder of Ginnie Green. Did you leave Frank on account of Ginnie Green?"

"No. No! I wasn't even aware —" Her hand went to her mouth again. She chewed on it some more.

"You weren't aware that Frank was having an affair with Ginnie Green?"

"He wasn't."

"So you say. Others say different."

"What others? Anita Brocco? You can't believe anything *that* woman says. Why, her own father is a murderer, everybody in town knows that."

"Your own husband may be another, Mrs. Connor. You might as well come clean with me."

"But I have nothing to tell you."

"You can tell me why you left him."

"That is a private matter, between Frank and me. It has nothing to do with anybody but us." She was calming down, setting her moral forces in a stubborn, defensive posture.

"There's usually only the one reason."

"I had my reasons. I said they were none

of your business. I chose for reasons of my own to spend a month with my parents in Long Beach."

"When did you come back?"

"This morning."

"Why this morning?"

"Frank called me. He said he needed me." She touched her thin breast absently, pathetically, as if perhaps she hadn't been needed in the past.

"Needed you for what?"

"As his wife," she said. "He said there might be tr—" Her hand went to her mouth again. She said around it, "Trouble."

"Did he name the kind of trouble?"

"No."

"What time did he call you?"

"Very early, around seven o'clock."

"That was more than an hour before I found Ginnie's body."

"He knew she was missing. He spent the whole night looking for her."

"Why would he do that, Mrs. Connor?"

"She was his student. He was fond of her. Besides, he was more or less responsible for her."

"Responsible for her death?"

"How dare you say a thing like that?"

"If he dared to do it, I can dare to say it."

"He didn't!" she cried. "Frank is a good man. He may have his faults, but he wouldn't kill anyone. I know him."

"What are his faults?"

"We won't discuss them."

"Then may I have a look in your garage?"

"What for? What are you looking for?"

"I'll know when I find it." I turned toward the garage door.

"You mustn't go in there," she said intensely. "Not without Frank's permission."

"Wake him up and we'll get his permission."

"I will not. He got no sleep last night."

"Then I'll just have a look without his permission."

"I'll kill you if you go in there."

She picked up the garden shears and brandished them at me — a sick-looking lioness defending her overgrown cub. The cub himself opened the front door of the cottage. He slouched in the doorway groggily, naked except for white shorts.

"What goes on, Stella?"

"This man has been making the most horrible accusations."

His blurred glance wavered between us and focused on her. "What did he say?"

"I won't repeat it."

"I will, Mr. Connor. I think you were Ginnie Green's lover, if that's the word. I think she followed you to this house last night, around midnight. I think she left it with a rope around her neck."

Connor's head jerked. He started to make

a move in my direction. Something inhibited it, like an invisible leash. His body slanted toward me, static, all the muscle taut. It resembled an anatomy specimen with the skin off. Even his face seemed mostly bone and teeth.

I hoped he's swing on me and let me hit him. He didn't. Stella Connor dropped the garden shears. They made a noise like the dull clank of doom.

"Aren't you going to deny it, Frank?"

"I didn't kill her. I swear I didn't. I admit that we — that we were together last night, Ginnie and I."

"Ginnie and I?" the woman repeated incredulously.

His head hung down. "I'm sorry, Stella. I didn't want to hurt you more than I have already. But it has to come out. I took up with the girl after you left. I was lonely and feeling sorry for myself. Ginnie kept hanging around. One night I drank too much and let it happen. It happened more than once. I was so flattered that a pretty young girl —"

"You fool!" she said in a deep harsh voice.

"Yes, I'm a moral fool. That's no surprise to you, is it?"

"I thought you respected your pupils, at least. You mean to say you brought her into our own house, into our own bed?"

"You'd left. It wasn't ours any more. Besides, she came of her own accord. She wanted to come. She loved me."

She said with grinding contempt, "You poor groveling ninny. And to think you had the gall to ask me to come back here, to make you look respectable."

I cut in between them. "Was she here last night, Connor?"

"She was here. I didn't invite her. I wanted her to come, but I dreaded it, too. I knew that I was taking an awful chance. I drank quite a bit to numb my conscience —"

"What conscience?" Stella Connor said.

"I have a conscience," he said without looking at her. "You don't know the hell I've been going through. After she came, after it happened last night, I drank myself unconscious."

"Do you mean after you killed her?" I said.

"I didn't kill her. When I passed out, she was perfectly all right. She was sitting up drinking a cup of instant coffee. The next thing I knew, hours later, her father was on the telephone and she was gone."

"Are you trying to pull the old blackout alibi? You'll have to do better than that."

"I can't. It's the truth."

"Let me into your garage."

He seemed almost glad to be given an order, a chance for some activity. The garage wasn't locked. He raised the overhead door and let the daylight into the interior. It smelled of paint. There were empty cans of

648

marine paint on a bench beside the sailboat. Its hull gleamed virgin white.

"I painted my flattie last week," he said inconsequentially.

"You do a lot of sailing?"

"I used to. Not much lately."

"No," his wife said from the doorway. "Frank changed his hobby to women. Wine and women."

"Lay off, eh?" His voice was pleading.

She looked at him from a great and stony distance.

I walked around the boat, examining the cordage. The starboard jib line had been sheared off short. Comparing it with the port line, I found that the missing piece was approximately a yard long. That was the length of the piece of white rope that I was interested in.

"Hey!" Connor grabbed the end of the cut line. He fingered it as if it was a wound in his own flesh. "Who's been messing with my lines? Did you cut it, Stella?"

"I never go near your blessed boat," she said.

"I can tell you where the rest of that line is, Connor. A line of similar length and color and thickness was wrapped around Ginnie Green's neck when I found her."

"Surely you don't believe I put it there?"

I tried to, but I couldn't. Small-boat sailers

don't cut their jib lines, even when they're contemplating murder. And while Connor was clearly no genius, he was smart enough to have known that the line could easily be traced to him. Perhaps someone else had been equally smart.

I turned to Mrs. Connor. She was standing in the doorway with her legs apart. Her body was almost black against the daylight. Her eyes were hooded by the scarf on her head.

"What time did you get home, Mrs. Connor?"

"About ten o'clock this morning. I took a bus as soon as my husband called. But I'm in no position to give him an alibi."

"An alibi wasn't what I had in mind. I suggest another possibility — that you came home twice. You came home unexpectedly last night, saw the girl in the house with your husband, waited in the dark till the girl came out, waited with a piece of rope in your hands — a piece of rope you'd cut from your husband's boat in the hope of getting him punished for what he'd done to you. But the picture doesn't fit the frame, Mrs. Connor. A sailor like your husband wouldn't cut a piece of line from his own boat. And even in the heat of murder he wouldn't tie a granny's knot. His fingers would automatically tie a reef knot. That isn't true of a woman's fingers."

She held herself upright with one long rigid

arm against the door frame.

"I wouldn't do anything like that. I wouldn't do that to Frank."

"Maybe you wouldn't in daylight, Mrs. Connor. Things have different shapes at midnight."

"And hell hath no fury like a woman scorned? Is that what you're thinking? You're wrong. I wasn't here last night. I was in bed in my father's house in Long Beach. I didn't even know about that girl and Frank."

"Then why did you leave him?"

"He was in love with another woman. He wanted to divorce me and marry her. But he was afraid — afraid that it would affect his position in town. He told me on the phone this morning that it was all over with the other woman. So I agreed to come back to him." Her arm dropped on her side.

"He said that it was all over with Ginnie?"

Possibilities were racing through my mind. There was the possibility that Connor had been playing reverse English, deliberately and clumsily framing himself in order to be cleared. But that was out of far left field.

"Not Ginnie," his wife said. "The other woman was Anita Brocco. He met her last spring in the course of work and fell in love — what *he* calls love. My husband is a foolish, fickle man."

"Please, Stella. I said it was all over between me and Anita, and it is."

She turned on him in quiet savagery. "What does it matter now? If it isn't one girl it's another. Any kind of female flesh will do to poultice your sick little ego."

Her cruelty struck inward and hurt her. She stretched out her hand toward him. Suddenly her eyes were blind with tears.

"Any flesh but mine, Frank," she said brokenly.

Connor paid no attention.

He said to me in a hushed voice, "My God, I never thought. I noticed her car last night when I was walking home along the beach."

"Whose car?"

"Anita's red Fiat. It was parked at the viewpoint a few hundred yards from here." He gestured vaguely toward town. "Later, when Ginnie was with me, I thought I heard someone in the garage. But I was too drunk to make a search." His eyes burned into mine. "You say a woman tied that knot?"

"All we can do is ask her."

We started toward my car together. His wife called after him, "Don't go, Frank. Let him handle it."

He hesitated, a weak man caught between opposing forces.

"I need you," she said. "We need each other."

I pushed him in her direction.

It was nearly four when I got to the HP

station. The patrol cars had gathered like homing pigeons for the change in shift. Their uniformed drivers were talking and laughing inside.

Anita Brocco wasn't among them. A male dispatcher, a fat-faced man with pimples, had taken her place behind the counter.

"Where's Miss Brocco?" I asked.

"In the Ladies' Room. Her father is coming to pick her up any minute."

She came out wearing lipstick and a light beige coat. Her face turned beige when she saw my face. She came toward me in slow motion, leaned with both hands flat on the counter. Her lipstick looked like fresh blood on a corpse.

"You're a handsome woman, Anita," I said. "Too bad about you."

"Too bad." It was half a statement and half a question. She looked down at her hands.

"Your fingernails are clean now. They were dirty this morning. You were digging in the dirt in the dark last night, weren't you?"

"No."

"You were, though. You saw them together and you couldn't stand it. You waited in ambush with a rope, and put it around her neck. Around you own neck, too."

She touched her neck. The talk and laughter had subsided around us. I could hear the tick of the clock again, and the muttering signals coming in from inner space.

"What did you use to cut the rope with, Anita? The garden shears?"

Her red mouth groped for words and found them. "I was crazy about him. She took him away. It was all over before it started. I didn't know what to do with myself. I wanted him to suffer."

"He's suffering. He's going to suffer more."

"He deserves to. He was the only man —" She shrugged in a twisted way and looked down at her breast. "I didn't want to kill her, but when I saw them together — I saw them through the window. I saw her take off her clothes and put them on. Then I thought of the night my father — when he — when there was all the blood in Mother's bed. I had to wash it out of the sheets."

The men around me were murmuring. One of them, a sergeant, raised his voice.

"Did you kill Ginnie Green?"

"Yes."

"Are you ready to make a statement?" I said.

"Yes. I'll talk to Sheriff Pearsall. I don't want to talk here, in front of my friends." She looked around doubtfully.

"I'll take you downtown."

"Wait a minute." She glanced once more at her empty hands. "I left my purse in the — in the back room. I'll go and get it."

She crossed the office like a zombie, opened a plain door, closed it behind her. She didn't

654

come out. After a while we broke the lock and went in after her.

Her body was cramped on the narrow floor. The ivory-handled nail file lay by her right hand. There were bloody holes in her white blouse and in the white breast under it. One of them had gone as deep as her heart.

Later Al Brocco drove up in her red Fiat and came into the station.

"I'm a little late," he said to the room in general. "Anita wanted me to give her car a good cleaning. Where is she, anyway?"

The sergeant cleared his throat to answer Brocco.

All us poor creatures, as the old man of the mountain had said that morning.

Index of Titles and Authors